EDDIE MACON'S RUN

Also by James McLendon

FICTION
Deathwork

NONFICTION
Papa: Hemingway in Key West
Pioneer in the Florida Keys: The Life and Times of Del Layton

EDDIE

MACON'S RUN

James McLendon

THE VIKING PRESS   NEW YORK

Copyright © James N. McLendon 1980
All rights reserved
First published in 1980 by The Viking Press
625 Madison Avenue, New York, N.Y. 10022
Published simultaneously in Canada by
Penguin Books Canada Limited

LIBRARY OF CONGRESS CATALOGING IN PUBLICATION DATA
McLendon, James
Eddie Macon's run.
I. Title.
PZ4.M1642Ed   [PS3563.A3184]   813'.5'4   79–22865
ISBN 0–670–28855–1

Printed in the United States of America
Set in Linotron Caledonia
Maps by Paul J. Pugliese, GCI

FOR

My Precious Children
STACEY, IAN, CAITLIN
Smallest Runners
Strongest Hearts

AND AS ALWAYS FOR
My Wife, Ann
The Run Gets Sweeter
By the Day
LADY ANN

AUTHOR'S NOTE

This is a work of fiction and the author has taken certain liberties with respect to chronology, geographic features, time zones, and certain facts of U.S. history. These are obvious and were done to enhance the storyline of the novel. It should also be noted that any scenes involving real people, living or dead, are purely fictional.

CONTENTS

Eddie ran his finger slowly north to south on the colorful map. His heart pounded. He could feel the land. He could hear himself running. He could feel . . .

freedom.

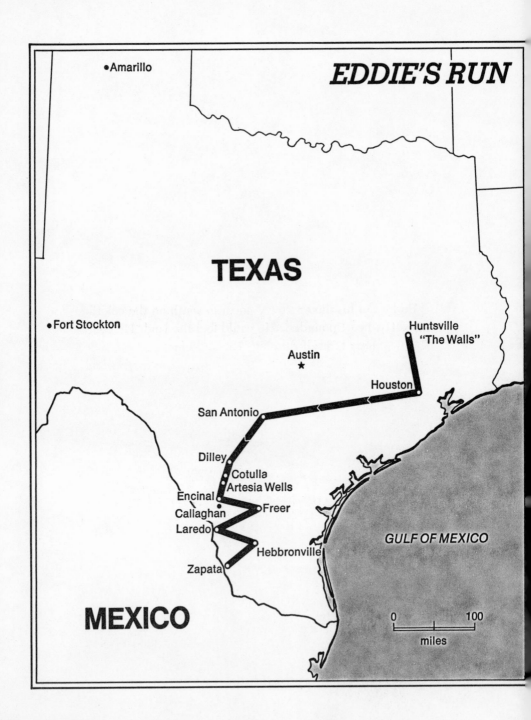

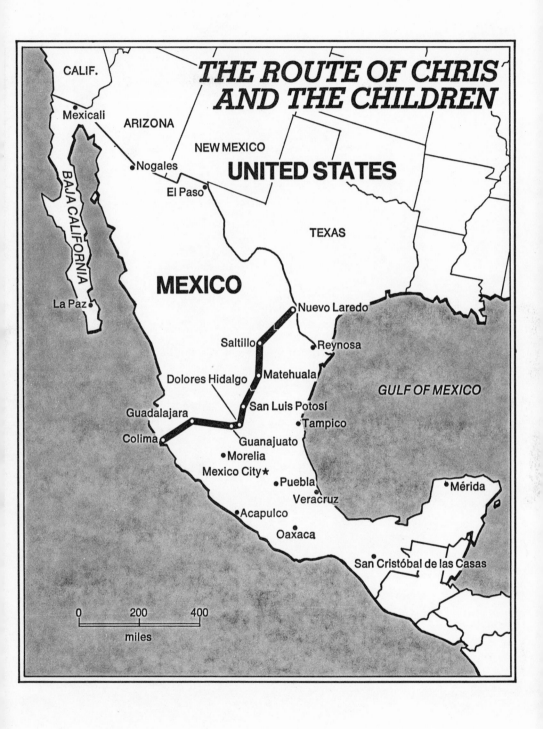

Y SO EASY SO EASY

Texas State Prison: "The Walls"

Huntsville, Texas

Sunday, October 28, 3:30 p.m.

See what Eddie saw. Feel what Eddie felt as he limped out of the noise and dust of the chute area into the cool, muffled dampness of the stadium stockpens. Already they were bringing some of the trucks and trailers into position at the edge of the ramps. It is his second escape from prison; if he is caught he will spend the rest of his life in a cage.

Eddie, in coarse black-and-white prison coon stripes, keeps on with his limping as he makes his way past guards and convict rodeo hands to the calf trailer whose truck doors are marked: L-BAR-T RANCH, COTULLA, TEXAS. *The roar of twenty thousand spectators beyond in the stadium rises and falls, and the saddle-bronc-riding finals continue.*

They'll go on for another thirty minutes, *Eddie tells himself.* By then I'll be gone, or caught, or dead.

The possibilities seem as one to Eddie as he limps on toward the trailer, eyes straight down but taking in everything.

The L-Bar-T stock trailer: thirty feet long, open bed, steel railings, with an eight-×six-×three-foot storage box at its head.

Freedom, *Eddie's mind drums as his eyes fall on the box that is less than fifty feet away.* Freedom.

A sergeant in uniform grays, checking the storage area. Long-handled stainless-steel flashlight in one hand, hardwood walking stick in the other. Poking at the scattered gear inside the storage box with the cane, probing with the light. The sergeant, with half his mind on his work, half on the Texas Prison Rodeo outside. Closing the steel doors of the box; turning, striding on the trailer bed in slow, resentful steps. Jumping down from the trailer, cursing as his boots hit the ground. Then waving the driver of the truck permission to back the final foot until the trailer touches the edge of the stockpen ramp.

Eddie, now forty feet: limping, face twisted into a curl of pain that is not, like the limping, an act. The sergeant at the rear of the trailer. The red-faced cowboy driver of the L-Bar-T truck making his way back to the sergeant. The sergeant giving grudging permission for the loading.

"Get it done," *he mutters, turning from the ramp gate, walking off toward the sunlight of one of the stadium entrances.*

The silent cowboy, face red from part of a fifth of Early Times tucked under his driver's seat, engaging the gate latch; then a line of calves charging out of the pen and into the trailer, grunting, mouths frothing, heads butting. The loading over in seconds. The tough rodeo calves wedged in head-to-tail.

Eddie now at the head of the truck, making his way around the far side, a part two feet from the concrete-and-steel wall of the stockpen. A last quick look.

Nobody watching—move!

Eddie partially hidden.

Move!

Eddie's stomach is acid. His knees are weak. Edging down the side of the truck, flashing past the narrow opening between truck and trail, knowing he has only seconds.

Seconds!

The driver securing the gate latch, then the latch on the trailer's gate; shaking it out of habit. The sixteen calves inside the trailer shuffling, settling down into a routine they know well. The driver turning from the gate, striding back to the truck in a tough, liquor walk. Eddie at the far side of the trailer now, peering around the end.

Nothing! No one! Go! Go!

The sergeant at the stadium entrance fifty yards away, smiling, sucking on the stub of a hand-rolled cigarette, watching a bronc named Saddle Billy pound a black car thief from Odessa into the dust.

Eddie's hands on the trailer's latch. Opening it. Pulling himself inside. Jamming his straw cowboy hat low over his forehead; banging into calves, kneeing them out of his way, elbowing. Then his hands through the slats, and the gate is latched once more.

Seconds! Seconds!

Eddie wheeling around digging his way through the calves, fighting for the storage area.

Go! Go! Go!

Now at the storage compartment. Opening it. Kicking calves out of his way.

Seconds! Only seconds. Move!

Pushing off a calf, using another as a step.

Go!

Now up and inside. ˙

I've got it! Holding! I'm inside. I'm . . .

The truck's motor starting. A jerk on the trailer. Eddie's head banging into the steel wall of the storage box. Truck and trailer moving. Calves lurching forward: hooves pounding on the steel trailer bed. A wail of grunts and bleats. Eddie in darkness, counting to himself.

1 . . . 1,000; 2 . . . 1,000; 3 . . . 1,000 . . . *going to 47; knowing the exact second the truck should pull up to the outside prison gate.*

Truck and trailer stopping. Calves reeling and grunting once more. Eddie frantically wedging his head against the wall, feet against gear; straining with every muscle to keep the compartment doors shut. Now, voices. A guard. The truck driver. More sounds.

Jesus!

Eddie's eyes shut tight in the close darkness of the compartment.

Jesus!

A dank silence. Then a bang on the wall by Eddie's head.

What? What?

New motion. Truck and trailer moving again. Gates clanking as the vehicle moves past. Eddie like granite. Balled in a fetal knot; holding on to the compartment door, no feeling left in his hands. Counting again to himself. Counting to five minutes, and Interstate 45—due south to Houston.

Now downhill. The motion shoving Eddie into the wall once again. The compartment doors held together on their own by the motion as Eddie searches the clammy dark for a piece of rope or twine. His hands finding a small piece of rope near his crotch.

Hurry! Hurry! Move! *Eddie's mind is screaming as he works with the rope; securing it to the ends of the latch bolts inside his steel box.*

On! It's on! Tied! *Truck and trailer level off on the great interstate for Houston.*

The driver pushing 85 mph; wheels singing under the strain. Eddie settling back against the wall. Blood starting to circulate in his fingers again; his right hand still holding the rope end. But his mind and body are still fire and hysteria.

Six hours! *Eddie is thinking now that the first hurdle has been cleared.* I need six full hours! Six, till I'm counted again. Jesus God! Six! Six! Six!

He cannot block the number from his head. It keeps hitting him like a fist.

Six hours to go 90 miles south to Houston, then 178 miles west to San Antonio, and then 54 miles south again to the Frio River Bridge—322 miles in six hours!

But through it all another thought starts to sink in on him. The number six is replaced by two words. Two small words that almost make Eddie laugh out loud there in his black box.

So easy, *he begins to say to himself.* So easy.

Suddenly it all begins to seem so easy.

But that is escape from prison. At any point there are only two choices: you get caught, or you get away.

So easy, *Eddie kept saying to himself.* So easy.

DAY ONE DAY ONE

Sunday, October 28

1

Eddie / 9:23 p.m. / Frio River, Texas

Eddie was damp from the river, but it felt good. Cool and refreshing in the small chill of the October night. He could see well in the full moonlight. Before him was the seemingly endless southeast Texas desert. He could just detect the far side of the valley where a flat ridge met the black-yellow lunar skyline. He took in everything from his vantage point on the high bank of the river. He paused a second more where he stood, tightened, and then he began to run in long clean strides as he had prepared. For an instant, as he began, Eddie thought of Chris and the children. But he rid himself of all images. *The run. The run. The run,* he chanted to himself as he moved. All around him the only sounds were those of the beating of his heart and the *pat, pat, pat,* of his running shoes on the stone-hard desert floor.

Ahead lay a 108-mile run. He had five days to cross the Mexican border. Four nights running totally on his own with no contact until he reached the border at Laredo, Texas; then half a day in Laredo before he could cross into Mexico and freedom.

There was a simple truth about escapes: *Contact means capture*, the old con saying went. Freedom was doing everything on your own and doing everything right. There could be no slipups. If there were any, the odds were that you got caught. No contacts. No slipups. Freedom by escape was as simple and complicated as that. Words; but more to Eddie. He had run away again. Escaped. He had challenged TDC to come and get him: to catch or kill him.

TDC, he said silently and bitterly. Then his mind formed a new word, a word that shook him and dulled his step for a moment.

Marzack, his mind blazed. *The Hounder, the . . .*

But he forced the name and all the dread it possessed back into the depth of his mind, and in the manner of a long-distance runner, now, he did not look back. What was behind was so bad it didn't matter. It could drive a man mad if he thought about it. As it was for other runners, for Eddie now there was only the finish line. Nothing else mattered. Like Marzack, it could not be dealt with until it happened.

So he ran on, the physical act keeping madness and his family from his mind. And he did not allow himself to feel free. Because he was not. He was only running. The last time, he felt free from the start and he had been captured in less than ten minutes. The last time, he had made contact. He had slipped up. He had gotten caught.

As he ran now in the cool, clear night Eddie felt strong and kept a cadence in his mind like a song.

Run, he sang to himself. *Run. Run. Run.*

He had never, in all the six years of his imprisonment, given up, and now he was proving that to everyone. He had prepared for the run for two years. He was in control. Now he knew where he was going and he knew how to get there. Now he *could* win. But victory was a long way off, and Eddie knew that totally as he ran on over the flat landscape that was broken only by thick mesquite and short, thorny prickly-pear cactus.

Run . . . Run . . . Run . . . he sang to himself for comfort.

2

Marzack / 9:34 p.m. / Huntsville, Texas

Marzack, whose name was Carl, but who had been called "Buster" since he was twelve years old because he liked to bust heads, walked out of the officers' dining room at the Walls and adjusted his ancient trench coat against a damp chill.

With the coat tied at the waist, a short-brimmed felt hat centered on his forehead, and a habitual green Optimo cigar in the corner of his mouth, Marzack moved off down the unheated hallway that led to the administrative offices. There was no one as he passed through the hardship visiting area and moved up before the two barred gates that led to the Outside. He was just past the hallway entrance when the alarm went off.

Eh, he muttered thickly to himself as his shoulders tightened at the alarm's grating drone. He looked up at the two officers in the elevated central control booth. One caught his eye and held up a finger meaning "One in the bush."

Marzack shook his head and walked into the narrow exit corridor and turned right for the stairs that led to the control booth. There was another barred door at the opening to the stairs. He pushed the buzzer at shoulder level on the right and waited for a voice to materialize over the small, square speaker above the buzzer.

"Sir," a voice said.

"Marzack."

"Come," was the nasal reply, as the electric door hummed open.

Marzack took all fourteen steps at a steady clip. At the top there was another barred door; it opened after the same procedure. Joe Logan, the duty lieutenant, a big man with a tough cowboy face, was on the phone when Marzack came into the long, narrow room that was hot and filled with cigarette smoke.

"Goddamn you," the lieutenant yelled into the phone's receiver; the words peppered Marzack ten feet away. "Sergeant, if you've got liquor on your breath, I'll have your ass and job together."

A short silence then as the sergeant fumbled for words.

"How long uncounted, dammit?" the lieutenant demanded.

Another pause. This one still shorter.

"Sergeant—dammit!"

A long pause, the lieutenant's eyes revealing words on the other end of the line.

"Bullshit. Give me a time," the lieutenant said; Marzack held his position by the door, watching, listening.

"Fuck!" the lieutenant bellowed. Three-thirty? That's six goddamn hours!" He looked first to Marzack, then to his shift officer. "That's fuckin' impossible," he said, astounded.

A second's hesitation.

"Screw the goddamned rodeo!" the lieutenant raged in obvious protest to lame words from the sergeant. "No con in TDC ever went uncounted for six hours."

By the door, Marzack couldn't resist a hard smile around his cigar.

"All right. All right," the lieutenant said, dancing with anger as he shuffled his weight from foot to foot. "Check the rest of the late rodeo crew in and then, goddamn you, you get your ass over here!"

The lieutenant cracked the phone back onto its base, then turned red-faced toward Marzack, who was standing with his hands jammed into the pockets of his trench coat.

"Six hours?" the lieutenant said again in genuine disbelief. "He let one of the rodeo *ahos* go uncounted for six hours. There ain't no way something like that could happen. I been chain-gangin' twenty-four years and I never heard of an asshole uncounted for six hours."

His eyes left Marzack and his gaze fell blankly on his littered control-room desk. Marzack let the silence stand for a few seconds; then he broke it with a question.

"Name of asshole, Joe?" he asked, with no real interest, trying only to ease the lieutenant's pain.

"Macon. Edward J.," the lieutenant replied with an equal lack of interest; still staring at the desk, lost in thoughts of the button-up he was about to begin.

The name stung Marzack like a slap. His chin shot up and his fists tightened inside his coat pockets.

"Say again?" he asked in a voice louder than he intended.

"Macon. Edward J.," Logan repeated, his eyes searching Marzack's face for recognition. "Welding-shop aho. Saddle-bronc hand. You know the boy?"

"Sonofabitch!" Marzack choked, avoiding the question and Logan's eyes. "Bastard," Marzack went on bitterly.

"Hey! What does the boy mean to you?"

Marzack looked across the room at the lieutenant. On impulse he rubbed the scar over his right eye, but said nothing for a moment.

"He's run before," Marzack said, finally unclenching his fists in his trench-coat pockets. "I nailed his ass a block from my house. Fuck-up from the word go," he added bitterly.

"Shit-my-ass," the lieutenant said. "Two times in the bush, and six hours gone. He'll be con-wise this time, and hell to take. You may get some work here," he said flatly, and directly to Marzack.

Then Lieutenant Logan once more turned his attention to the button-up, as Marzack stood back and watched and burned with an anger that made him uneasy.

There were three TDC button-up routines when an escape was on: one for mornings, when cons were showering or being fed or transported to work; one for afternoons, when most cons were at work; and one for evenings, when most cons were in their cells. All three button-ups could be accomplished in less than ten minutes, and with all three routines eight basic things happened: all cons were locked up; tower guards switched to machine guns instead of rifles and shotguns; off-duty correctional officers, housed in state quarters on the prison reservation, came out armed; the prison's administrative staff came out; the warden appeared as soon as possible; the TDC prison director was notified; the prison's dog pack was brought out; and city, county, and state lawmen in the vicinity of the prison were notified and placed on alert—the eighth part of the routine came much later.

Within minutes all thirteen of the other TDC prison units were also on standby alert with the escaped prison, forming a solid north-south gauntlet across East Texas. But it was in the escaped prison itself that the situation was the roughest. Guards began rounding up cons like cattle, herding them toward their cells. Tension flashed like lightning. As at no other time, the lines between guard and guarded were drawn during an escape. Escape was a finger held in the face of the whole prison system. Riots brought out hate and fear. Escapes were insults. They brought revenge to the surface, and in prison, revenge is the most violent emotion of all.

Lieutenant Logan was busy with the phone when the brass—the warden, deputy warden, and the shift major—bolted into the control room, all three irritated and anxious, seething with anger and embarrassment. Since it was the last night of the rodeo, there had been a big party for TDC officials and their guests at the prison director's mansion. The escape had not only disrupted the party, it made TDC look foolish before the public. Logan ended his phone call almost immediately after the warden, a stocky hard-faced man of forty-three, entered the room. Logan faced the warden and chewed on his words as he delivered them.

"One gone," he said. "A rodeo hand named Macon: white male, thirty-six, welding shop—trusty. Second time gone." Then Logan paused for an instant and delivered the last part of what he had to say with even more difficulty. "Gone six hours," he choked out.

"The hell you say!" the warden bellowed. "Goddamn—six hours! That is not possible, goddamnit. That is not possible."

"Six hours," Logan repeated with painful finality.

The warden was a block of stone who lived by the word "discipline."

He looked about him at the men in the room, then turned back to the lieutenant.

"I'm going to my office," he said slowly and deliberately, his anger stilled, his mind now holding only strategy. "I want the boy's duty sergeant in three minutes; two minutes after that I want to hear from you that the button-up is complete and that my officers are here and the dog pack is outside."

When he finished, the warden didn't wait for an answer. He wheeled toward the control room's door, the deputy warden and the major in step behind him, avoiding Marzack, not out of rudeness, but embarrassment. In TDC it was the warden of each unit who lost an escaped convict, and it was the warden who was responsible for getting the con back. The officer only lost his ass, as the saying went; the warden lost face. But Marzack was different. He was the eighth part of the button-up. "The Hounder," as he was known in TDC. He, Marzack, was the one who got the con back if he eluded even the bloodhounds. He was the one who went beyond the grasp of the warden and the prison.

Marzack remained after the three men left. The lieutenant returned to his phones and the button-up. Finally Marzack caught his attention.

"I'll hang around in the lobby for a while. What the hell," he added with strained goodwill. "Maybe the bastard broke his ankle and is sitting on a park bench downtown waiting to be picked up."

Joe Logan tried to smile but couldn't.

Marzack turned, chewed on the two inches that remained of his green cigar, and waited for the door to be released by the duty officer. Behind, there was an agony of tension in the room; like all escapes, there was no comfort to be had until you got the runner back.

Marzack was an ex-New Jersey cop, but no cartoon-character ex-cop. He was a mass of contradictions, and, in a pro cop's way, it seemed he intended it that way. To some he looked like a bouncer in a down-and-out Las Vegas nightclub, to others like a tired ex-jock in a business suit; yet there was just a slight touch of elegance if the

observer knew where to look. On the surface, however, Marzack was
still so much a New Jersey cop and so out of place in the Texas
Department of Corrections that he gave the appearance of a cartoon.
He had "cop" written all over him as surely as if he carried a sign
marked "The Heat."

Marzack was born to be a cop. His uncles were cops. His only
brother was a cop. His father would have been a cop too but he never
learned enough English to pass the one-sheet entrance exam the
Passaic Police Department required in the late twenties.

His father, Stefan Marzanski, and his mother, Maria, came to the
United States on a steamer from Bialystok in northern Poland, fifty
miles from the Russian border. Like the legions that came before and
after, Stefan Marzanski had his name shortened by a customs official,
ending up, for no particular reason, with the label Steve Marzack.
Steve and Mary settled in the Polish section of Passaic, a thirty-
minute train ride from downtown Manhattan. Buster was born four
years later; a year after that, Steve Marzack brought his two younger
brothers over from Poland with money he saved as a policy runner.
Until he went into exile in Texas at age thirty-six, Buster Marzack's
world was the tough northeast Jersey tank towns of Paterson, Clifton,
Belleville, Hackensack, East Orange, Newark, Jersey City, and
Passaic, with an occasional two weeks in Fort Lauderdale, Florida.
There was no "Garden State" where Marzack lived, only the spillover
from New York City on a line across the Hudson River from the
Bronx. Marzack was a star tackle for three years at Passaic High
School, a buck sergeant in the army, then a cop on the Passaic police
force. When he went into exile in Texas, his wife of twelve years
divorced him rather than move out of Jersey, took their two children
to her mother's house in Clifton, and married a milk-delivery man.

Marzack got to Texas disgraced and marked for life as a bad cop
for one wrong move he made on a liquor-store stakeout that cost the
lives of three other cops. He had $22,000 in cash from a safe-deposit
box he acquired soon after being made a detective, and nothing else.
He got a job as a prison transfer man in Texas through the only friend
he had left in the Passaic Police Department after the fatal mistake.
Five years after he arrived in Texas, he was promoted to lieutenant
and put in charge of the TDC inmate-transfer detail, a promotion on

merit that never sat well with any of the five Texas men he
commanded. But they never openly opposed him for fear Marzack
would live up to his nickname with them in private.

Marzack was six-two and forty pounds overweight at 230, but he
carried his weight well, like an ex-jock. He shunned prison housing in
the TDC compounds in Huntsville and lived instead in a one-
bedroom wood-frame house on the corner of Ninth Street and Avenue
I that he bought for $9,500 because it was a marginal neighborhood
with some black families. He had lived in the house since he came to
Texas, and on the outside it seemed a little shabby and in need of a
new coat of white paint. But on the inside, as it was with Marzack
himself, things were different. The inside of the house was sparsely
furnished with good sedate modern furniture. The walls were freshly
painted and decorated with well-framed lithographs of what had
become Marzack's favorite pastime: hunting. The walls were filled
with excellent drawings of deer, antelope, game birds, and bear.
There were photos of Marzack standing with some of his trophies,
several good racks of horns, and in the living room there was a huge
Kodiak-bear rug from Alaska. There were books and magazines—*New
York* and *Sports Illustrated*—a seventeen-inch color TV, and two
upright gun cases. It was a man's house, a place where a woman could
have felt uneasy. But then, no one, woman or man, ever came to the
house. When Marzack wanted the company of other men, he went
hunting; when he wanted the company of a woman, he picked up one
in a bar. The killings at the Passaic liquor store and the loss of his
detective's shield and his family put a permanent wedge between
Marzack and the rest of the world, and he just left it there.

As for the elegance, you had to look closely. Weathered, sad,
composed eyes surrounded by soft, baggy pouches gave it away. The
slightly chubby fingers with their well-groomed bachelor's nails. The
thick, limp, light brown hair that was worn full and parted, with bushy
graying sideburns that came down to the base of his ears. The way he
sat with his legs crossed: slumped back, but erect at the same time,
with one elbow resting on the arm of a chair, the open hand holding
the side of his face. It was a look you didn't ordinarily find in TDC, or
any other prison system.

In TDC, the look was generally pure cowboy: working cowboy for the guards, cattleman for the officers; or gaudy Middle American double-knit sports clothes for both. Marzack was the opposite. He always wore suits: dark wool in winter, light linen in summer; and always a good, dark Dobbs business hat: felt in winter, straw in summer, a New Jersey detective's costume. Like all good cops, Marzack was mean and street-smart and aloof, and had only one thing on his mind: his work, a work that had been taken away, then given back after a fashion.

As he waited in the lobby of the administrative offices of the Huntsville unit—"the Walls," as it was called because of its high brick enclosure—and watched the lines of guards and officials pour in for the manhunt, Marzack sat and thought of Eddie Macon. Cop impulses that had lain dormant for years were taking over in his mind; they made him feel good, satisfied him.

Six hours gone, Marzack said to himself as he sat waiting, and chewed on a freshly lit cigar. *That gives him some time to maneuver and me some time as well. First I find out how he got out; then I figure where he's going. It will be sweet,* he kept on thinking, rubbing the scar over his right eye, *to run up against him again, sweet indeed,* he thought as he watched the lobby fill up with noisy and aggravated men whose Sunday night had just been ruined.

It was not hard to spot the offending sergeant as he entered the corridor. Everyone left the man alone as he made his way quickly and stiffly to the warden's office. When the sergeant came out again in twenty minutes, head down and ashen-faced, followed by the deputy warden, Marzack could guess most of what had gone on in the office. The sergeant, a twenty-eight-year veteran, would not be fired for failing to keep Eddie Macon counted, but it was certain he would be busted to correctional officer one and go on the Walls' garbage detail. In TDC—in all prison work—you were either right or wrong, up or down, caught or loose; there was no middle ground.

But as he watched, Marzack didn't want to merely guess at what went on in the warden's office. He cornered the deputy warden, who was making his way out of the building to the party in the prison director's mansion across the street, where he would personally give a situation report to the TDC prison director and the board-of-corrections members. The deputy warden, horseshoe bald and fat, stopped and gave Marzack the details without much reluctance—a good sign, a sign that told Marzack his name had already come up.

"A fourteen-karat-gold mess," the deputy told Marzack. "Boy fakes going lame in the saddle bronc finals, lays low, then hitches a ride out the back gate on a stock trailer. At least that's how we make it now. There were twelve of them, twelve trailers going to Oklahoma and Louisiana and seven Texas towns."

"What towns?" Marzack asked automatically.

"One end of the state to the other," the deputy answered with genuine exasperation.

"You got a line on where he might be headed?"

"We're squeezing every stooge Inside and sweating the boy's cellmate in Meditation. But right now we got nothing."

Marzack shook his head and held his pleasure inside.

"It's a pisser," the deputy said. "Prison board's across the street with a party on, and we put one in the bush. Sweet Mary's ass!" He turned for the door and his mission.

Marzack's eyes casually followed the deputy warden out the door, but his mind dwelled on only one piece of the deputy's information: that Eddie had *faked* going lame.

Fake-lame, Marzack said to himself. *Fake-lame*.

The idea intrigued Marzack and would not leave his mind.

Lame like a fox . . .

Something strange was happening in Marzack's mind: some bond, some link to Eddie that Marzack did not understand. It had been there from the first moment Marzack heard Eddie's name spoken by the duty lieutenant. It was as if Marzack could feel something between himself and Eddie. As if he could feel Eddie somewhere out there waiting just for him.

But where? How? Marzack asked himself as he stood in the lobby. Suddenly he felt cold and alone in the middle of the hot and crowded room.

What? his mind kept on probing, without the slightest hint of an answer.

3

Eddie / 9:48 p.m. / Frio County, Texas

Eddie was pleased. The knapsack rode well on his back. Chris had padded the shoulder straps so that they didn't dig into his underarms. She had washed his jeans many times to make them soft, yet protective, with the suede leggings sewn to the knees. His leather running shoes were new, but they needed no breaking in. The holstered .38 pistol on his belt did not rub his leg because it was a snub-nose and was no more bother than a sunglasses case. Chris had hidden the knapsack well and placed it in exactly the right spot under the eaves of the Frio River railroad bridge. There had been no trouble slipping off the stock trailer when it stopped at the Frio River weight station. No trouble crossing the four-lane divided highway and sliding down the grass bank to the river and the great wooden supports of the bridge. No trouble in making his way up to the knapsack. No trouble in burying his prison clothes with rocks in the river, then floating downstream for a mile or so. No trouble at all. Everything was working. Eddie was moving very well and making good time even though the terrain was more dense with mesquite bushes than he had imagined from Chris's descriptions.

Chris's rhyme for this part of the run had been: *"From Otley to Dilley it's a little hilly."* He remembered that exactly. But he knew she had not been able to cover the exact lay of the land. She had viewed parts of the land from positions on roads that looked out on a distance of two or three miles into the country where he was running. On I-35, from Otley to Dilley all Chris had been able to see was short, rolling hills that buckled the desert floor where Eddie would run. On the maps it was the same: rolling hills and a clear eight-mile run from Frio River to Martin Branch Creek. Running now, it was different. Not big differences, but different. And that meant surprises, and surprises meant great caution.

There was good light, and Eddie had no trouble sidestepping cactus, and the suede leggings took care of the ones he missed. But something was not right. Eddie sensed it for several minutes before he saw it: the mesquite growing much more dense, small plants in bunches, a softening of the ground, then a few short cottonwoods. There was water ahead; water he had not counted on. But the backbone of his plan was to run straight. Sidetracks to avoid obstacles could add another day. So he kept an even stride toward the water. He saw it from thirty yards as he entered a clearing.

It was a broad irrigation ditch. The kind that wouldn't show on a map. A shiver of fear swept through Eddie as he ran on toward the water.

How many would there be during the 108 miles? One? Two? Ten? Fifty? He shut the leaden thought from his mind and kept on running. There was nothing he could do about it.

Take it as it comes, he told himself. *Level off and take it as it comes. You're doing fine. You're doing just fine.*

He stopped fifteen yards from the ditchbank, crouched on one knee behind a thick mesquite bush, and looked from side to side. There was no one. He held his breath and listened. The only sounds were the crickets and frogs along the ditch, and a distant screech owl. The wild sounds reassured him there were no humans. But he was careful, moving to the ditchbank in a low crawl.

The ditchbank sloped down at a solid forty-five-degree angle. It had been shaved clean of vegetation when it was dug, but that had been years ago. Now the sides were covered with tall grass and weeds. Eddie got down flat on his stomach and looked at the ditch. It went on as far as he could see in both directions, and he judged it to be a good thirty feet across. The water was still and slimy in the moonlight. Eddie thought it looked shallow, but he could not be sure. It didn't matter anyway. It was water, and he could not get his clothes and gear wet. He turned around from his vantage point, looked side-to-side again, and then quickly and quietly made his way back to the mesquite bush for cover.

Eddie's procedure for all water was the same: strip naked and pack his clothes and pistol inside the knapsack; then cover the knapsack with a plastic garbage bag to keep out the water as he swam. Only his leather belt, that he cinched to the covered knapsack and looped around his neck, would get wet.

Behind the cover of the mesquite bush Eddie followed that procedure, and then, looking about once more, scrambled to the ditchbank in a crouch. He was down to the water in seconds. Close up it smelled stagnant and no longer seemed shallow. Eddie stared at the water for a few blank seconds; then his mind took hold of his actions.

Move! he commanded himself. *Move right now. Go!* he shouted in his head. *Go!* In a second more he was in the water, which he found bathtub-hot and over his head.

He moved cautiously through the rancid water—the leather belt looped twice around his neck—picking his way along at a dog paddle, arms barely moving. The unexpected water had thrown him off stride. It had not been right from the first; now, as Eddie moved out into its middle, he began to sense danger. The instant after the thought of danger invaded his mind he saw the thing in front of him. He stiffened and felt his penis disappear in the jelly that moved down through his stomach. There, illuminated by the clear moonlight in the ditch five feet before him, riding the alloy surface like a rope, was the head and top body of a snake: a deadly cottonmouth water moccasin. The big-headed snake was coming straight for him—moving with terrible ease and deliberation.

Jesus!

Eddie's mind and body jerked as he stopped himself dead in the water. On an equal level with the TDC searchers, snakes were what Eddie feared most on the run. Like the searchers, they were something he could not anticipate or defend against.

God! he screamed in his head as he watched the snake move in on him, the reptile's big glassy eyes shining in the moonlight like devil's horns.

Act! Act! his mind cried, as he pushed the knapsack out in front as far as the belt would allow—paddling hard with his legs to remain stationary and afloat. When the snake made its first strike, it bounced off the plastic like a waterlogged stick. For a second there was nothing. Then Eddie heard a *swish* in the water. He wheeled 180 degrees to face the sound. The snake was coming back. Eddie could see all of the reptile now: it was as big around as a baseball bat and five feet long.

The cottonmouth shook in the water before him; a motion like an angry bull's. Then Eddie could see the big snake's tail pulsating. It was getting ready to strike again. Eddie held on to the plastic-covered knapsack with both hands and watched the snake's mercury eyes. All at once he and the serpent were at a standstill, each sizing up the other; then, with the speed of an arrow, the snake struck again in blind rage.

Schwoop was the sound the snake made as it hit the plastic this time. But with equal savagery Eddie clubbed the snake with the bag, an upward punch to the right that sent the fat black-orange reptile sprawling in midair.

Swim! Swim! Go! Go! Eddie cried to himself, as he plowed frantically through the water, the belted knapsack tugging at his neck like an anchor.

Eddie beat wildly for the far shore. He was ten yards from the bank when the snake hit him: a smashing crack into his neck like a gunshot.

"Yaaiii!" Eddie screamed aloud, the strike rendering him half-unconscious with fright as he beat the water in an insane frenzy for the shore.

When he came out of the water the snake was dangling from his neck, its body wrapped around his chest, tail flailing at his stomach. As he planted his feet on the muddy shore, Eddie's mind was a fiery ball of light. He could feel the poison rushing through his brain. He righted himself on the bank and instantly his hand shot up for his neck and the snake. Without thinking that it might pull his neck open, Eddie groped for the snake, took hold of its gritty body, and ripped it from him in one sweep. Eddie's hands came back instantly and dug at his neck. He sank down on both knees, expecting to find a hole in his neck, expecting to black out or die at any second.

But nothing happened. Suddenly Eddie was aware that he was not in pain. His eyes were open and clear, and although he was warped with fear, he seemed okay. But how could that be? He had been hit by the water moccasin. He had pulled the thing from his neck. There should be a hole in his neck. He should be dying. But he felt nothing. Again his hands frantically searched his neck. There was no hole, no fang marks. His mind was clearing. There was total silence around him for a second more; then Eddie heard the snake land in the ditch. Then he heard the sound of the serpent as it thrashed in the water a few feet in front of him. The sight and sound brought him out of his daze. With the plastic-covered knapsack dangling from his neck, Eddie turned and scurried up the soft ditchbank on all fours like a scared dog.

What? God, what? what? he wailed inside his head. *It was on my neck! It hit me! What? What?*

At the top of the bank he stopped and pushed himself down flat on the grassy ledge and looked in all directions. There was no one, but in the distance, to the east, he could see the lights of a house no more than a mile away. The house, not the snake, now dominated.

Did they hear? Will they come?

With his chin pressed into the grass, Eddie waited and watched the house and the open field before it. Minutes went by, but lying perfectly still in the grass, he saw no one and heard nothing. Finally he felt secure enough to touch his neck again. Nothing. Now his mind was completely clear.

But how? How?

He sat up cautiously, naked on the grass, sitting just below the bank's rim. He took the belt from his neck and held the knapsack between his legs. In the sharp moonlight his questions were answered. The snake had hit the belt; both lethal fangs were still lodged in it. In the distance now, Eddie could hear the dying snake churning in the water.

The belt! For Christ's sake, the belt!

Eddie's whole body went limp. He could feel himself breathe again. Once more he could feel the sex between his legs.

"Ho!" he screamed in a wild laugh. "Ho! Ho! Ho! Jesus! The belt! The con belt I made to show the screws at the Walls I was a good little rehabilitated slob. My con belt saved my life! How about that— assholes? How about that! My con belt saved my life!"

But all at once he was no longer laughing. Suddenly he was crying.

"No, God. No . . ." He sobbed, his head bowed in his hands. *God, no. Oh, God. So close. So close. Why? Why?*

But of course, no answers came, and after a few moments more Eddie opened the knapsack's plastic covering, and then the knapsack itself, and reached inside and began taking out his clothes. He dried himself with his damp shirt and then put on his clothes, careful, as ever, to make sure there was no gravel or sand on his feet before he put on his socks and shoes. Out in the water he heard the snake die in a final frenzy, as he completed his dressing by securing his holstered .38 pistol on his belt; his lifesaving con's belt. He jerked with fright as he clinched the belt tight; the short hair on the back of his neck bristled as the ditch became silent again.

Don't think, he told himself. *It's a luxury you can't afford. Just perform, like an actor.*

An actor, he repeated to himself as he stuck the plastic bag inside the knapsack and closed it. *An actor whose role is to run . . . to run,* he said, as he slung the sack on his shoulders.

He did not let his mind play with thoughts. He stuck to his own reality. *Just run,* he said with silent finality, as he started his stride again across a great stretch of flat and open desert.

Run . . .

4

Marzack / 10:00 p.m. / Huntsville, Texas

Marzack watched. It was like the start of a foxhunt. There was sexual anticipation in the air, and a tangible venality.

The searchers were gathered in front of the Walls' main gate. The party at the prison director's mansion, one house down on Fourteenth Street, had moved out onto the lawn and some of the guests had walked the half-block up Fourteenth Street and were standing on the edge of the lawn of the warden's house, waiting anxiously with their drinks.

In the dog truck, a high-beam three-quarter-ton Ford with prison markings and a thick wire cage that took up the entire flatbed, the bloodhounds, seven rangy, muscular thoroughbreds imported from Missoula, Montana—"The Bloodhound Capital of the World"—paced and grunted. All up and down in front of the Walls' main gate, the guards, some dressed only in gray TDC uniform shirts with Levi's and

26

cowboy hats, milled around in small bunches, armed with shotguns and rifles and pistols. Like the dogs and the guests at the prison director's party, the guards were wild for the thing to begin.

Only the four men on the dog truck were steady. The driver of the truck, a coal-black bloated trusty who had driven the truck for twenty-five years, slumped sleep-worn into the steering wheel; the dog boys —two tall, skinny black trusties who ran with the dogs—stood at the rear of the truck bed, erect and cocky in freshly starched prison whites; the dog sergeant—an ancient and honorable position in TDC—a tough old cowboy with a bush mustache who had run the Walls' dog pack for thirty-seven years, stood on the street beside his seated driver, watching the main gate. When the dog sergeant saw a trusty emerge from the gate's cavernlike brick entranceway, he turned and made his way to the rear of the truck, where the dogs waited in their cage.

In his hands the trusty carried Eddie's workshoes and pillow. The convict went straight for the dog sergeant and held the three items out to him. The sergeant took both shoes and in turn brought each up to his nose. He selected one and handed the other back to the trusty. Then he moved up to the thick wire mesh of the dog cage and presented the shoe to each wet and throbbing nose that was thrust through the wide openings. When that was done, the sergeant handed the shoe to one of the dog boys, who instantly carried it to the truck's driver for safekeeping. Then the dog sergeant took Eddie's pillow from the trusty and examined it carefully, smelling it as he had the shoes. He carried the pillow to the dogs. They had the smell now and put up a great howl as they tore their noses into the openings of the mesh for another scent of their quarry. When each dog had the second scent of the pillow firmly in his nose, the dog sergeant brought the pack to a frenzy as he baited them with thrusts of the pillow up into their cage. The hounds bellowed and mauled each other for a fresh noseful of the scent. The air filled up with wailing *aaaahhhhooooooooos* from the dogs and shouts and curses from the guards.

"Let's do it!" a guard shouted.

"Yeah, boy!" somebody answered.

"Let's get that rabbit!"

"Sit on his ass—good!"

"Rabbit done ruined a whole night's drinkin'!" somebody else chimed in.

Then, as the lieutenant in charge of the search party came out onto the main gate's steps, one of the black dog boys at the end of the truck had his words amplified as he spoke to the other dog boy the instant the guards fell silent at the sight of the lieutenant.

"Man run from TDC twice," the black trusty chanted. "That man a dumb sumbitch."

The lieutenant eyed the black convict for a few silent seconds; then he spoke to all the searchers.

"Boy's right on the money," the lieutenant said in slow, even South Texas tones. "Con runs from TDC twice *is* a dumb sonofabitch."

There was rough laughter and agreement from the group; then the lieutenant gave his brief instructions and a final admonishment.

"So," he said, his hands on his hips. "We go get him and we get him quick, and rough if we have to. But we get him."

With that the group broke up like a military formation, the dog sergeant moving first, striding off to his truck's cab with Eddie's pillow tucked securely under his arm. In the shadows just inside the main gate's entranceway, Marzack went unnoticed as he watched the cars and trucks roar off into the cool and misty hill-country night.

Hi-o fucking Silver, Marzack mouthed sarcastically to himself as he watched the lieutenant's car lead the procession on Fourteenth Street past the mansions of the warden and prison director, and the small half-drunk cheering crowd assembled on the lawns, for a circle of the prison grounds and then out of Huntsville on State Road 190, eight miles to Phelps and a sweep over the back roads of the Sam Houston National Forest.

All show. Just spinning wheels. Marzack, like the searchers themselves, knew that until they got a blip—some sort of information on the escapee from a second source—they had nothing to go on. Stolen clothes off a clothesline. A stolen car. Guard dogs barking out of the ordinary. A kidnapping, or someone seeing the runner loose in prison garb. A blip usually came from some private citizen who heard the news of the escape on radio or TV and noticed something out of the ordinary. But Marzack and the searchers knew there was little chance of an early blip on this escape.

This rabbit, Marzack said to himself, moving out onto the main gate's steps and descending them with his hands in his trench-coat pockets, *is beyond the bloodhounds.*

He won't be coming back with chewed trousers. Marzack laughed sourly to himself. *This will take more than cowboy antics; a lot more. This will take a cop.* And as he moved off to his car, Marzack was well aware he was the only cop in TDC. Although he never allowed his mind to form the words, he knew that he was the Hounder, something very different from a hound.

5

Eddie / 11:03 p.m. / Martin Branch Creek, Texas

Eddie was six miles due east of Dilley. He could see more hills, and in the sharp moonlight, a great valley floor that reached to the black horizon. Ahead, he could also see the first breaks of Martin Branch Creek.

The Martin was a southern offshoot of the Frio River, a swift black stand of water that formed a slingshot V with the Frio toward I-35 and Dilley. Eddie planned to ride it southeast for a mile or so as a diversion, as he had done with the Frio itself an hour and thirty-two minutes before. That was before the snake. It was still so vivid in his mind Eddie could feel it dangling from the belt around his neck. Eddie jerked with fright as he ran toward the water, but as he raced on, a new and greater concern entered his mind as he saw a thin line of lights just past the stand of cottonwoods that guarded the lazy bend in the creek to the east.

Ahead, the woods began to thin out as Eddie approached the creek bank. He could see the lights plainly. Lights meant people. People meant contact. Eddie slowed to a cautious shuffle; then fifty yards from the creek bank he began to pick his way through the widely thinning trees and shrubs in a fast, deliberate walk. At the last brush cover he stopped and surveyed the creek and the fish-camp settlement of Rash beyond on the far side of Drumon Bridge. He was breathing hard and his face and neck boiled. But he knew it was not his conditioning; he had seen to that. It was the snake and the new water before him.

You'll go in the Hole for five years minimum. They'll stick you in the Hole and bury you. You'll be forty-one when you come out to daylight and sixty-five when you walk out the gate. . . . You'll . . .

"God," Eddie grunted out loud, his fists and arms and neck flexed in anguish.

"Let it stop! Let it be all right! Please! *Please!*" he muttered in a fierce whisper. He was down on his knees. Not for prayer, but praying. He held on to his words and braced himself with rigid arms and neck and waited for the fright to pass.

Don't think, he said to himself as control came back to him. *Don't think. Just act. Just do as you've planned. Keep to the plan. Keep to the plan. Keep to details. Details . . .*

He caught himself and stopped cold.

Do everything right or get caught, he said silently and simply in answer to his own prayers and fears.

He held his watch faceup to the clear gray-yellow moonlight and looked at the time—11:07 p.m. Right on the money to reach the Martin. In a way the incident of the snake suddenly meant nothing. Escape is like the score at the end of a football game. It doesn't make any difference which team plays the best, which holds the noblest ideals, or who plays the fairest, or who *deserves* to win the most. There were only winners and losers. Eddie lowered his watch arm and surveyed the tree lines on either side of him. Then he returned his gaze to the high and open creek bank and the bridge. With no more hesitation he forced his body to inch past the tree line and out into the open moonlight of the bare creek bank.

Once he was exposed, Eddie dashed over the tall carpet of thick grass on the open space. In seconds he was at the cliff edge and groping his way down the twenty-five-foot drop to the swift-moving water. The lights and sounds of the town of Rash were crystal clear as he moved toward the water. Eddie could hear the sounds of car motors starting fifty yards away where the town began on the south side of the creek bank. When he reached a dense clump of reeds and cattails, where the water and land met, Eddie froze as his mind filled the swift creek water with a thousand deadly snakes. His body was stone, and his mind raged with terror, but just over his own breathing, the loose, juicy sounds of country music from a jukebox floated down to him from a ramshackle wooden bar that sat on the far side of the creek. The music broke Eddie's spell. For an instant he even saw the mad humor of it. But there was no time for thought. If there were more snakes, all he could do was fight them as best he could.

Act! Act! The plan! The plan!

Eddie surveyed his position professionally. A narrow thumb of land stuck out from the south side of the creek for twenty yards, and it seemed about fifty feet high: a fifty-foot promontory topped by the massive and crumbling estate once owned by General Timble E. Rash, the Confederate infantry officer who settled the town a year after the Civil War ended. The estate, which took up the entire peninsula, was dominated by the three-story Gothic ruins of the general's wood-frame mansion and smaller rotting outbuildings that were plainly visible in the strong lunar light. There were no boats on the creek that Eddie could see, and no movement on either side of the creek bank that he could detect. A car clanked north across narrow, wooden Drumon Bridge and then disappeared into the town. Eddie could not hear any other car motors along the town's one street. It was time to move again.

Act! Act! Eddie shouted in his mind as he shed the knapsack and began to undress.

The water was fast and cold. It refreshed his naked body, but Eddie kept the bagged knapsack out in front like a shield, the grinding memory of the snake blocking any comfort the water might afford him. But Eddie moved well in the water, dog-paddling with his free hand and drifting out into the creek toward the edge of the thumb that struck out before him like the bow of a ghost ship.

I'm okay . . . I'm okay, he told himself, his eyes darting madly, searching for snakes.

Out on the long open porch of the bar where the jukebox music drifted, Eddie could just make out the forms of two men standing under a strong neon light. But he could hear their conversation as if he were the third person standing with them. The two men were talking about pussy. They were drunk, and each kept trying to top the other's lies. Eddie had heard the same conversation a thousand times in prison. As he saw the men and heard their voices, a new fright sent the image of the snake from his mind. Eddie dug hard into the water with his free hand and moved as quickly as he could to the security of the far reeds that began in the water in front of him at the start of the thumb of land.

Can they see me? Eddie's mind flashed. *Can they hear me?*

The new angle of the thumb's fifty-foot promontory blocked the conversation of the two men on the bar's porch, and Eddie was again surrounded by the safety of the creek's ripple and his own breathing. His eyes darted left and right, searching everything in sight. But he saw nothing, heard no more human sounds. Slowly, with the knapsack in front of him, Eddie began to move east around the tip of the thumb. He moved with absolute quiet just outside the ring of reeds: a movement through the water as if he were no more than a floating leaf. As he came around the end of the thumb, the drunken voices of the two men droned down on him again.

"I stuck it right up her ass!" he heard one of the men bellow. "Jesus, it was like brandin' a fuckin' dog. She let out a howl that woulda woke up her husband in the next fuckin' state!"

Both men roared with laughter. Eddie dug in close to the creek bank and kept on moving with the contour of the thumb so he would not expose himself in the clear light that shone on the surface of the water between him and Drumon Bridge, thirty yards away to his front. For a few seconds, as he began moving straight with the even line of the creek bank again, Eddie was pelted by the laughs of the two men who stood fifty feet directly above him. He hugged the reeds, and in seconds negotiated the distance to the first bulky concrete piling of the bridge. As he reached the sanctuary of the bridge, Eddie was acutely aware that if the two men on the porch had been looking for him they could have seen him. As he paddled in the water, Eddie could look up and see their faces plainly beneath the glare of a strand of pink neon, big-gutted cowhands wearing jeans and white T-shirts and straw cowboy hats with the bills flattened down in front as a defense against the South Texas sun. As Eddie watched them, he took care to get completely under Drumon Bridge before his head came out of the water.

Under cover of the bridge, Eddie's eyes searched his surroundings with a frantic intensity. He saw nothing and heard only the voices of the two drunken cowhands above him. But suddenly the voices of the two men stopped. Eddie dug into the reeds where he was and strained to hear.

Did they see me? Hear Me? Am I caught? Jesus! Am I caught again?

Eddie's mind burned, and in the vacuum silence, he heard what he thought was the bar's screen door slamming shut. He kept wedged into the reeds, and his ear strained for more sounds. But there were none.

They're coming for me. That's why the door slammed. They're coming for me. They're . . .

Eddie waited for the sound of another slamming door: for the sound of men racing down the hill like dogs. But there was nothing; only silence, and the terror of his mind.

Move down the creek! Go! Go! Go! he screamed at himself.

He obeyed the pounding thoughts and silently pushed himself away from the reeds and began once more to paddle down the creek, the knapsack in front as a shield, the sex between his legs lost from cold and fright, his teeth chattering beyond control.

He moved southeast down the deep creek as the bank made a big lazy U-bend past the town of Rash. He was stopped only once, but only for seconds as he negotiated the small municipal plank dock just past the last fishing shacks of the town. There was no one on the municipal dock's sagging planks. The only sounds were the slaps the several skiffs made as they banged rhythmically against the dock. It was Sunday night. The fishermen had all gone home.

It's working, Eddie told himself as he moved on with the swift creek. *It's working. It's working.* He was pulled along by the swift cold water, farther and farther away from the dying sounds and lights of Rash, farther on into safety.

God, please let it be working, he prayed, reality and fear descending upon him once more as he paddled on into the darkness, the bagged knapsack held before him as his only defense.

God . . . Please . . . Please.

6

Marzack / 11:15 p.m. / Huntsville, Texas

Marzack drove through the damp, empty streets of Huntsville and listened to both his radios: the AM-FM and his police band. A local radio station was playing soft 1940's swing music; the police radio crackled with occasional news of the escape. As he drove, closed up inside his solid, warm Olds 88, Marzack paid the AM station little mind; his mind was on the police radio. He had forgotten how good the police band sounded to his ears. It had been a long time since he had really listened to it; focusing on it now reminded him of the old days in Passaic, cruising in his unmarked detective's sedan.

He stopped for a light on Sam Houston Avenue before the Walker County Courthouse. There were no other cars at the intersection and no one moved on the streets. Like most Southern towns, Huntsville, Texas, rolled up its sidewalks at six p.m. six days a week and all day on Sunday. When the light changed, Marzack turned right and drove three blocks on SR 190, then turned left onto Avenue I. Two short blocks later he turned into his narrow dirt driveway on the corner of Ninth Street and Avenue I. Streetlights gave a ghostly yellow hue to Oakwood Cemetery and Sam Houston's grave across the deserted street. He sat in his car with the motor off and listened for more news of the escape; when none came, he turned the radio off and got out of the car, locked it from a cop's force of habit, and walked into his house.

It had started as another dull, melancholy Sunday with Marzack putting in an appearance at the prison rodeo, his annual TDC function. But now at a quarter past eleven Marzack found himself as keyed-up as in the old days when he came off a shift with the Passaic Police Department. He hung his trench coat and hat on a rack to the right of the front door and went into the kitchen for a beer. He took an ice-cold Coors and a plate of salted peanuts back into the living room and turned on the TV for the late news. The TV anchorman was coming to the end of the eleven-o'clock news. Marzack sat and wondered if the station would pick up the escape. After a few cool sips of beer, scenes of the day's prison rodeo appeared on the screen. Marzack watched, certain the escape would be passed over. He set his beer on the coffee table before him and took an Optimo from his coat pocket and lit it; with the short green cigar in his hand he massaged his eyes with a soothing, practiced U he made with his thumb and second finger. He sat back on his heavy canvas-covered sofa, absentmindedly watching the rodeo film. When the TV anchorman appeared again, Marzack got set for the pro-football scores, but the anchorman went quickly into a speech that was delivered like a comedy routine.

"Yes . . ." The anchorman smiled. "The annual TDC rodeo *is* fun for everyone, or *almost* everyone," he quipped, broadening his TV smile. "Seems at least one of the inmates at the Walls had such a bad time he decided to leave. Edward Macon, a North Carolina man doing forty-one years for assorted charges, was apparently so disgusted with his losing performance in the saddle-bronc-riding event that he felt he couldn't face his guards or fellow inmates. So Mr. Macon departed the premises at about three-thirty today, according to prison spokesmen. As yet, Macon is still at large. Prison officials believe he may have stowed away on one of the many stock trailers that left the prison today with rented rodeo stock. When he's caught, prison officials indicate"—the anchorman ended with a controlled TV chuckle—"Macon will have more than his losing rodeo performance to apologize for."

As a commercial appeared on the TV screen Marzack leaned forward on the sofa and reached for his beer on the coffee table. He drained the remainder of the can in two long swallows and placed it back on the table and sucked on his already half-spent cigar.

Apologize, Marzack grunted to himself in contempt of the TV words. *He'll have to be caught before anybody gets an apology. And that will be about as difficult as getting the apology itself. Apology— shit.* He sat watching the screen with no more interest.

Suddenly the images on the screen caught Marzack's eye. Once more he gave the TV his total attention. It was a detergent commercial. There was a mother on the screen. One by one, her children paraded into the laundry room with dirty clothes and threw them into the washing machine. The woman was smiling and saying she didn't mind if the children got dirty because she had the miracle detergent of the age to clean their clothes. The children, dressed only in their undershorts, stood around her smiling. Then the father entered the picture with his clothes covered with dirt. The mother smiled at the father and took his dirty clothes and put them in the washing machine; then the father and his children stood around the washing machine in their undershorts and waited for their clothes to get clean—the whole family smiling fake TV-commercial smiles all the while.

Marzack's mind was turning with images of his own. The last frames of the commercial, the family standing around the washing machine in sparkling white clothes, solidified his thinking, bridging a gap that had nagged at him all evening.

The family, Marzack said to himself, the words almost erupting into sound. *Macon's family.* He pushed forward on the sofa with both hands on his knees.

"That's the key," he said out loud to the empty room.

His mind could see Eddie as clearly as if Eddie were in the room with him. Instantly he had a lifelike image of Eddie running down Ninth Street in front of his house that summer day six years before.

Marzack could see himself leaping up with surprise from his porch, giving chase, throwing a bone-crushing tackle on Eddie. Then the fight, the scar over his eye, and finally Eddie tied to his porch with handcuffs—crying.

Crying, Marzack said to himself with pleasure. *Crying for his wife and children.*

Marzack had never seen it before or since, and the scene, like the scar he carried over his right eye, was always in his mind, ready to be called up with anger. But now the thoughts had his mind dancing.

The family's the key, he said silently, sucking on the last dead half-inch of his cigar. *Get a line on the family, and you put a collar on Macon.*

He pushed up off the sofa with his hands on his thighs. "Homesick," he said out loud as he walked into the kitchen for another beer, dropping the spent beer can and his cigar butt into an open metal garbage container by the kitchen sink. *The bastard was as homesick as a kid on his first day of school.*

He took his second beer and walked back into the living room and stood and watched the TV set from ten feet; the pro-football wrap-up was on now, and Marzack watched the screen, but his mind had room for only Eddie.

Going fake lame and riding out in broad daylight in a stock trailer takes either great brains or great stupidity, he told himself as he stood holding his beer to his chest watching TV.

He was stupid last time. He won't be stupid two times. And you can bet your ass his wife won't be stupid or easy to find either. It's his deck, and he's dealing all the cards. The only way to beat a bought deck is to knuckle down and wait for a wild card—a blip.

A blip, he repeated as he stood with his weight on one foot, watching the pro scores only as images on the TV screen.

Marzack was still wearing his suit coat. As he watched the TV screen and sipped his second beer, he started to get hot. He moved over to the sofa once more and took off his coat and threw it on a nearby leather-and-chrome chair. Then he loosened his tie and automatically went for his belt. He undid the buckle in one motion, and in a second quick motion he had his holstered .357 Colt magnum revolver in his hand. He bent down and laid the big holstered pistol on the coffee table. Then he rebuckled his belt and reached behind his back and unsnapped his handcuffs from the belt and laid them on the table beside the pistol. Finally he took his leather-covered lead slapstick, a thing like a big flat spoon, from his right back pocket and laid it on the table with the other objects of his trade. He stood back for a few moments and looked down at the table and the three objects. As he looked, they took on meaning for him. A special meaning. An old meaning. He sipped his beer and looked at the hardware and felt very satisfied for the first time in a long while.

A late movie came on TV. Marzack sat down and reached for a fresh cigar. He lit it and sat back into the sofa, got comfortable, and started watching the movie. A new thought entered his mind, momentarily blocking out Eddie's image. When the thought fully materialized, Marzack could not help but laugh out loud, a small laugh, but an excellent one. He had not curled up before a TV late movie with a few beers and a cigar for years. He was usually in bed by eleven. He couldn't remember the last time he had wound down before a TV set with beers and cigars. Probably, it occurred to him, it had been in the old days, after work—after police work, or before the last Hounding.

He sat and watched TV and drank his beer and smoked his cigar and thought of Eddie. He didn't know where it came from, but he knew he felt a bond with Eddie and the escape.

Tomorrow, he told himself. *Tomorrow I'll get on the mother and the children. Find them, and I'm on my way to finding my homesick con.*

Homesick. My homesick con, he repeated to himself, feeling very good.

It was about to start again. He had not been called in. It might be days before that happened. But he was sure it was about to start again. A Hounding. It had been years: two, three? He wasn't quite sure. But it was going to happen again.

I know it. I feel it. I feel . . .

7

Chris and the Children / 11:34 p.m. / Guanajuato, Mexico

Chris checked the children a final time. They were sleeping together in the single bed beside hers. Both lying on their sides. Angie's head on the pillow to the right, her long ebony hair done up in one large ponytail for the night, a child-woman appearance. Bobby to the left, his head off the pillow, his small hand just touching Angie's shoulder, left thumb perpetually in his mouth as he slept. As she stood beside the bed and watched them, Chris was aware that she never stopped marveling at the peace and serenity on their young faces. They had always, she thought, been immune to the thing that had happened to the family. She envied that very much, because she did not feel immune at all.

For a few seconds more Chris's mind lingered on her children. She adjusted the covers around their necks, smoothed their hair, touched their sleeping faces. But her thoughts were never really off the radio on the large carved wooden table between the beds. She had KGL on her oceanic-band radio, and every half-hour since six she had listened to the five-minute news. There had been no news of Eddie's escape. But because she had lived there, she knew the Houston stations always picked up news of escapes in Huntsville; now, near midnight, Chris was drying up with anxiety for news. Abruptly she left her children and sat down on her own bed and wrung her hands and stared at the radio and waited for the words she wanted to hear.

They came in the last thirty seconds of the eleven-thirty newscast. Chris lurched from the bed as if hit by electricity. Suddenly she found herself standing once more between the two beds: arms locked across her breasts, fingers digging into her sides, eyes locked on the radio, ears devouring the announcer's words.

"The convict," the announcer was saying in a disinterested radio monotone, "Edward J. Macon of Blowing Rock, North Carolina, apparently fled the Walls in Huntsville today in one of the dozen stock trailers that carried rented rodeo stock from TDC's annual Texas Prison Rodeo. Macon, a onetime escapee, is believed to have escaped sometime after three-thirty this afternoon. He is still at large at this hour, prison officials say. But a three-state manhunt continues for Macon, a convict TDC officials describe as 'dangerous' and serving a forty-one-year sentence for a variety of charges including felonious assault."

The words Chris had waited for disappeared then as a commercial jingle materialized, and she was left standing with a dominant feeling of emptiness in the midst of the emotions of fear and relief that Eddie had truly made his break.

Dangerous, and serving a forty-one-year sentence for a variety of crimes including felonious assault . . . were the words her mind kept.

Good God! she raged to herself. *Will it never end? Will we never on this earth get what is rightfully ours? Goddammit!* Her fists were clenched at her sides now. *To hear him spoken of like that—like some wild animal, some . . .*

Chris went limp with the "wild-animal" implication and unclenched her fists and sat back down on her bed in resignation. She looked at her watch. It was 11:36 p.m. She knew exactly where Eddie should be: Martin Branch Creek. *Swimming and running: like a wild animal.*

She pushed herself back on the turned-down bed and stared blankly at the high ceiling in defeat.

They—someone else—always have the words. Words that always have the hurtful sound of truth. And, always, the ringing of tin, Chris said as she gave up looking at the ceiling and turned over and held on to her pillow with both arms.

God, how I hate this! How I've always hated it! God . . .

She and the children had left the interior of Mexico on Wednesday, October 10. Two days later they crossed the border and spent the night in a motel in the border town of Eagle Pass, Texas. The next morning Chris bought Eddie's running supplies at an army-navy store, a health-food store, a pharmacy, and a grocery store in Eagle Pass. She had crossed the border with fake Canadian papers, but she used an Ohio driver's license with the name Mrs. Mary Jean Nicholls when she bought Eddie's .38 pistol and ammunition—all the fake papers obtained on the black market months before in Houston. From Eagle Pass Chris drove on Highway 57 through La Pryor and finally connected with I-35 at an interchange ten miles north of the Frio River Bridge, where Eddie would begin his run. She left the knapsack supplies under the eaves of the Frio River Bridge at eight o'clock on the night of Saturday, October 13, and then, with the children, drove on to Laredo and registered at La Posada as Mrs. Christine Lanson of Windsor, Ontario, Canada. She spent the night, and in the morning made Eddie's reservation for the first of November, put his fake Canadian papers and money in a La Posada safe-deposit box, taped the key behind the dresser mirror in Room 216, and drove east and crossed the border back into Mexico late in the afternoon of Sunday, October 14 from Rio Grande City, Texas, to Reynosa, Mexico. She and the children spent the night in Reynosa and then moved south to the Gulf of Mexico for a week in a beachfront suite in a Tampico motel. On Sunday, October 21, they moved again, arriving inland in the colonial city of Queretaro at midmorning on Monday, October 22. They stayed in a hotel in Queretaro for a week and were in place to begin the northerly pickup route for Eddie when he ran from the Walls on Sunday, October 28. Like Eddie's, Chris's plan during the escape was one of motion; one that provided maximum confusion to the enemy, which was everybody and everything.

It was as secure as any plan could be, but Chris felt helpless as she lay on her bed.

Helpless, she said to herself, momentarily defeated. *Dammit, I hate this. . . .*

God! Do you hear me! she boiled in her mind, eyes shut tightly against tears, fists balled under her pillow. *Do you hear me? Do you?*

Do you hear me—dammit! she raged uncontrollably, her thoughts almost spilling over into words. *I hate this! I hate it and I'm through with it!*

But she caught herself. She knew she was not through with it. She knew that it had just begun.

God, God, God. God, I hate this. . . .

But she thought of Eddie, and in a while she let her rage go and went to sleep to be strong for the morning and the days ahead.

DAY TWO DAY TWO

Monday, October 29

8

Eddie / 6:30 a.m. / La Salle County, Texas

Eddie was tired but happy. He had been running for eight hours and fifty-two minutes. Dawn would break in thirty minutes; already the night was giving way to the gray-purple glow of first morning.

He was almost to the end of his first twenty-seven-mile run, and through all his happiness he was bone-weary. Since a man could fast-walk a mile in twenty minutes, to cover twenty-seven miles did not seem so severe at first glance. Simple math would tell you a man could walk two miles an hour with twenty minutes left over to rest, thus covering the whole twenty-seven miles in fourteen hours. But there were catches to that easy reasoning: in the first place, there were not fourteen hours of covering dark in which to run; second, it was not a simple case of running two miles an hour, but twenty-seven miles a night; and third, it was not twenty-seven miles per night, but 108 miles in four days, all without proper food and water. It was like running four Boston Marathons back-to-back on a half-empty stomach

with a pack of wild dogs chasing you. But the wild-dog factor was on
Eddie's side. If he was to complete his run, the dread of the TDC
searchers would make him run with the bare minimum of food and
water needed to sustain energy and life. So he kept on running, his
arms and legs fiery with exhaustion, but kept at the correct arch for
best running. He moved over the desert floor as if he were something
that belonged there, as if he were some species of animal that ran for
survival. But he was not such an animal, he was a frightened man a
long way from the time and place of his birth doing something he had
to do to stay alive, to stay free. As he ran, to ward off the exhaustion
and fear that were steadily chipping away at his body and mind, Eddie
played a very simple and direct game with himself: he set his life up in
his mind and held it before him, as real as the wild and serene desert
that was beginning to take shape before him as he ran toward his first
stopping place.

He had been born Edward Jubal Macon in the small Blue Ridge
Mountain town of Blowing Rock in western North Carolina. His
family were mountain people whose ancestors had been poor in
England when they immigrated to Georgia with Oglethorpe in 1733,
and poor from the moment the first Macon arrived in the Blue Ridge
after the Revolutionary War in 1783. Eddie's father, Jack, was a
handyman, a slot some of the 800 local people in Blowing Rock, called
"townies," fitted into, relegated to that position by the "summer
people," as the 5,000 Floridians who made up the economic bulk of
the community were called.

In Blowing Rock, there was very little middle. You were either a
summer person or a townie, a have or a have-not. That was the first
lesson any local kid ever learned, and because most assumed they
could do nothing about it, like the generations before them, most
simply knuckled under to the shallow reality, or, like Eddie and
Chris, got out at the first possible chance.

In other places there was the cliché of being from the right or wrong
side of the tracks; in Blowing Rock it was the *ledges*. When the Blue
Ridge Mountains were formed four hundred million years before, the
mountaintop that became the incorporated town of Blowing Rock was
laid out as if some hand had ordained that two kinds of people would
live there.

As you came up the nineteen winding miles to Blowing Rock from the foothills of North Carolina's Piedmont past the industrial city of Lenoir, you knew you were entering one of nature's truly peaceful domains. Everything seemed in harmony. The town was pin-clean and laid out in the form of an elegant suburb, with $200,000 mountain villas as much a part of the scene as the evergreens and great poplars. Divisions were the farthest thing from your mind. But as you entered Blowing Rock itself you saw the divisions immediately. There were ledges everywhere you looked.

In the west there were three distinct ledges that faced the sunset from a thousand-foot gorge and looked out across a broad valley of 3,000-foot peaks for a full hundred-mile view. The same was true for the south side of the mountain, and equally true in the north, where ancient mile-high Grandfather Mountain stood like a prehistoric guardian of the sunset. West, south, and north, everything was sculptured and lovely; the ledges themselves inviting order, ease, and grace: "Box seats," the local chamber of commerce touted, "to the wonders of nature." But to the east everything was different. To the east there were no ledges and there was no view; everything was cramped and disjointed. On the other three sides of the mountaintop, things seemed to flow together. On the eastern side there were sharp angles and disorder. The west, south, and north were reserved for the summer people. The east was for the townies.

In the pattern of most of the resort towns of western North Carolina, the original settlers lived on the warm southern side of the mountains, but when Florida's superrich discovered the cool pleasures of the Blue Ridge in the early 1920's, they of course wanted the best side of the mountain. The settlers willingly sold out for what they considered a big profit and moved to the almost equal western side of the mountain. But as the years passed, the settlers were bought out on the west and then the north, leaving them with only the harsh and cramped eastern side—the side nobody wanted.

By the end of World War II, the townies had used up the big-profit money and were surrounded by mansions and money they could not really comprehend and people who saw them as "quaint locals" on one level, and more realistically, servants, on a final level. The sharp deal their grandfathers made became the instrument that kept most of their descendants in a poverty cycle not unlike that of the European system of serf to feudal lord. "Tater Hill," as the townies' side of Blowing Rock was called—like their British and Irish ancestors, each family raised potatoes as the staple of their diet—became the classic Appalachian hard-luck community of slatboard houses with rusting washing machines on front porches, packs of bony dogs roaming at will, snot-nosed kids, outdoor toilets, and junk cars parked on forty-five-degree-angle rock driveways.

As he ran on, although he knew he should not, Eddie let the image of the town dissolve into an image of Chris—her and their childhood together, their hopes and dreams, what they *hoped* to become. He set his feet down firmly on the hard earth and did not feel anything but joy as he let the woman he loved come into his mind.

He had been born in a five-room Tater Hill shack with an outdoor toilet on Russell Street. Chris was born a quarter of a mile away on Lewis Street in a four-room shack heated by a single potbellied wood stove. Both their fathers were "pickups," men who picked up whatever work they could in the summer and then served at twenty-five dollars a month as caretakers for the town's mansions or as day laborers in the furniture factories of Lenoir or Hickory during the winter and spring. A "hard-by-the-bone" world, as the saying went, where five thousand dollars a year was a big income.

Eddie and Chris were only two weeks apart in age. They played together as children and then went to Blowing Rock Elementary School; then they were bused eight miles to Boone to Watauga High School. Chris was valedictorian of the class, Eddie was a star football and baseball player—adolescent honors that might have launched them on lives with sound, secure futures. But futures required means: money and standing; Eddie and Chris had neither.

They dated casually during their freshman and sophomore years at high school, but in their junior year, Eddie and Chris started going steady. They made love for the first time on the warm June night they graduated, and after they finished, they sat naked on a blanket on a deserted country road on Grandfather Mountain and held each other and looked at the moon for hours. As they started to drive away, Chris held on to Eddie in the front seat of his family's battered eight-year-old Plymouth and she started to cry.

"*Goddammit!*" she sobbed, using the first profanity Eddie had ever heard her utter. "Is there any hope at all for us? Anything really good?"

Eddie faced her close in the dark of the car and answered quickly and deliberately.

"Yes," he said with a resolve that quieted her tears.

Two weeks later Eddie went off to the service and Chris went to work as a summer clerk in one of Blowing Rock's boutiques. They agreed to write every day and to marry when Eddie's four-year enlistment was up. Eddie had a plan, but he knew it would take money to put it into action. And for the poor, money means time.

Plans, he thought as he ran. *Always so many plans. So many hopes.* With all his will he kept the desperation of where he was and what he was doing from wrecking his mind and body. He concentrated on the reality of where he would be at the end of all those plans and hopes, and just kept on running.

He was breathing hard but well, and the chill of the night was giving way to the first warmth of morning as the dim, false daylight grew stronger with each second and each step he took.

He and Chris, they had wanted so much. They had planned for so much. They had worked for so much. They were so hungry, so desperately hungry; that thought he could not keep from his mind as he ran on.

So hungry.

Eddie was an eighteen-year-old and his head spun with ideas, but all he knew for certain was desire, distinct feelings he could trace back to a sun-filled summer day when he was nine years old. One afternoon he had stood before the magical candy counters of Jackson's Ltd. in

the center of Blowing Rock and watched a summer father and his
summer son moving about the store. They were both dressed all in
white: gleaming white tennis shirts and shorts, white socks, and white
tennis shoes. Every hair on their heads was in place, their teeth were
straight and white, their bodies plump and pink-brown and spotlessly
clean. To Eddie they looked like babies. They were as cheerful as
babies too, smiling and looking at one another, touching, laughing,
moving with a rubbery ease. Eddie stood back and watched them.
They were buying things. Anything they wanted they casually
dropped into the small wicker shopping cart the father pushed. One
by one Eddie saw the things he considered life's treasures—candies,
fruits, toys, comic books, soft drinks, rolls of sausages, blocks of
cheese, long sticks of bread—tossed into the cart as if they had been
the lowly potatoes he and his father deposited in their rickety wooden
wheelbarrow.

Finally the father and son were even with Eddie at the counter.
Eddie pushed himself back against a wall, out of their sight, and kept
on watching them. Near the counter there was a final array of
treasures, the things Eddie considered the most sacred: baseball
gloves, balls, bats, yo-yos, games, and best of all, official deep blue
junior New York Yankee baseball caps. While the father set the
contents of the shopping cart on the counter, the son walked over to
the treasures. Eddie's eyes never left the boy for a second as he
approached the items and began picking from them with the same
nonchalance he had used for the comic books and sausages. At first
Eddie went red with anger. But almost at once the anger was replaced
by fascination as the boy filled his arms with two gloves, a bat, and two
boxes of balls, ending with two of the lovely and sacrosanct Yankee
caps.

How? Eddie said to himself as he stood and watched the spectacle.
How is it possible one person can have so much?

But then came the most miraculous part of the whole scene, the
part that remained most vivid for Eddie for the rest of his life. The
sight of the boy walking back to the father with his arms crammed full
and the father smiling, *laughing*. No reprimand. No screaming. No
cursing. No violent slaps. Smiles and laughter, *happiness* that the boy
was choosing so much.

Eddie left Jackson's that day, after the father and son got into their long convertible and drove away, and although the summer day was thick with heat, and he was in the place of his birth, he felt cold and alone. It was a feeling that never really left him from that day on.

Never once did Eddie really feel completely warm or completely a part of his home. It was as if his poverty uprooted him; a feeling of total vulnerability. In his youth he had not even been allowed the small luxury of momentary ease and warmth that came to the sons and daughters of townies who were taken in as "pets" of the summer people: "cute little primitives" to be fussed over and tolerated as do-gooder projects for bored wives or fathers whose sons and daughters had long since departed on summer-people courses of their own.

Although he was brighter and more inquisitive than the other townie children, Eddie was not petted because he was not cute. He had the hard, lean, muscular, tough-cocky look of exactly what he was—a dirt-poor Appalachian kid. He did not have a pinkish side the summer people could reach out to and coddle. He was always the observer, always on the outside looking in. But not merely the hungry voyeur with his nose pressed against the restaurant window numbly wanting his belly full; Eddie was the observer who also wanted to know about the food on the inside. For Eddie, as unlikely as it appeared at first, the sea always seemed to be his key to the inside.

Keys, he thought as he pounded on over the desert floor, which was bare and free of cactus and mesquite now. *So many keys.* For a long time he thought that his keys were the ones that would unlock the doors to the secrets and the places that he longed for. He was still not sure he had been wrong. For a long time now he had not been sure of reality at all, because the reality that had been forced on him was so different from the one he had prepared for.

So different. So different, he said in his mind as he ran.

You remember strange little flashes, strange quirks as a child, and like the memory of the long-ago summer boy and his treasures, Eddie's mind—from age nine—held a single image more dearly than any other: the image of a flying fish. A beautiful, serene little creature able to move in all worlds with equal ease, always aloof and majestic. For any farmboy daydreaming at a school desk in the mountains of North Carolina, a textbook picture of a flying fish and the sea was a narcotic. But for Eddie it was much more. It was something magical, Eddie's great childhood fantasy.

His older brother and sister died as infants, so Eddie had a room of his own in his family's small wood-frame house. In the way of so many children, the room became his kingdom, the place where a tangible existence was played out on walls in color drawings and photographs clipped from books and magazines. To enter Eddie's room was to enter the far-off and esoteric world of the sea; and to a child, it never mattered in the least that it was simply a paper, fantasy world. But as he grew to early manhood, the sea images remained in Eddie's mind, and then it began to hurt that they were fantasy. Eddie began to look for ways to make them real. The way to do it was obvious: the sea services, the Navy, Merchant Marine, and Coast Guard. Eddie ruled out the Navy as being too big and filled with too many chances of no sea duty; he crossed off the Merchant Marine and their big ships as being too impersonal. From age sixteen on, Eddie knew the Coast Guard was exactly right for him. Years later he could laugh about the pest he became at the Coast Guard recruiting office in Boone. But the two years he haunted the office, in the company of a salty old chief petty officer, whose uniforms were lined with rows of brightly colored and mysterious service ribbons, and rank and insignias, was the most meaningful time in Eddie's young life. By the time he reported for recruit training at the Coast Guard Training Station at Cape May, New Jersey, he had all but committed the *Seaman's Manual* to memory.

For the other sons of the families who lived in the squalor of the Tater Hill section of Blowing Rock, the military service was the one great encroachment the outside world made on their small and ignorant lives. But for Eddie the military was not only a great adventure and the culmination of years of dreams, it was first and last his way out of Tater Hill, and he grabbed the chance with all the youthful vigor and anticipation he possessed. He sensed that from all the possibilities there was one classic reason why people succeeded away from home, and that reason was simply that there was nothing for them *at* home. For this reason alone Eddie graduated as the honor seaman of his training squadron at Cape May and thereafter held the top rating of proficiency and conduct throughout his Coast Guard career.

Eddie liked everything about the Coast Guard and his new surroundings. Where others might have found the quarters Spartan, Eddie saw them as wonderfully clean and modern. He liked the food, the clothes, the fresh disinfected smells. The order and discipline and the indoctrination into seamanship were all the "higher learning" he ever desired. He had no frame of reference that would let him imagine that his contentment overstepped the bounds into being trite and wholly predictable. All Eddie knew was that he felt happy and fulfilled for the first time in his life. When he was assigned to the seven-man Coast Guard Station on South Caicos Island in the Turks and Caicos Islands chain in the British West Indies, one hundred miles south of the last Bahama island, his mood unashamedly overflowed into euphoria.

To get to the Turks and Caicos Islands you caught a Navy plane out of Opalacka Naval Air Station in Miami for Grand Turk, the seat of government for the islands, 550 miles south of Miami in the Caribbean. Grand Turk and the Turks and Caicos Islands were one of the last of the stiff-upper-lip, Union Jack–waving colonies left for the British around the world. To Eddie, the tiny, drowsy dot of an island was a London of history and geography books rather than a down-at-the-heel Lyme Regis. When he reported on a humid September day, Eddie was supposed to be billeted at the small Grand Turk U.S. Naval Air Station for the weekend before being taken by launch to the Coast Guard Station on South Caicos, thirty miles to the northwest. But he spent his own money to stay at the two-hundred-year-old Turk's Head Inn in the heart of the colonial section of the island. Grand Turk had virtually no tourists: there was a local British joke that nothing had happened from the October day in 1492 when Christopher Columbus sailed by until the Loyalists fled America after the Revolutionary War, and that everything had gone steadily to hell since 1836, when Britain abolished slavery, and the salt-raking business became a victim of the artificial-salt industry in the 1950's. But all of this was unknown to Eddie; he saw only what the first-time foreign traveler sees—the awesome difference of another land.

In boot camp, Eddie put on twenty pounds, had his habitually bad teeth fixed, and replaced some of his cockiness with a steady, if not solid, self-assurance. As he roamed Grand Turk's narrow, dusty stone-wall-and-bougainvillea-lined streets and haunted its cool, dark bars that served gin and tonic in wine goblets and warm ale and bitters in heavy pint-sized facet mugs, he began soundly, for the first time in his life, to find himself, to try to determine what the world held for him personally, his ideas, his hopes and dreams. Of course he found no definitive answers that first time, but in that first trying, Eddie discovered an almost tangible happiness that replaced his newer contentment, a happiness that reminded him of the look on the face of that long-ago Blowing Rock summer boy. And in that same happiness, from among the more than six hundred letters Eddie wrote Chris during his four years at sea in the Coast Guard, Chris always reserved a special place for the first short letter he wrote her from the balcony of his room at the Turk's Head Inn.

Honey,

I feel different. I know that's not the right word, but it's the way I feel—different. I miss you and you know I love you, but I don't miss you and home. Blowing Rock doesn't even seem real.

How can that be?

I want you so badly and want you here with me right now, but I don't feel homesick or lonely. Please don't take this the wrong way and get upset or worried that anything has changed between us, because it hasn't and never will. But I just feel different. Like I'm about to find out something and I don't really know what it is. Different—that's the only way I can describe it.

All my love and kisses,
Eddie

Chris, his mind said to him as he ran, and he felt refreshed by the sound of the name and the image it conjured up. *Chris, Chris, Chris,* his mind sang to him in a sweet song.

They had been so close, so perfect, so much a part of each other you could not tell where one left off and the other began.

And even now, after so many years apart, it was still so painful to think of the parting, of the great gap the separation created in his mind and body.

Chris! Chris! Chris! he shouted in his mind to ward off the devils of separation.

Eddie was the first and only man ever to make love to Chris, and when she let him have her she did it knowing she was giving herself over to him for life. There was never a second from that time that she doubted his complete love, never a time she doubted he could make a place for them, a better way of life for them. But that first letter made it all official, sealed it more so than their marriage contract. The letter, as juvenile as it was, set down in black and white exactly the way Chris felt too—*different.* They were two of a kind, and "different" was the only hope they had for a better life. Eddie's plan for making a better life for them was complicated, but it came under a very simple heading: "Operation Flying Fish," Eddie called it.

The flying fish was not only Eddie's abstract symbol of breaking from his past; it also had a very concrete meaning in his life: the flying fish was the chief bait used in the taking of billfish, sail, marlin, and broadbill swordfish. And that was the way Eddie intended to make his way in life—as a charter-boat captain at the wheel of his own fishing machine, a sleek, gleaming white forty-two-foot cruiser, framed by dual outriggers and topped by a flying bridge and a tuna tower. He and the flying fish would be as one. He would learn the ways of the sea and the craft of boats in the Coast Guard; then he would hire himself out as a mate on a charter boat in South Florida or the Florida Keys and he would settle in and learn the art of big-game sportfishing for billfish and the giant tuna that schooled in the Gulf Stream between Miami and Bimini. He would learn fishing and at the same time learn the ways of the super-money anglers who followed the sport. He would make contacts and establish himself. He would save for a boat of his own.

The top of the line, a handmade Rybovitch or Merritt sportfisherman, would cost a minimum of $250,000. These fishing machines were reserved for the always rich. But a good used forty-two-foot production-made Trojan or Chris Craft could be had for about $50,000; made like new for another $5,000; and outfitted with an adequate fish finder, depth gauge, and radios for another $5,000. To start on your own, you would need a kitty of another $5,000 for expenses and living money until the charters were regularly booked. In all, you needed $65,000 to get into the charter-boat business on a cash basis, but if you knew what you were doing, you could get by on $40,000, by paying half on your boat with a bank note for the other $25,000 payable over seven years.

Under the terms of Operation Flying Fish, during the four years Eddie was in the Coast Guard, Chris would attend the University of North Carolina at Chapel Hill on a full academic scholarship, with Eddie sending her money for clothes and Chris working part-time for spending money. Chris would take a degree in elementary education, and when they were married she would teach school and they would live on her salary and save $100 a week of Eddie's mate's salary toward the boat. It would take them seven years and seven months to save the $40,000 they needed. Seven years, seven months, plus four years of college and the Coast Guard; almost twelve years in all. The fact that they were two penniless eighteen-year-olds working on a plan that would affect them until they were thirty, a plan that had only an outside chance of working, never once entered their minds. The plan was their hope, their salvation. Without putting the thought into words, Eddie and Chris knew that without the plan they were doomed to the second-class citizenship of Blowing Rock's Tater Hill.

Eddie struck, as the Coast Guard termed it, for a job as a boatswain's mate on South Caicos, and three months after he reported for duty, he was promoted to boatswain's mate third class. When he left the station a year later in August, he was a BM-2 and had a sound working knowledge of the station's forty-footer; he was beginning to learn the sea and its ways and moods. Before he reported to his next duty station, Eddie took his annual thirty-day leave with Chris in a cottage at the foot of Mount Mitchell. The cottage cost a hundred dollars for the month and was ninety miles from Blowing Rock, a place they no longer considered home. They registered as "Mr. and Mrs. Edward Macon of Chapel Hill." Of course they were not married, and they were not from Chapel Hill. But they were together and no longer from Tater Hill.

When Eddie went off to the service and Chris entered Chapel Hill, the break with home was complete. From that moment on, they declared their independence of Blowing Rock and its Tater Hill stigma, and broke irrevocably from their families. Chris was aware that her family regarded her as an "uppity whore." Eddie's family saw him as "stuck-up." It was not easy for Eddie and Chris to break completely with their families, but they knew it had to be done and held to a firm rule never to speak of the break or the little they had left behind.

"We pretend we're orphans," Eddie decided for them with juvenile resolve. "*We're* our family," he said. "It's all the family we'll ever need. It's the family we will give to our children."

Their summer month together was magic. Two grown-up children playing house, enjoying the ripeness of sex and love like two primitives suspended in time and space. Each shared their strange new worlds with the other, each built on the other's plans. They had no car and little money and no need of either. They had each other. The first year had passed and they were on schedule with their plan. They were both alive in every fiber of their beings, as only people with a far-reaching goal can be. In September Chris returned to her dormitory and Eddie departed for his Coast Guard duty station in the Florida Keys.

In Marathon, the big, sprawling, noisy fishing center of the Middle Keys, Eddie began in earnest to learn the charter boatman's trade, hiring out whenever he could on his off days for twenty dollars and tips as a fill-in mate on one of the many cruisers moored at the

Hurricane Charter Boat Docks. The first day Eddie fished for money
in November, he knew absolutely that it was what he wanted to do for
the rest of his life, that he had made the right choice.

If the *why* of the thing was obscured from Eddie's vision, what he
saw before him he understood and reached out to completely. In
Marathon he wrote to Chris:

> Honey,
>
> It's all so great. Every bit of it. The guys, the boats, the fish. All of
> it. I just feel like giving out with a war whoop all the time. Today I
> went out for the first time. I got a boat called the *Shooting Star*,
> with a captain named Homer Bishop. A big tough-looking man with
> twenty years of sun on his face and hands and neck.
>
> It's a whole new world. I know I'm not telling it right or letting
> you know really what it's like. It's just all great and new. The guys
> dressed up in Bahama straw hats or long peaked-bill fishing
> caps—khakis, white tennis shoes, cut-off jeans. Everybody sun-
> tanned and healthy-looking, not white and milktoast-looking like
> back home. Everybody talking with Yankee accents. (I'm trying to
> get one myself, but not having much luck!) And the boats. If you
> could see the boats! Rybovitches and Merritts all over the place, like
> they cost five thousand instead of a quarter of a million. But also
> plenty of fine-looking Chris Crafts and Trojans. And through
> everything, like somebody standing back and having a great belly
> laugh, everybody is having a ball. Fun, just like a Fourth of July
> picnic back home. Fun all the time. If you were just here, that
> would make it all complete.
>
> All my love and kisses,
> Eddie

If you were here. Eddie thought of Chris as he ran on, a thought that
had dominated his entire adult life in one way or another.

For a futile few seconds he tried to imagine her beside him, both of
them gliding free and wild and untouched through the vacuum space

where he ran. But it hurt too bad to imagine her so close and still not be able to reach out and touch her.

If you were only here, his mind kept gnawing at him as he dug his arms in close to his sides and pumped them, as his legs kept up good knee motion and his feet beat at the desert floor like a machine.

If you were only here.

When he left Marathon two years later, Eddie was twenty-one years old and a first-class boatswain's mate. He was a man. He knew the sea and boats, and the art of fishing for money. And he knew where he wanted to practice the art of big-game fishing.

Because it seemed to answer all their needs and because it fascinated him as if it had been a person one could talk to and know, Eddie chose Key West, Florida, for him and Chris. During his first summer in Marathon, Chris rode the bus from Chapel Hill to the island city and Eddie met her at the depot at the head of Duval Street. It was Chris's initiation to the Florida Keys and to the world of fishing and the sea that Eddie had described to her in letters. Eddie presented it to her the way one might show off a new baby. Nothing in his life until that time, and few things after, was as sweet as showing Chris his new world, their new world, for the first time.

Key West was a feast, as much an idea as it was real. To Eddie and Chris, the low-level little wooden seaport town was Madrid and London and all their fantasies in between. The nine-square-mile city set 120 miles out at an apex between the Atlantic and the Gulf of Mexico had been fought over for two hundred years before it was sold to an American named John Simonton in 1821; it had always remained half-Latin, half-English in tone, and completely unto its own in stubbornness and charm. As the southernmost point in the continental United States, it was the end of the line for end-of-the-liners, a place of whitewashed homes, bougainvillea and poinsettia and loonies crammed in with the military establishment and the locals, who were called "conchs," after the pronouncement by their white Bahamian ancestors that they would rather eat conch meat, the flesh of a Bahamas and Keys shellfish, and relocate in the Florida Keys than eat

English beef in the Bahamas under the harsh British colonial rule of the mid-1800's.

Eddie and Chris took a three-room second-story apartment on Eaton Street: a big, open kitchen with a six-foot-long sink and a tiny two-burner gas stove; a small, boxy living room paneled with knotty pine and furnished with big overstuffed pieces that were slightly frayed; and a bedroom that had a fourteen-foot ceiling, a four-poster bed, and a narrow porch with no screen that ran the length of the three rooms and looked west several streets to the end of the island and the shrimp docks along Caroline Street. After so long without each other, their time together was one of renewed discovery and fascination. Each could see the changes in the other, and with that knowledge they began to see the changes in themselves. They had been running blind with an idea; now their vision was clearing.

Most obvious of all, they looked different. Their conversation was different. Their manner had changed. Chris had always worn her dark hair below her shoulders, the typical "fan" style of Appalachia. Now her hair was bobbed to a boyish length. She had replaced her uniform of simple cotton and wool dresses with colorful skirts and single-color cotton blouses that she wore open two buttons at the throat, and her shoes were Indian-toed sandals. She was alive: smiling, laughing, inquisitive, not cowed and dull like the young girls and women of Tater Hill. Eddie was an even one-sixty now, all hard-packed on his five-ten frame. He was sea-brown with fisherman's sun creases already beginning to form on his neck and forehead and hands. He possessed great self-assurance. His eyes no longer searched, they began to *look*, to inquire. He sported a $350 Rolex watch, a sportfisherman's tool that he bought from a Key West jeweler for twenty-five dollars a month for fourteen months; cut-off Levi's; tight-fitting white T-shirts; and battered white slip-on tennis shoes. His hair was cut military-close, but he had already begun to sport a thin petty officer's mustache that delighted Chris and was dubbed by her his "Clark Gable paste-on." And if it is true that the conversations of down-and-out country people revolve around their mutual distrust of the outside world and of their own grinding, hapless problems—the conversations Eddie and Chris had grown up with—their words came to be built on expectation and, if not total trust of their new world, anticipation of it. They shared things, an act they never saw played out by their parents or childhood acquaintances. In the sharing they made the transition into companionship that most people take completely for granted, or never come close to achieving. Their conversations, their lovemaking, everything they did, were not ritual. They became totally involved. Eddie and Chris would spend whole mornings and nights playing with each other's body; whole afternoons eating and drinking and talking. To the untrained eye their actions might have seemed simple or even mundane, but for them it was fulfillment, total happiness.

A year in advance they made arrangements for Chris to take a job teaching third grade at José Martí Elementary School in Key West and took a postdated year's lease on a small Bahama-style house at the end of secluded Baker's Lane off Elizabeth Street in the center of Old Key West. Then Chris returned to Chapel Hill for her last year of school and Eddie reported as officer-in-charge of the five-man caretaker unit at the Coast Guard Station on Lighthouse Key in the Dry Tortugas Islands between Key West and Cuba. Chris graduated from the University of North Carolina on the sixth of June a year later; Eddie mustered out of the Coast Guard fifteen days later.

A line from the last letter Chris received from Eddie before they were married in July summed up all they had worked for the past four years, and solidified all Eddie had pointed them toward.

"I think," the line read, "we are ready to begin."

Of course, Chris felt the same.

They were married on a crisp summer afternoon in Chapel Hill, North Carolina, by a justice of the peace, with Chris's college roommate and her boyfriend serving as bridesmaid and best man. After the ten-minute ceremony the four young people adjourned to a nearby college tavern and had a pitcher of draft beer, cheeseburgers, and french fries, and made strained conversation for half an hour. Then—Eddie always remembered the time exactly—at five p.m. he and Chris were on their own: married and headed for their new life together. As they started south for Key West, Eddie made the halfhearted observation that it had taken them twenty-two years to make it from Tater Hill to Chapel Hill, but that, in the frame of reference of North Carolina, was no small accomplishment in itself.

"Let's just not take another twenty-two years before we get to the next plateau," Chris joked.

The remark stuck with them, and as they drove out of Chapel Hill's polite and manicured streets and started south, although the idea was buried deep inside them, they both felt very much alone and brittle. But as always there was anticipation and excitement, and plans— always a plan. And the idea that everything was going to work out beautifully, with no one to interfere.

Suddenly Eddie let all his thoughts go, and he smiled. Ahead, in the near-daylight, he could see the first breaks of Characo Marrano Creek. Finally the first run was over. His heart soared and he felt a flash of relief as he bolted for the tree cover at the bank of the narrow creek as harsh, full daylight suddenly materialized around him like stadium lights. His heel strings ached and the nerves and muscles at the base of his back were on fire. His head pounded with the pain of ten hours of running. His forearms were heavy as lead and they hurt. His eyes were red and burning with sweat, and for the past two hours he had been nauseated. But now it was over. He had reached his first objective. He had not made contact. He had not been captured.

Where he came to rest, the Characo Marrano made a lazy fist north to south. There were tall cottonwoods on both banks, whose slopes were a full twenty feet to the water's edge. It was plain that the creek had once been a forceful stand of water but now it was muddy brown and slow-running and no more than fifteen yards across at its widest point. As he made for the cottonwoods, Eddie saw no one and he heard no sound other than the wild sounds of birds who were out for their morning feeding.

I'm having luck, he allowed himself to think as he entered the trees and stopped.

Thank God, I'm having luck. He let himself go on even though he knew the words were wrong because they gave him a false hope and confidence he could not afford. On impulse his mind shifted to the reality at hand.

Go! his brain demanded. *Get to the water! Get into hiding! Quick!*

Go! In seconds he was at the lip of the bank and then down it like a rat.

He found a thick patch of gallberries just at the water's edge, a ready-made nest fronted by a long line of high reeds; quickly he slipped inside and was hidden from view. In the center of the gallberry patch there was a small clearing just big enough for him to lie down, a spot that some other animal clearly had used before. Eddie picked his way through the bushes to the clearing, jerking nervously at the crackling sounds the branches made. When he reached the clearing he stopped dead still on his hands and knees and listened. There was vacuum quiet around him, punctuated only by the occasional shrieking of birds.

In the bushes, now that he was still, Eddie began to sweat. The pain of his body flooded in on him. His nausea returned. He gagged, holding back the retching sounds behind clenched teeth and tight lips. He felt the knapsack. He had carried it for so long that it seemed like part of him. Now he could feel the straps cutting into his armpits and the weight pushing down on his back. For a second he thought he was blacking out. But he fought with all his powers to beat the pain and the nausea and lightheadedness. His body shook against the pain; he pushed himself up on his knees. He shed the knapsack in two shoulder motions; then he fell back on it, limp and exhausted. His eyes closed and his brain went numb. He drifted off into a gray fog and did not have the power to bring himself back.

He was out for only minutes, but when he came to, the gray pain and exhaustion were gone, and in their place Eddie saw blue—the crystal blue sky—and he felt refreshed. The sweat had dried on his forehead. His clothes—blue sweatshirt and jeans—were soaked through to the skin from the run, but they were drying in the early-morning sun that came in quickly from a dominant position in the east. Eddie opened his eyes fully and took in the cloudless blue sky above him. He lay and looked at the sky and stretched his arms and legs as if waking from a long and excellent sleep. And he smiled. He couldn't hold back the smile. He looked at the bushes around him, waxy green leaves with gray-green trunks, and smiled. He sat up and looked at the free-world clothes on his arms and legs, and the free-world shoes on his feet, and smiled. He looked at the rich soil by the water's edge, and at the creek's water beyond, and smiled. He could not stop exploring the place he was in, and he could not stop smiling. At first he did not fully understand his joy. He thought he was simply giddy with exhaustion and fatigue, or mad with fright. Then the reason behind the joy occurred to him: he was happy to be in the free world.

Being happy. Such a simple act. But a totally new emotion for him, a reflex that had not been fully triggered in his mind for six years. For a while Eddie just sat in his nest inside the bushes and rubbed his sore legs and allowed himself the luxury of being happy, the luxury of blue sky instead of walls and bars, the luxury of natural ground instead of concrete, the luxury of jeans, not TDC prison whites. But before very long he stopped himself.

No! No! he raged in his head. *Don't. Don't let yourself slip. Don't start to enjoy what is not yours until it is yours to keep. Don't enjoy it until you're free. Not until you're free and gone! Stop,* he told himself, bringing calm to his mind. *Do the things you have to do and then rest. Do the things now, and do them well, and that will put you one step closer to real freedom. Thoughts of freedom are nothing.* He reached for his knapsack and undid the top flap. *Freedom is freedom,* he repeated as he opened it and got ready to eat and repair the damage the twenty-seven-mile run had done to his body.

In Eddie's knapsack Chris had put eight one-pound packets of high-carbohydrate foodstuffs. That would give Eddie two pounds of food a day—three short of what he needed to get up the energy to cover twenty-seven miles—but he could not run with twenty pounds of food in his knapsack. To compensate for the three pounds of lost food a day, Chris had added small packets of dextrose tablets that would give Eddie quick energy, and salt tablets to ward off exhaustion. The requirements of the run stretched Eddie's endurance and health to the bone, but he possessed a motivation that no marathoner ever had: the fatal desperation of capture, and life in prison.

Eddie had eaten one of the food packets at the start of the run; now he took another from the knapsack. It was a simple system—eat one food packet at the start of the run and one at the end of the twenty-seven miles—but in no way did they satisfy the monstrous hunger he felt. Each packet was a sealed plastic bag only half full. Eddie took his empty canteen down to the creek edge and filled it and quickly returned to the cover of his nest. Under cover again he put a halazone tablet in the canteen to purify the murky brown creek water; when it was purified he poured the water into the half-empty food packet. The contents of the packet were dehydrated apricots and peaches, dehydrated cooked beans and corn, dried cereal, cashews, and dried honey and molasses. Eddie stirred the mixture with his knife, turning it into a viscous brown lump; then he ate it with his fingers without thinking about its miserable taste. He drank two more canteens of water, and when he was through, he sat and rubbed the calves of his legs. They felt like concrete, and that worried him, but he had expected it.

All I need is rest. By night my legs will be okay. Rest, that's all I need, he told himself as he felt his mind closing off again.

He lay back and got comfortable in the shade of the bushes. From where he lay he could see the creek's water clearly and he could hear it as it rushed by. He watched the water and the sun on its ripples; they were the next-to-last thing he remembered as he fell asleep with his right hand holding his .38 pistol. The last thing he remembered as sleep came on was the lovely image of his flying fish.

So beautiful, he thought as he passed into a deep sleep, his head easing—like a child's—down into the warm hollow of his left arm.

9

Marzack / 10:00 a.m. / Huntsville, Texas

Marzack let Ray Bane sit in the holding room for a full twenty minutes before he went in, let him sit there in the small stark room and worry. Bane would know it had something to do with his escaped cellmate, but since he had been questioned for hours the day before, and since in truth he knew nothing about the escape—a fact he thought he had communicated to TDC officials—he wouldn't know exactly what was in store for him. And when he saw Marzack, whom he would know by reputation, there would be genuine fright. But above all—a constant between con and guard—Marzack would have the simple and devastating element of surprise, of time itself.

As Marzack anticipated, the dog sergeant and the TDC search party returned empty-handed to Huntsville just after sunup. They nonetheless made a great show of their return, by circling the downtown courthouse square and parking on line in front of the Lone Star Café

for coffee before moving on to the officers' dining room at the Walls
for a free breakfast.

Marzack waited until nine-thirty before going to Meditation Row,
where Bane was being held. He knew the tough sergeant who ran the
eight-to-four Meditation shift, a man who had become dissatisfied
with his stationary life on the punishment block at the Walls and who
longed for a job with Marzack's transfer unit. He would ask no
questions about Marzack being there, and would have nothing to say
about the visit or what happened between Marzack and Bane; he
would be *expecting* Marzack.

Marzack stood outside the holding room's door and peered through
the small one-way window and watched Bane for the last five minutes
of the twenty before he jerked the door open and burst inside,
red-faced and venal. Bane was on his feet the second the door opened,
standing with his hands by his sides, cowed, his wide eyes half on
Marzack, half on the bare concrete floor.

"Mornin', boss," Bane mouthed with desperation he could not
control, even though, like the sergeant, he had been expecting the
Hounder.

"Sit down," Marzack ordered, checking his stride so that he was
one step from the narrow metal table that separated him and Bane in
the tiny box of a room.

"Yes, sir, boss," Bane said immediately, dropping onto the bench
on his side of the table, as if his legs had been clipped from under him.

Marzack stood rock-still and watched him. As soon as Bane was
seated, he spoke again. His tone was like a hammer.

"My name is Lieutenant Marzack," he said with New Jersey
sharpness. "Lie to me once and I'll take your fucking head off."

Bane started to plead cooperation, his eyes darting toward
Marzack's face with apprehension, but Marzack stopped him cold with
the raised first finger of his right hand. When you question a con, you
expect him to lie to you—that is a sure reality—so you beat him by
establishing a pattern of obvious truth versus obvious lies; then pick
the less obvious lies apart one by one. It took only five minutes in the
soundproof room in the heart of the Walls for Marzack to establish the
lie-truth pattern with Ray Bane.

"So you didn't think anything about it that a hick like Macon wanted to rodeo?" Marzack questioned calmly, hunched forward across the table so that his face was less than a foot from Bane's.

"No, sir, I sure didn't," Bane lied, easily put off guard by Marzack's matter-of-fact tone.

But suddenly the ease was erased; suddenly there was motion and a sickening slap.

Whap! came the thudding sound.

Bane never saw the right cross that sent him plunging to the floor. But seconds after the blow, his eyes and head still filled with nauseating yellow circles, Bane felt Marzack's knee on his chest and the big man's hands on his throat and in his hair.

"Aaaugh," Bane groaned, his hands flailing uselessly, like a dying chicken's legs. "I . . . I . . ."

"You lying pile of dog shit, answer me straight or you'll piss blood for a month!"

Bane was hurt and confused. He had gotten crushed for one of his smallest and most insignificant lies. He struggled to clear his head, his eyes focusing on Marzack looming over him like a mad bull.

"*Answer!*" Marzack stormed, crooking Bane's neck upward with a jerk on his hair.

"Boss! Please, boss! I . . . I . . ."

"Suckhead! Answer the fucking question!"

"Boss, I thought it was funny . . ." Bane struggled with the words. "But we didn't talk. He never said *nothing*, boss. I swear to God, boss. He kept to himself. I didn't know he was gonna run. Boss, I'd a come to my sergeant," he went on quickly, his hands half-raised. "I swear that on God, boss!" he begged.

Marzack's eyes drummed into the convict. He jerked his hair roughly again and let his head fall, then pushed himself up with a grunt, jabbing a heavy knee into the tall, wiry con's chest. Bane rubbed his swollen jaw and lay stiff on his back and waited to be told what to do, a slow trickle of blood coming from his cut lip.

"Get up and sit down," Marzack instructed as he backed away to his side of the table.

Bane, weak-kneed, scrambled up as fast as he could, his wide eyes never once leaving Marzack.

"One more lie," Marzack said evenly, his hands perfectly still on the tabletop, as Bane seated himself shakily, "and they'll carry you out of here to the hospital."

Bane forced himself to sit ramrod-straight on the bench, holding his prison-white hands on the tabletop to quiet his shaking.

"I swear the truth, boss," he choked out.

"Four questions," Marzack came back, like stone, his eyes finding Bane's and gripping them.

"One: did you ever see or hear anything that might tell you where Macon is headed?"

Bane's neck twitched. He hesitated for a brief second, then spit out his answer, his fright-swelled eyes glued on Marzack's hands.

"He went to the library a lot. But I never went!" he protested. "Not at all," Bane went on urgently. "Beyond that, I can't say where he's goin', boss, God help me I can't," he stammered, expecting a fist.

Marzack didn't move.

"Two: did you ever talk with his wife in the visiting area?"

"No, sir! No, sir! We never visited together. You can check that, boss! You can check it!"

Still Marzack didn't move.

"Three: did he ever do anything out of the ordinary? Any hobbies or athletics. Anything."

Bane considered the options a few seconds and then burst into animation when he discovered he had something to give Marzack.

"He ran," Bane exclaimed, grinding his hands together nervously. "He ran all the time. For hours in the courtyard. For hours." He looked up at Marzack like a wet dog waiting to come in out of the cold.

Running. Running. Marzack gave Bane no hint of appreciation or even recognition at the information, and methodically went on to the final question, holding the word "running" in his mind's eye.

"Four: was Macon building anything? Anything at all?"

Bane relaxed slightly, his shoulders and head dropping a fraction.

"No, sir," the convict responded, his voice eased too. "No, sir. He never built anything."

Again, Bane never saw the punch that fell on him. But this time the blow took him out completely.

"You lying sonofabitch," Marzack said to Bane's unconscious body as he stood slowly, with absolutely no emotion. "He made a belt. One belt in six years, you lying asshole. Pay attention to detail." He turned and walked to the door and opened it. "Save your ass, and me, a lot of trouble."

Outside, the duty sergeant waited by a far wall that led to the short row of meditation cells. He pushed himself from the wall and came toward Marzack, smiling.

"Boy in there," Marzack told him as he moved by on his way out, "fell down and hit his head. Boy's stupid. Clumsy."

"Git the fuck up!" Marzack heard the sergeant bellow as he started down the cellblock corridor. "*Shit!* Get your ass moving!" Then, just as he reached the cellblock door, he heard the sounds of Ray Bane vomiting. But what he heard even louder in his mind was: *Running. Running.*

Marzack had gone through Eddie's file at the Walls' record office at eight-thirty and he had gone through Eddie and Bane's cell before he interrogated Bane; now, after leaving Bane, Marzack went back to the cell again, looking for something he might have missed the first time.

All fifteen hundred general-population cells at the Walls were **exa**ctly the same: fourteen by fourteen by nine feet, with two bunks, one over the other; two stationary metal desks and benches; an aluminum toilet with no lid; and an aluminum washbasin. The ten meditation cells were also the same size, but they contained only a toilet. All the cells were painted a dull industrial gray. People didn't live in them, they only existed. You could see they were planned for that. A total punishment, twenty-four hours a day, 365 days a year. As Marzack made his way through the cons in the cellblock hallways, they parted, and the guards, who stood bull-faced and tough, eyed him with rural envy and suspicion. All along his way there was the odor of urine and disinfectant and cheap tobacco smoke. Texas prisons worked. They did not have as many repeaters as the other forty-nine states. In Texas you got your ass kicked, physically and mentally. The convicts all had the look of old-time Parris Island marine recruits, scared, cheaply dressed, and with clipped heads. On J-wing/L-4, he came to Eddie and Bane's cell near the head of a line of fifty identical cubicles. All fifty of the electrically controlled doors were open; only the floor bull, a young red-faced guard, and the convict sweeper, a sixty-year-old black with only a left ear, were on the block. Marzack entered Eddie's cell without acknowledging either of the two, whose eyes secretly followed his every move.

Again Marzack went over the cell, inch by inch, piece by piece, as he had an hour before. Again he found nothing that gave him the remotest clue as to what Eddie had in mind or where he might be going. After fifteen futile minutes, Marzack sat down on Eddie's bottom bunk, as he had before; but now his eyes examined an object on the metal table, three feet away from the bunk, that he had passed over lightly the first time.

Like every other con at the Walls, Eddie had a mural. Murals were photos of your family and what you left outside. Part of a con's status depended on his mural, and, as it is inside or out of prison, murals were part fact, part fiction. But on the inside you took a con's mural at face value. You never asked him to prove his mural the way people on the outside make you produce the goods.

Marzack couldn't know it, but Eddie's mural was all fact. It was small by comparison—eight by ten inches, containing only four wallet-sized photos and a small magazine drawing in the center. Ray Bane, a wiry six-footer from Lubbock, who had held up a loan office in downtown Dallas on his twenty-first birthday, had a fifteen-by-twenty-one-inch mural with ten photos and five magazine clips. Nothing on Bane's mural was fact. It was a "Pussy" mural—beaver shots from *Playboy* and color clips of motorcycles, and in the center, a photo of Bane standing beside a 940 Harley-Davidson outside a showroom in Fort Worth.

Marzack studied the photos on Eddie's mural: color photos that had turned slightly brown with age. The picture in the center was a crisp color line drawing of a small, delicate flying fish. The picture in the upper-left-hand corner was of Chris, staring straight into the camera, almost smiling, which was her look. She was wearing a bikini top. The photo stopped just at the top of her breasts and cut off the top of her head just above her high forehead and the long thin bangs that followed the contours of her face. From Eddie's file, Marzack knew that the shot had been taken in Key West. Chris was deeply tanned. She had a solid, hearty look, but at the same time, the look of a child. She was big, but she wasn't big. She was beautiful, but she wasn't beautiful. Her face, like many of the country faces of Appalachia, was high-cheekboned, with an Oriental hint as it moved from wide cheeks to a pointed chin. The records had also shown that she had been a cheerleader at Watauga High School, and she had the look of a bobby-sox dream girl, with cream-brown hair and big blue eyes. Her hand was on her chin; her fingers were strong and solid and her wrist firm but delicate because there was only a wisp of sun-blond hair on it. She was wearing no lipstick but her cherry-red mouth, with her eyes, dominated the picture.

The photo in the right corner was of Eddie's eleven-year-old daughter, Angie. She was standing in front of the Judy Thomas Elementary School in Houston; the date on the back read November of last year. Angie's face was pale by comparison with her mother's photo, but she was Chris's double. Eddie liked to call them sisters.

In the lower-left corner was a photo of Eddie's son, Bobby. Marzack knew that the boy was now seven, but the snapshot had been made when Bobby was three in Key West. He was standing on the end of a dock with the island city's azure shallows in the background, sun-browned as dark as coffee, his thick, straight brown hair worn almost to his strong bony shoulders, hands on his hips in a mimic of Eddie; a beautiful little tough guy with a wide, self-conscious grin.

Eddie himself was in the photo at the bottom right of the mural. Standing bare to the waist in faded jeans, hands on hips and smiling, in front of their story-and-a-half Bahama-style wood-frame house on Baker's Lane. The house had been freshly whitewashed, and plants hung in colorful earthen pots on the porch; just to Eddie's left on the porch was a red-white-and-blue half-quart can of Budweiser.

The four photos were set at even intervals from the sides of the mural's frame, but the drawing in the center was slanted from left to right and was twice as long as the photos. It was one of *Sports Illustrated*'s excellent true-to-life color drawings.

Marzack could see that Eddie's mural varied in another way from his cellmate's. First of all, it was framed differently, a small matter to the Outside eye, but not to Marzack's Inside eye. In the vision of cons—what their eyes see—it's the little things that are most important,because in their world there are no big things. Eddie's mural was framed in a dime-store picture frame, the $2.95 kind with a thin black plastic border and a triangular pull-out stand in the back. Bane's frame was wide and imposing at first faraway glance, but up close it was plainly homemade. Homemade versus store-bought was not the issue. The difference was what the frames were made of and what that implied, and Marzack saw that difference, although he did not know what to make of it—yet. Bane's frame was made of varnished wooden match sticks scrounged in the Walls' exercise yard. The world of Bane's mural, like Bane himself, was totally encased by the prison. No matter how cheap Eddie's frame looked, it was of the Outside; Marzack saw that clearly.

Eddie and Bane had both been in prison for almost six years, Eddie with a forty-one-year sentence, Bane with twenty. Bane had lost sight of the outside world, the *free world*. Eddie had not stopped thinking of the free world for one second during his six years behind bars.

Suddenly Marzack was stung, and at first he did not know why. Then, as he stared at the mural, it occurred to him: *The family, his family . . . his, not . . . mine.* Suddenly it occurred to Marzack that the man he was hunting, the man he might kill—a man totally cut off from every link of society—had something he didn't: a family. After a few more seconds, he turned away; the memory and the reality of his family were too painful.

Eddie didn't talk to anyone in prison, guard or con. His mind was outside while his body was trapped inside. He was the prison ten-percenter, a fence man.

All Eddie had was his dream. But that dream, like the mural, was *not* fantasy, it was reality. The reality of freedom. Dreams were what Eddie had had for all of his thirty-six years. Sometimes it seemed to him—in prison or out—that he lived in a world apart from everyone else. No matter where he was, he was always somewhere else. No matter what he had in his mind, there was always something else. He was always searching, hoping, working, for a mythical something better. The fact that "better" never seemed to get one inch closer didn't stop Eddie for one minute of one hour, of one day. Marzack could not know these things, but like the mystical bond he had felt with Eddie from the first, images, *differences*, were starting to form in his mind—a pattern was starting to form.

Marzack sat and looked at the photos on Eddie's mural. He looked as deeply as he could. Of course, he could not see the abstract, *Something Better,* but he could see the drawing of the flying fish.

A flying fish? Bait fish? Lure? Deception? Marzack asked himself. *What? What does a fucking flying fish mean?*

Marzack lit a cigar and sat and looked at the drawing for a full five minutes. Then, in the fashion of a sumo wrestler, he put his hands on his knees and let out a roar.

"*Sweeper!*" In seconds the ancient black with one ear stood breathless and nodding in the doorway.

"Uncle," Marzack said evenly past his cigar, his eyes never leaving Eddie's mural, "I've got a question for you."

"Yessirboss," the black responded in an East Texas singsong, his trained con's eyes finding the object of his keeper's interest, huge hands gripping his mop for balance against worn-out legs.

"You see that mural there?" Marzack said.

"That one there on the table?" the sweeper said, his eyes on Eddie's mural.

"That's the one," Marzack replied, playing out the small amount of fencing the old con was allowed because of his age, his color, and his years in prison.

"I see that one, boss," the old man said, bringing the game to an end.

"I know what the family means," Marzack said quietly, his gaze on the mural. "It just means family. But, Uncle, I don't know what the fish means. Do you know what the fish means, Uncle?" His eyes at last found the old man's face.

The convict sweeper readjusted his grip on his mop, kept his eyes on the mural a few seconds longer, then turned his head to fully meet Marzack's eyes.

"That's the freedom fish, boss," the convict answered deliberately after another second's pause. "I akst the white boy what made that mural onst what kinda fish that was. He looked up at me and told me quick and straight: 'freedom fish.' I neva seed a freedom fish before that time, and not since." The old man turned his eyes wishfully to the fish for a second.

"Freedom, eh?" Marzack said, almost laughing, studying the fish and the mural a final time. "Ain't that some priceless information. Priceless." He stood up abruptly to leave the tiny cell. "Absolutely priceless." The old man shuffled back out of the doorway before Marzack as fast as he could.

At the doorway Marzack stopped and confronted the old man a last time.

"Uncle, how long ago did the white boy tell you about that freedom fish?"

The sweeper continued to choke his mop as he looked up at Marzack, screwing his face into a thoughtful pose that gave the appearance of mild pain. After an interval of about half a minute he answered Marzack's question.

"Two years, boss," he said. "Yessir, 'bout two years to the day, just after the boy come ova here from Ellis."

"Two years," Marzack repeated, his eyes fixed down on the sweeper. "That so. And during those two years, the boy ever do anything out of the ordinary? Anything *special?*"

"Yasa. He did a little leatherwork, and a whole lot of running. That white boy damn near run hisself to death, boss. Run all the time. Yasa. Run all the time."

Two years of running. He came here with the idea. More than two years pointing to yesterday. To the rodeo, to the . . .

Running . . . Rodeo . . . Freedom fish . . .

Marzack's thoughts trailed off as he bolted for the cellblock door, leaving the old black convict standing rigid, hands still on his mop.

And . . .

There was a single entry in Eddie's record that occupied Marzack's thoughts. Back in the Walls' records office he again took Eddie's bulky file from a disinterested white convict clerk and settled with the papers at a long conference table in the center of a big windowless room. The entry was on the next-to-last page of Eddie's personal file, marked in ball-point pen by his classification officer.

"No communication with family (visit or mail) after Monday, April 9." There was a further notation below; again in ball-point, and made by the same classification officer. "Doesn't make sense. Wife and kids have followed subject faithfully during term of sentence." Then a final notation: "Check into."

But there were no further notations. Like most in-house prison investigations, they never reached to the outside.

"Doesn't make sense" is as far off-base as you can get, Marzack said silently as his eyes stayed riveted to the paper. *Makes too much sense, is more like it.* He looked at the last entry a second more, then closed the folder so that he was staring at Eddie's side and front mug shots.

But it's too pat, runner, he said to Eddie's sad, frightened face of six years before, savoring the word "runner." *Maybe you couldn't help it; and it looks like you couldn't, because from what I've seen so far, you're a planner. But it's too fucking pat. People dropping out of sight. People who mean so much to you. Because you remember, runner, I'm the one who saw you bawl for those people, bawl for your wife and kids.*

The family—that was the thought that assailed Marzack's mind. *Where is Macon's family, and how do they figure in all this?* The word "family" jumped out at Marzack like a ghost, because he remembered that Eddie was different from the other cons he knew. Married or not, they were singles. But Eddie was obviously part of a whole, part of something that could not completely be locked up or out. It was something that Marzack had been cut off from a long time ago, something he had never completely been able to forget or forgive. His wife had made a single out of him, shutting him off from herself and his children.

The family, Marzack said, grinding the word into his mind. *Find the family and you find the key to the plan. Find the family and you find the runner.* His cop's mind kept churning with pain turned to pleasure now that he had his first tangible clues on which to build.

Runner: the word sounded very natural for Eddie, Marzack thought.

In his office, a boxy one-window affair in the rear of the TDC administration building, fifty yards across Avenue I from the Walls, Marzack sat at his bare desk and pondered his next move. He lit a green Optimo and sucked hard on it and thought. He had still not been called in on the escape, so what he had in mind was still outside his authority. *But soon, soon. It's coming, it's coming for sure, I know it*, he said happily to himself as he reached for the black phone on his desktop. *It's coming very soon.* He smiled.

It took the operator a full five minutes to locate Blowing Rock. It took another fifteen minutes to round up the town's police chief. When the man came on the line, he was out of breath and oversolicitous at being called by an out-of-state lawman.

"Chief Billy Joe Thatcher at your service . . . sir," the chief gushed in round, nasal hillbilly tones. "What can I do for you?"

"Need some help," Marzack replied, affecting bad English in an effort to sound down-home, but not quite pulling it off. "If you've got a minute," he added with manufactured good humor.

"Shoot!" the chief barked. "Anything you need. That's what we're here for."

"All right," Marzack said quickly, dropping all pretense. "We've got a convict. Eddie Jubal Macon—M-a-c-o-n. Ran from here yesterday at midafternoon; forty-one-year sentence, second escape. Considered dangerous, although he's on a bullshit sentence that started with a drunk-driving charge. We—"

Marzack got no further as the police chief cut in.

"Goddamn, mister!" the chief exclaimed in high-pitched tones. "You ain't the only one wants this Macon. By Jesus, the FBI and the IRS want him and his wife so bad they can taste 'em both."

"What the hell?" Marzack stiffened in his chair and leaned forward on the desktop.

"Damn straight! Wife's parents got killed in a car wreck last year.

Never had a nickel. But all of a sudden some land company buys the family farm, buys the sucker for a flat hundred thousand. Wife comes back here for a weekend, then hightails with the cash. *Cash,* by God, and nobody's heard shit since."

"Sonofabitch!" Marzack laughed into the receiver. "Sonofabitch."

"That's the word," the chief said. "That's the word, all right."

"And you got nothing?" Marzack said, no longer laughing.

"Not a damn thing."

"No family? No friends? No leads?"

"Family's all dead or don't know nothing. Not lead one. We closed the mess up a few months ago. Hell, what could we do? We ain't got money for things like this."

Investigation money. You're not the only one, Marzack thought to himself in disgust and frustration at his and TDC's inability to respond to the Outside wrinkles he was uncovering. He muttered a short thank-you routine that got him off the phone, lit another Optimo, sat back in his chair and settled in with his thoughts again. *Big money equals big plans,* he reasoned. *Wife and kids gone; a meet somewhere. But where? Mexico? South America? The Far East? Africa? Big money. Big advantage. Fake papers. Plane tickets. Disguises.* He smiled, enjoying the beauty of the thing, the challenge.

Then, on a hunch, he called the prison library. A nervous convict clerk answered in lisping homosexual tones. Marzack hammered at him for a few seconds, then asked if the clerk knew a convict named Eddie Macon, who used the library a lot. The clerk hesitated a moment. Marzack threatened him. Then the clerk answered Marzack's question. "Yes, sir," he said. "He read Texas history books. All we had. And maps. He looked at maps all the time. Lots of maps."

"What kind of maps?

The clerk hesitated again. Marzack threatened him again.

"I just don't know, boss," the clerk stammered in obvious truth. "I don't pry. The only reason I know about the Texas history books is because I checked them out. The maps they get on their own. You can verify that, sir," he said, as Marzack hung up on him.

Marzack again sat back in his chair and reflected. *Maps, running, flying fish,* he said to himself as he got up and walked out of the office, just as the noon whistle blew. *Flying fish—freedom fish. Hell! That's a damn bait fish. Okay, runner. I take the bait. Now, let's see what happens.* He walked briskly out of the TDC office compound to his car and headed for his house, feeling better than he had in years.

10

Eddie / 2:07 p.m. / Characo Marrano Creek, Texas

Eddie came awake with a start like a wild animal. Then, as he came fully awake, he saw he was in an animal's den, and he knew he was reacting like an animal, rolling up to all fours automatically, searching his four sides like a wolf. But there was nothing. No one. No sounds. He seemed totally alone in the middle of nowhere. Then he saw a tiny green water frog before him; all of a sudden he wanted to laugh. Once more he was graphically aware that he was not in prison. He was not free, but he was not in prison. As he looked at the frog, Eddie had to restrain the urge to jump and shout for joy.

But he settled down on his haunches and surveyed his position again, to make sure there was only the frog. *Nothing.* Then he concentrated on the frog once more. The gentle little creature seemed to be looking at him. Eddie wanted to reach out and touch it, but he held back.

"Good afternoon," he said aloud to the frog, not feeling foolish.

Then the words he was forming choked in his throat. He started to weep. He sat back on the ground and cried like a child. But he wasn't scared; he was happy. When he took his hands from his eyes, the frog was still there, still looking up at him. Eddie reached for him, but the little reptile jumped away in a flash. Eddie laughed out loud, a small, brittle laugh.

"Fair-weather friend," he said, still not feeling foolish, watching the frog bounce three times on land and then into the waters of Characo Marrano Creek. When it had disappeared, Eddie stood up cautiously inside the head-high gallberry thicket. It was a wobbly start, but after he massaged his legs for a few seconds he gained his balance. His clothes were stiff with dried sweat and they smelled ripe. He wondered with some amusement how they would smell in four days, but he let that thought go.

One day at a time. One run at a time, he said silently.

Then he made his way the few feet to the creek's edge, filled his canteen, and came back to the cover of the gallberry thicket. He put a halazone tablet in his canteen and reached for his knapsack for something to eat. His food cache looked deceptively full, but he knew that there were only eight packets of high-carbohydrate food; he reached inside for number three. The food tasted like numbers one and two—soapy beans and molasses—but like the others he ate it ravenously. When he finished, he was still hungry, wildly hungry, but he dared not indulge in more than another canteen of water. He drank it slowly, and sat back, enjoying the deep and excellent silence of his surroundings. Eddie smelled the clean, dry air and looked at the brown creek through the bushes before him. Suddenly he was a young boy again in the mountains of North Carolina, a young boy lying in the bushes and looking out at a creek, and Chris was beside him.

It was the summer before Eddie went off to the Coast Guard. They were in a broad mountainous valley, the Globe, it was called, that sat a thousand feet before Blowing Rock's four-thousand-foot gorge. Once, before the great 1940's flood, the Globe had been one of western North Carolina's great tourist attractions; people came from all over the mountains to swim in the Globe's river-wide creeks, whose clear waters flowed over smooth gray and brown pebbles.

There were more than ten classic swimming holes there, and Eddie and Chris were hidden in the hollow of a large evergreen thicket by one of those holes. The temperature was in the eighties and there was a thick, high-country heat-haze scent from the trees and the acres of summer corn on the opposite side of the creek, across from a wide clay road. Eddie and Chris were naked inside the thicket, holding each other, exploring their hard young bodies and kissing. Not making love, just nude and hugging and kissing; totally warm and happy. They lay there for several hours saying sweet, innocent naive things, just touching. Finally Chris wet her hand with her mouth and brought Eddie to a climax. They held each other awhile longer, then got up and started toward the water for a swim.

Suddenly they stopped—they heard something. Eddie looked out from the thicket across the road, and he saw three men get out of a truck and stand looking up and down the creek. He and Chris froze where they were, afraid to breathe or move for their clothes. The men were not fishermen and they did not look like farmers. They had on drab green uniforms with arm patches and they wore pistols on their belts. At the time, beyond the frightened, out-of-whack adolescent idea that somehow the men knew he and Chris were naked and were looking for them, Eddie had no idea who or what the men were. Only later did Eddie learn that they were federal whiskey agents looking for moonshine stills. Now, in another thicket, in the middle of Texas, with the picture of the lawmen in his mind, Eddie stiffened and pushed himself to his knees and began scanning his position again in all four directions, his picture of Chris shattered into oblivion. Instead, the image of Marzack, the Hounder, loomed before him as large and menacing as a prison wall.

Don't let down. Don't let your guard down for an instant! he drilled into his mind, as his eyes darted to the four corners. *Don't let go for a second . . . don't think. . . . Don't hope. . . . Don't dream.*

It was midafternoon. He had been gone almost twenty-four hours. In another twenty-four hours the time would be officially played out, and TDC would alert the Hounder.

Forty-eight hours: an unheard-of length of time for a con to be out of reach. A length of time that showed weakness on the part of TDC. In the delicate relationship of keeper and kept, the keeper could not afford to show weakness. If the keeper did, twice the amount of force was needed to compensate. Marzack was the compensator.

From the moment he began to plan his escape, Eddie knew he would have to face Marzack again. He meant to run away from TDC, meant to get beyond bloodhound reach, and he knew the consequences.

Eddie looked at his watch and saw he had less than twenty-seven hours to go before Marzack would officially be brought into the hunt, but he knew that Marzack would have been one of the first to hear it. He knew Marzack would be at the rodeo, knew he would eat in the officers' dining room at the Walls, knew that he knew his name: *Eddie Macon* would sting Marzack like a whip. As he sat hidden in the gallberry thicket now, Eddie began to sweat with fear as he felt Marzack rub the scar over his right eye. He felt the big man turn hot with anger, felt the hatred Marzack held for him, and knew Marzack would come. Knew it.

He sat in the gallberry thicket like a rat and let the thoughts of Marzack pass. They had slipped into his mind in an unguarded moment; he was not yet ready to deal with them. The time would come when he would have to deal with it, make plans to defend against the thoughts and the man behind them, but that time was still in the future—twenty-seven hours away in the future, to be exact.

One part of the thing at a time, Eddie told himself as he sat and ground his fists into his lap and waited for all the fears to go away. *One right thing, followed by another right thing, one plan followed by another plan.*

The scare had broken Eddie's happiness, but when the fears passed, he made himself settle down flat on his back in the thicket and made himself rest.

Rest. You must rest and you must watch. Rest until it's time for the next run. There will be a time for the other. Rest is all you can do to be ready, and you must be as ready as possible. The other will come in its time.

Above him the sun had arched well over the noon mark and was falling steadily to the west in a fiery orange ball that stuck out as if it had been pinned to the cloudless blue sky. It was such a beautiful sight, totally unobstructed past the thicket. Not a *free sight,* Eddie knew, but a sight of something that *was free*. The depression of that reality and the nagging venal presence of Marzack began to eat at his brain. To ward off the vision, Eddie played the game he had used before: he set his life up before him and examined it like a doctor looking at an X ray.

During his forty-eight months in the Coast Guard he had saved an even $5,000. The new VW sedan he bought when he and Chris were married cost $1,850 cash, the rent on the Baker's Lane house was $135 a month, and when Eddie and Chris made the first and last rent payment, got a telephone, paid for the utilities hookups, bought their first pots and pans and dishes and household items, and laid in their first groceries, they had $2,600 in the savings account at the Key West State Bank. They took out the $600 for checking, and left the remaining $2,000 in savings, as a start on their Operation Flying Fish bank account.

Since the beginning of the plan, Eddie had everything figured to the penny and the day. From July 20, allowing a six-week grace period to get settled into Key West before Chris drew her first check from the Monroe County Board of Public Instruction, and before Eddie could find a job as a mate on one of the charter boats at the Roosevelt Boulevard Docks, the seven years and seven months they would need to save $40,000, would end on an April Fool's Day, an irony Eddie never once considered.

At age eighteen it had seemed logical to plan for age twenty-two, because a neutral period of learning separated the four years, but as they settled into Key West, the reality of planning for age thirty took hold of both Chris and Eddie. The ancient island city was real and alive as no place else they had ever seen, and they wanted what they saw.

As it happened, their next-door neighbor on Baker's Lane was a well-known screenwriter, John Allen Doyle. Big and heavily bearded, Doyle, with his wife, Joanna, a stunning redhead who had enjoyed a brief career as a New York fashion model and later a minor Hollywood actress, shared the top ring of the Key West artists-and-writers spiral with the legendary Tennessee Williams, and the ghost of Ernest Hemingway. Doyle, the Harvard-educated son of a Bronx cabdriver, took an immediate liking to the young couple, and when he discovered

Eddie was an accomplished fisherman and seaman, the friendship cemented around Doyle's triple passion for billfish, tarpon, and giant tuna. Doyle needed someone to run his forty-eight-foot Rybovitch sportsfisherman and his twenty-foot Mako flats boat. A week after their arrival in Key West, Eddie went to work for Doyle as his full-time captain for a salary of $500 a month, plus the proceeds from whatever market fish they happened to catch.

Key West was a compact little ball of real estate and humanity and in its own stubborn way there was no really *best* section of *first* families. People and houses alike, you made your own way, with money considerably down the list of important variables. With Doyle's patronage, Eddie and Chris were soon included in the circle of cocktail parties that made up the bulk of the island's social life. They became fixtures in the scene they flowed through, but it was a start, and they delighted at being swept into the group. Tater Hill and their families remained blocked from their minds. They were on their own, and it seemed to them that they were indeed on their way to the mythical Something Better of their dreams. And from the start, they got a lesson about money. Close to Doyle, they got to see exactly how money works.

John Allen Doyle had his first big literary success at age twenty-seven with a detective movie entitled *The Kellmann Factor;* eight years later he won an Academy Award for a screenplay. When Eddie first met him, Doyle had been married to Joanna Price, a Boston Brahmin heiress, for five years. Eddie saw firsthand that such marriages were not only acts of love, they were also mergers. It was immediately apparent to Eddie that he and Chris had united their love in marriage, but all they had merged was their mutual poverty. There was no blockbuster super-money movie looming on Eddie's horizon, and no inherited fortune. He was finally seeing the summer people up close and mixing with them, but the proximity only increased his distance from them.

During those first years Eddie and Chris never got more from life. The house at 711 Baker's Lane was a one-bedroom conch bungalow, a classic little Bahama-style wood-frame structure with a living room that opened to a wide screened-in patio, which had potted palms and plants and the limbs of a great banyan tree overhead, the domain of a hundred lizards who daily came out to catch insects and then sun themselves on the twelve-foot concrete wall that separated Eddie's house from John Allen Doyle's property. The house was a rare little jewel, owned by a wealthy New Yorker who had inherited it. It was a pin-neat little dwelling filled with old but expensive furniture. The walls were lined with excellent art copies, and in the wide triangular bedroom, there was a tall English writing desk and a set of kudu horns on the wall. Beyond the bedroom was a second small enclosed patio. It was the perfect place for Eddie and Chris to begin to act out the life they had styled for themselves, a place to practice, a place to sit and reflect, a haven to store up strength and security.

Of course, they had plenty of ideas of their own, but in the beginning, what they did, although they did not intend it as such, revolved around imitating John Allen and Joanna Doyle. They would have early-morning breakfasts out on the living-room patio and dinner with inexpensive French table wine at seven-thirty, then long walks through the pleasant back streets of Old Key West from Truman Avenue west to land's end at the terminus of Front and Caroline streets. It was a routine that Doyle and the others in their circle took for granted, but to Eddie and Chris it was a completely different rhythm, a way of doing things that added new dimension to their lives.

It was all lovely, but the simple truth was that it was not free. Everything they did, even the walks, cost money, because as informal as Key West was, it was also a place of correctness. John Allen and Joanna dressed themselves from the shops along Fifth Avenue in New York and Rodeo Drive in Hollywood—Hermès, Brooks, Gucci, I. Magnin, Saks, Paul Stuart, J. Press. They drove a Mercedes and ate and drank at all the right places, a stance with which Eddie and Chris obviously couldn't compete, but something they could imitate and copy, a way to see good things and how they were used. Copying the Doyles was exactly what Eddie had pointed Chris and himself toward all their lives. Doyle went beyond the overt consumption and gluttony of Blowing Rock's summer people. Doyle was Correct, and all his life Eddie had wanted to be Correct.

The first bittersweet lesson Eddie learned in Key West was that while he was perfectly willing to copy Doyle, he had nothing to copy

him with. He and Chris did not even have the social basics—a dark
suit or a black cocktail dress, blue blazer and gray slacks, black shoes,
decent leather or canvas luggage—no trappings at all. During their
first winter season in Key West, Eddie and Chris spent over a
thousand dollars each acquiring the scant basics that would keep them
from standing out like sore thumbs in Doyle's crowd. At the end of
their first year in Key West, under the terms of Operation Flying
Fish, they were supposed to have saved $5,200. In their savings
account at the Key West State Bank Eddie and Chris had recorded a
balance of $3,700. As they sat and brooded over the money, Eddie
summed up their situation.

"I never realized we had so little," he said.

"We have something now," Chris answered. "So we tighten our
belts and go back to the plan."

For the next two years they managed to stay on the savings plan of
$100 a week from Eddie's salary, living chiefly off Chris's $8,000 a
year as a teacher. When their first child, Angelia Louise, was born on
October 7 of their second year in Key West, they had $11,800 in their
account. It was far from the $40,000 they ultimately needed, but its
five figures gave both Eddie and Chris a sense of security. Angie's
birth, however, immediately took $4,000 from their savings account.
The small, frail little girl was born with lupus, a strange cancerlike
blood disease; the medical expenses incurred went well beyond the
limits of a normal health-insurance policy. It was two years before the
child was healthy, and even with Doyle's generous help, by the time
Angie was finally released from outpatient treatment at a Miami
hospital, the Operation Flying Fish savings account had fallen to just
over $5,000.

The money was unimportant, the child's health was what mattered,
but Eddie could not escape the black thoughts that five years had
elapsed, and instead of having $26,000 in the bank, he had only
$5,000. Two years later, on the $40,000 payoff date of Operation
Flying Fish, Eddie had exactly $17,500 in his account at the Key West
State Bank. He had missed his goal by a wide margin.

Eddie and Chris both loved Key West and all that went with it, and
Eddie and John Allen Doyle had grown as accustomed to one another
as brothers. But the failure of his plan made Eddie desperate; his

mind started wandering to schemes of quick money. On June 29, seven weeks to the day after their second child—a small, handsome boy they named Robert Paul—was born, Eddie moved his family from Key West to the northeast Texas hill-country town of Palestine and took a job as a welder on a natural-gas pipeline that was being laid across East Texas. The salary was twelve dollars an hour. There was time and a half from forty to seventy-five hours, and double time thereafter. The work was seven-twelve—seven days a week, twelve hours a day; that earned a salary of $1,326 a week before taxes. Chris would not be working, but by living close, Eddie calculated he could save $500 a week during the two-year working life of the pipeline, a time span that could net him over $50,000. Finally he could get into the charter-boat business on a totally cash basis at age thirty-two, with $70,000 in his Flying Fish savings account.

The move totally uprooted Eddie and Chris in body, mind, and spirit. But as desperate as it was, Eddie reasoned there was no alternative. If he was going to have his own boat before it was too late, he had to make a move, for in Key West, no matter how good life was with John Allen Doyle, Eddie would always be an employee. With his own boat, Eddie could pull his own weight, he could have things on his own terms. But in Texas, on the day Eddie reported for work, disaster struck with a note of finality.

It was all I could do at the time, Eddie told himself as he lay back in the thicket, the misery of that long-ago defeat crushing in on him. *I was trapped, with no way out. I was desperate and I had to do something desperate to get out of the hole I was in. I went out there for money and I was willing to work like a dog for it, like a damn dog! It didn't have to turn out like it did*. He cringed under the weight of the truth of the images in his mind. *I didn't leave home to hurt anyone, I left home to help myself, to help my family.*

I . . . I . . .

He could not go on. It was either crying or apologizing, and he was sick of both.

Deep, deep inside, Eddie wanted to scream. But he did not know at whom, and would not have risked the sound if he had known.

Eddie had learned welding in the Coast Guard on a whim, and perfected it because it was a time filler. While he was stationed at the South Caicos Coast Guard Station, he made friends with the seamen in charge of the base maintenance shop. To pass the time the seamen tinkered with metal sculpture. Mostly as a joke Eddie started the haphazard project of assembling a scrap-iron dragon. But he soon discovered he liked puttering with metal, and whether he cared to admit it or not, learning the craft of welding was also a hedge to back up the grandiose plans of Operation Flying Fish. Although he dared not say it out loud, it padded his confidence that he could fall back on the welder's trade for the money if all else failed. Twelve years later, however, it ate at Eddie's pride that, after putting a sizable distance between himself and Tater Hill, he was forced to dip back into a dogged working grind to make Operation Flying Fish work.

Eddie presented himself at the pipeline company's offices on Highway 287 west of Palestine. There were acres filled with the awesome clutter of pipes and equipment, a stark, humid, treeless landscape at once foreboding but at the same time fascinating. The move from Key West and the temporary separation from the sea had been traumatic for Eddie, but as he entered the deliberate momentum of the construction site he felt better. He did the customary test welds and passed the welding X-ray tests with no problem. All that remained was the formality of being hired by the pipeline company, getting a pay number, and joining the local welders' union. Eddie's mood of apprehension had reversed itself and he had a sensation of purpose and resolve as he knocked at the welding foreman's trailer door to fill out his employment forms.

The welding foreman was a tall, bony man with a flat-top haircut. He had long, skeleton fingers with thick black hairs and he chain-smoked Camel cigarettes, lighting one with the other as if it was a profession in itself. He was a nervous, sour-faced man in his late

forties and he made Eddie stand in front of his desk for several
minutes before he acknowledged him. Finally, when he did speak, it
was with a thin, false smile that made wide horizontal cracks around
the sides of his mouth.

"So," the foreman said in a thick East Texas drawl. "You the fella up
from Florida?"

"Yeah," Eddie replied, smiling, making an effort to be pleasant. "It
was a long hot trip, but it looks like it's going to be worth it."

"For a fact, young fella," the foreman said, pushing himself back in
his short-backed swivel chair, elbowing the chair back so that it
reclined slightly. "Yessir, it's a fact that this kind of a job can be worth
one hell of a lot to a man. But a man," he added quickly, avoiding
Eddie's eyes, "that knows what's what."

"Well," Eddie said, "I haven't followed the trade as a job, but I
know my business."

The foreman's eyes darted cautiously up to Eddie's, and he pushed
himself up in the seat and planted his feet on the floor again. His face
got sour and his fingers drummed nervously on his desktop.

"Look," the foreman said. "I ain't got time for this. You don't know
your ass from a hole in the ground. *Shit,* boy, you don't just waltz your
butt into a pipeline office empty-handed and go out the door with
twelve or eighteen bucks an hour. You got to show up *with*
something." His eyes now searched Eddie's for understanding.

But Eddie still didn't get the point.

"I'm here to work," Eddie replied, puzzled, shaking his head.
"What else can I say?"

The foreman stared hard at Eddie for a few moments. Then he
answered in a hard, nasal voice, looking straight up into Eddie's face.

"Simple as I can tell you, it works like this. You new hands lay down
a hundred bucks before I give you your pay number; then every week
after pay call you *pay* me a little visit and drop off another hundred.
Damn, boy, you don't know shit, do you?" he added with genuine
indignation.

"Wait a minute," Eddie came back with no hesitation, hands braced
on his hips. "I've got to pay *you* a hundred a week to work here?"

The foreman smiled an almost pleasant smile at Eddie's understanding.

"Well, finally," he said with satisfaction. "I was beginning to think you was slow in the head or something." His eyes shifted down to Eddie's midsection, to his wallet.

For a second Eddie tried to keep his emotions in check, but he could not hold them back. "You miserable sonofabitch!" His hands were in front of him, ready to become fists. "Who do you think you're talking to? I may not have followed the trade for a living before, but I'm not a damned fool. Hell, I'm going to the supervisor here and put an end to your little game."

The foreman looked at Eddie in disbelief.

"You are slow, son," he said softly. "I'm damned if I ain't just real sorry for you." His tone changed abruptly, and he dismissed Eddie by going back to the stack of paper on his desk.

"You dumb bastard," he mumbled just over his breath without looking up. "The supervisor gets *half* of the fuckin' hundred! Now, get out of here before I call in a couple of the boys who *do* know which way the damn wind blows."

Eddie was undone. In an instant, the reality of the situation crushed him. It was Tater Hill all over again. It was as though he had never left. Suddenly it was as if all the effort of the past twelve years of his life had been for nothing. He wanted to curse, to cry, to strike out at the man before him, he wanted to hurt something. But he knew better. He knew the rules of Tater Hill completely. Finally, amid the gloomy silence of the small, smoke-filled trailer office, he simply turned and walked out the door, defeated.

It was just after ten a.m. when Eddie left the welding foreman's office. Palestine was in a dry county, but Eddie had a fifth of rum from Key West in his car's glove compartment. He drove around for two hours, drinking. At noon he had lunch in a small café in Tyler, fifty-five miles north of Palestine; then he turned around and headed back for the pipeline-company office. It would put him behind with his Flying Fish money almost $10,000, but Eddie knew he had no choice other than to pay the foreman the $100 a week in kickback money. He was drunk when he came back to the foreman's office, and he found the man as he had left him, chain-smoking and aimlessly sifting through the papers on his desk. But now the man was smiling, a broad, leering smile of satisfaction and victory.

The smile did it. Something clicked inside Eddie. Some dark, secret nerve of hate and resentment that had lain dormant for all his conscious years came to life like a mad dog cut from his leash. His drunkenness aided the flow of anger. With that smile, it would have spilled over if he had been cold sober. In an instant Eddie was on the man, clubbing him with his fists, beating him onto the floor. Later he did not even remember being pulled off by two burly pipeline-company men. He did not remember fleeing the construction site in his car. The first thing Eddie remembered after striking the foreman was the sound of the Texas highway-patrol car behind him. He saw the black-and-white Dodge behind him, saw the lights flashing, heard the siren blaring. Then the realization of what he had done came in on him and Eddie panicked; it took the trooper more than five miles to run Eddie off the road and into a ditch on Highway 84, east of Palestine.

It might have been a simple fighting-and-drunk-driving charge, with a $500 fine and loss of his driving license for six months, but Eddie's anger had not run its course. He struck out at the trooper and had to be pistol-whipped into submission. The episode had become a tangled legal nightmare: assaulting a police officer with intent to commit a felony, felonious assault and battery on the welding foreman, unlawful flight to avoid prosecution, and finally, drunken driving. Eddie was charged in Anderson County Criminal Court and faced a total of twenty-five years in prison and fines of $10,000. In his county-jail cell, sick-drunk and aching with cuts and bruises, Eddie went into shock. All he could do was lie on his bunk and stare dumbly at the ceiling. For the first time in his life he felt abjectly beaten and totally at a loss as to what to do about it. Finally and at last, it had proven to Eddie that he was a nobody.

Chris tried frantically to reach John Allen Doyle, but he and Joanna were in Japan on an extended holiday. She was able only to acquire the legal services of a second-rate ambulance chaser who wanted a $5,000 cash deposit before he took the case. When Eddie refused to sign the joint withdrawal slip on their $17,500 Flying Fish savings account at the Key West State Bank, his sorry fate was sealed. He was declared indigent, and a youthful Anderson County public defender was appointed to take his case. On July 25 he was found guilty on all counts of the indictment against him and sentenced to twenty-five years in the Texas prison system.

"Straight out," his attorney told him after the trial, "they made an example of you. Something to keep the other pipeliners in line for as long as they're around here."

Eddie listened to the young man's words in the same disjointed fashion he had viewed his trial proceedings. It was like something unhinged from reality. But it was all very real. On August 1, Eddie was transported ninety miles south and placed in the custody of the Texas Department of Corrections at TDC's inmate Diagnostic Unit outside Huntsville; he would be eligible for parole for the first time in twelve years.

He was facedown in the thicket now, balled in a knot again, his eyes wedged shut against the devils of his mind that were all around him.

They had me. People I didn't know, people who didn't know me. People who wouldn't have given a damn if I'd of blown up in a pile of smoking guts right before their eyes. People who are sure everything and everybody beyond their own front doors is shit. They had me, it's just as simple and deadly as that.

They did what they wanted to me and put me where they wanted me. I had to adjust; had to—period. And I did. But nothing they or anybody else ever did to me before or since equaled what he did to me—what the Hounder did to me.

He wasn't part of them; he was like me. That's what made it hurt so bad and last so long.

Just like me: as strange as that sounds, Eddie went on thinking as he forced himself to turn over and face the sky once more.

Just like me.

Prison had been the farthest thing from Eddie's mind. He had never even had a speeding ticket, and like most people from poor circumstances, he viewed the law with a mixture of distrust and

indifference. But that was from a distance. When he came face to face
with the reality of TDC, all Eddie felt was fear.

The first weeks of prison were as much a torture for Eddie as if he
had been spread out on a medieval rack. He was completely
unprepared for the prison experience. Convicts are losers and they
know it, so consciously or unconsciously they prepare to lose. When
they finally get to prison they are ready for it; in a way, they've
worked for it, they've reached their goal—prison, the zenith of losing.
But since it was the exact opposite with Eddie, prison was all the more
painful and confusing.

He broke all the con rules. He let others see him cry. He couldn't
eat and he got sick, which meant he couldn't pull his end if there was a
riot or a fight. He couldn't work, which meant his work had to be
divided among the other cons in his section. He screamed in his
sleep, which got others to thinking deep and twisted night thoughts.
In his tests and interviews during the two-week indoctrination into
the prison world of TDC at Diagnostic, Eddie went blank, which
showed overtly that he was beaten, and with his defeat, that all cons
were beaten. The convict code seemed like a great mystery. The
guards, the prison, the system were firmly in control; the only hope a
con had was when he stayed tough and aloof and gave the appearance
of independence and defiance. When you gave up, as Eddie did, it let
the Outside have a true picture of the Inside, and that was the one
thing a con could not afford to give away, because it was the only thing
he had.

But while he was at Diagnostic, Eddie was never really aware of the
taboos he was breaking. He remained lost between the fantasies of his
Something Better dreams and the physical reality of the prison.
Locked away in his cell and in his mind, Eddie tried to figure where
he had gone wrong.

He had not aspired to be the president of the U.S. or even
president of a bank. He had not wanted to write a great novel or an
opera. He had not longed to discover the secret of an ancient
civilization or probe the mysteries of science. He simply wanted to
make a better, more secure place for himself and his family. He
wanted to live out a life, not of affectations, but of simple good taste

and ease: a life of correctness. The Good Life of a Somebody. And he would have done it as the captain of his own charter boat, a profession that catered to style. His was a reachable, obtainable goal for a person with his background. Locked away in the misery and separation of prison, he could not—*would not*—let go of the idea. Whatever had brought him to where he was, it was not as simple as folly, Eddie decided. But even though his tortured mind accepted that fact, it was no help to him. He was lost in despair.

For the other cons, there were two distinct worlds, the Inside and the Outside, and whichever sphere they were in at the time was the one that got all their attention. And above all, when you were Inside, everybody, family and friends on the street, lived like the cons lived in prison—alone and tough. But Eddie could not let go of his family, not for one second. He worried about them day and night. He couldn't separate the Inside from the Outside. All he saw was that he was not supporting his family, he was no longer providing for them, they were no longer under his protection. His thoughts were on them instead of on taking care of himself in this hostile prison environment. But for a new con that wasn't possible, and Eddie knew it. All he wanted was out, but no new con could beat the system on his own. It would take a fluke, a twist of fate—lightning, the cons called it. But in the ups and downs of his disoriented life, Eddie got his lightning.

The date was August 9. Eddie had been at Diagnostic eight days. He was still in shock, a zombie, and as homesick as a lost child. It was four p.m. on a hundred-degree day with no breeze, and Eddie and twenty-five other new inmates were on a white TDC bus on Highway 247 inside the city limits of Huntsville, bound from the prison hospital back to Diagnostic. The air inside the bus was thick with dust, and Eddie sat handcuffed by a barred window in the rear. The bus was moving along the highway at a fast clip so the convicts could make the 4:30 p.m. count at Diagnostic. The only sounds inside were coughs and the muffled whir of the tires on the burning hot asphalt. But all at once there was a screeching of the bus's tires, a dry silence, then a crash. Finally there was a violent surge as the bus slipped over on its side and lunged headfirst into a telephone pole on the northeast corner of the intersection of Highway 247 and Seventh Street. Before

Eddie fully realized what had happened, he found himself running, charging off wildly with no sense of direction or purpose, like a scared rabbit.

All Eddie knew about Huntsville at the time was that Chris and his two children had taken a little trailer in the rear of the gas station off Highway 19 in the northeast section of the city. As he ran from the wrecked bus, Eddie had no idea of how to get to his family. All he saw before him as he raced along Seventh Street was a line of boxy frame houses, and before him, where Seventh Street ended and became Eighth Street, there was a cemetery.

Eddie did not remember seeing the man who stood up on the thin porch of the house at 903 Ninth Street, but as he rounded the corner of the cemetery, Eddie's mind froze on the words: "Hey! Sonofabitch! *Boy!*" Words shouted with surprise and just a hint of humor.

Eddie's head popped back in the direction of the sounds, and he saw the speaker coming off the porch, making for him like a pro lineman pointed for a halfback. Eddie broke into a frantic run but could hear the big man closing in on him for a jarring tackle. They rolled on the dusty ground beside the street and fought, but there was no contest. Eddie was handcuffed, and his attacker was twice his size. But Eddie got in one good shot before it was over. Just as the man was dragging him to his feet, Eddie turned his fists palms-out and made a tight chain of the short link of steel between his handcuffs. He caught the man over the right eye, and the last thing Eddie saw before he was knocked unconscious was blood spurting from the right side of the man's big, dirty, sweaty face.

When he came to a few minutes later, Eddie found himself chained to the man's front porch by another set of handcuffs. The man was standing over him on the porch, holding a wet towel on his right eye, glaring, while a group of children gathered to watch. Eddie's head ached from the clubbing blows of the man's fists, and his nose was bleeding. You could see that the man was holding back because of the children. It was obvious by the sour look of hate and pain on his face that the man was capable of killing Eddie, and that he wanted to kill him. The two men eyed each other on the porch while the children looked on: the big man, edgy, his violence about to spill over; Eddie, subdued on the porch floor, hands strung up over his head, feet splayed out in a limp V, blood spattered all over his Texas prison whites. Suddenly it all began to seem crazy to Eddie. In a traumatic rush the events of the past five weeks overwhelmed him and Eddie collapsed into tears—choking, burning tears that turned his face grotesque with pain and blanked his mind to all but his suffering and madness. He had come to Texas to achieve his life's dream; five weeks after his arrival he was doing twenty-five years in state prison and now faced the prospect of doing another sixteen years because of an escape—forty-one years of prison time for fighting and drunk driving! That reality became a cancer in his mind.

How? How? How was it possible that a man whose whole life had been built around the iron-willed motto of "Something Better" could have come to such a sorry end? How? How? How? He began to slip deeper and deeper into the warm, comforting liquid of madness, but the willing slide was stopped by the sound of a name and a child's voice.

"Mr. Marzack! Mr. Marzack!" Eddie heard one of the children shout. "Look, Mr. Marzack. The convict's crying. Look! He's crying!"

Then Eddie felt a sharp kick on his left thigh. His eyes came open again, stinging and blurred from the tears.

"Here. Dammit! Stop that. Stop!" Eddie heard the man's voice order. *"Stop!"*

When he focused on the man, Eddie saw his hard-block face looming down into his own, the man's teeth clenched, his fists balled and ready to strike. But the man's name, not his menacing presence, or the child's voice, was the thing that rode the crest of Eddie's consciousness: *Marzack. Lieutenant Buster Marzack:* the Hounder. Marzack's reputation preceded him even in the Diagnostic Unit for new inmates. Men on their second or third trip to TDC would tell you, "Make your move if you want, but hope two things—one, that you don't get caught; and two, if you do, that Buster Marzack don't catch you!"

With the realization of who the man standing before him was, Eddie became a con again. The luxury of insanity passed and the understanding of where he was and what he was hit him like a smothering wet blanket. Texas ran the tightest prisons in the U.S., and after only nine days in the separate world of TDC Eddie knew what a convict was. The definition went *"When I say shit, you say, 'How much, boss?'; and when I say jump, you say, 'How high, boss?'"*

On the porch floor, Eddie flinched back into reality before Marzack, wiping his eyes and nose on his shirt sleeve, trying to straighten up before the prison lieutenant. Finally, with great effort, he spoke to Marzack.

"I'm sorry, boss," he said, "I lost myself. I'm sorry. I—"

"You ain't half as sorry as you're going to be when we settle up about this," Marzack cut in with a rough grunt just over his breath, moving the wet towel away from his eye to reveal a deep three-inch gash just over his right eyebrow.

Eddie flinched again as he saw the cut and the look of hatred and disgust on the big man's face. He squirmed on the floor and looked pleadingly at Marzack.

"I shouldn't be here," Eddie said in words he knew he shouldn't use but could not hold back. "I don't belong in prison."

"Shut your mouth!" Marzack ordered. "Shut your mouth and sit still until the bus comes for you!"

But Eddie was unable to hold back his words. There were things he had to say to Marzack, things he had to make clear to someone in TDC, things he stood for and could not let go simply because he had a prison number and prison time to do.

"I came out here to work," Eddie said in a cracking, excited voice. "To work! I'm a fisherman. A charter boatman from Key West, Florida. I came out here to work on a pipeline to get money to buy a boat, a forty-two-footer." The handcuffs dug into his wrists as he sought to make the point with his raised, trussed hands.

"I've got a wife and children." The thought broke the thin line of pride and defiance in his tone. "I don't belong here. I came to work! I've got a wife and children! I'm no criminal! I . . . "

He couldn't go on. Tears and homesickness overwhelmed him and he broke down again. Marzack turned away from the sight, unable to watch. He had no frame of reference for Eddie or what he was doing; he had never seen a con cry. Eddie's emotions repulsed him, but the tears and the homesickness stayed in his mind. They were so foreign, so different, Marzack couldn't shake them. And there was the matter of settling the score for the scar over his eye.

Eddie had stopped sobbing when the TDC pickup bus came for him at Marzack's house, and as the neighborhood children watched, Eddie was led away roughly by two burly guards in TDC grays and cowboy hats. As he was taken to the rear of the small prison bus, Eddie turned and squared off toward Marzack and spoke to him a last time.

"I don't belong here!" he shouted again in a defiance that surprised him as the words came out. "I came here to work! I've got a wife and children! I'm no con! You hear me! I'm no con!"

Eddie had more to say, but that was all he was allowed. The two guards pushed him inside the bus and locked the doors behind him and drove away. A week later, as Eddie sat in a meditation cell at Diagnostic, Marzack came to see him. The Meditation-shift sergeant opened the door of Eddie's cell and locked Marzack inside with him and came back in ten minutes. When Marzack left, although there was a part of him that always fought it, he had beaten the word "con" into Eddie. Marzack left no outward marks on him, but Eddie urinated blood for a week, and it was almost two months before his ribs healed. The Buster knew his work well.

Marzack was the one who was openly marked for life by the purple three-inch scar that formed over his right eye, and that was a sort of victory, but it was Eddie who had the real mark, and that reality took away any victory that might have been his. But that is the con's lot—never to win, no matter what the luck. Never. That is the way prison works. Always. When you could stand it no more, you had only three choices: you gave in to it, you killed yourself, or you ran away from it.

So I learned to lose, Eddie said to himself as he lay back and looked up at the lovely blue sky, trying with some success not to feel any emotion at the thoughts that had been a reality to him for six years.

I learned to point my head down instead of up. The neck wants to let the chin fall away, so it was not much of an effort.

No! That's a damn lie, his mind raged. *It was the hardest thing, the greatest effort I ever expended in my life. My neck was different. The feel of my chin on my neck was the most sickening sensation I ever felt.*

I had to think about it all the time to keep my head down, the way you think about it underwater to keep from breathing. Just that way, and just that out-of-place. And it got harder and harder all the time, to keep my head down.

Damn you for that! Damn all of you to hell for that! Eddie said bitterly as he made himself keep looking at the beautiful sky.

Eddie was transferred from Diagnostic to the Ellis Prison Unit thirteen miles north of Huntsville on September 21. Ellis was the "dumping ground," the toughest maximum-security prison in Texas. Seen from the air, Ellis was six quarter-mile-long brick cellblocks; each with three tiers; a boxy administration building dividing the six cellblocks in half, with rectangular factory buildings to the west and a rectangular chapel to the east, all connected by a central two-mile-long brick corridor and surrounded by two thirty-five-foot-high Cyclone fences topped with electrically charged barbed wire. There were brick guard towers—miniature forts—at each end of the fence, and the bare ground from the buildings to the fence was crisscrossed with electronic sensors that set off an alarm the moment pressure was applied to them. Everything about Ellis was awesome, efficient, modern, sterile, and crushing.

Eddie drew the standard two weeks in Meditation at Ellis for escaping. Meditation was in D-9, a row of cells off the main corridor on the eastern side of the compound, as the numbering system of the cellblocks went: B, C, D to the east; and G, H, J to the west. In Meditation you were supposed to "get your mind right." You were also supposed to learn a lesson about fighting back, about bucking the system—a lesson "jackrabbits," escapees, learned in the dark.

In Meditation Eddie went truly Inside, like a con, for the first time. But it was hard for him because the Outside was still so real. For the first three days of darkness Eddie sat in a corner of his cell, wrapped in a blanket, cowed like a frightened child in a horror movie, his mind coming apart from the grief of being separated from his family and everything else in the world. But on the fourth day, as the guard brought him his breakfast of bread and water, Eddie suddenly

found something to laugh at—a small, deep, hidden laugh, close to
madness, but a laugh. He was having the ultimate joke played on him:
a strip cell in the toughest prison in Texas. He could go no lower in
life. As it had been since his birth, he could only go up. His whole life
had been directed around plans, and all the mechanisms were still
there, waiting to form in his head; it only remained for him to get
another plan in motion again. And for Eddie, alone in the darkest hole
in American prisons, with forty-one years to serve, a plan meant only
one thing: another escape.

On that fourth day in Meditation Eddie also started doing push-
ups, sit-ups, and leg exercises. The exercises became his work, a
bridge between the Inside and the Outside, a filler while he worked
on his escape plan. Eddie began with twenty-five push-ups and
sit-ups a day and at the end of his two-week stretch he was up to one
hundred and fifty a day.

In Meditation, life for Eddie took on a new perspective. He learned
the con's lesson that life in prison is not a series of events as it is on the
Outside, it is only time—seconds, minutes, hours, days, weeks . . .
years. On October 2, when he was released from Meditation, Eddie
was assigned to B-2-6—B wing, second tier, Cell 6. Two days later he
went before the prison review board and became part of Ellis' 2,100
general-inmate population as a close-custody inmate assigned to the
field squad. Up until then, he had not seen Chris and the children
since August 1, and he had not been allowed to write or receive letters
from his family. But as a general-population inmate Eddie could have
two two-hour visits a month and could write and receive as many
letters as he wanted. On Saturday, October 7, he and Chris and the
children saw each other for the first time since he had been sent to
prison.

Chris had tried to prepare herself for their first prison meeting; she
had steeled her mind with all her will; but that was not enough. When
she saw Eddie, she broke down and wept. Angie and Bobby cried.
But Eddie did not cry. He sat on his side of the steel-and-glass
partition, stone-faced and vacant, waiting for them to stop. His mind
had held as much sorrow as it could hold, and he had used up all his
tears. Finally Chris and the children stopped crying, and she sat and
looked at Eddie without speaking, the children holding on to her sides

in confusion, staring at the father that they could not touch. He looked so strange to her, like someone she vaguely knew from an old snapshot. He was healthy and unhealthy at the same time—tanned and drawn and muscular, totally humorless and stiff, dressed in prison whites with his hair clipped short in an irregular crew cut.

"Oh, God," she said when she at last found words. "It's all so unfair. Eddie, it's so unfair."

"Fair is not the question," he answered quickly and woodenly. "In here there are no questions, and there are no answers; just what is. That's all," he told her. "Just what is. Don't talk about anything in here, ever. Talk about what you and the children are doing, about what happens on the outside. Nothing happens in here. Nothing. Everything is always the same. And it's always bad."

Chris looked down the long line of cheaply and gaudily dressed wives and children seated on benches to her left and right, and she looked past the steel-and-glass partition and saw the haggard line of cons seated on either side of Eddie; without effort or thought, she could see how bad it was.

Visiting at all Texas prisons is done "no-touch." Once a convict came into TDC, he had only two chances to touch a relative until he walked out the gate with his sentence served. On Mother's Day, each male inmate got to hug his mother and pin a flower on her; on Father's Day, each female inmate got to hug her father and pin a flower on him; the second opportunity came if the family lived more than five hundred miles from the prison where the inmate was kept.

At first Eddie tried to get Chris to divorce him and go away and make a new start for herself and the children with the $17,500 Flying Fish money. But she refused, and until Christmas of that year she remained in Huntsville, working as a waitress so she could be close to Eddie. In January of the new year, she moved herself and the children ninety miles south to Houston and took a job as a public schoolteacher; with her $9,500-a-year salary the three of them lived well in an apartment complex in the northern section of the city. Eddie adjusted to being alone on the Inside; Chris adjusted to being alone on the Outside. They had to sit and wait until things got better, something they had done all their lives. But it went much deeper than that—at the bottom of all their plans and hopes, Eddie and Chris were all each other had. They had to keep on trying, because if they quit, no one would care. It meant everything if they tried; it meant nothing if they failed or quit. By the first of the new year, Eddie was off the field squad and faced with an irony he did not care to consider: he was assigned to the Ellis welding shop. Chris was teaching sixth grade at Judy Thomas Elementary School in West Houston.

For four years, from the time he came to Ellis until he was transferred to the Walls, Eddie stayed as low as a convict can stay. On the surface he was a dog. But inside he was planning, working, always, for the elusive *Something Better*. He went about his work with his head down, dead quiet; he was almost invisible. But in his cell at night he kept himself lean and tough and hard with exercise. And he read. He read everything that had to do with Texas history and geography. Since escape was never really far from his mind, Eddie had determined that he would never again make the mistake of not knowing exactly where he was. At the end of the four years Eddie knew Texas like a scholar, and in a scholar's way, he looked for ways to use the information he had gathered. But his answers were a long time coming.

A *God's long time in coming*, Eddie said to himself as he lay in the thicket. *A God's long time*.

But he could not go on with the images of his mind, and he could not look at the beauty of the free sky any longer. He rolled over on his stomach and crooked his right arm under his head for support and turned the focus of his tired mind on Chris. She would refresh him. She would be comfort, company in the lonely and solid time he had left before he would run again.

Chris. Chris. Chris, his mind said, as her image came up inside him.

Chris, he said to himself with deep pleasure.

11

Chris and the Children /
6:31 p.m. / Dolores Hidalgo, Mexico

Chris felt a sensation of icy fingers on the back of her neck. The translucent hairs on her arms stiffened. She smoothed the hairs and massaged the back of her neck as the sensation retreated to the depths of her emotions. Then her mind reached out to bring the sensation into focus. She saw Eddie—not clearly, but she saw him. Her mind strained to bring him into focus as she straightened herself in her chair.

She was sitting on a leather-covered chair on the short, narrow pink-granite patio of her second-story room at Hotel Cocamacan across the Hidalgo Plaza in the center of Dolores Hidalgo. The city was so colonial in look and feel it could have represented the whole Mexican colonial mystique. Angie and Bobby were playing tag with several Mexican children in the small, serene, unadorned plaza across the street; from a private house behind the hotel on Guerrero Street there was the music of a soft guitar and a muted trumpet.

Chris looked at the children playing and heard the music, then shook her head, thinking she had merely imagined Eddie out of concern and loneliness. But his image was now firm in her mind. She saw him clearly, as if he was with her on the patio. For a second she thought she could reach out and touch him. She even reached out her hand, pulling it back quickly out of embarrassment, even though she was alone on the patio. Eddie's image would not go away.

Suddenly it was gone. Chris jerked her head back and forth, her eyes finally fixing on the brown afternoon dark of the large master bedroom of her suite. Her eyes dug through the room until she found Eddie again. He was standing by the open door to the tile bathroom opposite the king-size bed that was covered by a great red-orange-and-brown-striped Indian blanket. He stood there as she preferred to remember him: lean, hard, suntanned, and cocky. Now a warm glow replaced the shiver she had felt, and Chris turned fully to face the room and Eddie. Her mind leaped years into the past to Key West and an afternoon of the same color in their first apartment.

She was sitting on the bed naked, waiting for him to shower; when he came out he was nude and his hair was damp.

"You smell nice and fresh," Chris said to him as he sat down close to her on the bed. She was lying on her back as innocent as a baby, her legs spread open slightly.

Eddie reached out and touched her face with the fingertips of his right hand. Her skin was soft and tanned, her white breasts standing out as if in a painting. She took his hand and pulled him down and they kissed. She took command, moving her tongue inside his mouth and over his lips. He returned the kisses. She had a thick female odor in the taste of her mouth, a smell that fascinated him, he liked to tell her.

"I am going to be so good to you," she whispered to him, holding him close.

He kissed her gently sagging breasts and she held his head and moved it expertly over them. His hand moved down between her legs.

"Oh, yes," she said. "Yes," she repeated into his neck.

They rolled on the bed and kissed deeply. Her hand went down between his legs, her mind racing in a thousand directions, images flashing wildly before her—legs, arms, chest, hair, muscles, the bed sheets that were rich with his smell, and most of all, the wild excitement of the serpentlike curve of his penis. She slid down between his legs and began to move over the muscular snake with her mouth. He quivered and shifted his weight from side to side. Then she saw the angle of the serpent change as Eddie turned and mounted her in two swift moves. She felt his thick pubic hair on her stomach, the tenderness of his mouth, the security of his arms on her sides. Then she stopped thinking and was simply pulled along by what she was experiencing, completely warm and satisfied. She was barely conscious of Eddie moving on top of her, of his lunges in and out of her. And when she came, it was as if part of her body was somewhere else, as if it was no longer a part of her at all. Afterward, she felt cleansed. She became aware of her entire body, empty but at the same time full. She felt totally a part of Eddie, even after he withdrew from her and lay on his side facing her, his penis—to her, elegant in limpness—against her leg.

On the Mexican patio Chris held on to the image of Eddie's elegant limp penis for as long as she could. Finally she lost it and all she could do was sit and look at the empty bed, a miserable sight she had seen for six sterile years. She shuddered as before, but this time there was no sharp sensation, only the dull pain of loneliness that she knew so well. She crossed her arms over her breasts to ward off another shudder and turned from the bed and again faced the plaza across the narrow rutted gray street. Angie and Bobby were still running on the cobblestones between the palms and firs of the small park, shouting happily in Spanish to their new playmates. Chris sat and held on to herself and watched them and tried to block out all else by watching them run. But there was Eddie and his run. That thought invaded her mind. Off to the west, directly behind the park, she sat and watched the last of the day's sun disappear behind the jagged, treeless peaks of the Sierras. In seconds the sun would be gone; in minutes more, Eddie would be running again. Suddenly she thought she understood the reason for his image; he was trying to tell her something.

But what? What? her mind raged, her hands jutting out to the wrought-iron railing of the patio, gripping it like a vise. *What?*

As she held on to the railing, her mind flashed a thousand images to her: caught . . . *killed . . . wounded . . . hurt . . . or simply: scared and alone?*

Oh, dear God! she pleaded, almost audibly. *God, will it never end! Will it never end!*

But she knew, like countless times before, that there would be no answer to her question. She knew, as always, that all she could do was sit and wait. But she knew too that she was coming near the end of waiting, that she *personally*—with Eddie, or without him—could not wait anymore. She made herself let go of the iron railing and sat back in her chair and began watching her children again as the sun finally disappeared like a shimmering fingernail over the far mountains. Waiting was all she could do for now, and she knew that completely.

In minutes, he will be running again. May he be protected, she said deep within her mind. *May he . . .* But she was forced to give up the thought because it became too painful.

Goddammit! Eddie, I want to help you so, but there is nothing I can do. Nothing. Goddammit! Nothing!

All she let herself see was her children playing on the Mexican street below, as a new and much calmer thought formed in her mind.

But I can help myself, she said silently, feeling only slight guilt at the words. *I know how to do that.*

12

Marzack / 6:36 p.m. / Huntsville, Texas

Marzack was a very happy man. He sat alone at one of the tables in Aldo's Restaurant, a big pink-stucco affair on the south side of Huntsville at the corner of Sam Houston Avenue and Avenue J. The restaurant was movie-set Italian: red-and-white-checkered table-cloths, hanging potted plants, wall posters of Italy, dripping candles wedged into straw-covered Chianti bottles, and Neapolitan music piped in from a hi-fi. But the food was good, cooked and served by an Italian immigrant family who abandoned New York City after twenty hostile years. Before Marzack on his table there was a huge plate of veal *francese*, a deep dish of spaghetti covered by a light garlic sauce, and a half-empty bottle of Valpolicella. Having begun with an order of steamed clams and a draft beer, he nursed the main courses, savoring the excellent taste of the basil in the pasta's garlic sauce.

But the food was not the chief cause of Marzack's happiness. He knew he would go on alert tomorrow. He knew all his duties on the transfer detail would be temporarily taken over by his sergeant. He knew he would be free to indulge himself in his own pleasures; free to be a cop again—not the Hounder, that was TDC's word. Cop was his. The main pleasure of the moment, though, was the fact that all leads to Eddie's whereabout were dead. As far as TDC knew, Eddie had simply vanished. Marzack twisted his spaghetti into the hollow of a large spoon, brought it to his lips, swallowed it, and then washed it down with a long swallow of the mellow Valpolicella. As he set his glass down, Patrolman Mike Shorter of the Huntsville Police Department took a seat opposite him.

"Whatever he's having, I'll take," Shorter said, his voice almost devoid of an East Texas drawl. "With my booze in an ice-tea glass," he added quickly to one of Mario Aldo's fat married daughters who hovered over him the instant he sat down.

"You better be prepared to stay all night," Marzack said, taking another drink from his wineglass. "I went the whole route tonight."

"Suits me just fine," Shorter said, elbows on the tabletop, rubbing his eyes with the balls of his palms, then looking over at Marzack. "We've had one public drunk, two fender benders, and a goddamned lost cat." There was disgust in his voice as he fingered the full, well-trimmed mustache on his meaty face.

Mike Shorter was twenty-six and going through hell, serving an apprenticeship on the HPD before he could move on to Houston or Dallas. Like an army of other East Texas boys, he played mediocre ball on the Sam Houston State University football team and took a degree in criminology. From there he went directly to TDC, first as a correctional officer, then as an administrative trainee, a step that plugged you into the TDC power structure. But Shorter floundered in his trainee's slot. Prison work was not for him. He wanted action. He wanted to be a cop. Before he was forced to resign from TDC, he was assigned for six months as a fill-in on Marzack's transfer detail. That had been two years ago. On the transfer detail, Shorter learned about Marzack's exile from the Passaic PD. Marzack had no friends, but over the past two years he and Shorter had become solid social acquaintances.

"So what's the momentous occasion of your buying me dinner?"

Shorter asked, smiling slightly, his forearms coming to rest on the tabletop.

"A bribe, pure and simple," Marzack said around a tasty mouth of veal.

The policeman's clams arrived, along with his beer in a tall dark blue ice-tea glass that concealed its contents well. Shorter drained half the glass immediately and then launched into the steaming clams.

"That's against the law." He grinned as he munched one of the rubbery clams.

"No, sir," Marzack said, dead serious. "That's what the law's all about."

Then, with the wine and the meal starting to take effect, Marzack told Shorter exactly what he wanted him to do; when he finished speaking ten minutes later, the youthful policeman was on fire.

"I'm in. I just wish to hell I could go with you," he said longingly. "That is," he added, instantly regretting the slip, "if you go."

"Oh, I'll go," Marzack answered, smiling. "I'll go," he repeated with pleasure.

13

Eddie / 6:52 p.m. / Characo Marrano Creek, Texas

Eddie sat on his haunches and waited as the early night came in around him. The temperature began dropping, and in the slate-gray sky the thin outline of the moon began filling to a bright yellow ball. He waited quietly and patiently, like a long-distance runner awaiting the starter's gun. In ten, no more than fifteen minutes, he could put his plan into action again; he could begin to run again.

There was no way to count the hundreds of hours Eddie had lain awake planning in his cell, or daydreaming as he worked, on how to escape. He never spoke of it to anyone. But he was always quick to observe any conversation that had to do with escape. In his four years at the Ellis Unit, Eddie heard ideas that ranged from science fiction to utter stupidity, but never once did he hear an idea he thought had a hope of succeeding. As a maximum-security prison, Ellis was a total-search lock-up. All visitors, children included, got a naked search, and at the slightest inclination or provocation, the matrons would give the female visitors a vaginal wipe, looking for contraband dope or smuggled pistol parts. Everything was completely controlled, totally sealed off. The only hope of escape was a merit transfer to a medium-security prison. After four years of an act that could have been played on a Broadway stage, Eddie got his merit transfer to the medium-security Walls Unit thirteen miles away in the center of downtown Huntsville.

At Ellis, Eddie put his emotions to sleep while he carried out his dogged submission. Even though he still had no clear escape plan, at the Walls it took all his powers of restraint to contain his renewed sense of hope and anticipation.

How could you truly escape from prison? Eddie pondered the question endlessly. The prison had all the guns, guards, dogs, and a count system that pinned you down to a spot almost hour by hour. The prison had bars, walls, cages, and a retribution system of punishment for escape that hung like a noose around every con's neck. The stock con answer to the question of escape was there were three ways. In the first, you waited for the right moment, the time when the system slipped up—a moment that might take a lifetime to find. In the second, you just grabbed a gun, a chair, a stick, a knife—anything you could find—and went for a guard and tried to hardnose your way out. In the third way, you developed a plan— simple or elaborate—that kept you as far away from outside contact as possible. But the truth was that the three ways usually did not work.

The key, Eddie decided, was finding a fourth way, something so totally original, so unheard of, that it would work because it could not be defended against by the prison. On the first Sunday night in the fifth September of his sentence, the fourth way came to him. It was three in the morning and Eddie had to stick his head under his pillow to keep from howling out loud with joy. He, like every other con, had said it to himself a million times: "Someday I'll run away."

Run away! Jesus Christ! he howled with delight to himself that night. *That's it! I'll just run away! Run! I'll just run away! It's as simple as that!*

There was obvious beauty .and simplicity in deciding to run, but once that decision was made, where to run became Eddie's next problem. It was soon clear that Mexico was the destination, but if Mexico was so clear to him, Eddie knew it could also be clear to the TDC prison officials.

It was common knowledge among old-time prison officials that most American prisons were "country clubs" where convicts could come and go as they damn well pleased. But not so in Texas, and in Texas escape was the dirtiest word spoken. The trick, then, was to get away from TDC first and then begin your run. That meant he had to have a means to get in place to run.

The idea of running came to Eddie one month before the start of the annual Texas Prison Rodeo—"the roughest rodeo behind bars," as it was billed. The rodeo became the X factor that let all the other pieces of Eddie's growing puzzle fall into place, because it was the rodeo that presented the way for Eddie to get into place to run.

At six o'clock the next afternoon—sixteen hours after the idea of running had come to him—Eddie was out on the concrete exercise yard on the eastern side of the Walls' brick enclosure, jogging. For almost four years he had done his push-ups and sit-ups, busywork to keep him fit and sane, but now Eddie was beginning something that might set him free. He gave himself over to the jogging as never before with anything in his life. In various ways he had been running all his life; now running became his life.

The prison rodeo was open to all inmates in TDC's thirteen prisons. During August and September of each year, convicts answered an ad in the various prison newspapers and applied as contestants for the rodeo events. The applications were screened at each prison, with the individual wardens having the final say as to who was allowed to enter from each prison unit. For no specific reason, Eddie had applied for the past three years, but he had been turned down each time because of his escape. For those three years, like the security risks from all the other prisons, Eddie had been bused from the Ellis Unit to the Walls as a spectator for one of the rodeos that were staged each Sunday in October. Like the other cons, Eddie sat behind the caged-in section on the west side of the twenty thousand-seat rodeo arena adjacent to the Walls and watched the rodeo. But unlike the others, Eddie was

not interested in the rodeo events; he was interested in the movements in and around the arena itself. As he had watched every other
movement of his prison existence, Eddie watched the arena, looking,
as always, for some crack, some flaw in security or procedure that
would provide him with a means of escape if he were ever transferred
to the Walls.

Of course, he didn't know exactly how to use it at first, but from the
moment it entered his mind, Eddie sensed that something connected
with the rodeo was the flaw he had been looking for, a time when the
prison stopped being solely a prison just for a few hours. He applied as
a rodeo contestant immediately after coming to the Walls and
volunteered his services as a welder with the trusty crew assigned to
revamp the rodeo stadium. As a medium-security prisoner he was
allowed to enter the saddle-bronc-riding event a week after he
applied; by that time he was as familiar with the stadium as if he had
built it himself, and by then he was certain he could use the rodeo as a
means of escape. But *how* he would use it did not come to him until
the last Sunday of the rodeo.

Until then, Eddie had followed everything: the coming and going of
the prisoners from the other units; the professional entertainers that
were hustled in and out of the rear area of the stadium; the
movements of the guards . . . the hours he was left uncounted. But
the one thing he had not seen by that last Sunday was something he
could not have seen until then—the departure of the rented rodeo
stock. All the stock—more than a hundred bulls, calves, steers, and
horses—left the prison after the rodeo ended late on the afternoon of
the last Sunday. There was great confusion as the animals were loaded
into stock trailers at the rear of the stadium. An open space lay bare
between the stadium and the Cyclone fence gate where the trailers
exited to the Outside. There were a dozen trailers and they went off in
different directions: some to other parts of Texas, some to Louisiana,
some to Oklahoma. After a month of rodeoing, on the final Sunday
there was the maximum opportunity for human error. A chance for
the prison to slip up. Something large or small that might even the
odds just a little toward Eddie's side.

So, it can be done with the rodeo, Eddie thought as he surveyed the scene for the last time before he was locked up on the final rodeo Sunday. *But, how? And where will I run?*

No easy answers came. As always in prison there was only time, a vast dead space to sit and scheme.

For nine months Eddie said nothing to Chris. For nine months he ran five miles a day—an activity that did not arouse the least suspicion, as there were many other cons who ran and lifted weights in the exercise yard—and did his other exercises and replayed the last rodeo thousands of times in his mind. Finally in July he went to the Walls' library, a small space filled with virtually the same material he had used at Ellis. But as he again searched through the volumes on Texas history and geography, Eddie had a purpose. Now he was looking for definite answers, a diversion, the ruse ultimately needed to pull off an escape. And because it is true that escaping meant doing everything right, it had to be an escape plan so complicated, yet so simple that it erased margins for error. There was no middle ground with escapes. In the middle you slipped up, you made contact, you got caught.

Eddie began with the two basic problems of a ruse and not making contact with the outside world as he went to work on his escape plan. Texas geography provided him with the basis for the solution to both problems.

East Texas meets the Mexican border for three hundred miles, with exactly the same coned silhouette as the rhino's front horn. Eagle Pass sits in the west, Brownsville to the east on the Gulf of Mexico, and Laredo squarely in the center, with the Rio Grande River, a muddy ditch, between the two countries. On the map, if you drew a straight line across the base of the rhino's horn from Brackettville in the west, past San Antonio in the center, to Galveston in the east, from the air, the twenty-two million square miles of the horn would look like a badly kept baseball diamond. Excellent running country. But Eddie was not in the horn. He was dead center in the rhino's eye, Huntsville, the heart of the East Texas hill country. He was locked away on the forty-seven acres of the Walls, behind the thirty-foot-high brick walls that gave the prison its name; surrounded for a hundred miles in all directions by endless rolling hills and thick pine forests, a landscape broken by hundreds of small towns and ranches and crisscrossed by a beehive of busy roads and highways. He, and the other cons, were prisoners of TDC, nature, and civilization, a perfect and devastating holding combination. To escape, Eddie had to get out of the rhino's eye and into the rhino's horn.

It was easy to decide to use the rodeo to get to the horn, and easy to decide to use one of the stock trailers as a means of escape, but in early July Eddie knew it was impossible to single out one of the trailers. He would have to wait until late July or August before the grapevine, with all its catalog of information, knew which stockmen would supply the October rodeo. His first order of business would be to decide the logical places to run from and then match the locations with the hometowns of the stockmen. In the prison library in early July, Eddie pored over East Texas maps; at once he could see a distinct pattern from among the light red secondary roads, the dark red primary roads, and the thick, dark green Interstate highways. I-45 ran 90 miles due south from Huntsville to Houston, where it met I-10 for a 197-mile stretch due west to San Antonio; I-10 met I-35 for the final 160 miles south to Laredo and the Mexican border. In the rhino's head, everything was bunched together. But in the horn, past San Antonio, the land opened up on the map and became vast, unobstructed white spaces to the Mexican border. From all the little towns that fanned out from San Antonio around I-35—Uvalde, Devine, Poteet—there was good running room. But the mileage was off. It was 150 miles to Mexico. A run like that might take a full week. On your own you couldn't hold out for a full week. You'd die trying, or get caught as weak and defenseless as a baby. Eddie looked deeper at the maps.

It's got to be about a hundred miles, he told himself. *A hundred miles and four days. No more than four days on the run. Four days running is all you can take, back-to-back.*

On his map Eddie took the forefinger of his right hand and moved it from Uvalde in the west, on an arc, to the town of Three Rivers in the east; squarely in the center of the arc his finger made was I-35 south to Laredo, beginning with the little town of Dilley. Eddie's mind raced to add up the miles from Dilley to Laredo. By the Interstate highway the figure was 83 miles. Eddie's heart pounded as he added the mileage of running out from the Interstate through open country. In seconds he had the rough figure of 108 miles. His hands trembled on the map as his eyes bore down on the little dot that Dilley occupied. Then suddenly his eyes saw something else. His mind burned with anticipation. Just above Dilley, not more than two miles, there was a river. An excellent little black line of a river that flowed on an arc almost equivalent to the path his finger had just taken to cover the town of Dilley.

The Frio River. Eddie's eyes kept moving from the river to the town. *The running distance: the cover of the river as a starting point; the landscape from Dilley to Laredo: all perfect!* he said silently in the midst of his euphoria.

But then, as suddenly as the euphoria had come in, it disappeared as he studied the map further. His heart sank as he saw the huge gap from Huntsville in the northeast to Dilley in the southwest. At a glance it seemed to be four hundred miles or more. When Eddie computed it, the figure was 322 miles exactly. At an average hard driving speed of seventy mph, it would take one of the stock trucks five hours and twenty-five minutes to get from Huntsville to the Frio River. And to average seventy mph, the driver would have to push eighty most of the way. Texas still "unofficially" allowed the old speed limit of seventy mph, so eighty was possible, but it would take a wild man, and somebody with enough clout to get out of speeding tickets, to make eighty.

Loopholes, Eddie considered as he debated the matter with himself. *Three hundred and twenty-two miles to cover in about five and a half hours,* he said in grim silence. *Five and a half hours to go without being counted by TDC. Loopholes and questions. And with both you get caught.*

Something else blackened his mind.

How to stop at the Frio River Bridge?

In the end, as he sat in the prison library, there were four big questions that immediately confronted Eddie.

Could you make it from Huntsville to the Frio in five and a half hours?

Could he go that long without being counted at the Walls?

Was there a highway weight station near the Frio River Bridge where a stock trailer would be forced to stop?

And was there a stockman who would pass over the Frio River Bridge on his way home from the prison rodeo?

The answers for two of the questions came easily, and when Eddie had them, his hopes again began to soar. In the prison library, after much searching through the free state- and federal-government publications that were used as stuffing, he found there was indeed a highway weight station at the northern end of the Frio River Bridge, placed there as a checkpoint for Texas–Mexico commerce flowing in and out of San Antonio. Second, he satisfied himself as much as he could that it was possible to make the drive from Huntsville to the Frio in five and a half hours, provided the right driver was in the seat. But the answers for the other two questions eluded Eddie. But during the last week of July he got a break. The prison grapevine sorted out the company names and towns of all the stockmen who would supply the current rodeo. It was a useless bit of information, but cataloged like everything else by the grapevine simply to show TDC that the information could be gotten. Eddie studied the names and towns frantically. There were a dozen stockmen: three from Oklahoma; two from Louisiana; and seven from Texas. The Texas hometowns were: Dallas, Fort Worth, Victoria, Bryan, Orange, Kerrville, and Cotulla. The last town on the list sent a shockwave through Eddie's brain.

Cotulla. He dived for a map in the prison library, and as his finger slid down the green line I-35 made from San Antonio to Laredo, he found the town: nineteen miles south of the Frio River Bridge, right on I-35. *Cotulla*, he kept repeating to himself with great pleasure as his finger bore into the spot the cow town occupied on the map. *Cotulla*.

But again his joy was eroded, because the answer to the fourth question—could he remain uncounted for five and a half or six hours?—could not yet be answered. He would have to wait until October and the rodeo to be sure. That meant he could not escape until October of the following year.

Fifteen more months Inside.

He would have to stay low and build fifteen months before he could escape. There was no other choice. All the loopholes had to be plugged before he made his move. He had done over four years. Now he would be Inside six years before he could run. Eddie wondered if he could make it. Each year, Inside got harder and harder, put a great wedge between him and the Outside—between him and Chris and the children.

Then a fifth question surfaced. Was the driver of the Cotulla stock trailer a man who could push his truck and trailer 322 miles at eighty mph? And a sixth question. If Eddie could go uncounted, how would he finally communicate the escape plan to Chris? The answer to the sixth question came easily. If he was going to actually talk to Chris face-to-face in at least semiprivacy, she and the children would have to move five hundred miles from the prison; then they could visit in the administration lobby of the Walls. So many questions. So many loopholes. And all Eddie could do was lie low and build time.

Time, Eddie said to himself as he pondered his fate. *Time . . . time . . . time . . .* And he had the feeling that, for him, time was running out.

In August, Chris was a month away from resuming her teaching job at Judy Thomas Elementary School in Houston. If she began in September she would be contractually obligated to remain until June of the following year. As infant as his plan was in August, because of the Outside checks that could come if she broke her contract, Eddie could not see Chris bound to legal entanglements. It was painful and clear: Chris and the children had to move five hundred miles from Huntsville. He had to be able to talk to her face-to-face when the right time came.

Eddie went back to his maps in the prison library. To the east of Huntsville, five hundred miles reached almost exactly to Mobile, Alabama; to the west, to Fort Stockton, Texas. He stopped searching when the name Fort Stockton surfaced. It was a perfect, anonymous little West Texas town set in a valley and surrounded by five thousand-foot mountains, right on I-10, a workable day's driving to Huntsville and the Walls. When Chris and the children came for their regular visit on Saturday, August 5, Eddie had only one thing to say to them before he got up from his bench behind the glass-and-steel partition and walked back to his cell.

"Move to Fort Stockton, Texas," he said in a low, barely audible voice from his place in the center of a line of other cons. "Take a job as a waitress and come and visit me in September after you get settled."

Chris sat stunned as she watched Eddie get up and walk away. Finally, she too got up, and with the children she drove back to Houston, resigned her teaching job, vacated her apartment, moved to Fort Stockton, and took a job as a day waitress in a chain motel off I-10 on the eastern end of town. Seven weeks later, on Monday, September 5, Chris and the children again visited Eddie, but this time the visit was just inside the main entrance of the Walls. They were in a boxlike room formed by highly polished solid-brass bars, a holdover from the old days when the Walls was the only Texas state prison and brass was dirt cheap. At one end of the room you could see the front door of the prison that led to the Outside; from the other end you could see the maze of newer gray steel bars that led to the Inside. The steel-and-glass visiting shield was gone, and in its place there were four wooden tables with short benches. There were no guards to directly supervise the visit. Chris and the children were thoroughly searched before they were allowed to enter the room, but once in, only the shift guards in the central control booth saw them from twenty feet, and with no real interest. Since an inmate with family more than five hundred miles could receive only one visit a month, on any day the family could come, the visit was for four hours and allowed to take place in a relaxed atmosphere, an atmosphere that tolerated touching. For the first time in five years Eddie and Chris and Angie and Bobby touched each other. Five years. Just short, deep hugs that would not cause the guards or passersby to stare. Only brief kisses. Then the touching of hands across the visiting table as Eddie took up his position on one side, with Chris and the children on the other. But it was so sweet, so good—so warm for all of them. For a long time they sat and looked at each other and lingered over thoughts of the touching, all near tears and not touching. Eyes and fingertips drinking ravenously. When Eddie finally broke the spell by speaking in a low and hushed voice, Chris knew exactly what his words would be.

"I'm coming out," he said, looking directly into her searching wet eyes.

Chris pleaded with him at first, in words she had prepared, but his touch was too close, his kiss still too much with her; his smell, his *feel* too alive. She wanted him. It had been so long. Not five years of memory, but five years of empty time. She gave in and listened to him, the children sitting silently beside her as she had instructed and rehearsed them.

"I don't yet exactly know how I'm going to do it," Eddie told her. "But I know where the run will take place. I know the area by heart from maps. But what I don't know is the *land*. That's where you come in. First, you have to be my eyes and ears. Then, when I've figured out all the details, you have to be my hands."

For the rest of their four-hour visit, Eddie went over the details of the escape he had worked out to that point. Step by step he took Chris over an imaginary map from the Frio River Bridge to Laredo; then, point by point, he told her what he wanted to know about the land. Finally, when their time was up, they touched again. The touch and the escape, and with both, the thought of once again being together, never left Eddie and Chris for a second until they saw each other again on Monday, October 30, the day after the last rodeo Sunday— the day when all of the questions blocking the assembling of the pieces of Eddie's puzzle were at last answered.

It was simple enough for Chris to cover the territory Eddie would use for his run. She left the children with a baby-sitter in Fort Stockton and drove to San Antonio and spent the night. The next day she drove on I-35 to the Frio River Bridge, and then she began meticulously to catalog all the information she could about the land just to the east of the highway, two or three miles out into the hard desertlike terrain. At every opportunity she would leave the Interstate and drive out onto country roads for firsthand looks, and then back to the Interstate itself. She tested the ground for hardness and she made careful notes on the vegetation and on water whenever she found it. The scouting trip took a full day, and there was no problem in getting all the information Eddie might need. The hard part would come when she presented the information to Eddie. She could not write it down, and he could not receive it on paper or make notes himself because of the constant searches and shakedowns at the prison. The only way Eddie could get the information was to memorize it, something he did not do well. Before her next visit, Chris had arrived at a workable idea to transmit the facts she had gathered.

"Nursery rhymes," she told Eddie on October 30.

"What?"

"Nursery rhymes," she said. "From my years teaching school," she added. "I've already committed most of the facts to memory. What I do is tell them to you, and you repeat them until you get them right," she added, making an attempt at humor, her first in all the years of his imprisonment.

He reached out and took her hands and held them tightly and tried to laugh.

"Until I get it right. That's the key," he said, words that held no humor at all.

On Sunday, October 29, the last day of the annual Prison Rodeo at the Walls, the stockmen left with the rented rodeo stock. Eddie was there in the stockpens at the arena waiting to help with the loading; from the second he saw the Cotulla stock truck and trailer—marked in bold black-and-gold letters on the sides with the brand: L-BAR-T RANCH, COTULLA, TEXAS—and met the driver, Billy Bob Turner, all the pieces of his escape puzzle finally fell into place.

Billy Bob Turner was standing beside the truck cab when Eddie first saw him, standing with one foot on the ground and the other on the truck's running board, with one hand resting in the truck's window and the other on his hip. Everything about Turner was physical and dominating. Eddie did not have to look twice; beyond his cowboy exterior, Billy Bob Turner had the clear look of Blowing Rock's summer people. As Eddie stood quietly sizing him up, Turner's eyes caught his and spoke before Eddie could turn away.

"Hey, son," Turner called in an easy South Texas drawl. "How 'bout shakin' over here and lendin' me a hand."

Eddie responded without thinking. "Yes sir, boss," he called, jumping toward Turner.

Turner pushed himself away from his truck's cab and started striding for his stock trailer. "You can knock that 'boss' shit off with me," Turner instructed, without looking at Eddie. "I just need a hand, not an ass."

Eddie forced a half-smile and fell in step with Turner, helping him load a dozen wild young calves from one of the holding pens; his eyes studied everything about the man, and his truck and trailer; his mind committed all he saw to permanent memory.

Billy Bob Turner was the youngest son of William "Lightning Bill" Turner, a legendary Texas oilman and ambassador to Saudi Arabia during the administration of fellow Texan Lyndon Johnson. In Texas, the initials LBT were almost as well-known as the initials LBJ. But both sets of initials meant the same thing: big money, and big power. San Antonio was the Turner birthplace and power base, but Billy Bob Turner preferred the family's many ranches, chiefly the two-thousand-acre spread just east of Cotulla. Billy Bob was a loner, a hell-raising hardhead who tolerated his wife and four children but who enjoyed the company of his ranch hands and the business of raising rodeo stock—bucking horses and roping calves—and breeding fighting bulls for Mexican bullrings. He was alternately good-natured and savage and was known to lawmen in Texas as someone to leave alone. In short, the L-Bar-T brand on his truck was a license to do as he pleased on Texas highways, with the name Turner adding a wide berth for his business and social life.

Turner and Eddie were almost the same age, but the differences between them were the old Tater Hill/Blowing Rock summer-people gap, a distance that ate at Eddie with renewed acidity during the five Sundays of the rodeo. Turner was five-ten and weighed one-ninety, a thickset man with big features all around—big hands, big neck, ample girth, and a broad forehead with short, receding salt-and-pepper hair, and a full, graying beard that was expertly trimmed. He was a man of style and swagger and you could see he took considered interest in his dress, affecting conservative cowboy shirts with pearl buttons, a wide rattlesnake belt with a gold L-Bar-T buckle, whipcord trousers, and expensive custom-made cowboy boots. But through the cowboy facade and his tough-friendly liquor-marked face, Turner had the look and stance of the always rich.

Turner had been a fixture at the Texas Prison Rodeo since his mid-twenties. People moved when he said move, with no questions asked. He was perfect for Eddie's purpose.

The first information Eddie passed to Chris on their meeting, the next day, was of course about Turner. "I've got my ticket out," he told her, unable to keep from smiling. "Whether he drives or not, the truck . . . the *initials,* will do it."

The second thing he told her was about the count. "I can go uncounted for six hours," he said.

"Are you sure?" she questioned, her eyes wrinkled with concern.

"Yes," he answered with assurance. "It was six hours on the button yesterday when we helped with the reloading of the stock. Six hours on the button."

"Good," Chris said quickly, her eyes still showing fear. "The count is my greatest worry."

Eddie didn't reply. The count was also his chief concern, but like so many other things about the escape, he had no control over it. For the next twelve months he had to continue training himself as a runner and refine his escape plan; learn the land-form nursery rhymes Chris was transmitting to him once a month, and stay low until the next October, when he could finally escape. All the pieces of his escape puzzle were set; but Eddie had to sit for a year and hope the variables remained constant.

Chris and the children had their November visit on Thursday the twenty-third, Thanksgiving Day, eleven months from the escape date. They were supposed to return to the prison for their December visit on the day after Christmas. Eddie waited all morning in the visiting area, but they never came. By noon he had to go back to his job in the Walls' welding shop. In all his five years in prison, Chris had never missed a visit. For two days Eddie moved from his job to his cell like a robot, his mind exploding with the grim possibilities: *wrecks, sickness . . . death.*

It would have been a simple matter for Eddie to go to the prison chaplain and request a phone call, but there was his escape plan to consider; a call, anything out of the ordinary, might jeopardize his plan. So Eddie did nothing on Wednesday or Thursday. On Friday, December 29, at two p.m. he was taken from his job at the welding shop and escorted to the administration and visiting area of the prison. His heart pounded as he moved ahead of his sullen guard. Eddie had convinced himself that Chris and the children had been in an automobile accident; he could not shake the idea once it came into his mind. As he walked toward the administration building he was sure he was about to hear the grim payoff of his thoughts. In his mind Eddie was already a dead man himself. But all the terrible visions passed from him as if drawn out by a vacuum as Eddie came into the administration corridor from the east exercise yard of the prison; there in front of him, seated at one of the visiting tables to the right, were Chris and the children, loaded down with Christmas presents and smiling ear to ear.

They embraced at the table, taking full advantage of the relaxed Christmas atmosphere. Chris and the children played out the holiday ritual with ample enthusiasm for a quarter of an hour, but Eddie could see there was more behind Chris's eyes than the holiday. Since their new touch visiting privileges began at the Walls in September, Eddie and Chris had built safeguards and signals into their conversations as a setup for whatever information they were transmitting; the children, who had grown up with prison visiting, were equally attuned to the secrecy. After a quarter of an hour of merriment, staged chiefly for the benefit of the guards in the administration control room who might be looking on, Chris took Eddie's hand and leaned forward and started the real conversation she had come to the prison to make.

"I've got a very good excuse for being late," she said, unable to hold back a true smile that Eddie had not seen in five years and did not understand. "Today there'll be no nursery rhymes. Today, the topic of conversation is money."

Eddie looked across the table at her in genuine bewilderment. The children were quiet, but they too were smiling broadly at their father.

"We're rich," Chris told him just over her breath. "Rich." Then she held his hand tighter and kept looking straight into his eyes and told him a story that seemed like something out of a fairy tale.

Chris had been at the end of her lunch shift at the Fort Stockton restaurant where she worked when the mailman, a rural carrier who had visions of making time with her, unknowingly delivered the news of the money in a large manila envelope, marked in bold black letters: Sutton, Currier, Lowe & Ames, 2187-B West King Street, Boone, North Carolina 28607.

There was a mass of papers and forms inside the envelope, all under the specific letterhead of Hugo Lowe, Esquire, one of the firm's senior partners, but of all the items on the various papers, two pieces of information leaped out at Chris.

> . . . and so it is my sad duty to inform you of the death of your parents in the tragic automobile accident aforementioned . . .
> . . . it is also my responsibility to tell you of the offer by the Collins Development Company of Blowing Rock, North Carolina, of $100,000 cash for your parents' seventy-five-acre farm near said Blowing Rock . . .

There had been no contact with her parents in all the five years of Eddie's imprisonment; suddenly Chris was told that they were dead and that they had a seventy-five-acre farm. She held the letter in her hands and looked at it and tried to feel a sense of loss, but couldn't. She felt only dullness. At first there was the same feeling about the news of the $100,000; then Chris's emotions polarized as she automatically saw the money as a reprieve for Eddie. With $100,000 behind her, Chris reasoned, she could go to a respected Texas lawyer and have Eddie's case appealed. She accepted the $100,000 offer on the day she received it, and the Blowing Rock development company, which had dickered with her parents for two years over the property, promised immediate payment. Two days after receiving news of the money, Chris took Angie and Bobby with her to the Texas state capitol in Austin and sought out the services of the legendary Andre Lipowski, a former Texas U.S. senator and U.S. attorney general. After much insistence, Chris was granted a short meeting with the regal silver-haired Lipowski. She gave him a capsule version of her life and of the constant struggle she and Eddie had mounted to better themselves; then she told him of the events in Texas for the past five years. Lipowski listened carefully, with interest and sympathy; then he made the pronouncement that Chris most dreaded.

"I might be able to clear up the original charge," he told her. "There might be a small chance of that, but I cannot—one cannot— clear up the matter of escape. *Parole*. Parole is the only answer. And with a forty-one-year sentence, your husband will do at least ten more years before he can seriously apply.

"I'm sorry," Lipowski said, his face pained. "Very sorry."

Chris sat for a moment without speaking; then, without showing any emotion, she thanked Lipowski, got up, and took her children back to Fort Stockton. On the way home, for the first time, she totally committed herself to the escape.

All right, she said bitterly to herself as she drove home. *If there's no help from God, man, or the law, then we'll help ourselves. We've always been on our own, and now, with a hundred thousand dollars, there will be a cushion, a way to make things work out. We will prevail. Goddammit! We will prevail!*

Eddie sat and looked at Chris and tried to fathom exactly what she was telling him, tried to let the figure $100,000 and what it meant to them sink in. But he couldn't. He had been behind bars for five years: fed, clothed, and housed like a child, and doled out twenty-five dollars a month canteen money from the funds Chris deposited. He knew he wanted out of the prison and he knew he could pick up where he left off, but he also knew that prison and his five years Inside had put a terrible gap between him and the Outside. All he could do at first was sit and listen and wonder.

"I'm late," Chris told him, "because I went home for the money. I brought it back to the bank in Fort Stockton and talked with one of the officers. He said I could put it in savings at five and three quarters percent until April, then we have to pay taxes on it. Inheritance taxes and capital-gains taxes," she added with words that were foreign to both her and Eddie.

Eddie followed her words closely but could not form words of his own.

"We'll lose about half of it with taxes. That is, if the kids and I stay in the States till April," she added, searching Eddie's eyes.

"I don't understand," he said, rubbing his forehead out of frustration. "You lost me a long way back."

"If we leave the States with the money before April 15," Chris answered, "then who's to make us pay taxes?"

"Exactly," Eddie said quickly, responding to a sudden flash of understanding and anger. "Then you'll end up in here with a number on your butt just like me."

Chris took his hand again. "No," she told him evenly. "They have treaties, but they don't extradite from Mexico for tax evasion. I've already checked."

Eddie held on to her hand and searched her face. For an instant he went cold with sadness. During all the years of his sentence, he and Chris had resisted the changes that prison brings to a family. But, admitted or not, there had been changes. Chris's words chiseled that fact in Eddie's mind. But he let the coldness go; prison had taught him that, too.

"So we change our plan a little," he answered, forcing a smile. "You and the kids hightail it to Mexico before tax time."

"Perfect," Chris broke in, not giving him a chance to change his mind. "The money is our war chest, pure and simple. Now we can stay in Mexico and not drift all over Central America with you doing pickup work. Now you can have your boat or anything else you want.

"The kids and I will go down and get things set up and come back and get you in October," she said, smiling, trying to make the whole thing seem logical—like a business trip instead of the ten-month nightmare web that lay between them.

But she instantly stopped pretending. "Honey," she said, as she held Eddie's hand. "There's fate in this somewhere. Money coming in like this, at this time. It's got to be fate. Or just something good.

Something good after all this *shit*." She broke off bitterly, her nails digging into Eddie's hand as he stared back in hard silence.

Chris and the children came again in January, and in February, and March, and for the last time on Monday, April 9. By then Eddie had memorized all the land-form nursery rhymes and the escape plan had been set. From April 9 until November 1, Eddie would not see his family. He would run and train at the prison. He would stay low and out of the way of con and guard alike. He would make himself ready for his escape and for the 108-mile run from the Frio River to the Mexican border. He would do everything he could to make his plan work, but as he and Chris and Angie and Bobby said good-bye at the Walls on the afternoon of April 9, all four knew it would be their last meeting if the escape failed. After April 15, they would all be on the far side of the law. Eddie said it best as they parted and prepared to go their separate ways.

"That's where we've always been," he told them. "The far side. The trick is to cross over on our own terms and stay there."

"But first," Chris said, holding on to Eddie for a last, long defiant time before the guards, "we have to make one last plan work."

The plan was absolutely beautiful. Complicated and simple. And possessed of the perfect ruse. And the money, the glorious $100,000, made it all so sweet; at times, Eddie thought he could taste the greenbacks.

Stowing away on the stock trailer from Huntsville to Cotulla was the ruse; TDC officials would be searching for trailers and on the main roads, not the desert from the Frio River to Laredo, where Eddie would be running. Chris's land-form rhymes and Eddie's map and book knowledge from the prison library at the Walls supplied the needed guides for the run—the whereabouts of creeks and rivers, larger hills, open desert spaces, and finally telephone and TV towers out from I-35. Eddie would be in southeast Texas running alone in the desert, and TDC officials would be looking for him in the congested areas of north-central Texas or his home state of North Carolina.

And there would be no contact. Chris would leave the knapsack filled with running and survival gear for him under the railroad bridge across the Frio River, where he would start the run.

There would be a full moon at the start of the run, and Eddie would move at night in the good lunar light and sleep under cover by day. He would run a quarter of the 108-mile distance every night, and on the morning of the fifth day he would clean himself as best he could in a service-station restroom on the outskirts of Laredo and then walk into the city and take a room at La Posada Hotel near the entrance to the International Bridge to Mexico. Chris would have reserved a room and a safe-deposit box for him by number and she would leave the key to the safe-deposit box behind a mirror over the dresser in the reserved room that she would use after she stored the knapsack at the Frio River. Eddie would get the key and claim the contents of the safe-deposit box—$1,000 in cash and a fake Canadian passport and papers. He would buy a simple change of clothes in downtown Laredo and then he would go back to the hotel and bathe and change into the clothes, and at noon on the fifth day he would cross the border into Nuevo Laredo, Mexico, under the name of Edward J. Lanson, of Windsor, Ontario, Canada. In Morelos Park, just inside the city of Nuevo Laredo, Chris and the children would be waiting to take him back into the interior of Mexico and their new home in Colima, where she and the children had been living for six months.

Simple and direct. Eddie running south through Texas to the border, Chris and the children driving north through Mexico; all meeting at the border for a clean, swift getaway. A plan of continual motion and no contact until the very end. A plan of running that would once more start the clock of Eddie's life running.

Eddie waited for his eyes and body to become adjusted to the night's cold and half-darkness and then he stood up and shed his clothes and put them in the knapsack and covered it with the plastic garbage bag and prepared to cross Characo Marrano Creek.

The fear of the water moccasin from the irrigation ditch the night before gripped him like a vise as he stepped into the water, and Eddie found himself flailing wildly across the creek. He crossed in seconds, but he made noise. As he crawled up the far bank, he made himself promise he would cross the next water with a calm head.

Don't be afraid, he told himself. *Just do what you planned. You have no control over the rest. No control.* He started to dry his shivering body and dress again for the first part of the night's run. *Act! Just act! Just run!*

He filled his canteen, something he did not want to do because of the weight, but he would be well into the second night's twenty-seven-mile run before he came to more water. For the first seven miles of the run there would be only open, exposed desert until he reached the cover of the first hills south of Cotulla. Chris's rhyme guides for the second night's run were mostly about hills and roads and muddy creeks. But one of the rhymes summed up the major pitfalls of the distance: "Dry as a bone, and far from home," she had said.

As he stood at the top of the creek's far banks and surveyed the flatland ahead of him, ground that seemed to go on forever in the yellow dark, Eddie felt very far from home and Chris and the children. He thought of them for a brief moment, but he gave up the thought. Then he thought of the searchers from the Walls and Marzack; he gave that thought up too.

Don't hope. Don't be fearful. Don't think. Just do what you are supposed to do; just run, he told himself as he adjusted his knapsack and pistol and checked his shoes before the ordeal began again.

He bent down and rubbed the calves of both legs; they were stiff, but they felt strong. In an hour they were loose and he was running well, with the stiffness gone, replaced by a numbing mind block that let him feel only the spring of his jog across the hard desert. By eight p.m. Eddie was moving mechanically in good clean strides across the land. He was more than seven miles from Cotulla. There were outlines of several big ranch buildings off to his right, the west, but they held no light this October Monday. As he ran, there was not a foreign sound anywhere. For half an hour, as he ran, Eddie had the giddy idea he was the only person left on earth.

Just let there be four of us, he said silently as he moved. *My family is enough*.

Above him the moon suddenly seemed a forbidding wild gray-yellow, his shoes on the ground sounded like lonely drumbeats, and his family seemed on another planet.

Tuesday, October 30

14

Eddie / 12:15 a.m. / Near Tuna, Texas

Eddie froze. Three things hit him at once: the sound of a truck's motor, the flash of a truck's headlights, and the halting jolt of a shotgun's blast. Then, after a split second of vacuum silence, he heard words.

"Right there, *fucker!* Move a muscle and go straight to hell!"

Eddie froze convict-still in his tracks, hands automatically raised over his head. In the blinding headlights he could not see what was before him, but he knew it was the searchers from the Walls or sheriff's deputies. He started to go for his pistol but he knew he had missed the moment for self-defense. Before he had time to reason that he would rather be dead than caught, someone was on him like a bull, jerking Eddie's pistol from its holster, then sending him to the ground with a one-handed blow to the chest with a shotgun butt.

"Thievin' cocksucker! I oughta kill your ass on the spot. Where's the

rest? *Goddammit!* Answer me! Where's the rest of your fuckin'
bunch?"

Eddie held on to his stinging chest and tried to focus on the man
above him.

"It's just *me*," Eddie managed, confused, grunting painfully. "Who
are you? What do you mean? Just me." He cut his words off sharply as
it suddenly became clear to him that the man over him did not know
he was an escaped convict.

"Don't lie to me, you bastard, or I'll kill you right here," the man
barked, jamming the barrel of his .12-gauge automatic shotgun in
Eddie's face. "Where's the rest? Answer, dammit! *Answer!*"

"Mister," Eddie gulped, "I swear to God I'm by myself.
I'm . . . I'm camping. Good God"—he made a weak and unsure try at
indignation—"I'm just out camping. Running and camping. I don't
know what you're talking about." A second man, holding a scoped
hunting rifle, came into his vision. This man, although a hulking giant
like the first, seemed more in control of himself.

"Ease off, Daryl," he said. "Ease off and let me see what we got
here."

Daryl hesitated, then grudgingly took a half-step backward and
raised the barrel of his shotgun away from Eddie's face.

"Son, we ain't in no mood for bullshit," the second man told Eddie.
"I want one story from you and I want it quick. What the hell are you
doin' out here on me and my brother's land?"

Eddie could see the men plainly now. They were both over six feet.
The bigger of the two—Daryl—looked to be about two-twenty or
two-thirty, a fat, tough-looking man dressed in a white T-shirt and
jeans, sharp-toed cowboy boots, and a straw cowboy hat with a bright
red bandanna sweatband. The second man was about two hundred
pounds, thick and muscular, dressed in a plaid short-sleeve cowboy
shirt with pearl buttons that flashed in the dark, jeans, cowboy boots,
and a cowboy hat with a wide snakeskin sweatband. Both men were
black-mad and anxious. Eddie saw they might kill him if he did not
satisfy them with his answer. He looked at the second man squarely
and spoke.

"I just told you my story, mister," Eddie said, trying to smile and
sound convincing. "I'm on a week's camping trip. Back to nature, like

the kids say. My wife thinks I'm nuts, but I just wanted to get out of the office and back to the land for a week. I'm an accountant from Dallas. I didn't mean any harm trespassing on your land. I'll pay you for the trouble. I—"

"How the hell come you're runnin' the fuck around at night if you're campin'?" Daryl broke in, sticking his shotgun barrel back in Eddie's face. "How the fuck come *that?*"

Eddie looked at the second man for help but found none.

"Answer my brother's question. How come?" he demanded.

"Well," Eddie fumbled on, "I just couldn't take the heat of day. Too much time pushing a pencil behind my desk," he added quickly, trying to force a small laugh. "I've been running a little at night just to get the feel of the thing, and walking and sleeping in the daytime."

"Shit," Daryl said, looking at his brother in disbelief and disgust. "This cocksucker's one of 'em. Fuck it, let's kill him and take his lying ass to the sheriff. He's got cattle thief wrote all over him. Lemme kill him, Rudy. Lemme shoot him now." He seemed to get excited at the thought.

"Hold back, *dammit!*" Rudy instructed, elbowing his brother. "We just can't *kill* somebody outright. Hold back. *Shit!*" he muttered, perplexed, eyeing Eddie frozen on the ground.

Eddie kept his eyes on Rudy, hoping for understanding, and looking for an opening to break and run, but not expecting it. They both seemed crazy, and he could smell the thick, vomitlike stench of bourbon whiskey on their breath. Rudy stared back at Eddie and pondered the situation, the opening of his hunting rifle's barrel pointing directly at Eddie's nose, moving up and down an inch each way with his breathing.

"*Hell!*" Rudy erupted suddenly, the rifle barrel flying past Eddie's face. "Let's just get his ass to the house and then decide what to do. *Campin' an' runnin'*—if that ain't the biggest crock of horseshit I ever heard." Suddenly he turned directly back to Eddie again, leveling his rifle barrel on his face for emphasis. "Get up slow and easy, cattle thief. Slow and easy, or I'll kill you dead."

"You've got me all wrong," Eddie started protesting in a subdued voice as he slowly did as he was told. "I'm just out for—"

"We know goddamned good and well what you're out for," Rudy

cut him off. "You and your bunch have took two hundred head from me in the past three months, and I'm fuckin' sick of it. I'm gonna kill your sorry ass and teach your bunch a lesson."

"But not before we find out where the rest of your crowd is," Daryl injected, poking Eddie in the stomach with his shotgun barrel. The words brought an instant howl of approval from Rudy.

"Damn right, Daryl," he said quickly. "By God, you hit the nail right on the head."

Daryl, a dim-witted giant, swelled with the praise. Eddie stood before the two men and waited for them to give him orders. He was a convict again. The feeling came without effort, but with great pain. He considered running and letting them end the pain, but on impulse, he held back. Like prison, you waited, you hoped; you looked for an opening. After a few seconds more the men herded him to their pickup truck. Rudy drove and Daryl got in the open flatbed as Eddie's guard.

"Keep your fuckin' nose on the floor," Daryl grunted, "or I'll gut-shoot you right in the ass." He poked Eddie in the rectum with his shotgun barrel as the truck bounced over the field.

Eddie pushed his nose hard onto the steel floor of the truck bed and started to think, to plan.

12:30 a.m.

The Potts brothers' two thousand acres was one of the largest ranches in La Salle County. They kept eight hundred head of beef cattle, but that wasn't what made them the richest men in the county; their millions came from natural gas.

The two thousand acres was cut up into nine fenced-off sections; Section 12, a two-hundred-acre pancake-flat expanse in the southeast corner of their spread, was one of the richest private natural-gas holdings in the West, yielding about $5,000 per day in net revenues.

Rudy and Daryl Potts were "sand millionaires"—semiliterate, crazy rednecks. Rudy, forty, was the elder and less volatile; Daryl was thirty-eight, a man-mountain with a brain that functioned on the level of a slow child's. Even in the boondocks of La Salle County, the Potts brothers and their Bar-P Ranch were to be avoided. Rudy's wife, Kay, a thirty-four-year-old chesty bleached blond whom he found in a Dallas massage parlor, was the only one of the family generally seen in La Salle County. Most of the time Rudy and Daryl were drunk at the ranch or in Dallas or Las Vegas, or big-game hunting in Wyoming or Montana or Central America.

The Bar-P Ranch, run by a professional manager and nine Mexican ranch hands, had everything money could buy. The main house could have been part of the movie set of *Gone with the Wind*. It had been furnished by a Dallas decorator with $100,000 worth of gaudy period furniture and Old South antiques, and authentic portraits of Confederate generals and politicians were hanging everywhere; for Rudy and Daryl Potts the trite Rebel bumper-sticker slogan "Forget Hell" was a living maxim. The Potts brothers' money had literally bought them a piece of the Confederacy; to them the Civil War was as real as yesterday.

As the brothers drove up in front of their four-columned mansion, Kay Potts was standing on the long, open front porch in a see-through pullover and red short-shorts, her blond hair teased and piled high on her head. She was barefoot and smoking a cigarette, holding a drink and grinning.

"Oh," she gushed in her nasal Arkansas drawl. "You got one! Oh, goodie. *Goodie!*" She waved, her heavy breasts dancing inside her blouse as if water-filled.

Rudy Potts blew the truck's horn wildly. Eddie pushed his nose hard against the floorboards as Daryl began to give out war whoops.

The Bar-P Ranch was isolated, almost bisected by a southern curve of the Nueces River. It was bordered to the west by the 500-population town of Tuna and I-35, and to the east by range country. The ranch manager's house and the bunkhouse were half a mile from the mansion. The two brothers, under the giggling, half-drunken approval of Kay Potts, shoved Eddie up the steps and into the mansion, all knowing he was theirs to do with as they pleased.

"*God!*" Kay giggled, dancing on her toes, edging close to Eddie as the brothers kicked and pushed him into the huge living room. "You really did it! Just like in the movies. You caught a rustler. God!" She was clearly fascinated by Eddie. "Are you gonna *hang* him, like in the movies? Baby, that would be such a kick!" Her nipples showed· hard through her blouse, and she shivered with excitement.

Daryl felt the full weight of Kay's arousal; before Rudy could answer her question, he bolted from the room in search of a rope. "Whooew . . . shit!" he whooped, trotting out of the room, carrying his shotgun down at arm's length like a baseball bat. "Sheeit!"

Kay reached out and squeezed Rudy on the arm and then took the last sip of her drink to steady herself.

"Oh," she moaned, pulsating on her bare toes. "God, to hang somebody right here in our own living room. Oh!"

"Hang 'im!" Daryl Potts bellowed. "*Son of a bitch!* That's a helluva idea. Shit!" He came booming back into the room with coil of rope in one hand and his shotgun in the other. "Hang the prick just like in the movies!"

Daryl and Kay were getting swept up in the idea like evil children; they looked to Rudy for approval. A small crooked smile on Rudy's face was all it took to send them into a frenzy.

"Goddamn! We will hang 'im!" Daryl snorted to Kay.

Eddie stood helpless before the three, held at bay in their huge and gaudy room by Rudy's rifle and Kay and Daryl's insanely curious eyes. It all seemed like a bad dream, some nightmare he'd conjured up under the strain of the run and the possibility of capture. But it was real. Eddie searched his mind frantically for words that would help him.

"I'm just camping!" he began to protest, his hands shaking, his eyes trying to find Rudy's eyes. "You've got the wrong person. I'm an accountant from Dallas, on vacation. That's all," he pleaded, using his hands.

Rudy held his rifle level with Eddie's stomach and thought for a moment.

"What building's your office in?" he asked with contempt.

Eddie searched his mind for the name of a big Texas bank.

"The First National Building," he said quickly, his voice showing some relief.

Rudy studied him; Kay set her glass down on a tabletop and sucked on the last of her cigarette, obviously disappointed at Eddie's factual answer.

"What street's the bank on?" Rudy hammered, pleased with himself for the question as he leaned forward menacingly for the answer.

Eddie turned pale. He drew a complete blank. He started to stammer the name of a random street that came to him, but Rudy stopped him cold.

"You lyin' fucker. *You're one of 'em!* One of the bastards that's been stealin' me blind. Bastard!" he screamed suddenly, holding his rifle in Eddie's face. "You're gonna die right here in this room. Right *here,* right *now!*" He jammed the rifle barrel into Eddie's nose, his finger tight on the rifle's trigger.

Before Rudy could make himself shoot Eddie, Daryl let out another of his war whoops.

"No! It's hangin' time, by God!" Daryl roared, shaking the rope in Rudy's face.

The war whoop broke Rudy's will to shoot Eddie; he shook off the thought and replaced it with words.

"String 'im up, then, goddammit. I wanna see the bastard wiggle." Rudy snorted, jerking his rifle barrel out of Eddie's face, wedging it into his chest.

"Oh, my gosh!" Kay screamed, pushing in toward Eddie. "This is the most fun we've *ever* had. Oh, Rudy . . . Daryl."

"Please!" Eddie begged, his eyes racing between Rudy and Daryl. "Okay, so I lied about being an accountant from Dallas. I just said that because it was the first thing that came into my head. Something that sounded right. Something quick," he kept on, pained and scared, his hands waving in front of his waist. "I'm a charter-boat captain from Key West, Florida. I live on Baker's Lane. I keep my boat at Garrison Bight. I—"

"Shut the fuck up!" Rudy Potts yelled, reversing his rifle, sending Eddie unconscious to the floor with a butt stroke to the side of his head. "You bullshittin' motherfucker. Shut up!" He started to shoot, but again he stopped short. "String 'im up! Goddammit! String the bastard up and we'll have ourselves a good old-fashion' hangin'," he told his brother.

"Oh, thank you, Rudy!" Kay chimed in from behind, throwing her arms around his back, kissing his neck. "I'm so *glad* you didn't shoot him."

On the floor, Daryl Potts went to work on Eddie, tying his hands behind him, hobbling his feet together, then stringing the expertly made noose, with the regulation thirteen loops, around his neck. Rudy stood Eddie up while Daryl threw the other end of the long strand of rope over one of the thick exposed beams near the top of the twenty-foot living-room ceiling.

"Yessir," Daryl said as he got the rope over the beam and started to pull it tight. "Hangin' time! Just like in the movies." Before he could go on, Kay broke in, wide-eyed and grinning.

"Jesus!" she exclaimed, clinging tightly to Rudy. "This will always be the room we *hung* somebody in. Nobody else around here can say *that!*"

"Right!" Rudy beamed. "We're gonna turn the living room into the dyin' room!"

"Yeah," Daryl said. "We'll have something you can't even order from Neiman fuckin' Marcus." The three of them laughed wildly, as Eddie started to regain consciousness, trussed up before them like a pig.

Rudy, Kay, and Daryl came into Eddie's view as three shimmering balls of painful light. As he began to see them plainly, Eddie vomited and choked on bile when the rope jerked his head back; then his knees buckled as the reality of what was happening poured over him like scalding water. Suddenly Daryl pulled the rope tight from the ceiling beam and Eddie began to do a gallows dance in the center of the living room, his toes just touching the heavily carpeted floor. Before he had time to contemplate death, Eddie started slipping into it as if going down a playground slide.

"Oh, Jesus!" Kay Potts shrieked with joy, holding on to the sides of her blushing face. "This is beautiful. God, it's just beautiful!"

"Look at him jig!" Rudy yelled, his fists balled at his shoulders.

"Do the twist, boy. Do the friggin' twist!" Daryl bellowed, holding on tightly to the stiff rope.

"Look at his eyes!" Kay screamed with pleasure. "They're rollin' back into his head and poppin' out! Is he dyin', Rudy? Is he? Is this how it looks to *die?*" She was clapping her hands with joy, her eyes flying between Eddie and her husband.

"Fuckin'-A," Daryl said. "He's gettin' his lights turned out right here before us. Dyin' deader than hell," he said with great satisfaction.

Rudy said nothing. He stopped, suddenly sour on the whole idea.

"Screw this!" He bristled. "This is a crock of shit . . . killin' somebody in your own living room. Shit on this!" He moved over to Eddie, supporting him so that the rope's lethal tension was stopped.

"Sonofabitch!" Daryl shouted, banging his fist and hand together savagely as he let go of the rope. "He just had a few more seconds to go. Fuck! We could'a seen him die!"

"Rudy!" Kay Potts bleated defiantly. "It was over too soon!"

"Shut up. Both of you!" Rudy commanded. "Daryl, get the rope off his neck before we have a damn corpse on our hands. Now, dammit! Do it right *now!*"

Daryl jerked his shoulders in resentment and lumbered over to the rope as Rudy let Eddie fall heavily to the floor. Then he was on Eddie, still unconscious, wrenching the noose free of his neck. Eddie's bound hands jerked to be free, and his neck muscles strained under bulging blue veins as he gasped for air.

"Here!" Rudy ordered, looking over his shoulder at Daryl. "Help me get him over to the pool. The sonofabitch looks like he *is* dyin'. Move your ass, goddammit!" he shouted when Daryl failed to jump. "You get his feet and I'll take his arms. Come on, move! Shit, the sonofabitch may already *be* dead."

Eddie's mind was on fire, his brain filled with exploding flashes of purple that turned white as they started to disappear. He could feel himself being handled; he had the idea his arms were being pulled off like the branches of a dead tree.

An indoor swimming pool monopolized the whole near side of the living room behind the stairs and twin formal libraries that had been turned into TV rooms. The marble pool was thirty-five feet long, twenty feet wide, and tapered off from a depth of ten feet. They carried Eddie across the room to the pool's shallow end. Rudy got in up to his waist, then Daryl stood Eddie up and pushed him in facefirst. For a split second, just before Daryl pushed him, Eddie became half-conscious and saw the swimming pool and the water. He became fully conscious the instant the water's stinging slap hit him in the face. Again there were the purple and white flashes of suffocation. Eddie flopped sickeningly, trying to gain some sort of bearing so he could stand in the bath-warm fluid that enveloped him. Before he found his footing, Rudy had him standing and was holding his head by his hair, beating the water out of his lungs with hard slaps to his back. Eddie was sure he was about to die. Suddenly, by great force of will, he began to fight.

"Damn you!" Eddie shouted, finding the words with surprising ease inside his frenzied mind. "Damn you bastards. You've got the wrong man. Bastards!" He raged into Rudy's face, his hands tearing at the ropes that held his arms behind his back. "I didn't do anything to you!" A hard scowl formed on Rudy's face. "I didn't do—"

But he didn't get another word out before Rudy dropped him into the water like a bag of garbage.

"Drown, you prick!" Rudy snorted. "Drown, fucker!" He held Eddie under the water in the vise of his hands.

"Oh, Rudy!" Kay shrieked from the pool edge, leaning forward with her hands on her knees. "This is better. So much better. Drownin' him in the pool. Oh, Rudy, it's perfect."

"Shitfire!" Daryl laughed, moving forward for a better look. "He's wigglin' like a bass on a cane pole. Hell, you always got the best ideas, Rudy. Shit! Look at him go. Wiggle, you bastard—wiggle!" he called down as Eddie fought madly to stand and breathe.

But again, as he watched Eddie, Rudy soured on the killing. He was callous and mean, but he was not a killer; that was something else entirely. He brought Eddie out of the water, Eddie's wrists bleeding from the effort to free his hands, his frantic mouth gasping for air.

"Please! Please, stop! Please!" Eddie choked. "Please! I beg you, *please!*" The eye of death was on him now, and Eddie was out of control.

"You cuss me again, sonofabitch, and you're dead for sure," Rudy shouted into Eddie's pale face, his hands holding Eddie up by his ears. "You hear me?"

"Yes sir, boss," he said without thinking, his face thick with pain.

The word "boss" went past Daryl and Kay, who stood by resentfully, feeling cheated out of seeing death once more, but the word settled instantly on Rudy.

"Boss?" he questioned, dropping his grip on Eddie's ears, holding him at arm's length by his shirt. "You sure as hell ain't no Dallas accountant," he, said, eyeing Eddie closely. "You're a goddamned cattle thief for certain, and you've done time, too. Am I right? You've done time."

Eddie started to deny it, but he gave up and dropped his head without speaking.

"Hey!" Rudy bellowed into his face. "Where'd you do time? Ellis? Ramsey? The Walls?"

Eddie couldn't find words.

"You wanna take another swim, asshole?"

Eddie's head snapped up; words materialized.

"Ellis and the Walls," he mumbled. "But not for stealing cattle. For assault. You've got the wrong man. For Christ's sake, can't I make you understand that?"

"No-sirree-bob," Rudy replied with equal speed, his words forceful. "We got the *right* man. And before we're through with you, you're gonna tell us where every damn one of your bunch is, and we're gonna get the sheriff and go clean them cocksuckers out. You can bet your boots on that, pardner." He pushed Eddie back to the shallow end of the pool, letting him fall back on his knees in two feet of water.

The fear that Rudy, Daryl, and Kay instilled in Eddie was more intense than his first desperate fears of prison. After six years behind bars Eddie thought he was shock-worn and con-tough, but now he knelt in the pool and trembled openly as he watched the three of them.

Rudy leaned forward, his breadloaf gut flexing out at both sides.

"You're a dead sonofabitch. You know that?" he said, smiling sardonically. "Dead as hell if you don't tell us where the rest of your bunch is. If I was you, I'd just belch up with the right answers and save my ass."

"While I had an ass to save," Daryl injected quickly, with a thudding laugh.

"I'd save my ass too, sugar," Kay Potts purred, patting her half-covered nylon butt, then giggling like a schoolgirl to Rudy.

"Well, asshole?" Rudy wasn't smiling anymore. "What's it gonna be? Ass or no ass?" His eyes got small and wild like Daryl's and Kay's.

Eddie shook visibly in the water and searched the three unfeeling faces leering at him from above. Words stuck in his throat.

"You're just beggin' to get yourself drowned," Daryl snarled impatiently.

"I don't *know* anything. I'm not the person you think I am. Damn you!" he grunted in defiance, his head coming erect and steady, his bleeding wrists again tearing at his ropes.

"You a goddamned suicide," Rudy said, his neck and shoulder muscles stiffening. "You just tryin' to get yourself killed."

"An' we right here to oblige," Daryl added.

"Oh, sugar," Kay giggled in Eddie's direction. "It's gonna be fun watchin' you drown. Do it now, Rudy," she shrieked suddenly, jumping up from her chair, her face twisted with anticipation. "Do it now, honey. Do it now!"

"*Now*, Rudy!" Daryl roared, his eyes straight on Eddie. "God-dammit, let's drown him *now!*"

Rudy held back for a moment, taking a long swallow of his drink. He sat the glass down hard on the marble pool edge and looked at Eddie a second more. Then, without warning he jumped out of his chair like a prizefighter coming off a ring stool; Kay and Daryl were right behind him. Eddie went wild with fright.

"Godddd, nooooooo!" he screamed, trying to get to his feet. Rudy's massive bulk loomed in front of him, and before he could stand, everything went sickeningly purple and white again. Then, as earlier, everything went black, and all the pain and noise stopped.

3:30 a.m.

When Eddie came to, he was again lying on the living-room carpet, hands still bound behind, his feet still hobbled together. He was on his right side in the center of the floor, facing the bar across the room. The noose was around his neck once more, but the rope hung loose over the ceiling beam. He regained consciousness limply and with no sound. At first, because of the throbbing, sickening pain in his temple and neck, Eddie thought he had gone insane when his eyes finally cleared and he could see the Potts brothers. They were both wearing uniform jackets and plumed hats. For a few moments Eddie could not make out what kind of uniforms they were; then it hit him: they were Confederate tunics and plumed calvary hats.

Daryl had passed out and was sprawled back against the seat of a long sofa in his tunic and underwear, his huge bare legs splayed out before him. Rudy was a few feet away, sitting in a big armchair with his bare legs turned sideways. Kay was in front of him, in her pullover and panties, doing a contorted dance to loud music that came from behind the bar. She was blind drunk and flopping around like a chicken; her wet blond hair was plastered to the sides of her face, and her melon breasts jiggled. Eddie could hear her moaning as she danced. Suddenly he saw her catch herself in mid-motion and tear her panties off with two heavy tugs at either end of their thin side straps. Rudy let out a howl as Kay bared her thick black bush. Then Eddie saw her flop over to Rudy and bend down between his legs, her head buried at first, then starting to bob up and down with rhythm. When Eddie saw Kay stop to slide Ruby's underwear off and sit down on his lap, he went to work on his ropes, the hemp biting into his raw flesh. He worked furiously while the two grunted and moaned against each other on the other side of the room. Eddie had lost track of time, but as he worked against his bonds, he was sure he had been held captive for hours.

Two or three hours at least, Eddie thought, his mind clearing with the intensity of the pain. *If I can just get my hands and feet free, I've got a chance. I've got some hope. They're sappy drunk. If I can just get my hands and feet free before they see me, I've got a chance. A chance . . .*

Eddie was talking to himself again, urging himself on. He had not done that since the Pottses had captured him. It made him feel much better, stronger.

Hurry! he screamed at himself. *Hurry! God, hurry!*

Kay and Rudy Potts were rolling on the floor, drunkenly banging against each other, when Eddie finally got his hands free. It took him ten minutes, and his hands were bloody and numb when he saw them again. Rudy and Kay were completely naked now, thirty feet from him, half-hidden from him behind Rudy's high-backed armchair. He watched them carefully while he brought his feet up under him with his knees pressed hard against his chest. Silently he untied his hobbles and then took the noose from his neck. He was free. He lay stone-still for a moment and surveyed the three people across the room.

Daryl was still wedged back against the sofa, passed out, his mouth open. Kay and Rudy were deeply into their marathon sex bout. Eddie's eyes searched for weapons, looking hard for his pistol, which Rudy had stuck in his belt when he was first captured. Finally he located it on the bartop beyond Kay and Rudy. Eddie felt his stomach go limp with fear; he didn't know if he could make it to the other side of the room without Kay or Rudy seeing him, or Daryl waking up. But he did know that when they sobered up, they would kill him. After what they had done to him, they would have to kill him. Slowly Eddie flattened himself on the rug and started to inch his way toward the bar and his pistol. Before him, Kay and Rudy were coming to a climax, howling like cats, and tearing at each other as if they were fighting. In seconds they would be through. Eddie was too scared to think, he could only act, only crawl and hope they didn't see him. Rudy finally rolled off Kay and onto his side; he was facing Eddie from five feet. Both men went wide-eyed with shock; Eddie moved first.

"Aaaaaaahhhhhaaaaa!" he roared as he pushed himself to his feet, leaping toward the bar. Blindly his hands searched for the gun as he heard Rudy stumble to his feet. At last his grappling hands found it. He turned on Rudy, who was almost on him, lunging hysterically.

"You bastard!" Rudy screamed. "You'll—"

But Rudy got no more words out. There was only the blast of Eddie's pistol, a crack that sent Rudy back with sledgehammer force. He groaned, hands reaching for the hole the bullet had torn out of the top of his left shoulder, his blood and pieces of skin and bone spraying out in a circle that caught Kay in the face as she finally got to her feet.

"Oh, God!" She gagged, wiping at her face. *"Rudy!"*

Daryl was moving now, shaking his shoulders in a hoglike motion, grunting and trying to clear his drunken eyes.

"Wha? Wha the . . . Wha? Hell . . ." Daryl coughed, immediately silenced by his name.

"Daryl!" Rudy cried, his back flush with the wall to the side of the bar, starting to slide down it as blood gushed from his open wound. "Daryl! Kill the . . ." Rudy coughed, passing out in shock before he could finish, falling on his side with a heavy thud.

Facing the three, Eddie tried to see everything at once: Rudy, Kay, Daryl, every move they made, and all the doorways and windows of the great room.

God, who'll come now! With the shot, who'll come now? But there was no time for answers. Kay was coming at him now, hysterical, and Daryl was trying to get up, his eyes still only half-open. Eddie sidestepped Kay so he would not have to shoot her; as she lunged by, Eddie could see Daryl up on his knees, trying to get oriented in the midst of his stupor. But Eddie was ready for him. In an instant more, Eddie squeezed his pistol's trigger and Daryl crashed back to the floor, shot in the right thigh.

"Gaaaaaaahhhh!" Daryl choked, his hands grabbing for his bloody leg.

Then Kay was on Eddie, holding a thin jagged piece of metal sculpture like a knife. She was nude, but Eddie never saw her

nakedness, only her eyes, which seemed yellow with madness. As she
came in on him, Eddie faked a fighter's bob to the right and stepped a
half-step to the left. He caught her squarely in the nose with the side
of the pistol. Without even a whimper, Kay went down unconscious,
falling like the iron statue she held in her hand. For a second then, it
seemed to Eddie that everything came to a complete standstill—Rudy
against the bar wall, Daryl screaming on the floor, Kay out cold in
front of him, the noose still hanging over a ceiling beam, the
swimming pool rich with his blood, the smell of blood everywhere.
But the frozen mood broke, and suddenly Eddie was running again.
He tore out of the room into the entranceway and out the front door.
He paused at the pickup truck to get his knapsack, but was stopped
short by lights coming on, and sounds of people running in the night.

"Stop! Stop!" he heard a man shout. "Stop!"

The speaker was big, and Eddie thought the man had a stick or a
knife in his hand. He ran from the truck, only his pistol held vise-tight
in his hand as he moved frantically.

Oh, God! Eddie cried to himself as he ran, hearing the sounds
intensify behind him at the doorway to the main house. *God, no! Now
I have nothing. It's over. Finished. Oh,dear God!*

Ahead there was only the black night. Eddie's mind was eaten up
with misery. All he could do was run, stagger on like a robot. He
believed it was over. He had made contact. Without provisions, it
would be only a matter of time before he was caught again.

God! God! he kept on crying to himself as he ran. *Jesus God!*

15

Marzack / 8:30 a.m. / Huntsville, Texas

Marzack, shallow in sleep but resting perfectly, heard the telephone
on its first ring as he lay warm in his bed. He let the device sound five
times before he stirred slightly from under the covers to answer.

The man on the other end of the telephone registered Marzack's
clipped "Yeah."

"What the hell have we got here?" the speaker said. "Fucking
Sleeping Beauty?"

Mike Shorter's voice made its impression on Marzack, and he
pushed himself up and back against his bed's headboard, waiting for
what the Huntsville policeman had to say.

"I didn't get through with my eight-to-four tour yesterday till
almost ten; now I'm back pounding the streets and you're still in the
sack."

"Yeah . . . right," Marzack said. "Speak to me." He was wide-
awake now.

Shorter shifted gears, his voice becoming hard and businesslike.

"You know that word 'blip'. you used last night—'looking for a blip,' you said."

"Yeah."

"Well," Shorter said, "I think I got your blip."

The policeman got no further before Marzack cut in forcefully. "Anybody else know?"

"No. Hell no," Shorter protested immediately. "And it doesn't look like something anybody around here will pick up. I just want you to remember where it came from, is all, and that it will be my ass if anybody ever finds out I held it back or gave it to you. Okay?"

"Say your piece, governor," Marzack replied. "I'm reading you loud and clear."

"Well, it's South Texas, like you thought. La Salle County. Cotulla, the county seat. Off I-35. Little berg called Tuna."

"I know the place," Marzack said, massaging the back of his neck.

"A shooting," Shorter went on. "Two big-time ranchers and a woman. Routine, but here's where your blip may come in."

"So?"

"So," Shorter said, "the assailant left on foot. No known vehicle coming or going."

Marzack listened to the rest of the information Shorter gave him from a Texas-wide police teletype, but he was sure he had heard enough from the beginning.

Left on foot, he repeated to himself as Shorter kept on with the details. *Left on foot. Left like a goddamned rabbit.* Marzack smiled deeply to himself as he continued to massage the sleep from his neck.

Like a rabbit. . . .

8:40 a.m.

The call from the warden of the Walls came five minutes after Marzack hung up with Mike Shorter. Like always, the call was bitter and brief, and this time it came seven hours before the usual forty-eight-hour deadline.

"He's all yours" was all the warden said.

8:50 a.m.

Marzack stepped out of the shower stall into the soupy warmth of the bathroom and dried himself, using the thick towel roughly as a form of massage. He opened the bathroom door slightly and the steam from the shower cleared in the small room, but he had to wipe the wet mirror dry with toilet paper. Ten years after his stint with the Passaic PD he had mellowed, or maybe it was fairer to say his interests had shifted. Before, as a detective, his mind had been filled with his work; now, as a prison transfer lieutenant with TDC, he had time to think of himself. At forty-six, Marzack was worried that his 230 pounds were beginning to sag on his six-two frame. But he was a man who had always favored his pleasures, and so he had decided to live gracefully with his excess pounds, using the device of wearing his thick brown hair full, cutting his bushy and graying sideburns just below the center of his ears, and covering his bulk with good suits and his ever-present trench coat.

He shaved carefully before the mirror, taking pains to see that his sideburns were straight and even, then dried his face, slipped on his battered green flannel robe, and padded into the bedroom for some after-shave lotion. When the biting liquid had been applied, he moved into the kitchen for a breakfast of cream cheese and a tin of date-nut bread and coffee. The food was only half on his mind. The blip Mike Shorter reported shared the other half. It was exactly what Marzack was looking for, and as he ate he could see the blip as plainly as if it had shown up greenish-yellow on a radar screen. South Texas had been Marzack's first choice, with Southeast Texas, Beaumont or Corpus Christi, as a close second.

A Texas or Louisiana seaport or Mexico, Marzack said to himself as he happily chewed a large wedge of cheese and sweet bread. *Tuna, Texas. Assailant left on foot. No vehicle. So Mexico it is.*

You sonofabitch, he said, shaking his head. *I'll give you balls, if not good sense.*

Then, as Marzack's mind released the words, a new thought replaced them instantly. *"Balls" spelled backwards, as a Passaic PD precinct captain used to say, is "desperation."* That suited Marzack just fine, though; in fact, it was just what he was looking for, what hounding was all about.

Go, little desperate rabbit, he said silently, drinking the last of his coffee. *I make you two days away from mama rabbit and the little rabbits. Just run and get tired and stretch your desperation. Break your balls a little.* He smiled, almost laughing out loud.

Then we'll spell "desperation" my way.

9:45 a.m.

Marzack packed carefully: two extra suits and shirts, underwear, socks, an extra pair of shoes, and some rough gear—lace-up boots, khaki shirts and trousers, and a war-surplus leather jacket. He thought he would need both kinds of hunting clothes.

He dressed with equal care—a steel-gray lightweight wool suit, light blue button-down shirt, navy wool tie, and a pair of brown smooth-toed lace-up shoes—a fine big-city-detective outfit that made him feel good as he surveyed himself in the closet door's full-length mirror.

When he was dressed, Marzack walked into his living room and stood before the two glass-fronted gun cases studying the considerable contents of each before he made his selections. Finally he chose an Ithaca 7-mm hunting rifle with a hooded ramp front sight, for long-range shots; a .12-gauge pump shotgun for close in; and for a handgun he decided to use his favorite, a Smith & Wesson .357 magnum pistol with carved walnut handgrips. He put the pistol in its holder, on his belt, between the second and third loops; then he took the rifle and shotgun from the racks, sheathed them in their leather carrying cases, and got the appropriate cleaning gear and ammunition for each. As an afterthought, Marzack stopped and took a medium-sized stainless-steel case from one of the cabinets. Inside the case there were four rifle grenades and a tear-gas gun. After deciding on the gas gun, Marzack was sure he had covered all possibilities. He loaded the weapons, cleaning gear, and ammunition in his dark green Olds 88 in three trips; then he put his single leather suitcase and trench coat on the back seat. The final items to go in the car were two boxes of cigars, two fifths of Myers's rum, and a small black leather box he had taken from one of the gun cases—a last item of insurance.

Everything was ready, and first-class. For a man who made $16,000 a year, Marzack lived very well, concentrating only on quality items, things that gave him a sense of security. He was ready to go, but there was one final thing to do before he left. He went to the living-room phone and dialed the number of the duty officer at the Walls. He did not know the lieutenant on the other end of the phone, but when Marzack said his name, he got the other man's complete attention.

"Just checking in," he said, knowing he needed no more explanation. "Then I'm on my way."

"Yes, sir."

"Anything shaking on the Macon escape?"

The lieutenant had to look through his duty sheets; Marzack took that as a very good sign.

"No, sir," the lieutenant said. "Cold, it looks like."

"Okay," Marzack replied impersonally. "I'm on my way."

"Yes, sir," the cowboy lieutenant on the other end of the line replied coldly; like TDC's other cowboys, he was taking the escape personally.

Marzack's hand was shaking when he hung up the phone.

All mine, goddammit! All the fuck mine!

He locked his house, walked happily out to his car, got in, and drove up Avenue I to the center of Huntsville, then out to I-45. Just past the entrance to the Interstate he stopped and put metallic TDC PRISON TRANSFER UNIT decals on both doors of his Olds 88. Then he turned on the police band and his own AM-FM radio. He lit up a green Optimo and he was on his way south to Houston, then west on I-10 to San Antonio, then south again to Tuna on I-35. The TDC

decals would get him ninety mph with no trouble at all, and his TDC
lieutenant's badge and the warden's orders would be all the hunting
license he needed for Eddie.

As he drove off, Marzack felt on top of the world. He felt like a cop
again. Just to celebrate, he would stop in San Antonio long enough for
a great Mexican meal at Santiago's on the canal near the Alamo. An
excellent meal of guacamole, *tacos de pollo*, and *quesodillas*—tortillas
filled with Monterey Jack cheese, roasted over an open flame until the
cheese melted, and then filled to the brim with fiery hot chilies—all
washed down with sweet, ice-cold Mexican beer. To drive 350 miles
because of a single thread of information seemed fanciful, but
Marzack's cop sense told him it was the exact right thing to do. As
often happened in police investigations, it was a hunch that paid off, or
you got nothing and the suspect got away scot-free. In Marzack's mind
there were no doubts at all as he pushed his Olds to ninety on the
Interstate and settled back with his cigar, possessed of an enormous
sense of well-being and the immediate anticipation of an excellent
meal.

On foot, he said, repeating Mike Shorter's words. *Running?* He
could not be sure yet—whatever lay 350 miles south would hold *that*
answer. But with each passing minute of the escape, the word
"running" seemed to take on a more pragmatic meaning.

16

Eddie / 2:00 p.m. / Nueces River, Texas

Eddie did not think he was hurt too badly, but hunger had made him sick for the hour he had been awake. His wrists were the only part of his body that showed injury; they were cut with rope burns, and Eddie knew he would have to find a way to clean them or risk infection. His neck was stiff and his nose was sensitive and burned at the touch. His body seemed an endless mass of aches and pains, but nothing appeared to be broken.

He was sitting back against the wall of a shallow limestone cave on the banks of the wide, blue-brown Nueces River, rubbing his neck and legs as he had been doing for an hour. He was disoriented and weak, and although he knew he was on the Nueces, he had no clear idea of where exactly he was. In his confusion, Eddie thought he had strayed much farther to the south and east, as he knew the Nueces made a wide bend down past Artesia Wells almost on line with the next I-35 town of Atlee. In any case he knew he was still a good fifteen miles from his second night's destination of Giaman Creek, a point halfway between Artesia Wells and Atlee. He also knew that the fifteen miles could not be made up even if he had his knapsack and all its supporting gear and provisions. Sooner or later Eddie knew that he would have to steal a car if he was to make it to Nuevo Laredo in time to meet Chris and the children at noon on Thursday. That thought alone, beyond the despair of his physical condition and the loss of his knapsack, had kept him immobile in the cave since he awakened just before one.

The Potts-brothers incident—the hanging and the near-drowning, their mad eyes and animal rage—was still with Eddie like a fever, the images coming in and out of his mind like grotesque fantasies. The same feelings applied to his four-and-a-half-hour run from the Potts brothers' ranch to the Nueces—a mindless stumbling across the desert. He had crossed the Nueces once just below the ranch as he fled, and again as he came to rest where he was at daylight, both times with his clothes on, both times not even remembering going into the water or coming out of it. Now, instead of being, as Chris's nursery rhyme for this part of his run went, "Near Atlee and halfway home to the kids and me," he was lost and injured, his clothes caked with dirt and mud and torn from his aimless, frightened running. Now he was faced with the reality of survival instead of his sure path of escape. The run, the single most important thing in his life, now took second place to the fundamentals of finding food and water and some sort of medical care. The irony crippled him and kept him hiding in his cave.

He had come to the hiding place just as daylight broke from the north side of the Nueces over a barren, unpopulated stretch of desert exactly eight miles from the Potts brothers' ranch. The river's north bank was twenty-five feet high and bald. He judged the river gorge to be fifty to seventy-five feet wide, with the bank on the south side slightly more than twenty-five feet. The south side was a high wall of pearl-white limestone topped by an immense stand of cottonwoods. The trees were a perfect cover, and Eddie knew that where there was limestone there would be a cave. He found the cave, a small bear's den of a hole fifteen feet from the water's edge, as soon as he crossed the river. He crawled inside just as full light was dawning, and he fell asleep, knotted like a cold baby. As Eddie sat in the cave now and looked from its damp darkness to the dry white afternoon light outside, he was scared. It seemed he had run a hundred miles from the Potts brothers' ranch, but he had the horrible feeling that he was no more than a few miles away.

If they have dogs, he thought, his hand going to his mouth in terror. *If . . . if they have dogs . . . And with the shootings, someone has to come. Someone has to . . .*

He couldn't go on with the thoughts; they turned his mind to mush. They were soon replaced by a single word, which appeared before his eyes like a glowing neon sign. The word was "fantasy," a word as ironic as his situation.

The word blocked out all else. For a while, he thought he could reach out and touch it. Fantasy: right then and there in his cave in the middle of the Southeast Texas desert it dawned on Eddie that his whole life, all thirty-six years that he had been alive on earth, had been playacting, a sorry-assed fairy tale. He hadn't lived life; he was one of the world's greatest planners, and it finally hit him that not a single one he had ever formed had worked out start to finish. The reason for his failure hit him too.

I am always the object of the future—never a man of the present. The realization crushed him as if the cave's walls had suddenly fallen in on him, and Eddie threw himself forward on his face and wept uncontrollably, crying out in agony to the God he had believed in, for mercy and understanding. But his God did not use words, and so there was only the gravelike silence of the cave and the deep, mournful sound of his own misery. He didn't know how long he prostrated himself and wept. When it was all over, he got up and walked outside the cave and stood looking at the sun, not looking around to see if he was alone. Then he moved slowly down to the river's edge, sat down, and looked at the water. After a while, a small alligator turtle surfaced in the water, came ashore ten feet away, and dried himself in the sun, with no notice of Eddie.

"Ha," Eddie said in a mock laugh to the turtle, his voice broken from the crying. "I'm all screwed up." He was sitting with his dirty hands folded in his lap, one on top of the other, his legs crossed, speaking in a soft voice. The words had no effect at all on the reptile.

"I just wanted something. Something . . ." He shook his head. "I wanted something for my wife and kids, and me. I wanted what was mine. What I thought was mine . . . theirs. . . . I never had anything; nothing. So I wanted everything. All the time. For me and my family. God, doesn't that count for something? Doesn't that get you some sort of break?" he said to his wordless God.

"No, guess not," he answered himself in the silence.

"I'm not alone in that," he said, his voice rising, hands tightening just short of fists, eyes staring straight out over the water's alloy surface. "People want. Everybody wants. *Something*."

Then he sat and thought for a while before he spoke again.

"Point of view," he said evenly to the turtle, his hands limp and back in his lap once more. "I've always been down, so I've always seen from down. The trick is to see from up, no matter how far down you are."

Once he had said these words, Eddie fell limply into himself, his chin falling down on his dirty chest, arms like putty, eyes becoming glued to the turtle's spiny brown back. It was the lesson of a lifetime, and to learn it beside a muddy river in the middle of a Texas desert, a hunted convict, alone, beaten, scared stiff, and starving to death, was a hell of a note, Eddie observed to himself. *But better than not at all,* he added deep inside his mind.

"Point of view," he repeated to the turtle after a long silence. "Point of view," he said again as he began to stiffen, a new concrete thought forming in his mind.

"Have a plan, a goal, of course," Eddie told the turtle as he slowly began to push himself to his feet. "But seize the moment." He moved slowly and silently to the turtle, who held its position as if staked to the sandy riverbank. Eddie reached for the turtle, who moved finally and frantically, but too late.

"And you, my friend," Eddie said to the turtle as he grabbed the reptile's shell and swooped it up into the air in one motion, "are here and now, and my moment." He held the turtle at arm's length and looked at it for a brief moment; the reptile's pointed yellow-and-black head had disappeared inside the long brown shell.

"And like everything else bad that happens to you and me in life, an apology doesn't count for shit," Eddie said as he raised the animal over his head and sent it crashing into a nearby rock the size of a door.

"No," Eddie said, his voice strong and firm but not loud as he picked the broken, dying turtle up from the rock, "I won't insult either one of us by apologizing. Apology means nothing. Now is the only thing that counts for either one of us," he said.

He sat down on the door-sized rock and finished killing the turtle, opening its shell and legs up for the thick white meat that was inside. Without gagging or thinking about it, Eddie ate the raw turtle meat so that he could get strong and run again and do what he had to do—for *now*.

2:30 p.m.

Eddie bathed in the river and washed his clothes in the partial cover of a reed bed and then laid them to dry across the center of the reeds. Naked, holding the pistol, he walked north and south along the bend of the river, looking for anything that could help him. He found an old gray long-sleeved workshirt, a capped and empty plastic quart milk jug, an empty sardine can, and an empty king-size 7-Up bottle.

The shirt made a good loincloth and a place to holster his pistol and could serve as a makeshift pack if he found food. He walked back to where he had killed the turtle and sat down and carefully notched the bottle so that he ended up with the neck intact for a handle and half the side of the long green bottle exposed as a knife blade.

A *perfect con's shank*, he thought with no emotion as he smoothed the two jagged sides of the knife and sharpened the glass to a razor's edge.

When he had molded the objects into shape for his purposes as best he could, Eddie set out to look for makeshift food and medicine. He had prepared well in the prison library at the Walls and he knew that he should be able to find tuna cactus to eat, and chia seeds for food and medicine. He felt like those people who had built their houses in hurricane paths, and then one day find the houses have been blown down and they are faced with the prospect of starting all over again. But Eddie had an edge on himself, on *his old self*, because those were the people who said, as he had once said, "It can't happen to me!" He

knew for certain now that it could happen to him, and he was doing
something about it, without thinking, and without plans. He was
going about it with heart.

Eddie stored the milk jug and the sardine can in his cave and then
swam the Nueces with his pistol and bottle-knife held over his head,
wrapped in the old shirt he had found. On the north side he dried
himself with the shirt, fashioned it once more into a loincloth,
holstered his knife and pistol, and then walked deliberately up the
sandy twenty-five-foot cliff of the far shore.

It was a warm fall day with no wind and few clouds; as his eyes
cleared the top of the cliff, Eddie could see no one and could hear no
sounds. As far as he could see, there was only the flat desert he had
run through the night before. He entered the desert at a lope, looking
for tuna-cactus patches and chia flowers.

The early ranchers in the Southwest called the tuna cactus the
pricklepear because of the long, thorny spines that cut the legs of their
cattle; the early farmers called the same plant the Indian fig, but all
three groups—ranchers, cattle, and farmers—ate the plant's fruit to
survive in their harsh environment. The fruit, which sat atop the
uneven ovals of the cactus, turned a bright, unmistakable red when it
was ripe. It was the size of a big plum, and it had a fig's sweet-bland
taste. You got the mushy insides of the tuna by cutting off both ends
and peeling down the skin. Less than a quarter of a mile from the
riverbank, Eddie found a large patch of ripe tunas weaving into a high
mesquite thicket; he decided to eat all he could and then store the rest
in the shirt. The tunas would not satisfy his hunger, but Eddie knew if
he could find chia flowers, the seeds would sustain him and serve as a
medicine for his wrists and neck. Feeling only slight hope, Eddie set
about cutting the tunas from the tops of the cactus.

I might make it as far as Callaghan tomorrow morning, he told
himself as he ate the fruit and spit out the hard, slimy black seeds.
*I might make up the fifteen miles by cutting west diagonally across
the desert, close to Callaghan. Then I'd be back on target for my*

last night's run and crossing into Mexico at noon on Thursday.

But he stopped his thoughts savagely, his right hand closing like a vise around his bottleneck knife. *Stop it!* he screamed at himself. *Stop. Don't plan. Don't scheme. Just function. Do the best you can for now. Dammit! Let "now" be your new word. . . . Now!*

He ate a dozen of the ripe tunas and stored thirty-five more in his shirt, tying the ends of the sleeves up and carrying the makeshift pack by the shirttails. Then he ran on into the desert in search of chia flowers. It took him half an hour and almost two miles before he found a small stand of the plants, which looked like dying goldenrods. He gathered four handfuls of the pinhead-size brown-white-and-gray seeds by beating the dry flower tops on a rock, and stored the seeds carefully in the flapped shirt pockets. Then he quickly retraced his steps across the desert to the riverbank. At the Nueces again, he swam the river with the shirt and all its contents held high and carefully over his head, and went straight for his cave to do the work he had to do. It was after three-thirty now; he had been out of the reach of TDC for forty-eight hours. The Hounder would be on his way now. Eddie had known that all along and he had made no defense for it. But now he had one. He had himself; for the first time in his life, he had made peace with himself, and that peace would be his defense against the Hounder and everything else.

In the cave Eddie laid the tuna fruit out on the bare ground. He spread the shirt out and carefully placed the chia seeds on it; from his reading at the Walls Eddie knew the seeds would be the key to his survival on what was left of the run. The seeds would sustain his body and put off his making contact until the last possible moment when he had to cross the border and meet Chris and the children.

Chia is a member of the mint family of plants, but its seeds are almost tasteless. In Mexico, chia is used as a food and drink, even in Mexico City restaurants. When the Spanish conquistadores came to Mexico, they found the Indians eating the seeds, and when the Spanish conquered the country and enslaved the Indians, a teaspoon of chia seeds was often all an Indian worker had to eat at the end of an eighteen-hour day in the gold and silver mines. The Indians mixed a spoonful of seeds with a cup of water and made them into a milky gruel, or, with more water, a cooling drink. Chia seeds also purify water, and a paste made from the seeds is an effective poultice for gunshot wounds and general cuts. Chia is also a medicine for diarrhea and upset stomach.

The information on chia that he'd read came back to him like a prepared speech. He made a paste in the open sardine can and applied the medicine to the shallow cuts on his wrists, bandaging them with the cuffs from the shirt. He rubbed the rest of the paste on his neck, and put a few seeds in the quart milk jug, which he filled with river water, waiting a few minutes for the seeds to take effect. He had his first safe drink of water in twelve hours, a drink that would also quell the diarrhea he was beginning to feel. Finally he mixed himself a gruel of chia seeds and water in the sardine can and ate it with his fingers.

Once his meal had been eaten and medical needs met as well as possible, Eddie fashioned the found shirt into a knapsack and arranged his tuna fruit and chia seeds in it. He would eat more seeds and tuna an hour before the run was to begin again, and he would drink more water. He knew Gaiman and Los Almos creeks bisected his line of run south to Atlee and Encinal and maybe Callaghan, if he got that far before sunup of the next day, so he wouldn't need water. His clothes were drying before him in the strong afternoon sun, and he had four shells left in his pistol, and some food. He was not so sick that he couldn't run. He estimated he had lost about fifteen pounds, and he did not have the proper nourishment to combat the weight loss, but at least he had food; at least he was still free and able to run. He no longer considered what might come of the shooting of the Potts brothers, and he would not allow himself to think of his family or Marzack. He was doing all he could, and all that remained for him to do before sundown was to sit and rest in the cave and get as strong as he could in the time he had. As he sat back and rested, Eddie's new thought also gave him strength.

We all have to do the best we can, and for ourselves. We don't help others unless and until we help ourselves. We don't alter the future unless we deal with the present, he said to himself as he sat motionless, looking out of the cave toward the smooth and flowing river that had no sound as it moved in the midst of the vast and empty desert.

17

Marzack / 4:15 p.m. / Cotulla, Texas

Marzack parked his car in front of the La Salle County General Hospital in Cotulla and picked up the small black box on the seat beside him. Inside the box there was a gold badge that bore the words "Federal Bureau of Investigation." More than once, as a Passaic, New Jersey, detective, the black-market FBI badge had opened doors for Marzack that would have remained closed. He pinned the badge on the inside breast pocket of his suit coat, got out of the car, now devoid of the TDC decals, put on his trench coat and hat, and walked briskly and officially into the big red-brick hospital.

At noon Marzack had listened for news of the shootings on the Houston radio stations, but he heard nothing. At three p.m. he was sure he would hear something on the San Antonio stations, but again there was nothing. This puzzled him and caused him considerable concern that he might be following a blind lead after all. But the

minute he entered the hospital lobby Marzack sensed what was going
on; the scene had the smell of scenarios he himself had played out as a
cop. The lobby was full of Cotulla city police and La Salle County
sheriff's deputies. Both groups were on Marzack the moment he came
through the door. Marzack knew instinctively they were shielding the
Potts family, and with connected families that meant only one thing:
there was something in the Potts story and about the crime that had to
be protected, something that had to be kept off the record.

"Hold it right there, mister," one of the deputies said, his hand
held out like a stop sign as Marzack approached the reception desk.

Marzack did as he was told.

"Get me the sheriff," Marzack told the hard-faced deputy before
the man could go on with his orders. "Now, please." He said it firmly,
officially, as the deputy's face turned red with anger. Marzack eased
his coat open and bared the FBI badge for a brief second, secure in
the knowledge that there were no actual FBI agents present, as it was
simply a local shooting and not a federal matter. The instantly
recognizable gold badge pacified the deputy.

"Yes, sir," the man said, his head bobbing with submission. "Right
away, sir." He turned on his heel, waving the others off.

The deputy passed through the crowd of other lawmen and
disappeared down a wide hallway to the left of the lobby. In two
minutes he was back with the sheriff, a grim, potbellied man of
Marzack's age, dressed in a ten-gallon hat and boots and a brown La
Salle County sheriff's uniform.

"Bill Nighblack," the sheriff said, extending his hand, leading
Marzack into a small nondenominational chapel off the right side of
the lobby. He closed the door and looked up at Marzack with eyes
that were pained and tired. "You're a bit off your graze," he said,
obviously nervous but trying to sound good-natured.

The reaction was all Marzack needed to know for sure that he had
the sheriff right where he wanted him; there was indeed a first-class
cover-up going on. He gave the sheriff a big manufactured tight-
lipped grin and went to work on him.

"Yeah, seems that way. I mean, what you've got here is just a local
shooting, right?"

"Oh, hell yes, absolutely," the sheriff said, emphasizing the point vigorously with his hands. "Goddamn mess. But just like you say—local as hell," he added.

"Yeah—local," Marzack replied, his smile fading slowly and deliberately, a gesture orchestrated to get complete attention. It brought about the desired response from the sheriff who stood before Marzack, his own smile turning sour as Marzack spoke again.

"Sheriff, you've got more than a mess here. We think you've stumbled onto something that may touch on an investigation straight out of the Washington office."

The words "Washington office" were all the sheriff had to hear to belong completely to Marzack; his sourness faded. All at once he was a fourteen-karat-gold patriot, about to receive his instructions from Washington and the ghost of J. Edgar Hoover.

"Anything," he said, stiffening to full height. "Just name it. Anything."

"Fine. Everything we say here is strictly in confidence. You are to tell no one we spoke, and your name and office will not be used in my report. This is head-office business, not regional FBI business," he added, covering his tracks in case San Antonio or Houston FBI officials were to wander into the case at a later date.

"I understand perfectly," the sheriff said with proper gravity.

"So," Marzack asked, "tell me why I haven't heard anything about this shooting on the radio."

It took the sheriff ten minutes to sputter through the garbled details of the cover-up. The Pottses, although they did not know his name, were saying Eddie came to the ranch house and forced his way inside with a pistol and held the three—Rudy, Daryl, and Kay—at bay for almost four hours, torturing and then beating and shooting them, before fleeing on foot when the servants were finally roused from sleep. It took another ten minutes for Marzack to extract what the sheriff believed to be the truth: that the Pottses had captured Eddie while looking for rustlers and had in fact beaten and tortured him, and that finally it was Eddie who managed to escape after a shooting spree and fight.

"Goddammit," the sheriff said, "I just don't know what the hell to do. I'm trapped. The Potts family are shit, but they're one of the powers here. If I catch whoever did this to them, then the whole damn mess will come out at the trial. Hell, I'm fucked either way I turn."

Marzack, playing his role to perfection, provided understanding right on cue.

"You're doing the only thing you can, and we understand perfectly," he said, as the sheriff slumped visibly with relief. "Just tell me three more things."

"Name 'em and they're yours."

"First, what blood type did you find in the swimming pool?"

"O positive," the sheriff answered quickly.

Marzack could not hold back a smile; that was exactly what he wanted to hear. He knew he had Eddie firmly in his sights.

"Second," he said. "Did you find anything at the scene of the crime that could have been left by the subject?"

"Not a thing."

"Third, I understand the woman was not shot. Where is she, and can she talk?"

"That's exactly right. The woman, Mrs. Potts, Rudy's wife, wasn't shot. She was beat up pretty bad, but she's okay. She's out at the ranch. I've got a deputy out there with her," he added, eyes asking for praise at his precautionary move.

Marzack provided the praise and made his final demand.

"Fine job," Marzack said. "All I need is a few minutes with her, and I'll be out of your way for good."

The sheriff agreed instantly, saying he would telephone ahead with instructions for his deputy to admit Marzack without hesitation.

"Oh," the sheriff said as an afterthought, "don't you want to talk with the Potts brothers?"

"No," Marzack replied. "That won't be necessary at all."

Marzack was a cop, and cops look for weaknesses in their investigations. Marzack knew the wife would be the weak link. Seeing the brothers would simply be a waste of time.

5:00 p.m. / Tuna, Texas

Kay Potts was sitting in the larger of the mansion's TV rooms, smoking
a cigarette and holding a tumbler of 101 Wild Turkey. Her eyes were
purple-black and her broken nose was bandaged. She was half-drunk,
nervous, obviously in pain, and when Marzack entered the room,
escorted by a La Salle County deputy sheriff, her nervousness
instantly turned to apprehension and gloom.

Since junior high school a saying had followed Kay: "Her tits are
bigger than her head." That was an adequate frame of reference.
When she quit school at sixteen, she had been to bed with more than
fifty men, having had sex for the first time with her fourteen-year-old
brother when she was twelve and a half.

Marzack had no knowledge of her background, but he could see
whom he was dealing with before Kay spoke; she had "slut" written all
over her, a fact the $300 Neiman-Marcus one-piece cotton dress she
was wearing could not hide. Marzack dismissed the deputy and closed
the door. Without speaking to Kay, he showed her his bogus FBI
badge, turned off the TV set, and started to pace the room slowly, his
big face as impassive as stone. He had decided on a completely
different tack with Kay, and when he saw her he knew it would work
like a hammer on a nail in soft wood.

"Miss," he began in a strong and demeaning tone, as Kay's wild
eyes followed him up and down the room, "you and your husband and
brother-in-law are in a hell of a lot of trouble."

"Just one second," Kay shrieked. "I want my lawyer. I know my
rights!"

"Bullshit!" Marzack replied, turning to face her, his pointing finger
sending her back down to her seat on the fat orange sofa. "I want to
know what happened, and I want to know *now!*"

"What happened!" Kay retorted indignantly. "Goddammit, look at
me. This is what happened. I was pistol-whipped and my husband was
shot, and Daryl was shot. That's what the hell happened!" She took a
long drink of bourbon and a thick drag on her cigarette and held her
forehead in mock disgust. Marzack jammed his hands back in his
trench-coat pockets and stared her down, unmoved.

"That's what *looks* like what happened," he said. "I'm waiting to know what *really* happened."

"We got shot and beat up!" she said, stubbing her cigarette out in a large cut-glass ashtray.

"How does life in prison sound for all three of you?" Marzack asked, his eyes directly on hers.

She took another drink and squirmed on the couch like a child, her mouth twisted with confusion.

"I want my lawyer!" she bellowed. "You're crazy. You can't talk to me like this in my own house."

"Fine," Marzack came back quickly and quietly. "I'll take you to San Antonio and talk to you like this in the FBI office."

Kay went limp with dread. "You—"

"I can and I will."

"We were attacked!" she moaned. "By a burglar!"

"You kidnapped and tortured an FBI undercover agent," Marzack told her in even tones.

"Good God," Kay mouthed, slumping back into the couch.

"Tell me about it," Marzack said, ice-water-cold.

Kay Potts's garbled story more or less matched the true version of the incident the La Salle County sheriff had constructed for Marzack; when she finished telling it, predictably, she broke into sobs.

"I haven't got time," Marzack ordered, bringing the programmed tears to an immediate halt. "How bad was our man hurt? That's what I need to know."

Kay lifted her face from her hands, the weight of truth showing in her eyes for the first time.

"Not hurt bad," she said, with obvious relief. "He was like a wild man. I mean—"

"He had something with him," Marzack injected, with assurance. "You kept it from the sheriff's men. I want it."

Kay tightened visibly and hesitated, looking away from Marzack.

"Now!" Marzack roared, hands coming out of his trench-coat pockets. "Damn you, I want it now!"

Kay was on her feet in a split second, smoothing her bleached blond hair and holding on to the sides of her pasty face.

"Please," she whimpered, avoiding Marzack's fiery eyes. "Please
. . . I didn't have any part in it. Please . . . I just wanted them to
quit. I could see he wasn't a rustler. I could see he was different." She
led Marzack out of the room, past the deputy, down the hall to an
elaborate French-Provincial-style guest bedroom.

Marzack could barely contain himself as he followed Kay down the
hall. He reasoned that Eddie might be carrying equipment with him,
but he had not expected to find it at the Potts ranch; he had assumed
that Eddie had retrieved it before he left.

But there wasn't time, Marzack said to himself as he and Kay
reached the guest room. *He's out there totally on his own now. Beaten
up and without equipment. The odds are shifting, the odds are
shifting.*

With Kay Potts sitting watching from the bed, Marzack emptied
Eddie's knapsack on the floor and painstakingly went through the
contents one item at a time. Ten minutes after he began his
examination of the knapsack's contents, Marzack was convinced
beyond all doubt that the speculations he had made on the day after
the escape—after he had talked with Ray Bane and the prison
librarian at the Walls, and then the Blowing Rock, North Carolina,
chief of police—were true: Eddie was running. The knapsack also told
Marzack other things. Eddie's destination was unmistakably Mexico.
Chris and the children had disappeared from sight in April with
$100,000 in cash six and a half months before the run. That would put
her in Mexico hiding out from the IRS, and it would also put her back
in the U.S., probably under an assumed name, to plant the knapsack
at a predetermined spot for the run. There seemed to be food for two
days in the knapsack, and since Eddie was caught by the Pottses on
the second night of the run, that would mean Eddie had divided the
distance from where he started to where he was going into four equal
parts. But the knapsack did not contain false papers or money. Either
Eddie would have them with him, which was unlikely, or he would
have to pick these things up on the U.S. side of the border. Chris
would have to make another plant for him. Eddie would have to stop

at the border for a time before crossing. It all added up for a perfect catch by Marzack, and he had only a few more loose ends to tie up before he could get in place for the catch. He replaced all the items in the knapsack and cinched the straps tight and stood and faced Kay a final time.

"You see that this knapsack goes in your incinerator *today*," he told her. "And you make sure the deputy outside sees *nothing*."

Kay nodded and wrung her hands. When Marzack moved closer to her, she stiffened and held her hands tightly.

"You're off the hook," Marzack said. Kay's black eyes bulged with surprise. "You and your asshole husband and asshole brother-in-law walk away scot-free because I don't want my undercover man's identity blown any further."

Kay's face flushed bloodred and her indignation came back. "My silence for yours," Marzack told her. "Simple as that. But you tell your husband and brother-in-law that we'll be watching them, watching *you* too. One slip and you'll answer in spades for the shit you pulled."

"You bastard," Kay ventured cautiously, her chin down.

"What can I tell you, tootsie," Marzack said, grinning as he turned to leave the room. "What can I tell you," he repeated, easing effortlessly into a New Jersey brogue.

In the circular driveway before the mansion, Marzack took a Texas road map from the front seat of his car and spread it fully open on the hood. There were three more questions he wanted answered before he drove away.

Where is Eddie going?

That was easy. All Marzack did was draw a diagonal line up and down from the Potts ranch to the border. *He's going to Laredo.*

Where did he start from?

That was a little more difficult, but Marzack thought he found the answer.

He knew there was a stock truck that left the Walls for Cotulla. So he looked north of Cotulla for a place Eddie could have exited the

truck without being seen. He found the truck weighing station just
north of Dilley on I-35. Then he found the Frio River Bridge. *He
could have gotten off at the weighing station, and the knapsack could
have been left under the bridge.*

Marzack answered his final question, how many. days Eddie
planned to run, by drawing a line down from the Frio River Bridge to
Laredo and dividing the line in four equal parts.

He's probably off course now, Marzack told himself. *But with all his
planning, he'll get back on course tonight. And sometime tonight, he'll
cross Highway 44 from Encinal, out from I-35, to Freer. And that's
exactly where I'll be.*

Marzack refolded his map, got back in his car, and drove away from
the Potts ranch. He had things to do in the six and a half hours before
he would have to be in place on the highway outside Encinal.

You're mine, he said to Eddie as he drove off. *Wherever you are,
runner, you're mine . . . all mine.*

18
Chris and the Children / 7:30 p.m. /
San Luis Potosi, Mexico

Chris and the children sat at a formal table in La Virreina and waited to be served. She had felt contented and at ease for the first time in her life in Mexico. Both feelings had their roots in the money she brought with her, and the new land where she settled. Things had been so different in Mexico. Prison, Tater Hill, the misery of the past six years, the overriding misery of all her thirty-six years, even certain thoughts of Eddie had grown remote to her during the past six months. But now it was all rushing in again like a wild tide.

Prison teaches that there is nothing you can do on the Inside to change your situation. Chris learned that lesson with Eddie. But now Eddie was Outside again, now he had escaped, and the old misery of their down-and-out lives was beginning again. She had held Eddie Outside in her thoughts for all the six years, had plucked him from the Inside, but she had always been aware that it was an artificial act.

What hurt doubly now was that there had been nothing artificial about the last six months of her life in Mexico.

In Mexico everything had been real and concrete and lovely and easy for the first time in her life. In Mexico, sealed off from her past and insulated with $125,000 in cash, Chris had not been helpless; she had been somebody. Senora Christina Lanson, as she was known in Colima's small but elegant expatriate society, a lady of money and a rather mysterious past. But now she was Chris Macon again, she was helpless, and she detested it. The pain of the old reality brought bitter tears to her eyes.

The sum of $125,000 may not have seemed like much in America, where the government took away a large chunk for taxes, but removing it all to Mexico kept it a formidable sum, especially when you changed a $100 bill into Mexican money and got back 2,500 pesos. Chris and Angie and Bobby lived excellently on $500 per month, a sum that brought them a four-room suite in the city's finest hotel, three meals a day at the hotel restaurant, private school for both children, maid service, laundry service, gas for their car, and incidental spending money. In short, they had luxury, something Chris had never really known before. In seven months, including the secondhand Jeep station wagon, the fake Canadian identification papers, and Eddie's getaway equipment, Chris had spent only $10,000 of the Blowing Rock farm and Flying Fish money. At age thirty-six, she and Eddie and the children were set in Mexico for fifteen years if they never made another cent, a fact that gave her an ironclad feeling of security.

If the words "something better" summarized Eddie's life and the life he wanted for Chris and the children, then "long-suffering" were the two that unfortunately summarized Chris's life. But in Mexico, Chris had replaced those words with the single and, as she construed it, unselfish word "me." Her generation, America in general, and her region of Appalachia specifically, had taught her to be long-suffering. Even Eddie, without knowing it or wanting to, had taught her that. But now she herself had realized that there was no turning back. And it was not an issue of Causes, or Movements, it was a simple matter of Self, of Me, and not always Them, or even We or Us.

It was simple. She had decided to count, not separately from Eddie and the children, but for herself.

She sat in the restaurant and enjoyed its quiet elegance.

I am a part of this. Not just the sophistication. Not simply the richness. But the mood. The peace. The sweet, tangible peace. It is mine and I mean to have it, to stay a part of it.

Chris and the children had entered Mexico on the standard six-month tourist visa on Saturday, April 14, one day before the IRS deadline. That meant their visa would expire on Sunday, October 14, when they would have to exit Mexico for twenty-four hours before crossing the border again and routinely apply for and receive another standard six-month tourist visa. They settled in the city of Colima, the small, isolated capital of the small, isolated state of Colima, an unknown midget between the giants of Guadalajara, Jalisco, and Morelia Michoacán. It was a perfect place to settle or to move from, whichever Eddie decided when he arrived.

There were no real pretensions in Chris's new story. Mrs. Lanson and her family had come from the commercial city of Windsor, across from Detroit. They were workers, not social dilettantes; doers, not users. They were people of some style, people who simply wanted to be. In the depths of her heart Chris dared not think it through, but she hoped with every fiber of her being that they really could achieve that stance of being, once Eddie came home; if he came home. Because, with Eddie or without him, she meant to be.

As she and the children sat at a table in La Virreina, enjoying a thick corn soup before their main course of whole chicken stuffed with rice, green peppers, and chilies, Chris lingered over a glass of chilled Mexican Baja white wine and considered the elegant, ornate stone room and soft-glowing candles. She longed for Eddie in a way that went completely past words, a feeling only for the final region of the heart.

The main course arrived piping hot and fragrant, carried by two of La Virreina's liveried waiters and served up on heavy earthen platters painted rainbow colors, all to the delight of Angie and Bobby.

"Mama," Angie said as she waited to be served, "poor Daddy is having to eat that awful packaged food you made for him. Oh," she said in perfect innocence, "don't you wish he could be here with us tonight."

Chris had to turn away. She couldn't answer. All she could do was hold her breath and pray.

God! she cried in her mind. *Dear, sweet God, let him come to us and let it be all right when he gets here.*

Please, God. Please . . . I'm at the end of pretending, of hoping, of waiting.

19

Eddie / 8:00 p.m. / La Salle County, Texas

Eddie was starving. He had been sick and he tried to vomit, but there was nothing in his stomach to bring up. The running blocked the nausea out after a while. He was lightheaded, but he had beaten that; it even seemed to lessen the agony of running. He had been hungry since the run had begun, and he had beaten hunger as well. But he could not beat starvation. It was like the lights of a car going out; and when they went completely out, you were through.

Sunset was just before seven-thirty; Eddie left the south bank of the Nueces River the minute the sun disappeared. He had been running half an hour, but it seemed like all night. He was stumbling and falling, and the cactus was ripping up his legs. His night vision was bad, and he had lost the natural broken-field moves that had gotten him across the desert so expertly for the first two nights. He was running in a level desert trough formed by Gaiman Creek to the north and Los Almos Creek to the south; but everything was wrong. The shirt knapsack was attached to his back by sleeves that dug into his armpits. Instead of high-carbohydrate food and supplies, the shirt knapsack contained tuna fruit and chia seeds. In place of his canteen and water-purification tablets, there was only the empty plastic milk jug that flapped against his left leg, and more chia seeds for makeshift purification. Everything was makeshift, and he was fifteen miles off course.

The night air was in the sixties but Eddie was wet with sweat, and cold, where before he had simply been wet. He was chilled to the bone, and running slower than ever before. And he was stopping to catch his breath, something he had not even thought about before. The thought scared him to death. But he fought it with the only weapon he had left—the weapon of putting one foot in front of the other. *Run . . . run . . . run,* he told himself inside his heavy breathing. *Make it work . . . make it work . . . make it work,* he chanted, knowing if he didn't he was through. Finished.

9:30 p.m.

As Eddie swam jerkily across Gaiman Creek, his teeth beat viciously against the cold. When he came out of the water the fifty-eight-degree night air took his breath away and set him into a savage but comic dance for warmth.

Crossing water was a hideous ordeal now that his equipment was gone, now that there was no more plastic garbage bag to use as a water shield. As Eddie crossed water, he had to hold all his clothes and the makeshift knapsack and its contents above his head with one hand and pull water with the other. For a healthy man it was a nearly impossible task; for Eddie now it was simply unworkable, and each time he went into water his bundle sank a little deeper and got a little more soaked.

On the south bank of narrow Gaiman Creek, Eddie managed to dry himself with his half-wet sweatshirt, then dress in his cold and clammy clothes. He sat down on the water's edge and forced himself to eat and drink. The Gaiman Creek water looked thick and muddy in the moonlight as Eddie held a plastic jug of it up for inspection, but he thought the chia seeds would purify it for drinking. He drank half a jug of the water slowly and ate six tuna fruit and then lay back on the soft bank and closed his eyes for a few minutes, his head full of the same sickening purple the Potts brothers' noose had brought on.

As Eddie lay back on the creek bank, it occurred to him that this was the place he should have ended the night before; he was exactly halfway to the border. There was no way he could make up all the lost time, and there was no way he could last much longer in his present condition. It was only a matter of time before he collapsed or made contact. The alternatives were as simple and deadly as that.

Now he was no longer averaging two and a half miles an hour. Now he was lucky if he covered a mile and a half an hour, and he knew it would only get worse. He pushed himself up from where he lay and lunged his head forward into the creek's water to clear his head. As it had been at the first of the run, his hair was wet. But it no longer felt good. It only shocked him awake.

He got to his feet and adjusted the makeshift knapsack, and using the moon, headed off due south toward the border. It was more than five minutes before he realized the great change that had come over him. He was no longer jogging. He was walking. That, and the fact that he could do nothing about it, filled him with dread. But he didn't stop. *At least I'm moving, at least I'm moving,* he repeated, but not in the cadence he had sung before.

11:00 p.m. / Webb County, Texas

The thin plateau did not have more than a fifteen-degree incline, but when Eddie negotiated its hundred-yard rim he was heaving with exhaustion, unable to get his breath, and trying to vomit.

He was on line with the little town of Atlee now, a town situated on the edge of I-35, five miles to the west. After a while, as he sat on the top of the plateau, Eddie saw the small clump of lights to the southwest. A second clump of lights beyond was the slightly bigger truck-stop town of Encinal, eleven miles ahead. When Eddie's head had finally cleared he calculated his position exactly by using one of Chris's nursery-rhyme guides: "On a hill you see Atlee and Encinal, from there it is eight miles till water's your pal."

Eddie knew the water would be at narrow Venado Creek, halfway between Encinal and Callaghan, but sitting and looking at the two towns and the great open distance before him, Eddie did not think he could make it to water. As he thought about it, he didn't think he could move from the spot where he was. He lay back and just looked at the full moon and the little wisps of gray clouds that occasionally covered it for a few seconds. He gazed at the moon and the fleeting clouds and the billion stars for a long time. He didn't know how long, and he didn't care. For the first time in his life he was aware that he didn't care about anything.

Marzack . . . we are getting closer . . . he is out there . . . he is . . . But he blocked the words out and just lay back, taking in the view. He was not happy, but after a while he started to sing. The song he chose, "Oh, Susanna," seemed to fit the occasion perfectly, and, although he did not do it for that reason, the words pushed the name and presence of Marzack further back from his consciousness.

> I come from Alabama with my banjo on my knee.
> I'm bound for Louisiana, my true love for to see.
> Oh, Susanna, don't you cry for me . . .

He sang loudly and with abandon, not giving the slightest thought to anyone hearing him. Not thinking at all. Just singing. Finally he stood up, and then, as always, he moved off south again, but singing wildly like a fool.

> It rained so hard the day I left, the weather it was dry . . .

20

Marzack / 11:45 p.m. / Near Encinal, Texas

Marzack allowed himself the luxury of a last cigar before he got out of his car. By dividing the run distances on the map against a dark-to-daylight time frame, Marzack calculated he had about thirty minutes to go before Eddie would run into view, and he was in no hurry to finish the Optimo. He was in control and he knew exactly what he would do when he saw Eddie.

He had driven south from Cotulla on I-35 to Laredo and checked into a small motel on the north side of town. He had showered, slept a few hours, and eaten a good steak dinner. Back in his motel room he changed into khakis, his hunting clothes. He checked his weapons and chose the .12-gauge shotgun with number-six shot, and the .357 Colt magnum handgun with soft-nose bullets, a perfect long- and short-range combination. Then, at 10:00 p.m. he drove back to Encinal and turned off I-35 onto two-lane Highway 44, and drove four and a half miles east of town. He parked his Olds on the south side of the highway behind a large mesquite thicket; there he sat and waited.

When he had finished his smoke, Marzack got out of the car and took his shotgun and shell belt from the backseat and locked the car. He adjusted the shell belt and shouldered the shotgun and walked off quietly down the south side of the road behind the cover of other mesquites. When he had measured half a mile, he stopped and took up a position in the center of a short patch of mesquites, one that afforded a 180-degree field of fire and maximum concealment.

Because of the lay of the land, and the line of Eddie's run thus far, Marzack knew he was in the right spot. He could feel that Eddie would be his within minutes. The bond between them was about to close tight. Then he would take Eddie dead or alive—either way Eddie wanted it.

As he bent down on one knee and waited, Marzack felt wonderful, on fire, but at peace with himself. Just like the old days in Passaic. Just like the other houndings.

Come to me, runner, he mouthed silently as he waited. *Come to me.*

DAY FOUR *DAY FOUR*

Wednesday, October 31

21

Eddie / 5:50 a.m. / Near Encinal, Texas

Eddie had walked five miles in six hours. Things were blurred in his mind now, but he was aware that he had lost the shirt pack and the plastic milk jug sometime during the night, and it seemed he stopped at a cattle salt lick and ate some of the salt.

There was no mad bravado now with song, no indignation, no feelings of self-pity; no thoughts at all. Movement was all he had, and soon there would be no more of that; the senses of taste and feel were gone, his brain was numb—only the vague senses of sight and hearing remained as he stumbled along in the cold predawn light with his arms dangling limply by his sides.

Ahead, in the gray-yellow lunar haze of the false dawn, Eddie could see a wide clearing in the mesquite and cactus; when he entered the cleared area he was vaguely aware that he was walking over a series of rough dirt roads. He paid the roads no mind and walked on through the empty and defunct land-development project, but suddenly, twenty-five yards in front of him, something jarred Eddie's five senses back into motion.

First he saw the car—a gold 450 SEL Mercedes sedan—standing out in the harsh moonscape like an object in a Salvador Dali painting. Then, a moment after the grand car registered in his mind, Eddie heard a woman's shrill scream. He had been moving toward the car, but the scream stopped him cold. Then he heard words.

"You bastard!" he heard the woman rant in a tone only half-fearful. "You scum . . . *scum!*"

The words got him started for the car again, and instinctively Eddie drew his pistol as he moved. As he stumbled toward the car, he heard a fleshy crack and then he heard the woman cry out in pain. Both back doors of the car were open; six feet from one of the open doors Eddie saw what had made the crack sound: a tall, naked man was sitting on top of the woman's back, whipping her bare buttocks with a belt as if he were riding her.

"You cheap bitch," Eddie heard the man say. "You rich, fucking whore. Nobody gives me no shit! Whore . . . fucking whore!

"Ooooohhhhh!" the woman screamed. "Bastard!"

Eddie could see the man was about to strike again. "Hey!" he shouted. "Hey, stop!"

There was a second's dead silence, and then the naked man in the car whirled to face Eddie.

"What the fuck?" the naked man grunted. "Who is that out there? Fuck!"

At six feet from the car door, holding his pistol straight out in front at arm's length, Eddie jerked at the man's words, but held his position.

"Come out of there. Ah . . . *come out!*" Eddie said, fumbling for words of authority.

"*You motherfucker!*" the naked man yelled.

There was a split-second motion as the man bolted from the car and lunged toward Eddie, screaming, with a knife raised to kill. Eddie ducked the knife and clubbed the man squarely in the center of his face with the side of his pistol. The man fell to the ground without another sound, the knife still held tightly in his hand. Eddie stood in confusion and misery as he looked at the unconscious man and then at the dagger.

Who? How? Why? How can it be? How?

But there was no time for answers, and again, sounds the woman made jarred Eddie's senses back to the reality at hand.

"God!" he heard the woman moan. "What the hell."

Then Eddie was standing at the open car door looking inside at the woman. The inside car lights were on and he could see her plainly. She was the most beautiful woman he had ever seen. She looked like a movie star or a model or something out of *Playboy*. For a maddening, unreal instant, Eddie actually had the image of a *Playboy* centerfold in his mind—the woman was sitting up on the seat with her arms over her breasts and her legs pulled up under her exactly like a *Playboy* photo. Their eyes met. She saw his gun and he saw her nakedness. There was an eerie silence. Then the woman broke the spell with curses.

"Get the goddamned hell out of my car!" she yelled at Eddie, taking her arms down from her breasts, exposing their ampleness, as she searched the backseat for her clothes. "Get the fuck out of my car!"

Eddie was stung. He lowered his pistol and tried to find words.

"Was he . . . ? You . . . ?" he asked lamely after a pause, not able to finish his sentence.

"He was shit," the woman said instantly, finding her blouse on the floorboard. "And he was about to rape and kill me. But who the fuck are you? What is this, nut night? Goddammit, get out of my fucking car."

Eddie could see she was in shock; his mind blazed: *Unconscious man, car, woman, time, sounds . . .*

Then he saw the woman pull her thin blouse over her head and start to throw the man's clothes from the backseat of the car. Some of them landed on the man's body. Before Eddie realized what he was doing, he found himself racing for the driver's door of the big car. Then he was inside and the car was moving, the back doors slamming shut. And he did not hear the woman's voice anymore, although he was conscious of the sounds of her dressing as he roared off into the near-dawn over the moonlike landscape.

22

Marzack / 5:53 a.m. / Near Encinal, Texas

Marzack heard the sound of a car roaring away. It threw him into a rage of anger and panic. He had been certain that Eddie would cross Highway 44 no later than 12:30 a.m.; now, more than five hours later, he had not seen or heard Eddie—only heard a car. But he knew the car and Eddie .were one and the same. The instant he heard it, Marzack *saw* Eddie before him as clearly as if he had been standing in front of him—dog-tired, sweating—about to be caught.

You're right out there in front of me, runner, Marzack said silently to Eddie's image as he raced back the half-mile to his parked car. *You're right out there and you are mine.*

23

Eddie and Jilly / 5:55 a.m. / Texas Highway 44 East

Eddie was stiff with apprehension. He had not been alone with a woman or driven a car in six years; now he found himself speeding down the highway in a Mercedes, and with a woman whose very presence seemed to fill the space with unreality.

He was driving with his pistol held in his right hand on top of the car's padded big black steering wheel, his left hand tightly gripping the wheel. From his hours poring over maps in the prison library at the Walls, Eddie knew exactly where he was and the direction he was going: Freer, Texas, was forty-five miles east on the highway, and if you used Freer as the top of a triangle, Laredo and the Mexican border sat at the base of the triangle sixty miles to the southwest. Eddie's senses and faculties were alive again and he was desperately trying to figure out what to do as he drove.

Six in the morning. Unconscious man. Stolen car. Woman. Day early to Laredo. Can't check into hotel in Laredo until at least ten or

*ten-thirty. Four and a half hours to kill. Stay unseen. Man. People.
Police. TDC. Marzack . . .*

He didn't know what to do. All he could do for the moment was put
some distance between himself and the man. As he stared ahead into
the gray half-dawn Eddie jerked into a knot as he heard and felt the
woman coming over the car's high front seat. Automatically his right
hand came off the steering wheel and his pistol pointed at her.

"Whoa, there, Murder Incorporated," the woman said. The words
were flip, but the voice shook. "I'm the injured party, remember?
You're the knight in shining armor. Knights don't shoot damsels in
distress: *correct?*" Her voice began to take on authority now, Eddie
realized.

Authority? It didn't make sense. Eddie had no frame of reference
for it, and he had no frame of reference for the woman and her sweet,
musty-perfumed smells. Now she did not appear shaken by the
attempted rape or the fact that she might have been killed. She was
totally feminine, yet there was something mannish—something fierce
and exciting about her.

A *lion:* the word entered Eddie's mind and he could not shake it.
Her great head of champagne-blond hair seemed exactly like a lion's
mane to Eddie, like a lion's, not a lioness's.

He put his pistol hand back on the steering wheel and the woman
settled watchfully on the padded leather seat next to him.

"So," she said, "ass-kicker of heinous redneck rapists, what is your
sad story? And who the hell told you you could drive my car?" The
authority with which she spoke was undercut by a small tremor in her
voice.

Eddie cataloged the words and their tone, but they sounded like a
foreign language. He couldn't find words to say to her. After a while,
as they drove on, the woman spoke again, agitated this time.

"Look, strong silent type," she said, turning to face Eddie directly.
"This ain't the movies. Who and what are you?"

Again, it was a foreign language. Eddie grimly faced the empty road
ahead and tried to concentrate on what to do about going into Laredo
a day early.

"Look!"

Eddie turned to face her, his eyes cold.

"Okay . . . okay," the woman said, her long hand making the point. "So you're not a talker. But at least you've got a name. I'm nuts about names," she added, looking straight into his silence.

"My name is Jilly Buck," she ventured. "Jilly Buck and Donald Duck. Don't either one of us give a fuck," she added evenly, as if she had simply recited her name and address.

Joking? He was puzzled. *Joking?* Then, after a while, Eddie spoke, his voice on the thin edge of exhaustion and desperation.

"My name is Eddie Macon," he said, his eyes straight ahead on the road. "I'm an escaped convict and if I get caught, I'll be in prison for the rest of my life."

There was no reply.

24

Marzack / 6:04 a.m. / Near Encinal, Texas

Marzack spotted a small dirt road which cut a hole in the mesquite. It seemed to be pointing in the direction of the sounds he'd heard. He rammed his Olds into the opening and bounced along the road until a vast clearing opened up. He was only inches from running over the unconscious man's body before he saw him.

He slammed on brakes and raced out of the car to the naked body. His mind burned. He thought he was about to find Eddie dead; he would be cheated out of the kill or the capture. With great trepidation he turned the man over. It was not Eddie. It was a big man with a tough baby face, probably in his late twenties, and a workingman. Marzack could tell by his hands, arms, and neck.

Marzack studied the man for marks and scars; when he found nothing that interested him, he turned the body facedown and let the man fall roughly to the ground with a dull thud. Then he set about studying the surroundings. He saw the tire tracks almost immediately and would have bolted from the body and followed them, but there was the man's clothes to be examined. If Eddie was in the car, there were at least three directions he could have taken: north on I-35 back to San Antonio; east on Highway 44 to Freer; and south on I-35 to Laredo. Eddie had too much head start and too many choices. It would be a wild-goose chase, and it might be a long time before the man came to. So the clothes were the starting place.

Find out who the man is. Find who the car belonged to and the owner's story. Then get a line on the runner.

Under the glare of the headlights of his car, Marzack went over the man's clothes piece by piece. The garments were cheap sport clothes that told Marzack nothing, but in the trouser pocket there was a wallet. Marzack found eighty-seven dollars in cash in the wallet and no credit cards. The name on the Texas driver's license was Mark Earl Barnes. Age twenty-five. Home address: 6090 McCauley Street, Dallas, Texas. Inside the man's wallet, pinned to the leather, was a quarter-sized yellow button with red lettering that read: "#866/ZEB CONST. CO. DALLAS, TEX." Marzack got up from the man's body with the wallet in his hand and stood over him, putting together a picture in his mind.

Construction worker from Dallas. Knocked out in the middle of nowhere. Little cash. Cheap clothes. Naked. Rape? Woman? Second man Eddie? Tire tracks. Eddie and woman together? Whose car? Where to?

Marzack stood and looked down at the man a moment longer; then he went over to his car and wrote down the driver's-license and construction-company-button information on a small notepad he carried in his right inside coat pocket. Then he wiped the wallet and the metal button off with his handkerchief and threw the wallet back in the direction of the man. The wallet hit the man's head just as he was raising it from the ground, as he regained consciousness in a fit of groaning. He pushed himself up and turned to face Marzack and the headlights of his car.

"Just hold it right there," Marzack commanded, as he got his pistol out in one swift motion and leveled it at the man's face, ten feet away. "You got . . ."

"Gaaaaaaaaa!" the man roared as he plunged into the lights toward Marzack, a figure he saw as only a blur.

"Damn," Marzack said softly. He stood firm and took expert aim, so that when he fired, the round entered the man's face just at the bridge of the nose, a shot which took the entire rear of the man's skull out in a wad, leaving only a pencil-sized hole in his face.

Now when he hit the ground at Marzack's feet, the knife finally fell from the man's hand, sounding a thin metallic ring in the desert stillness as it struck a rock.

"Goddamn, you asshole," Marzack said to the dead man, as he holstered his pistol, feeling no emotion except frustration at not being able to question him. He turned from the corpse and stared off into the disappearing darkness in front of his car's lights, looking vainly for Eddie to appear. But he knew Eddie would not come. He knew Eddie had already arrived. He knew Eddie was in the car whose tire tracks flowed away from the scene. Marzack thought he knew something else, too: He believed Eddie was now pointed toward Laredo and the border one day early. That unexpected development would give Marzack the time he needed to retrace the dead man's steps and connect him with the car Eddie was driving.

You are still mine, runner, Marzack said to himself as he walked past the man he had just killed. He got back into his car and drove out to Highway 44, heading for I-35 and Laredo. *Enjoy your little ride. All it bought you is rested feet and a little time. You're still mine . . . all mine.*

25

Eddie and Jilly / 7:30 a.m. / Lake Casa Blanca, Texas

Eddie watched the shimmering ingot sun rise from the surface of Lake Casa Blanca but its beauty only increased his dread; he was not supposed to see it until tomorrow. Then he turned and looked at the woman. She had not spoken in the hour-and-a-half since he told her he was an escaped convict. She had simply sat and smoked, lighting her cigarettes, it seemed to Eddie, with a rectangular chunk of pure gold.

They had covered a hundred miles driving east on Highway 44 from Encinal to Freer, then southwest on Highway 50 back to the lake where they were now parked; two prongs of a triangle that had brought them only miles from the heart of Laredo. For an hour now, Eddie had decided to try and check into the hotel room Chris had reserved for him in Laredo. But there was the risk in being early; and the added danger of the early morning hour. You could not check into a hotel before ten-thirty at the earliest without arousing some suspicion, or at least some notice.

Three more hours exposed! Eddie's mind boiled as he stood at the head of the big car, looking out at the dead calm lake and the sun that was rising about it, gaining fiery strength and light with every second. *Three more hours of cat-and-mouse before I can hide again.* He was aware that his body was turning to stone with tension, weariness, and starvation.

But he knew his mind was his only defense, so he held on to the hood of the car and looked at the lake, trying to concoct a strategy that would get him safely into the Laredo hotel in three hours. From his map study at the prison library at the Walls, Eddie knew Southeast Texas geography and its highways with pinpoint accuracy. He tried to work up a mental picture of the highways out from his position.

Highway 359 east to Hebbronville; Highway 16 southwest to Zapata on Falcon Lake across from the Mexican border: another hundred-mile triangle; then a fifty-mile drive that would eat up the three hours, he reasoned. Three more hours of driving and staying awake and avoiding contact. Three hours . . . the woman . . . sleep . . . sick . . . He didn't know if he could do it, but he turned back from the lake's sunrise to try. Suddenly his breath left him because of the sight fifty yards behind the car. He froze like a mannequin. There, coming toward the car at a slow pace, was a blue-and-white Laredo Police Department cruiser with two uniformed patrolmen inside.

Jilly saw the cruiser a second after Eddie; she was out of the car before he could move.

Over, was the only word Eddie's blurring mind could grasp as he numbly watched the cruiser park beside the Mercedes and saw the policemen get out quickly and professionally. *Over . . .*

The two policemen were young and tough-looking, and both Tex-Mex. Eddie watched them walk toward the Mercedes; he watched Jilly walk toward them; as he looked on, the scene began to take on a sort of vulgar amusement for him—it was like being able to watch your own embalming.

So this is the way, he thought as he observed. *This is how it ends. These are the people who make it happen—two young cops and a beautiful woman.* Movement again became possible for him, his right hand moving slowly toward his right rear trouser pocket and the .38 pistol with which he intended to kill himself.

Just seconds more, he said silently, bemusement staying with him. *Over* . . .

Eddie watched what went on before him like a drunk: things came and went, sounds passed by him; everything seemed soupy and disjointed. There was Jilly laughing with the two policemen; they laughed with her, following her every move like two big obedient dogs. But it was more than Jilly. The two policemen seemed to be reacting to something else. Through his stupor Eddie could see they focused too long on her driver's license, exchanged too many glances over it, were too impressed by it. And the license plate. They looked at that too long as well, paid too much attention to it. Eddie did not understand any of what he saw, but he knew one thing for certain: his hand never reached the pistol in his back pocket, and after only a first hard look, the policemen never paid attention to him. And when he finally emerged from his stupor, Eddie again found himself at the wheel of Jilly's Mercedes, driving down the highway with the speedometer registering ninety mph. Like someone coming out of shock he was suddenly aware of Jilly beside him, the fact that they were in the car, and finally the speed of the car. It was her words that erased his stupor completely.

"Look," he heard her say. "I owed you one, so I bailed you out, but don't get us killed as a thank-you." There was a pause as she waited for a reply that did not come.

"For Christ's sake, are you on drugs or something? Slow the hell down. And say something, goddammit."

Then he saw her light another cigarette with the gold lighter; that small, newly familiar act broke down the final barriers in him, and Eddie was once more fully in command of himself. He was scared witless, his palms digging into the big black steering wheel.

"How is that possible?" Eddie finally heard himself say in words that seemed tiny and far away. "How can I be here? How can the police not have me?"

"Because *I've* got you, sweetie," he heard the woman reply. "Me and Sam-Seven. The greatest one-two punch in Texas."

The words didn't make the slightest sense to Eddie; what she said next also seemed incongruous.

"I am what I am, thanks be to old Sam," she said, like words from a poem that had no humor.

Eddie heard the words and looked at the beautiful woman and thought he was going mad or that he was already mad. He didn't know, but he did know he could not afford the luxury of stopping to find out. All he knew for certain was that by some miracle he was still uncaptured and moving. There was still hope. He was still functioning. He was sick and tired and fighting exhaustion, but still moving. The road ahead was almost a straight sixty-mile stretch to Hebbronville. Eddie concentrated on reducing the speed of the car to seventy, and focused on the white center lines and the passing telephone poles as his frame of reference. It seemed to take all his mental powers to remain awake and to keep the car in its proper lane. The sun was up fully now, and it was a cool, clear day with no wind. Eddie made himself think about the day and the driving, avoiding the strange woman beside him. But through it all he could not shake the words: Sam-Seven. They were like a siren call to him, a call that seemed somehow familiar but untouchable, unreachable.

Sam-Seven?

It was something for his mind to figure out, something to keep him awake at the wheel, so he played with it as he drove on in the clear and revealing morning light.

26
Marzack / 8:00 a.m. / Laredo, Texas

Marzack knew exactly what he wanted to find out first. He went to a small downtown Laredo café, struck up a conversation with the big meaty-faced woman who served him his breakfast.

"I got a little problem," he told the woman as she added his check.

She looked at him with the suspicion of a woman who has been abused by men's problems all her life.

"Me and another fellow were out drinking last night and I lost him early this morning," Marzack said. "Hell of a note, and me not knowing a thing about this town."

The woman fingered the check and shifted her weight on her feet. Her eyes looked right through Marzack to the far wall, an act that had nothing to do with magic or the supernatural.

"So I was wondering," Marzack pressed, "if you might know of a place around here that might be open, say, all night. Someplace pretty tough, if I know my friend."

"Huh!" The big woman snorted, hands moving to her chunky hips.
"That would be the damn Five O'Clock Club. Lost two husbands out
there. Worthless bastards stayed drunk twenty-four hours a day."

"You got an address?" Marzack replied quickly, his voice reverting
to his usual staccato New Jersey accent.

The woman took instant notice of the change in Marzack's tone.
Her eyes flashed across to him as he stood; she told him the address
and handed him the check in the same motion.

"You a cop or something?" she asked, no longer looking through
him, but at him.

"Or something," Marzack answered swiftly as he brushed past her
to the cash register.

A Five O'Clock Club; every honky-tonk town has one, Marzack said
to himself as he exited the restaurant for his car. *A woman being raped
at six in the morning half an hour from town. It fits perfectly.*

The Five O'Clock Club was a badly renovated barn on Saunders
Street near the Laredo International Airport. Now, at eight-thirty in
the morning, its vast asphalt parking lot was littered with beer cans
and paper. There was only a single car, an almost paintless, battered
'48 turtleback Mercury, parked near the enormous bloodred wooden
double doors of the entrance. Marzack parked his Olds beside the
rusting Mercury and walked up to the closed red doors and assaulted
the wood with the fleshy side of his fist. After three salvos, the doors
parted slightly and a black face peered through the narrow opening.
Marzack immediately went for his fake FBI badge.

"Outside," Marzack ordered the man as he showed him the badge.
The old man complied with indifference and resignation, avoiding
Marzack's eyes.

"Ain't nobody here, mister," the black man said in the direction of
his feet. "I'm the clean-up man. Nobody got no quarrel with me."

"Hold the phone, Pop," Marzack said, shoving the badge into his
pocket. "I just want a little information. You got no problems from
me."

The words raised the old man's eyes to Marzack's face.

"Yes, sir," the old man said with some relief. "What you need?"

"First of all," Marzack said, "I need you to keep your mouth shut about talking to me."

"You got that," the old man said, his eyes leaving Marzack's once more.

"Fine," Marzack said. "I'm looking for a man, a man who left here with a woman when the place closed this morning."

The old man shuffled his feet and waited for specifics that did not come. "Mister, this place is full at closing time," he finally ventured in the midst of Marzack's cop silence.

"Does the name Zeb Construction Company in Dallas mean anything to you?" Marzack asked. "Red-and-yellow button. Lot of guys wear them damn near all the time; bad-ass button, so to speak."

The old man considered the question and the information, and swept his feet lightly with his broom.

"Place's full of them fellas every night," he said. "All bad-assed and mean-drunk."

"Yeah . . . right. But this was a week night; not many of them out here on a week night? Just the hard drinkers, right?"

The old man agreed in silence with a slow nod of his bald head.

"You come on at closing. You see things. Tell me what you saw this morning."

"Just a bunch of drunk white folks," the old man said.

Marzack grunted a short laugh and stuck his hands in his pockets. "Go on."

"Couple of 'em was Zeb men. 'Course, I don't know 'em all."

"Right."

"Well, that's it," the old man said. "Just a couple of 'em was here."

"With women?" Marzack pressed.

"Yes, sir, I guess. I mean, they none of my business. I wasn't payin' 'em no mind, if you understand."

"The ones with women?"

The old man leaned hard on his broom and looked up at Marzack, his face wrinkled with frustration.

"With women? Maybe a woman with a big car and new tires," Marzack added, playing out the only real piece of concrete information he had gotten from the scene of the killing.

The old man tried to hold back, but his eyes betrayed him; Marzack caught the change the split second it occurred.

"Talk to me, Pop," Marzack demanded, his face flushing with interest.

"Mister, I just clean up this bar. That's all I do, and I don't bother nobody and I don't give nobody no trouble," the old man answered, his eyes on his shoes.

"You and me are going to have a big problem, Uncle, if I don't hear what I want to hear."

Both men hesitated for a moment, and then Marzack went for his wallet. But the old man stopped him before he could get it out.

"I don't want no money, mister," he said, his eyes coming uneasily up to Marzack's once more. "I just want to mind my own business."

Marzack did not give him another second.

"Tell me what you know, old man," he said sourly. "And don't waste another second of my time."

The janitor shook his head slightly and gripped his broom; then he answered.

"I don't know nothing. But then, you ain't asked me nothing I can give you an answer to," he added evenly.

Marzack watched and waited.

"But they is something," the old man picked up again, never losing his original thought.

Marzack nodded.

"But like you tell me to forget I talked to you," the old man said. "You forget I told you this."

Marzack nodded in agreement, and waited.

"They could be this. Lady out here last night, for the last couple of nights. Big car and new tires, like you said," he said with a slight and knowing smile. "Lady somethin' else; car somethin' else, too. License plate even more." His smile grew more smug with each word.

Marzack's face betrayed his interest. "Tell me all about it," he said.

The old man hesitated for a moment; then he looked Marzack squarely in the eyes for the first time.

"I'm go' tell you the license plate, then I'm go' get back to doin' what I gets paid for," he said. "What we talkin' 'bout here, I don't want no part of."

Marzack's mouth grew sour, but he kept silent, captivated by the little web of mystery the old man was spinning before him.

"Number: Sam-Seven," the old man said thickly, withdrawing his eyes from Marzack's face. "Sam-Seven. Blond lady. Merkadeez automobile. Number: Sam-Seven," he said a third time, his voice becoming knowing again.

Marzack eyed him for a few hard, silent moments, and then dismissed him with a lame thank-you, the license number buzzing in his head like the ringing of an unexpected phone call.

Sam-Seven, Marzack mulled silently as he turned on his heel for his car. *Sam-Seven*.

The initials and number registered dimly with Marzack, but he could not place them. But he knew who could decode them; he got in his car and headed straight for a pay phone. Mike Shorter bellowed an immediate laugh into the phone. For the first time, he had the upper hand on Marzack.

"Man, you are sure as hell out of touch."

"Shorter, you asshole, I am in no mood for fun and games. What the fuck is Sam-Seven? And why did it have that janitor standing at attention like a buck private on his first day on the drill field?"

"Shit!" Shorter kept on laughing. "He was standing at attention because old SAM was the commander in chief of *everybody's* drill field in Texas a few years ago."

Suddenly the initials registered in Marzack's mind.

SAM: Silas Allgood Montgomery. Governor Silas A. Montgomery. The man who received the government of the state of Texas from Lyndon B. Johnson. LBJ and SAM. Marzack felt like a fool.

"You got yourself a pretty important SAM, too," Shorter said.

"Explain."

"The old boy still awards his SAM plates to the chosen Montgomerys around Texas," Shorter replied. "God knows how many SAMs there are, but the first ten SAMs are the old man's inner circle of wife, children, brother, and a few kissin' cousins."

"Seven will probably come up a cousin, right?" Marzack asked.

"Hold the line," Shorter told him, "and I'll run a vehicle check and we'll see just which SAM you're on to."

In two minutes Shorter was back on the line.

"You ready to copy?" he asked.

"Shoot."

"You got a cousin, or a niece: niece, most likely," Shorter said. "Jilly Gayle Buck. Twenty-four. Single. Address: 42 Borg Street. Fort Worth, Texas. Car: gold Mercedes 450 SEL. Occupation: actress-model."

Shorter waited for Marzack to take down the information. "That help you?"

"Fits like a glove," Marzack replied without hesitation.

"What did you walk into down there? I thought you were on a simple con hunt."

"I was," Marzack said sourly. "But it looks like it just got complicated."

When he hung up on Shorter, he stood outside the booth for a few minutes and tried to string his pieces of information together.

Dead man. New tires. Heavy car. Woman out till five in the morning. Possibly picked up by construction worker. Possible rape or attempted rape. Jilly Gayle Buck, twenty-four. Actress-model. Gold Mercedes. Ex-Texas governor . . .

Blind leads. Dead ends strung together. But ends that seemed to connect in a cop's fashion of running blind ninety percent of the time; stumbling over real leads, stumbling over the real solutions.

Sam-Seven, Marzack thought. Favored status. A pretty little ass that had the old man's ear. Favored status that could mean trouble for me and a free ticket for my running if he is with her and she goes along with him.

It all added up to a long shot, but Marzack had been playing long shots and winning ever since he started, so he decided to shoot long again. He got back inside the phone booth and thumbed through the Yellow Pages to the "Hotel-Motel" section. It was immediately obvious from the ads that the new Hilton was the flashiest and most expensive hotel in Laredo, and so the most likely place SAM-7 would be if she were in town. He dialed the hotel's number and asked for Jilly Buck by name. There was a moment's hesitation on the other end of the line; then the desk clerk came back with the information that: "Ms. Buck does not answer her call."

Marzack smiled to himself and thanked the clerk and hung up.

Detective work was always a crap shoot, and for him everything was coming up sevens. He got back in his car and cruised the city looking for the gold SAM-7 Mercedes, but he knew he wouldn't find it. The time was nine-thirty, and he was sure Eddie and Jilly would be circling the city, waiting until at least mid-morning before coming in to either register in a hotel or motel or simply let Eddie pick up fake papers to cross the border. Marzack's cop's intuition told him it would be a hotel or a motel. Eddie's plans were too pat, too complete, not to fit that pattern. His wife had left the knapsack, and Marzack was convinced she had also planted papers and money for Eddie in Laredo. And he thought too that a hotel or motel would be the safest place for a plant. But the time for long shots was over. Marzack knew it was time for legwork. He would go back to his motel room and shower in place of sleep, and then at ten he would start making the rounds of the hotels and motels looking for the SAM-7 Mercedes. Eddie had arrived in Laredo a day early; there was time to maneuver. If Marzack's instincts held, it would be tomorrow, probably mid-morning or noon, before Eddie would be prepared to cross the border.

Enjoy your ride with the ex-governor's fluff, Marzack said to himself. *Tomorrow you'll be riding back to the Walls feetfirst or with your hands handcuffed under your legs.*

27

Eddie and Jilly / 10:30 a.m. / Laredo, Texas

Eddie pulled the gold Mercedes over to the side of Highway 83 just inside the city limits of Laredo. He and Jilly had been together for four and a half hours but they had only spoken twice. She had helped him once; but she had said she "owed" him. Now he was going to have to take her beyond any real or imagined debt; he was going to have to hold her, to keep her with him for the next twenty-six hours until it was time for him to cross over into Mexico. At last he was in Laredo, but everything was wrong; if he was to make good his escape, he had to start making things right.

"I don't know what you said to those cops this morning," he said directly to Jilly, his voice deep with fatigue. "I don't know anything about Sam, or whatever you said to me. And I don't mean you any harm, but I have something to do. Something I must do. And nothing can get in the way."

He looked directly at Jilly; she seemed to be studying his every word and movement.

"I've been in prison in Texas for six years," he began again, facing Jilly squarely. "I escaped three days ago from the Walls in Huntsville. I've been running for three days. I was running when I came upon you. I had one more run to go before I was supposed to be here. I'm not supposed to be here until tomorrow . . ."

Eddie's voice was breaking; Jilly could see he was about to collapse. He waved off his train of thought with his hand and spoke again, rubbing his eyes as the words came. "That . . . that doesn't make any difference, though. The story is not important. What I have to do now is all that counts."

She watched him with fascination he did not detect.

"I've got to go to a hotel room and try to register and get a room, and I've got to wait until noon tomorrow to cross into Mexico. My wife and children will be waiting for me."

Jilly sat and looked and did not reply.

"But now you're part of what is happening to me. You've got to stay with me until I get ready to cross, maybe even cross with me," he said, lifting his hand and searching her eyes for a reaction.

Jilly's icy, beautiful face gave away nothing.

"I didn't ask for this. I didn't ask for you. You've got to stay with me!" he said suddenly in a voice that was louder than he had intended. "You've got to stay with me and do exactly what I tell you."

Still she gave no reaction he could detect.

"Dammit!" Eddie erupted, reaching out for Jilly's wrist. "I'm talking to you. This is not a game. Not some damn joke. I'm telling you something you've got to hear, something you've got to do."

She jerked her wrist free and found his eyes.

"Which hotel?" she said with no emotion.

He looked at her for a few anxious moments and then sank back into his side of the car and leaned into the steering wheel. When he picked his head up, he was mad.

"This car. Your clothes. Your looks," he said, clipping the words. "You haven't heard a damn thing I've told you," he said directly to her. "But you can understand this." He pulled the pistol out of his back pocket and held it on the seat between them.

"You've seen me use this halfway before, and I tell you this for a fact: I will use it all the way to get across the border. This is my second escape; you don't get a third chance in Texas."

"What is the name of your hotel?" she asked again in the same monotone as before. "I've got a suite in the Hilton. We can use it if you like," she said, obviously hiding her true feelings.

Eddie's anger dissolved into bewilderment.

"I've got to use my own hotel—La Posada," he said, rubbing his eyes with his free hand, bringing the pistol back to his lap. "There are things there that I must have to cross the border."

Jilly made no reply. Eddie broke the silence after a pause.

"We've got to go to the hotel now. You've got to go to the hotel now. You've got to go in with me and do exactly as I tell you. Can you do that? I'm sorry," he added quickly. "But can you do that?"

"Yes," she replied.

He looked at her and registered the single-word answer; then his anger started to return.

"This is not a damn game," he said.

"I'm aware of that," she answered without hesitation.

"As long as you know that what I've told you is true and has to be . . ." he said.

"I hear you," she said.

Then they joined the morning traffic and moved off toward the center of town and the hotel. At the entrance to Zaragoza Street, Eddie could see the Rio Grande River and Mexico on the far side. But he could not pause to look; he had to get the car out of sight in La Posada's underground parking lot. He had to get himself and the woman to his room.

Eddie steadied himself against the wall of the small elevator that ascended the one floor from La Posada's underground parking garage. His vision was coming and going; he knew he could not stay awake much longer. He was holding Jilly by the arm. She seemed passive to the point of being disinterested; he could not figure her out at all. All he could do was hold on to her and hope for the best once they reached the hotel's lobby. When the elevator door opened, Eddie saw a small hallway that led to the left and two large French doors that opened out onto a large Spanish-style courtyard dotted with palms and bougainvilleas; in the middle was a luxurious swimming pool. He held on to Jilly's arm and steered her toward the French doors.

"Don't make trouble," he told her as they cleared the doors and stepped out into the sunlight of the patio.

As he expected, she made no reply.

The hour and the slight chill in the air kept all but a few of the hotel's guests from the patio, but those who were sunning themselves at the pool turned and looked as Eddie and Jilly walked past. He had a three-day-old beard, his sweatshirt and jeans were torn and dirty, and his leather running shoes were caked with mud. Jilly was the exact opposite in a deep red pullover, crotch-tight khaki slacks, and Italian leather sandals; her long champagne hair pulled straight back, to her shoulders, ample breasts dancing slightly as she moved, haughty and erect.

Eddie's .38 snub-nose pistol was concealed as well as possible inside his right trouser pocket, but there was nothing Eddie could do about his overall appearance; the only thing he could do was walk directly up to the registration desk with Jilly and ask for the room that Chris had reserved for him. If he was questioned about his appearance, he had decided he would say he had been on a hunting trip and had had car trouble and that Jilly had met him with her car. He would pose Jilly as his sister, and hope that worked.

The clerk behind the desk was. a thin and refined Tex-Mex with a cautious, professional smile. First he gave Jilly the once-over; then his attention turned to Eddie, and his smile disappeared as he made Eddie speak first.

"I have a reservation," Eddie said as forcefully as he could. "Edward J. Lanson of Ontario, Canada," he went on, holding Jilly by the arm, boring his eyes into the clerk's hardening face.

"Just a moment," the clerk said faintly with a prominent Spanish accent.

The clerk leafed through the cards in a small card file in front of him and came up with an evil, satisfied smile.

"I have a Mr. Lanson preregistered for tomorrow," he announced forcefully.

Eddie hesitated, but before he could speak, Jilly broke in with total authority.

"We would like the room *now*," she said, stepping up to the counter out of Eddie's grip. "I'll register," she told the clerk, whose smile faded into an uneasy look of attention.

"Here's my American Express card," Jilly went on, producing a gold card and her driver's license from her large suede purse.

The clerk took the two cards and looked them over for a second, then Eddie saw a look of submission pass over his face that was identical to the looks the two policemen had given earlier in the morning.

"Exactly as you say, Ms. Buck," the clerk told Jilly. "It's an honor to have you and Mr. Lanson at La Posada. I had no idea . . ." he kept on jerkily as he handed her a registration card. "Please forgive me."

Jilly gave the clerk a small smile in reply and quickly filled in the card and pushed it back to him. Eddie could only stand and watch in dumb fascination.

Who? What? his tired mind drummed. But there was no time for answers as they were led out of the lobby by a uniformed bellman to retrace their steps back to the elevator and to their room.

Eddie felt a wild rush of security when he and Jilly were finally alone and locked inside Room 216, but a flood of relief came over him as he moved to the dresser opposite the bed and dug his hands behind the mirror and found the safe-deposit-box key Chris had taped there the month before.

Here . . . here! his mind roared. *The last hurdles . . . The last barriers. Here . . . Now!*

The key meant Eddie had three final things to do. He had to take the key downstairs and retrieve the contents of the safe-deposit box in the hotel: one thousand dollars in cash and fake Canadian identity papers. He had to leave the hotel and buy some simple, new clean clothes to wear to cross the border. And last, he had to cross the International Bridge that separated Laredo, Texas, from Nuevo Laredo, Mexico, and present himself and his fake Canadian papers at Mexican Customs. Then he could cross the border to freedom. But those three things would take twenty-six hours.

Twenty-six hours. It would be the worst part. But one of the most necessary parts. He could not simply ride into Laredo and pick up the papers and money and get some clothes and clean up and then walk directly across the border to Mexico and freedom. He needed a cover. And that cover—like it or not, and he did not—was Chris and the two children. One man traveling alone in Mexico could be stopped and searched and questioned. Mexico and the U.S. had extradition treaties. They did not work most of the time, but they were there. There was a chance—no matter how small—that they might be observed. And Eddie could not afford chances. He had to sit and wait until noon the following day, when Chris and the children arrived in Nuevo Laredo, Mexico, and link up with them. Chris knew Spanish now. She could do the talking if there was a problem. But the odds were there would be no problem at all with a man and his wife and two children traveling in Mexico to their established home with a car that was already marked with Mexican visa stickers. Eddie had to wait. There was no alternative.

All at once the sanctuary of the hotel room polarized into the ragged horror of a cage, a pen in which to be trapped rather than hide for those twenty-six hours.

Jilly had watched Eddie grope behind the mirror for the key; then she saw him begin to search the room with wild eyes. With the key gripped tightly in his hand, Eddie roughly motioned her down on the bed and darted into the bathroom to search it; when he came out, Jilly saw that he could not last much longer.

"We're here," she said, her voice strong and direct. "Another five minutes and you're going to drop flat on your face."

He looked at her for an uneasy second and then took the .38 pistol out of his trouser pocket and sank down in the chair beside the dresser, placing the pistol down hard on the short table beside the chair.

"How about something to eat?" Jilly ventured, her eyes never leaving Eddie. "You look starved to death. For Christ's sake, give up this Jesse James bullshit long enough to eat; and a bath wouldn't hurt either while the food is on its way."

Eddie had his hand on the pistol. He picked it up and smashed it down hard into the wood. "*Shut up!* Shut your damn stupid mouth. You don't know what I'm doing. You said you understood this wasn't a game, but to you, to your kind, every damn thing in the world is a game. So just shut up . . . *shut up!*"

"That's a wonderful tough-guy speech," Jilly said. "But you still haven't gotten anything to eat, and you still smell bad."

Eddie let go of the pistol and rubbed his eyes out of anger and frustration and exhaustion.

"A long time ago," he said finally, looking over at Jilly where she sat on the edge of the bed with her long legs crossed, "I captained a fishing yacht in the Florida Keys. A lot of the people who fished on that boat talked just like you. And at that same time, I had a friend, another captain. And you know what that captain used to say about smart talk like yours?"

Jilly looked away disinterestedly at a far wall.

"Look at me when I talk to you!" Eddie raged.

She turned slowly and resentfully back to face him. Eddie waited until she faced him directly again before he finished what he was saying.

"He used to say, 'Big pile of nothing.' "

He watched her; she didn't show the least sign of recognition of the words, but he hadn't expected her to.

"Can I call for breakfast?" was her only response. "I'm getting a little rocky myself. After all, I'm paying for this. Jesus. The ultimate fucking insult: you pay your kidnapper's room and board and then have to beg for your breakfast. Huh?" She gave him a slight smile and a little shrug with her face and hands. "Loosen up a little. I don't hear any bloodhounds, or the sheriff pounding on the door. Breakfast?"

Pearly teeth and black mouths, Eddie remembered his friend saying. *Pearly teeth and black mouths.*

He looked at Jilly with disgust and puzzlement; then he gave in and nodded that she could call room service for breakfast, touching his pistol as a caution to her.

"I know . . . I know," she said, smiling sarcastically, "you'll *blast me* if I make any false moves or try to tip off the waiter with a secret code on the poached eggs."

Eddie said nothing in reply. He just sat and watched her making the call for room service.

Pearly teeth and black mouths. Just like Key West or Blowing Rock, where money is the weather. . . . Pile of nothing. Jilly gave her terse, precise breakfast order to the room-service phone clerk.

Eddie looked up from the last of a plate of scrambled eggs and ham that he had eaten without tasting, and did not think about it as he wiped his mouth with his hand the way you did in prison, where there were no napkins.

"How come everybody dances a jig when you say 'Sam-Seven'?" he asked Jilly, who sat on the edge of the bed and picked over half a grapefruit, toast, and coffee. "Is there some sort of magic I missed?"

She eyed him for a few seconds, then returned to her grapefruit when she spoke. "Definitely," she answered in a tone more haughty than she intended.

"You can save that social-register crap for the hired help," Eddie said roughly, poking his plate with half a piece of buttered toast. "Just answer the question."

"Truce!" Jilly said quickly, throwing up her hands. "And ease up on that social-register shit. I may be a dilettante; I've been called a hell of a lot worse"—she shrugged defiantly—"but never hard-core social-register. I don't even like the sound of it."

Eddie looked at her; suddenly he was back in his Key West days and there was a man he knew, a rich young man in his thirties from New York City. He had everything, but he was going broke; his inheritance was drying up after ten years of wild spending. Everybody in Key West knew it but the young man himself, and when the end finally came and he was penniless, the reality never really sank in on him; it was that, not the fact of a man going through over a million dollars in ten years, that always struck Eddie the hardest. The young man never understood what happened to him because he had no frame of reference to hang it on. That was exactly what was happening now before Eddie's eyes. He could get up out of his chair and walk over to the woman and punch her onto the floor and shut her mouth forever, but just like the man in Key West, she wouldn't understand why it happened; she had no frame of reference. *The weather of money,* Eddie's mind flashed. *It never rains. Not even when it's raining.*

The thought brought on a smile. Jilly saw it and she smiled back, thinking she had won him over. Eddie knew the difference, but didn't protest, and when the smile left his lips he asked her about Sam-Seven again and she told him. When he smiled once more, it was not a knowing smile, it was to ward off utter, total, and complete astonishment.

He sat looking across the room at her, and it all came back as she told it: SAM, the last of the great Southern political barons: "the Huey Long of Texas," the New York *Times* once dubbed him; but labeled forever "SAM" by all the big Texas papers. Worth half a billion dollars, with his tentacles in every good gas and oil pot in Texas, and most of the independent banks, whose charters he had begun approving from the 1930's on as, first, Texas banking commissioner, and later, two-term governor. SAM had it all—including Jilly Buck as official "Texas Governor's Mansion Hostess" in place of his deceased wife—MOM, Mary Owens Montgomery.

Eddie could see it plainly—the images passing through his mind from all the Texas history books he had read in prison. Jilly, courted by movie stars, Arab oil sheikhs, and rock superstars. Jilly, incredibly beautiful, chic, rough, and well-spoken in four languages—everything, and all the power and money in Texas behind her.

Everything, that is, until the *Playboy* centerfold. In newspaper and magazine parlance the incident was reduced quite succinctly by *Time* magazine to the "Bare Bottom Caper." It went deliciously further, though, including not only Jilly's lovely rear, but her ample front, including just a wisp of lovely V hair, all photographed in vibrant color in the Sam Houston Bedroom of the Governor's Mansion in Austin.

A month after the centerfold appeared and Jilly had left the mansion, the Houston *Chronicle* sealed the incident with a front-page photo of Jilly exiting the grounds in a chauffeur-driven Cadillac with the tongue-in-cheek caption: "The first First Lady to be hounded from office."

It was true that Jilly was hounded from office, but she was anything but hounded from SAM's affection. Two weeks after her official departure, Jilly was back in residence at the mansion for the weekend, spirited in undercover by state troopers. And after a private dinner that evening with SAM, the two adjourned to his private study for some serious bourbon drinking and a great, if not costly, laugh over the whole mess.

"Old Sam Houston would walk right out of his grave and come home to the Big House just for a look at your decorations in his bedroom," Montgomery roared that evening. "Honey, you're a goddamned pistol ball. What you did was funny, pure and simple. To hell with all the sob sisters and weak-knees. You're mine, and woe on the sad sonofabitch that crosses *my* line; *our* line," he added, smiling like the perfect Dutch uncle he had always been.

With the Texas governorship and SAM's money, and then the "Bare Bottom Caper" as a springboard—coupled with her looks and some talent—Jilly went into a two-year whirlwind of modeling, acting, and finally a world-wide tour with a leading rock star. But after the tour, Jilly dropped out of public view and came home to Texas, dividing her time between tending to SAM-1 in Fort Worth and her own private Mexican beach house in Veracruz. She had stopped in Laredo with brake problems on the Mercedes, and to pass the time she had had drinks for two nights at the Five O'Clock Club—a bored little rich girl looking for what was referred to in the trade as a "Blue Collar Thrill."

Eddie, and everybody else in Texas, was aware of the affection

SAM-1 had for Jilly and the absolute reach and power SAM-1 possessed. The realization jarred him, and Eddie dug through his dull sleepless mind for an appropriate response. When Jilly finished speaking, he was ready with a limp apology.

"Look," he said, cupping his chin in the palm of his hand, aware that it was becoming an effort to hold his head up and keep his eyes open. "I didn't want this. I mean . . . I didn't mean to get . . ." He couldn't go on.

Jilly saw he was about to collapse, but she did not move to help him. She watched him in much the same way he had watched her—with curiosity. Eddie caught himself on the edge of his chair and pushed back. For a moment he could not see Jilly—only ghostly, sickening, gaseous gray balls floating in front of his head. With all the strength and power he had left, Eddie brought his mind and body under control. He picked up the pistol and made himself stand erect.

"Sleep," he said to Jilly, waving the pistol in the direction of the bed on which she sat. "I've got to sleep. Got to sleep. I'm sorry," he said, moving toward her, still waving the pistol, his face becoming pained. "I've got to know you won't leave, can't leave," he said.

She looked at Eddie intently and said nothing as he approached her, his face becoming more pained.

"You've . . ." he stammered. "You've got to take off your clothes and give them to me," he went on, his face red with embarrassment and distress.

"I won't look at you," he said quickly, using the waving pistol again for emphasis. "But I've got to . . . you've got to . . ." He faltered in weariness, catching himself in mid-stride before the bed. "Please" was all he could end with. *"Please."*

Jilly sat impassively and looked at him for a moment; then she broke into a sincere smile of amusement and understanding. Eddie saw it, but his exhaustion devoured its intended effect.

"You're getting in with me, I presume," Jilly said, mugging.

Eddie's face was consumed with misery. "Please," he said again. "You'll be under the covers and I'll just be on the bed, *with* my clothes on. *Please* . . ."

"The captive princess always gets one request, my friend," Jilly replied, standing, beginning to take off her clothes before him slowly and deliberately. "Bathing first; sleeping second. You being the principal bathee."

Later, he was sure that it was a dream. That he was on the bed in his stinking rags with Jilly wedged in under the covers between him and the wall, naked with her clothes tucked under the bed for safekeeping. *Not* that they were both naked and standing inside a steaming shower stall, with her washing him with some care and concern. *Not* that he had flashes of seeing incredible nakedness before him; of touching it; smelling it. *Not* of being dried like a small boy and led to bed. *Not* of passing into warm, sweet sleep next to something he could finally only comprehend as a velvet lion. All of which came upon Eddie in the moment when he was finally cleansed, before his mind could focus on what he wanted most to focus on: Chris and his children.

28

Chris and the Children / Noon / Matehuala, Mexico

Chris sat on a pink-sandstone park bench in the little central plaza and looked at the ancient cathedral of the old Mexican mining town. There was a mood of peace and flow that she could feel, but like Mexico itself, explainable only to a point. If she looked at it through her own eyes, the eyes of an American, she would see poverty and misery. But as she got to know Mexico, the land and its people, she began to understand that her standards didn't apply. There was a measure of stoicism and joy here, a sense of life and its possibilities. And most of all there was slowness.

On the surface it seemed that the peasants of Blowing Rock's Tater Hill were no different from Mexican peasants, but they were different in every way, and the cornerstone of that difference was bitterness. In Tater Hill, people were bitter, while the Mexicans were not. But it wasn't a matter of resignation with the Mexicans. Of course, like all poor people, Mexican peasants knew they were poor and they were not happy about that, but in place of bitterness, they had long ago substituted the word "joy." Forced joy might not set a Mexican peasant free, but to be bitter was to stay in Tater Hill forever; it was as simple and uncomplicated as that. Chris had always known that she and Eddie were apart from most in Tater Hill because they had that quality of joy, but their demonic rush toward the elusive *Something Better* had led them squarely into the center of frenzy's whirlwind, and she had never really come to grips with that, or the absence of joy. But Eddie seemed to thrive on frenzy. He was a natural competitor, a born street fighter.

In Mexico, for the first time, Chris had been able to separate herself from frenzy and street fighting. The big money from the sale of her family's Blowing Rock farm and the remainder of the Flying Fish savings account had been the necessary buffer, but having money didn't remove frenzy and fighting; for most people, money was a springboard to a greater measure of the same. Chris, though, had reached out to the mood of Mexico like someone drowning, and it had saved her. But her joy was not complete. The missing element was Eddie. She didn't know if Eddie would stop fighting; she didn't even know if he *could* stop. All she knew was that she had stopped. Period.

Before her in the plaza, Angie and Bobby were standing together watching a monkeyish little Indian dressed in loincloth, with bright feathers on his head, arms, and legs, dancing near a mossy water fountain. The Indian was in his forties, but everything about him was childlike and innocent. As he danced, the Indian beat on a little bark-and-rawhide drum that he carried in the crook of his left arm. Chris watched children looking on in fascination, and she too became swept up in the little Indian's dance. The civilized world was losing its desire to dance; losing its capacity for joy. Chris understood this absolutely as she watched the small uncomplicated man dance on as if he were the only person in the world. But pain tore at her like a sudden thorn as she watched the scene; there was so much she wanted Eddie to see, so much she wanted to show him. The pain almost took her breath away as she watched. Her hands tightened and her eyes closed, and then it passed. When her eyes opened again, her children were standing in front of her, smiling.

"Mama," Bobby said to her. "He had real moccasins. The Indian had real moccasins and a little silver dagger."

Bobby's eyes were bright with fascination; his eyes, his hands, like Eddie's, always darting, always ready and alert. Chris smiled back at him, and at Angie, then reached out for their hands. There was no venality here. No dread. No hurry. No frenzy. No fighting. Only joy.

Oh, dear God, let him come. Let him be safe now and sleeping. And this evening let him start again and come to us. Oh, my dear sweet God, please do this, I beg you with all that is mine to beg. Sweet God . . . I'll show him the way once he gets here. Just let him come. I will make it right then. I . . .

Chris caught her breath so the children would not see the pain of her prayer, and brought them close to her; and all the while, the regal little Indian kept up his dance, his joyous and innocent dance.

29
Eddie and Jilly / 1:07 p.m. /
La Posada Hotel, Laredo, Texas

Eddie woke up frightened. Leaden with sleep, he did not know where he was, and in more confusion, he did not know *who* he was. When reality came back to him, it was like being stabbed.

Woman . . .
Bed . . .
Room . . .
Run . . .
Man . . .
TDC . . .
Marzack . . . Run . . . Man . . . Woman . . . Woman!

"Wait! Wait! Wait a . . . you . . . *you!*" he said audibly as words finally formed from the depths of his nightmare sleep.

He couldn't remember her name, and he couldn't find her.

No! Jesus . . . No!

His head popped from side to side, his eyes searching frantically for his pistol, which was on the bedside tabletop where he had left it.

What? What the . . . ?

He was sure the woman had left him, that the TDC officials, or even worse, Marzack, was coming for him; that he was at last through. Gun in hand, he pushed himself up savagely on the bed; twisting to face the room, he saw her. She was standing in front of the wall of mirrors in the bathroom. He leveled the pistol on her automatically.

"You wouldn't blast me while I'm making up my face, would you? Even the *bad* guys don't do that."

Jilly's sarcasm was the final link to his chain of reality. Eddie lowered the pistol and collapsed on the bed. As his eyes moved around the room again, he saw what was on the dresser and on the long tile counter in front of Jilly. There was a platter of ham-and-cheese sandwiches, a deep bowl of guacamole and a plate of hard tortillas, quarts of Johnnie Walker Black Label Scotch, Beefeater gin, and Maker's Mark bourbon, a tub of ice, mixers, and tall glasses. There were also men's and women's cosmetics and an electric shaver. Eddie balked at seeing the things; their presence flashed through his mind, and again he stiffened in bed.

Contact!

She's been out of the room.

People . . . places.

Contact . . .

But the articles were there in front of him; all Eddie could do was accept what had happened. He sank back down on the bed. Then he saw Jilly's nakedness for the first time. At first it was like seeing something from another planet. She was standing there in front of the wall of mirrors wearing only pink bikini panties. Her skin was velvet brown all over; her gently sagging full breasts brown, nipples wide and pinkish-red. It didn't make any sense, but the thought occurred to Eddie that she was standing there waiting for him to wake up, to see her! No sense at all. From the first moments in the car after he had come upon her in the desert, Eddie had attached a *Playboy* image to Jilly; now, as he lay back in the bed and looked at her, he understood why. Like the women in *Playboy*, she didn't have any flaws. Her female curves didn't end; they flowed together perfectly. He sat and looked unashamedly at her body, viewing it as if it were something in a showcase. But it wasn't in a showcase. It was there in front of him. The realization of her closeness suddenly jarred him. He turned away in sour embarrassment, and grief for not having seen a nude woman in six years. He didn't say anything. Instantly the shower came back to him—touching her body briefly in bed came back; then his own nakedness became apparent. He pushed himself up fully in bed and shoved his feet over the side with the sheet across his lap. He watched her as he moved, but she seemed to take no notice of him. When he was sitting fully on the bed, his eyes left her and he began to check his own body. It was a mess. His legs were scratched and scarred, his feet bruised and blistered. His hands were raw. His neck ached. His spine burned. He was nauseated. He was sure he had lost over twenty pounds, a loss that would put him between one-forty-five and one-fifty—too small, too weak to really defend himself if it came to a hand-to-hand fight. But it was all fact: this was the way he had ended up, and there was nothing he could do about it.

"At least there's nothing broken," he said just faintly over his breath as he sat and rubbed his sore and aching legs.

"We talking to ourself?" Jilly asked.

Eddie looked across the room at her as she went on fixing her eyes in front of the mirror, and didn't say anything for a time. After six years in prison he didn't really know what to say to anybody—man or woman—anymore. He had rehearsed things to say to Chris, things to do with her, but he didn't even know if he could say or do them when he saw her—at least not at first. How could he talk or be with someone like Jilly? Nothing about being with her made sense. All Eddie could say finally was something totally pedestrian, simple, and distant.

"Flip me a towel," he said, looking at her but still finding it difficult not to be embarrassed at her nakedness.

"Modest too? My, we are a find in today's crass old world," Jilly answered as she turned and took a towel off the rack beside her and threw it across the room, her breasts jiggling pleasantly.

Eddie took in the excellent sight and caught the towel, but his eyes ended on hers, and for a second she could not avoid him.

"Do you ever cut the crap?" he asked simply, his eyes straight on her face.

"Very seldom," she replied earnestly and with no hesitation.

Another world, he thought as he looked at her, but he was too tired, too concerned with other matters to protest. He stood up and wrapped the towel around his waist and walked over to the dresser and devoured half a ham-and-cheese sandwich in three gulps. Then he attacked the guacamole and hard tortillas. In five minutes he had eaten three sandwiches and a good portion of the guacamole. He was standing, looking at the row of whiskey bottles on the dresser top, when he felt Jilly's hand gently on his shoulder.

"*Huh!*" he said, startled, whipping around to face her nakedness, the towel dropping to the floor as he did. Seconds went by. Their bodies were only inches apart. Each wanted to move the inches to the other. Their eyes darted. Their hands tried to move. Still more seconds went by. Then it was Eddie who made the first move, a motion that surprised him as much as it did Jilly. But an *inner* surprise, because there was only Eddie's very slight and careful move, a motion that touched his limp penis to Jilly's stiff yet silky V hairs, a motion she responded to by coming up gently with her hands so that she was holding Eddie's firm waist at the sides; pulling her close to his penis.

Then Jilly's head went down gently to Eddie's neck, her mouth finding the crease where the neck met the shoulders. Her tongue was on the crease, then she felt Eddie's hands on her waist. Her hands moved up behind his back to his shoulders, a final motion that could have molded them together where they stood, with Jilly pushing up on her toes to receive Eddie fully.

But it did not happen. It had been too long since he had had a woman. And no matter how lovely and right and accessible this woman was, she was not the woman he wanted. Without speaking or moving, Jilly seemed to understand. So she just held on tightly to him.

They didn't move for a long time, and when they parted, Jilly kissed his neck and moved off to the side of the bed where her clothes were and began dressing. When she was through, she sat on the bed and adjusted her sandals. When that was done, she stood up and looked at Eddie and smiled, trying to be natural, accommodating, if not friendly.

A different world, Eddie said to himself as he looked at her and wanted her, and cursed himself for the thought. He thanked her for not making him speak of what had happened between them. *A different world,* he said to himself.

"I'm trying to figure out where I don't hurt" was what he said aloud.

Her face brightened.

"Have you discovered the places?"

"Yes," he answered, smiling lamely. "I think I've narrowed it down to the little toenail on my left foot."

It wasn't very much of a joke. And it really wasn't funny. But it was their first joke. And after a few moments they laughed at it soundly. Then they stopped. They had crossed a bridge. They had shared something. And they were aware of the sharing.

1:30 p.m.

"What are you smiling about?" she asked.

They were sitting on the two deep and comfortable chairs in the room, drinking, absentmindedly watching TV. Eddie kept on looking at the TV screen and smiling a few seconds more before he answered her.

"In prison," he said, straightforward, "about all the defense you have is fantasy. This was one of mine—everybody's. Motel room, booze, beautiful woman . . ." He caught himself. "Look," he said, "I didn't mean anything disrespectful. I—"

"What the hell kind of a fantasy would it be if it was respectful?" she said, amused and interested.

That gave them their second laugh. It was much easier than the first, and they shared it in that manner, again conscious of the sharing. But beneath his own amusement, Eddie had an acute sense that everything was out of place, out of order. He was in a motel room with a beautiful woman; there was booze; he had seen her nakedness; they had touched and been close. It was a fantasy situation. But it was to have been a fantasy he played out with his wife.

All so perfect, he said to himself. *It was all supposed to be so*

*perfect. Everything was supposed to fall into place just like I planned.
Just like I . . .*

But then it hit him that he had forever buried his plans back in the
desert. It came in on him once more that he would forever seize on
the Now, the step-by-step Now.

Now, he rolled in his mind as he sat and looked at Jilly. It was so
inviting, but it was not the Now he wanted at all.

2:00 p.m.

There was nothing on TV about his escape, and there was nothing in
the Texas papers Jilly had brought to the room. But TV and the papers
were meaningless; Marzack was out there somewhere. The press
didn't know about him. Eddie did. Eddie knew and Marzack knew.
That was all that mattered.

He'll come, Eddie said to himself as a shiver of fear shot up his back.
He's out there, and he'll come.

He pushed the thought out of his mind when Marzack's image
became so real to him that it seemed the big man was standing over
him with a club, ready to strike.

Let it go! Let it go! Just be ready. Just be ready! he commanded
himself.

Eddie had been asleep for hours with Jilly in the room. She had
sent out for toilet articles and had gotten room service, and she had
not turned him in. He couldn't figure her motives, but so far she was
with him, or at least not against him. There was still a lot to do. The
key, and the safe-deposit box with the fake Canadian papers, new
clothes. And he would have to attend to all this soon. What would he
do with her then? As he looked across at her, Eddie didn't know. He
got up from his chair and walked over to the dresser top and poked
through the remains of the ham-and-cheese sandwiches, which were
now dry.

"Touch not that sandwich," Jilly said, standing up and walking over
to the bedside table with the telephone on top of it. "It was intended

as a mere warm-up. I've had the kitchen primed for your recovery for two hours. Just say the word when you're ready for the main course."

He spoke without thinking, his face flushed bloodred with anger. "You still think I'm on some sort of . . . of . . . college-fraternity party or some nonsense. Dammit! I am fighting for my life!"

Jilly didn't seem hurt or angry, and her reply showed no emotion. "You run the escape, I'll run the kitchen and the bar," she said.

"This is no damn game," he stated firmly, the red flush dissipating from his face.

"We agreed on that point before," she answered simply.

He let the answer stand for a few moments; then he challenged it. "Why?"

"It's turning out to be a very slow Wednesday," she said as she picked up the phone and dialed room service.

Nothing ever bites.

Nothing . . .

2:25 p.m.

The meal was not elaborate, but it was also part of a con's fantasy: tender juicy steak, french fries, a big green salad with blue-cheese dressing, and several ice-cold beers.

Eddie ate in silence and Jilly had a salad and gin on the rocks. He had almost stopped trying to understand her, but he could not sidestep the issue of security. When he finished the meal, he looked up from the empty plates on the room-service table that had been placed between the two chairs out from the bed. He was still wearing the towel and he had wrapped the bed's spare woolen blanket around his shoulders; all of which, with his beard stubble and scars, gave him the look of someone rescued from a sinking ocean liner.

"I hate to seem like a bad guest," he said, twirling the last of his beer in his glass, watching the golden liquid and its white foam, "but do you suppose there's anybody in town who doesn't know this little party is going on?"

She took a short drink of gin and answered him evenly.

"If you're looking for protection, look no further. You're as secure as a baby, wrapped up safe and sound in what hotels call 'Silent VIP Service.'"

Eddie looked up, puzzled.

"Good service," Jilly came back, smiling thinly. "Simple as that. The desk screens all calls and callers and advises you ahead of time on who is about to knock on your door."

Eddie looked at her silently for a moment.

"Why?" he asked again.

For the first time Jilly hesitated. Like the shared laughs, they were both completely aware of the pause.

"Slow Wednesday, like I said," she answered finally, but unconvincingly.

She avoided his eyes completely as she stood and walked to the dresser to make herself another drink. He sat and watched her move. In all his life he had never seen a woman so beautiful. In a way she did not look real. But she was real and she was standing there before him. She had taken care of him, was hiding him. But she wouldn't make sense when she talked. She wouldn't stop, wouldn't link up, wouldn't take hold. On impulse, as he watched her standing at the dresser-top bar, Eddie spoke again.

"You know why I was out in the desert. What were you doing there?"

"Taking care of a slow Tuesday *and* slow Wednesday all in one," she answered instantly, looking around for her handbag and cigarettes.

She seemed strained and nervous, but Eddie didn't think that was possible. Rather than challenge her and give her an opening for another meaningless exchange of words, he sat quietly and drank the rest of his beer and looked at her as she lit her cigarette with her gold lighter. Finally the silence forced her to answer.

"I was down in Mexico for a month. Veracruz for fishing, Tampico for hunting," she said, standing in front of the dresser. "Hunting and fishing. That's it. End of mystery. I crossed the border three days ago with brake trouble. No real place to go right now. Maybe Paris for a few weeks, or watch some late leaves in Hot Springs . . ." She trailed off, intent only on her cigarette and new drink.

Eddię sat and watched.

"Is that what you do?" he asked finally. "Go places?"

"Yes," she answered blankly, moving over and sitting on the unmade bed.

His pistol was on the bedside next to her, with him halfway across the room.

"Shall I bring you your pistol, or would you like me to shoot myself and save you the effort?"

They were the same words, but there was just a little flicker of hurt in her tone, a tiny little flaw that had not been there before. For the first time—just for a split second—she did not seem so untouchable. There was a moment, a brief second when he might have said something, but Eddie let it pass. He had other things to do, things he had to do to cross the border. But he did not completely bury the moment in his mind. He let it float. She seemed to be doing the same. Something seemed to be different between them.

She wants to be a part of this.

Why?

How?

Of course, no answers came.

2:45 p.m.

He had eaten. He had had his first free-world drinks. He was beginning to feel rested and stronger, and his body no longer ached as much as before. Jilly was talking freely if not easily with him. But Eddie knew all of that counted for nothing against the requirements of the afternoon that lay ahead.

He sat on the bed and contemplated his pile of dirty rags on the floor. He would have to dress in them again and go downstairs and present the safe-deposit-box key in order to retrieve its contents. It had been relatively easy at ten-thirty in the morning with Jilly by his side, but now, at midafternoon, with the lobby jammed with fashionable people and Eddie by himself, it would not be so easy. And buying new clothes, exposing himself on the streets of Laredo looking like a bum, would prove even more dangerous. There were things that had to be done. But what would he do with Jilly? He sat and thought; when the answer did not come to him, he asked her directly. She was sitting in one of the chairs, smoking, looking at but not watching a movie on TV.

"The only thing that makes any sense at all," she answered him formally and with sincerity, "is for me to go for the safe-deposit box and your new clothes."

Her eyes left the TV screen as she spoke, but they stopped short of finding Eddie's eyes. He rubbed his bearded face and looked across the room at her. Finally their eyes met. He thought she looked like she wanted to help him. He thought she looked like she could be trusted. Eddie knew she was right and he wanted her help, but it didn't make sense that she was offering it.

Why? Why?

"Talk to me straight. Just give me one hard reason why I should trust you. One hard reason why you want to go out on a limb for me?"

Jilly sat up uncomfortably in her chair and drew on her cigarette.

"Dammit," she answered him, avoiding his eyes, "I don't have any straight answers for you or anybody else. I just offered. Don't take it. Big fucking deal. Go downstairs and get your ass caught and go back to prison."

He didn't say anything. He just looked carefully at her. She was big and voluptuous, and beautiful, and, like him, scared to death.

But of what?

Not me. She knows damn good and well I won't touch her.

Of what?

But she was right. It could be fatal for him to go down to the lobby for the safe-deposit box and the new clothes. Nothing was as it was supposed to be. No knapsack with its change of clothes. The timetable broken. Someone with him. It had all been planned so perfectly, and it had all turned out in reverse. But he was in Laredo. He could see Mexico from the windows of his hotel room. He was hidden. There was still hope to put the schedule right and cross at noon tomorrow. He looked at Jilly for a few seconds longer; then he reached over on the bedside table and picked up the safe-deposit-box key and flipped it across the room to her.

"I have a wife and two children that I have not been with in six years," he said. "That's enough to say. If that doesn't mean something to you, nothing else will."

Jilly didn't answer at first. She simply stood up and walked over to the dresser and put the key in her purse. When she turned to leave the room, she spoke.

"Write me down some sizes for clothes," she said tightly.

Eddie looked up at her; for a second time he saw the fright in her eyes. Just as she opened the door, he spoke to her again.

"In your pictures in magazines you always looked like you were having such a good time," he said. "You weren't, were you?"

"No," she answered in a small voice. "I was not having a good time."

She turned and left then, but as she left, Eddie seized on the word "time" as she had said it. It occurred to him that she had said the word exactly as he would have, that she said it as if time were also a sentence for her.

After Jilly left, a strange sense of contentment came over Eddie. In a way, it was like prison again, someone else having control over his destiny. But it went beyond that; it went back to what he had decided on the run. It went back to *Now*.

He went over to the dresser and made himself a scotch and ginger and looked at the room. It was big, with a high beamed ceiling, thick carpet on the floor, a big soft king-size bed, good Spanish-colonial art on the walls, good Spanish furniture, with the far wall across from the bed a solid mass of firebrick, and finally a short patio that looked out directly at the Rio Grande River and, beyond, Mexico. It had been made for comfort rather than containment. Eddie had to look at the room for quite a while before he fully understood what he was seeing.

He took his drink and pistol and walked into the large well-lighted tile bathroom. He took a sip of the drink and set it on the counter and looked in the wall mirrors at himself. Color was coming back to his face, and the dullness of exhaustion was leaving his eyes. His stomach had shrunk, and he had lost weight in his chest and neck, but he

looked strong and hard beneath all the cuts and bruises. He drew a
sink full of piping-hot water and toweled the three-day beard growth
on his face. Then he dried his face and applied preshave lotion and
hooked up the new electric shaver Jilly had bought him and went to
work. The shaver felt excellent, and after a few minutes Eddie began
to use it expertly, fashioning himself a neat full mustache that came
down from the center of his mouth and blunted off at the ends. After
he shaved, he showered, a long, steaming-hot shower that took the
final edge off his weariness and muscle aches. He dried himself and
combed his hair and admired his new mustache and then walked
naked into the living room with his pistol and made himself another
drink and got in bed. He was doing things on his own, with no one to
answer to or give him orders, and he was acutely aware of the total
pleasure in the simple acts. He lay back in the bed with its starched
sheets and soft wool blanket and colorful bedspread pulled up over his
chest and allowed himself to feel good. Under the covers his hand
held his pistol. He did not feel safe and secure, but he consciously
kept the feeling of *good* in his mind. He was growing stronger every
second, and just before he passed into a deep sleep, a humorous
thought occurred to him.

   *The initials LBT got me to the run; the initials SAM may just finish
it for me and get me across the border . . .*

   Before he could contemplate the power of the initials any further,
he fell asleep and his mind did not end on his wife and children, or the
Hounder, but on the fascination of Jilly's naked body, a marvelous
sight, the like of which he hadn't seen in six years.

30
Marzack / 3:18 p.m. /
La Posada Hotel, Laredo, Texas

Marzack turned left and down the hotel's narrow driveway to the parking garage. He was sweating with anger. Counting La Posada, he had only four more hotels and motels on his list. The thought had begun to creep into his mind that maybe he had missed Eddie. Maybe Eddie had just crashed the border and started running again in Mexico.

But the second Marzack turned his car a sharp right into the hotel's long basement parking lot, all his fears ceased. There in front of him, rudely obvious, was the big gold Mercedes sedan with its SAM-7 plates. Marzack stopped his Olds dead the second he saw the car and sized up the entire parking lot in two quick turns of his head. Eddie and the girl were nowhere in sight. The only person Marzack saw was an eager Tex-Mex teenager in a red jacket and shiny black trousers heading for his car, smiling broadly. When the kid came up to the car door, Marzack flashed him a half-smile and showed him his bogus FBI badge.

The badge broke the kid's smile and composure. He turned sullen and subservient and stood by the car door waiting for Marzack to speak. When Marzack fished a ten-dollar bill from his wallet the boy's smile began to reappear. Marzack held the bill up in front of the kid's eyes like a snake charmer.

"You see that car over there," he said, motioning toward the gold Mercedes with the bill.

"*Sí, señor.* Super *grande,*" the boy came back excitedly. "*Es un carro muy grande,*" he added, his eyes vacillating between the gold Mercedes and the green ten-dollar bill.

"English . . . *English,*" Marzack demanded.

"*Sí* . . . yes, mister," the boy replied, his eyes hard on the bill.

"Did you see who got out of that car?"

"Yes, sir."

"Describe the people."

"Two people, *señ* . . . mister."

"Go on," Marzack ordered, keeping the bill in sight.

"Pretty lady. Pretty, pretty lady."

"Yeah."

"And a gentleman," the boy continued, his right hand getting ready for the bill.

"The man. I want to know about the man," Marzack drummed.

The boy made a pained face. Marzack shook the ten-dollar bill.

"He looked bad, mister. He looked like he'd been in a fight, or working . . . or something."

Marzack showed the kid Eddie's TDC mug shot.

"Is this the man?"

The boy studied the photo for a few seconds, then answered, tight-lipped, "Yes, sir. Is he trouble?" he added quickly, unable to hold the question back.

Marzack turned sour.

"That doesn't concern you in the least," Marzack grunted, motioning with the bill toward his coat pocket and the FBI badge.

"You just forget we talked, or I'll have your ass in a sling so tight you'll think my foot is permanently on it."

The boy gulped and nodded in compliance. Then Marzack gave him another half-smile and the ten dollars. The kid took it warily, but had it in his pocket before Marzack fully saw it was gone from his own hand.

"The man and woman," Marzack asked, as the boy stood before him waiting to be dismissed, "have they used the car since they brought it in?"

"No, sir," the boy answered, shifting his weight from foot to foot, eyes on the concrete floor.

That was all Marzack wanted to know.

"Not a word to anyone," Marzack cautioned the boy as he put his car in reverse and started to back into a parking space and then pointed his car back out to the narrow driveway. "Not a word."

"*Sí, señor*," the boy answered, with all the defiance he dared.

"Yeah . . . right," Marzack grunted, smiling. "*Sí*."

"Okay," the boy said, smiling too.

Marzack found exactly the spot he needed in Saint Augustin Plaza across the street from La Posada. He parked his car facing the hotel on Flores Street. From where he was sitting he had a clear view of the hotel's main doors and the garage driveway. All he had to do was wait for Eddie to make his move. He lit a cigar and took a small drink of dark rum from the bottle on the seat beside him and started his stakeout.

A TDC con and an ex-governor's niece shacked up on the ass-end of an escape; sonofabitch, Marzack thought as he devoured his rum and cigar and looked at the hotel. *Sonofabitch. Enjoy, runner.* Full indignation dominated his thoughts. *Get yourself a little tail, because your own ass is still mine.*

Still mine. . . .

31

Eddie and Jilly / 7:00 p.m. /
La Posada Hotel, Laredo, Texas

Eddie stood on the patio and looked out across the Rio Grande to Mexico. The colorful lights of Nuevo Laredo were just coming on, and you could hear faint wisps of honky-tonk music from the bars and belligerent peals of car horns. From what little Eddie could see, the sprawling Mexican city looked to be noisy, dirty, and fun.

It seemed so odd to see the evening sky turn dark and not be getting ready to run. Eddie stood still in the French doors and thought about that, and about the past three nights of running. Like the years of misery in prison, and the first lightning moments of his escape, the four nights of running seemed so easy. No effort at all. Just time. And time that had passed. Now he was somewhere else, doing something else.

It's not that simple, he said to himself as he looked at the lights of Nuevo Laredo and listened to the music. *But it's that true.*

Three years after he had been sent to prison, Eddie became aware that he was no longer unhappy to be there. He was not happy, simply not unhappy. For the remaining three years then, he contented himself that life was more mental than physical, that you could actually live in your mind. But that had been when he was by himself and in the prison. On visiting days, when he saw Chris and the children, Eddie was not sure of the belief, and now, as he stood and watched the foreign city with Jilly in the room behind him, he was more confused than ever.

Mentally and physically, he said to himself as he looked across the river, *it hurts so bad while it's going on, but when it's over, there's just a hole, a black nothing that is filled up by the Now. Now . . .* he repeated solemnly as Jilly came up behind him and stopped short of touching him.

"Thinking of flying over on your own steam?" she asked, not as sarcastically as before, but not friendly either, a neutral tone.

He turned and grunted a little laugh.

"The thought hadn't occurred to me, but I'll take it under serious advisement," he said.

"Birds don't have to clear customs," she said.

He stood and looked at her seriously, then smiled a small inward smile.

"That was one of my great fantasies in prison."

Her eyes asked: What?

"That I would turn into a bird and just fly away. Simple as that. Just fly away and land on the other side of the prison fence and turn back into me again and keep on going."

He laughed a small laugh; she watched him silently as his face became solemn again.

"But that's just in fairy tales," he said, looking past her. "I didn't turn into a bird. I tried. Oh, my God, I tried. I . . ." He let the thought go, then picked it up again suddenly. "Just in fairy tales, never in prison."

Prison: you could see the word etched across Jilly's eyes. She was boiling with curiosity about prison, and about Eddie there. They had been together for thirteen hours, and from the moment he had first told her that he was an escaped convict, the curiosity had been there. Like a smoldering fire it was about to burst into flame. Eddie could not know it, but she had come back to the hotel room with his new clothes without so much as a thought of turning him in or leaving him in the hotel. He had something she wanted, and although she was not exactly sure what it was, she meant consciously to have it.

Eddie avoided her eyes and their wants and moved past her in the open doorway over to the dresser and poured himself a short straight scotch. The clothes Jilly bought had changed him. He moved in them with an air of command and authority. It was obvious to both of them that she had dressed him, but he did not mind in the least. Indeed, it pleased him. And it was a simple fact that the clothes she chose were the nicest he had ever owned. In her way of taking command of things, Jilly had returned to the hotel room two hours after she left with a pair of heavy tan corduroy trousers; a lightweight navy wool Pendleton shirt; tan, round-toed, street-heeled cowboy boots; and a soft dark brown suede coat that required no tailoring. Eddie was dressed in the shirt and trousers, with the shirt open two buttons at the throat. After he poured his drink he took it back to the patio doors and stood in the doorway and looked at Jilly as she leaned on the railing and watched, with no particular interest, the Mexican city beyond. Her curiosity finally exploded.

"Tell me about prison," she said. "I want to know what prison is like."

He searched her anxious face. "Prison," he said evenly, "is like being a child and being told to go to your room—for years."

She looked on with fascination and absorbed the words.

"But children don't go to prison. Adults, with all their feelings of freedom and movement and motion, go to prison."

Her look did not change.

"In prison," Eddie said, his words getting softer and slightly brittle, "everything about you has to slow down. When you finally realize how slow you've become, you're whipped."

He stopped suddenly and gave her a tiny, grim smile.

"Whipped," he repeated. "With no recollection of the pain."

She was drinking it in. She didn't want to talk; she wanted to listen. Eddie watched and understood, and deep in the center of his mind he sensed why Jilly was so interested in the idea of prison.

"It's not really all that physical. There are beatings from guards and from other cons, but that's only once in a while and can be avoided if you're smart. The real whipping comes inside your head."

Jilly was not leaning against the patio railing anymore; she stood up straight like a pupil and listened.

"The old cons," he said, "will tell you: 'Nothin' don't mean shit.' But that's only because they're old cons. After a while an enormous sense of peace begins to settle in on you. But it isn't peace; you're stir crazy. So for you everything *is* shit."

He stopped and took a small sip from his glass; he could see Jilly understood everything he was telling her, and that disturbed him.

"You get a label and a number, not a name. No matter what you do, good or bad, nothing ever changes. You can save the warden's life or put out a fire that's burning down the prison, but you're still a con with a con's number. *Convict:* it's all over you; like white waking up black or black waking up white. And it makes you so small. The smallest things in life—going to the bathroom, a change of socks, showers, cigarettes and coffee—all small things that take on big meanings. Because in prison all they give a con is small. That's part of the punishment of prison, a big part of the punishment.

Jilly just looked at him and waited for more.

"Words like 'nothing' and 'never' take on extra meanings. Convict. Not man, not child. But convict. A thing apart. It's like caring with every part of your mind and body and having nothing, having the caring count for nothing."

He looked up at Jilly; she still seemed to understand everything he was saying.

"Three more words come to mind. 'Lean.' Everything in prison is lean. Just the bare essentials. An exact replica of poverty. 'Group.' Everything done as a group. Never by yourself. Always the maddening group. And finally, 'motion.' Everything in prison directed to a single motion. Slow motion." His voice was hollow and tired.

She didn't say anything. She seemed to understand—understand firsthand. Her face said that plainly. It was painful to look at. Eddie turned away and walked back into the room. Jilly didn't say anything or try and follow him.

7:50 p.m.

"Money and fame," she told him later. "Four walls and a door with a key held by someone else."

She didn't have to say more. Eddie knew he was right about her. He had seen it many times with guests on John Allen Doyle's yacht, what charter-boat captains and others who serve the rich close up call "lock-up money."

It was simple enough to see that Jilly was fascinated with his stories of prison. But that couldn't be the real reason she was staying with him, why she was helping him, why, in the midst of her sarcasm and crassness, she seemed to actually care what happened to him. Eddie dwelt on the question as he watched Jilly make up her face again before the bathroom mirrors.

Why does she stay? Why does she care? Why does she let me see so much? Why never a straight word? Why . . . ?

No easy answers came, but the questions persisted. Another thought also fought for dominance in Eddie's mind. The thought that Jilly was the most beautiful person, the most beautiful *anything* he had ever seen.

But why? he said to himself. *Why someone like this? And so involved. So immediately, so easily involved with an escaped con. Why?*

As he sat and pondered the question and watched her, Jilly came over and took the chair opposite him.

"Food," she said, mugging. "The lady wants to eat food with the gentleman."

He smiled at the words and also at the fact that they were said to him. For the first time, she seemed almost pleasant.

To eat anytime he pleased, with whom he pleased, where he pleased—it was all so new to Eddie that he had to stop to reason out an appropriate answer.

"I guess more room service" was all he could finally answer.

"Lady no want room service. Lady want eat dinner with gentleman in restaurant."

"Gentleman not exactly prime candidate to eat in public place," Eddie said, trying with considerable effort to match Jilly's careless banter.

Jilly saw his uneasiness. She changed her tone.

"The situation is well in control. The hotel has a semiprivate club upstairs. I've already made arrangements with the maître d' for a private booth with a good view out but no view in."

Eddie looked at her in complete puzzlement. As before, he could not resist the direct question.

"Why?"

"Slow Wednesday," she said as before. "Just keep thinking: slow Wednesday."

The constant haughtiness seemed diminished, and some of the harshness was gone. But it had the reverse effect on Eddie. He bolted from his chair and stared down at her, almost shaking with anger. "You're just doing this for the hell of it, aren't you?"

She hesitated for a second too long and then answered. "Uh-huh," she said, trying for her haughtiness again, but failing. "Just for the hell of it."

Then she was out of her own chair and facing him head-on, her own anger taking the place of haughtiness.

"Look, goddammit," she barked, her eyes betraying pain, "what do you want me to say? That I'm doing this out of some radical-chic love of adventure, or a penance, or solidarity with my brother behind bars? Bullshit! This is Wednesday. *Wednesday!* Your little thing is filling up *Wednesday!*"

When she finished, her arms were braced across her breasts and her face was tight and red. There was no more need for words. Eddie went to the door and they went outside and to dinner without speaking or looking at each other. For an instant he started to go back in the room and get the pistol and papers that he had hidden in the inside of the toilet bowl's square back in a plastic boot bag, but he let the thought go. He had put the items there for safekeeping in case he was captured, with the thought that the authorities might link him and Chris together with the name "Lanson" and arrest her on the other side of the border if he were captured. The gun and papers would keep until he got back.

Everything will keep, Eddie allowed himself to think, in the face of Jilly's words. *Everything will keep. . . .*

32

Marzack/ 8:30 p.m./ Saint Augustin Plaza, Texas

Marzack sat and brooded, with one overriding thought on his mind: on that long-ago liquor-store stakeout in Passaic, New Jersey, his indecision had gotten three people killed. *Not a second time*, he told himself. *Not goddamned likely a second time*.

But there was SAM-7; Jilly Buck. SAM-1, the ex-Texas governor. Both a farfetched part of the thing, but yet there, and very real.

He had been on the stakeout for five hours. How long could he stay parked on the street and not at least be observed by the Laredo Police Department? They were not hick cops. Laredo was America's largest inland port, a teeming border city where five million automobiles crossed the border to Mexico each year, and a city with one of the highest crime and murder rates for any city its size in America. The police would spot him soon enough, and Marzack could not palm his fake FBI badge on them. He would have to show his TDC lieutenant's

ID, and that could cause him trouble. He didn't want to get Eddie as the Hounder; he wanted to get him as the Buster.

Marzack sat and looked across the small Spanish plaza at La Posada Hotel and kept on thinking. *Not a second time. Not a second time. But to storm the hotel? To storm their room? How would it end? How could I pull it off?*

Those answers didn't come to Marzack, but his thoughts drummed on in his mind, in his cop's mind.

Not a second time. Not a second time. . . .

33

Eddie and Jilly / 9:15 p.m. /
La Posada Hotel, Laredo, Texas

Eddie steered them across the courtyard and inside the arcade, where he motioned Jilly to the stairs. Her instinct was to take the elevator; he had a different frame of reference.

Dinner had gone well. They exchanged the stories of their lives as far as each wanted to go with the telling, but the meal had cemented Eddie's persistent thoughts that Jilly was *with* him for two shallow and clearly defined reasons: 1) he was different, an escaped con; and 2) as an escaped con he was an amusement. How long those two things would be enough to hold her, he didn't know, but Eddie understood clearly that it was something he had to watch constantly. When the amusement died, his troubles would start all over again.

Jilly accepted the stairs with only slight reluctance. They walked together up the stairs, but when they came to the head of the stairwell on the second floor, Eddie stopped her with his lowered hand.

"We ending the evening with a little melodrama?" Jilly goaded.

248

Eddie ignored the remark and moved silently to the edge of the short foyer in front of the elevator and looked both ways.

No one. But I'm sure . . .

He was relieved, but something was not right. He did not know what, but something: Marzack! Eddie could *feel* him, could sense his presence. He wanted to go on and search the long hall that met the foyer to the right, but he was not secure enough with Jilly to leave her standing alone on the stairwell. And there had been no Marzack. Reluctantly he turned and motioned Jilly to come up.

"We making a Grade-B spy movie?" Jilly asked, fashioning a half-grimace, half-smile.

Eddie started to reply, but Jilly was beside him before he found the words. Instead of speaking, he took her by the arm and in four quick steps ushered her to the beginning of the long carpeted hallway that was dotted with the doors of the rooms. Their room was four doors down on the right to the outside. He stopped short of the hallway's opening and cautiously peered past the wall, turning his head to the left.

Nothing. But I feel . . .

He turned to the right.

Everything in the world stopped! It was as if a six-year vacuum closed in on him. Eddie went slack-mouthed with terror. There, in the hall ten feet away and coming straight for him, was Buster Marzack.

Only Eddie's head and shoulders were in the hall, and then only for seconds. But it was view enough for both men. When Eddie jerked his head back behind the corner, the color was gone from his face; a second later both he and Jilly heard Marzack bellow.

"You sonofabitch! I see you, runner! I see you!"

The words pelted Eddie, and he tried to assimilate their tone as well as their meaning. But there was not time. He and Jilly both heard Marzack's feet pounding up the hallway toward them.

"You're mine, runner!" they heard, their eyes meeting for a single terrified second. "Your ass is mine!"

Runner! Eddie heard the word clearly above all the others. *Runner!*

He grabbed Jilly's arm and pushed her roughly down the stairs. In an instant of pure terror Eddie's mind whirled to the image of his pistol and fake ID papers hidden inside the toilet in his room. In spite of himself, Eddie's thoughts erupted and became audible.

"Wait! My . . ." he began.

But there was no hope of getting to the pistol and papers. Marzack was there like a lethal wedge. In an instant more, all Eddie could do or say was echo the words Marzack had just shouted.

"Run!" he screamed behind Jilly. "Run for it! Run!"

For once, there was no hesitation or protest. Like Eddie, Jilly began to dash down the stairs in blind fright, suddenly caught up in something neither she nor Eddie fully understood.

They plunged down the stairs to the garage and up the driveway's incline to the street. As they reached the street, Eddie heard Marzack burst out of the garage.

Out on the sidewalk to the right of the hotel, Eddie stopped Jilly; frantically he searched the street from left to right.

No one!

He searched Saint Augustin Plaza directly to his front.

No one!

To the left down Zaragoza Street was the International Bridge and Mexico. To the front was Saint Augustin Plaza, and beyond it, Laredo's business district. To the right on Zaragoza, past gleaming white Saint Augustin Cathedral, was the beginning of a shabby Tex-Mex neighborhood, a place of small houses and narrow streets and tree cover. After only seconds, Eddie shoved Jilly to the right and toward the tight little rows of streets and houses. But for one sick and heart-stopping moment Eddie hesitated on the sidewalk and looked back at the hotel while a thought flooded in on him again like a holocaust.

My ID papers! My papers and my gun. They're in the room! Jesus God, they're in the room! My papers! My papers . . .

But suddenly there was no more time for thought, only motion; Marzack was outside and coming after them.

"Runner! You sonofabitch runner!" Marzack roared into the night. "Your goddamned ass is mine, runner! You hear me, bastard. Mine!"

Eddie's stomach tightened into a knot as the words punched him from behind. And with each of Marzack's new assaults he could hear Jilly whine, terrible little sounds that seemed to echo fear itself.

Marzack panted heavily. It was cumbersome running in the suit and hat and trench coat, and he was out of shape. But the main problem was the streets and the lights. The streets were so narrow and the lights so dim he kept losing the two people in front of him, even though they were never more than a block away.

But always he heard them. The woman was having a bad time. He heard Eddie cursing her and urging her on. And as the run kept up, he too heard her whine. To Marzack the whine was like the sound cons made when they heard the goon squad come onto Meditation Row. He followed them west for six blocks through the residential section, and then, in the shallow glare of a streetlight, Marzack saw Eddie push Jilly right and north up still another narrow street lined with small houses. When Marzack got to the corner, he drew his pistol and took his first shot.

Toonk!

The lead ball whizzed past Jilly's ear.

Splat!

It struck a tree trunk three feet from her. Wood chips flew back and stung her face. "Ohh! I'm hit!" she moaned, sagging back into Eddie's rushing form. "I'm hit!"

"If you can talk, you're not shot! Now, *move!*" he answered, pushing her away from him roughly, sending her on down the half-dark street.

"Both of you! Hear me! Hear me good!" Marzack ranted behind them.

"Macon! Damn you, runner, hear me! You're a dead man! Jilly Buck!" he roared on, the words ripping apart the consciousness of both Eddie and Jilly.

"I don't give a damn who you are, bitch!" Marzack shouted. "Keep running and you're dead too!

"You're both mine!

"Goddamn you! Mine!" he ranted like a maniac, running with his pistol drawn, looking for an opening to make his kill.

"You hear me . . . mine!"

Eddie kept on pushing Jilly, but he knew she couldn't go much farther. Frantically he kept looking for something to develop, for some opportunity to arise that he could take advantage of. But no advantage came. Suddenly, to the left—the west—down a long narrow street he saw things widen. There were downtown lights again.

Downtown, with all its pitfalls, had been wrong at first, but now he was desperate; they had been on the run for over twenty minutes. In five . . . ten minutes at the most, he would lose Jilly, and then, whether she helped the authorities or not, it would all be over. He would not be able to go back to the hotel for his papers and gun. In desperation Eddie pushed her toward the downtown lights. Behind them he heard the leather of Marzack's shoes beating against the sidewalk like a hammer.

They raced down six streets at a dead run before Eddie shoved Jilly to the right and up a shop-lined street just off the Courthouse Square. They were right in the center of Laredo now, droves of cars moving down the streets; they bumped into people as they ran. Eddie knew he had to find something quick or they were through. At a narrow one-way street to his left, the opportunity he had been looking for finally materialized. There, coming slowly to the corner, was a Greyhound bus!

"There! There!" Eddie shouted behind Jilly. "Go for the bus! *Go!*"

Jilly obeyed in a frenzy, and in seconds they crossed the street and were at the corner where the bus was stopped, and Eddie was pounding on the door.

"Open! Open the damn door!" he shouted. "We missed the bus! Open the damn door!"

The bus driver, a fat man with a crooked face, looked down at Eddie for a moment and started to accelerate the bus, but then his eye caught Jilly and the doors wheezed open after only a moment's more obstinate pause.

"Express bus," the driver protested as Eddie and Jilly scrambled aboard. "Ain't supposed to stop an express bus."

"We missed it! We missed it!" Eddie babbled as he fished in his trouser pocket for his thousand-dollar wad of hundred-dollar bills.

It was only as he started to pay that he saw the destination of the bus printed in block letters on the eave over the driver's seat.

HOUSTON, the black and white letters proclaimed.

Oh, my God, Eddie's mind burned. *I'm going right back where I started from!*

The driver took his money, and Eddie and Jilly hurried to their seats in the back of the bus; it was just as they were seated in the dark security of the bus that they saw Marzack charge up the street, pistol in hand.

But he did not see them, and the people in the street seemed to pay him no mind. As Eddie and Jilly watched, it seemed all the more unreal to them; unreal, but true as death.

"Eddie," Jilly moaned, using his name for the first time. "That man . . . he knew who *I* was. He . . . he . . . was trying to kill you. Trying to kill *me.* I've never been scared in my whole life."

"It's awful, isn't it?" was all Eddie replied as they huddled close together in the dark bus, which moved off slowly on the dim street.

34

Marzack / Midnight / Saint Augustin Plaza, Laredo, Texas

Marzack looked through his car's windshield across Saint Augustin Park at the double entrance doors of La Posada Hotel and felt foolish. Eddie and Jilly were gone. He had no idea where. He had lost them. He had tipped his hand too quick. Rather than risk indecision, he had acted hastily, foolishly.

Now he was right back where he had been three hours before. Staked out, and waiting, but with none of the assurances of before. All he had to go on now were three things: 1) Eddie and Jilly were still together; 2) Jilly's car was still in the hotel garage; and 3) most important, Eddie's words just as he turned to run down the stairs: "*Wait! My . . .*" Eddie had said it plainly; the words instantly cemented themselves in Marzack's mind. Number three meant Eddie had left something in his room, something so vital his mind forced the thought into words.

Marzack couldn't bring himself to believe Eddie would leave something like fake papers or his gun in the room. But Eddie had been dressed well when Marzack saw him in the hall. It was dinner hour. Had he actually been to dinner with Jilly? Was she actually helping him? Helping him on her own?

Maybe the papers and pistol were still in the room, but could he risk entering the hotel again? Laredo police had combed the streets briefly after Marzack fired his pistol, but when he returned to his car he had not seen any at the hotel. That was understandable; fine hotels didn't like incidents. And, too, this incident had been minor, and confined to an empty hall and a deserted garage.

Finally, Marzack was left with this: there were too many questions to be answered and no real hope of answering them. All he could do was sit and wait and hope Eddie had to come back to the hotel for whatever he left in his room.

But he had forgotten how hard it was to sit in a car on a stakeout. You rode in cars when they were moving, and when they stopped, you got out. It didn't sound right, but it was true; cars were no good for sitting, especially on the driver's side, where the steering wheel got in the way of everything you did. He had been back on the stakeout for two hours now. He had eaten a pizza from a takeout café up the street. He had smoked six cigars. The two front windows were down, but Marzack's Olds smelled like an ashtray because he deposited the butts in a coffee can. You always took a can on auto stakeouts so the Other Side couldn't tell time by the number of butts you threw on the street. There were two things you always did: kept your eyes open, and tried not to attract attention.

For an instant—one miserable instant—Marzack had let go of both things, and three cops paid for it with their lives and he was finished forever as a cop. Now he had apparently blown another stakeout. He sat and brooded and wondered darkly if he really was the cop he thought he was, or if he was only the Hounder TDC thought he was—thoughts that only added to the hateful vision he had of himself at the moment.

A collar, he said grimly to himself. *To catch Macon; to prove . . .*

But he let the thought go; it was too distasteful. Thinking would do no good anyway. All he could do was sit and wait for Eddie. It would be a long night, but it could all swing back his way tomorrow. And he would be ready.

Tomorrow will be for keeps, he said to himself, trying to make himself feel better, but not succeeding. *Tomorrow . . .*

DAY FIVE DAY FIVE

Thursday, November 1

35

Chris and the Children / 7:00 a.m. / Saltillo, Mexico

Chris dressed herself in a finely pressed white cotton sun dress that came down just below her knees. The low-cut boat-necked dress was decorated on the straight short sleeves and at the skirt bottom with red, yellow, and orange flowers with bright green stalks. She wore no bra, and her breasts sagged well and pleasantly. Her brown hair was cut full at the sides of her face to her neck, with bangs that came down long and straight over her forehead. She wore a gold necklace and a thin gold anklet, and medium-heeled straw sandals. She was tanned and beautiful.

Angie was dressed in a short pink dress and white lace socks and black patent-leather shoes. Bobby had on tan trousers and a plain dark blue long-sleeved French pullover that he had rolled to the elbows, and he was wearing Mexican sandals. The blue-and-brown Jeep Wagoneer station wagon had been washed the night before by attendants at the El Camino Motel, and it stood sparkling clean before their room in the early-morning light. It was a lovely high-mountain, dry-season day. Not a cloud in the powder-blue sky. The temperature was already in the high sixties; it would be seventy-five when they reached Nuevo Laredo in four hours.

They had eaten a fine breakfast at El Camino and then packed and loaded the station wagon. Now they were ready for the last part of the trip. They were ready for Eddie.

They got in the car and turned right out of the tree-lined driveway past El Camino's elegant colonial-stagecoach sign onto Mexico Highway 57; two miles away she turned onto Calzada Presidente Echeverría for the loop around the northern end of Saltillo, and Mexico Highway 40 to Monterrey and Nuevo Laredo. She had done all she could, now she was performing the final act she would play out for Eddie. Her mind was eaten up with questions and anxiety, but she turned her emotions off and simply made the car go north. As it always was with her and Eddie, a third entity had control over what they did. But there was also relief deep within her; today, one way or another, that third entity would cease to exist forever.

She would arrive in Nuevo Laredo at eleven and stay until one in the afternoon. Then, with or without Eddie, she would leave for the interior of Mexico. Two hours did not seem like much leeway for a five-day run, but if Eddie was not in place to cross at noon on the fifth day, no amount of time would matter, and if he was in place, only a half-hour of the two hours would be needed before he and Chris and the children departed for the interior.

In three days we will all—the four of us—be safely home in Colima, or we will be parted for life, Chris said to herself in words so final they almost paralyzed her. The lovely Mexican autumn would begin soon; there was just a nip in the air, and a rare and occasional tree with red and orange autumn leaves.

36

Eddie and Jilly / 8:06 a.m. / Houston, Texas

Eddie awoke slowly at the sound of the bus driver's voice.

"Houston, all change here," the man's voice drawled with complete lack of interest.

Jilly was beside him; Eddie had to shake her awake. Her blond hair was in her eyes and she was turned sideways toward Eddie so that her breasts sagged down easily into his side. She was warm and lovely and she smelled wonderful. Eddie shook her gently a second time and sat and admired her beauty. But when Jilly's eyes opened they broke his spell completely. She looked terrified; her mouth twisted with fright, her eyes wide and searching.

"Where . . . what . . . what?" She choked out the words, turning more to him in her seat, her nails digging into his coat sleeve.

"We're in Houston. Everything is okay," Eddie answered, gently taking her hand from his coat. "We're fine. Fine," he repeated. "Let's just wait till the bus is empty and then get off and go inside and have some coffee and then decide what we're . . . I'm"—he corrected himself, avoiding her still-frightened eyes—"going to do."

She didn't reply. She pulled herself together and turned so that she sat straight in her seat. Only her hands betrayed her true feelings; she held them tightly on her lap as if she was making a great effort to keep her body from flying apart. But Eddie was composed. He had made himself get a good night's sleep. He had put everything out of his mind and had gone to sleep and rested for what was to come. Now, as the morning of the fifth day of his run came in, he was serene. His serenity came from the certain knowledge that today would be the great test of his life, and he had readied himself for it as best he could, and had blocked all thoughts that would interfere with the acts he would have to perform.

The run was like a Catholic Mass, and at the end of Eddie's Mass he would either go to heaven or hell. As he sat and stared out the window of the bus, Eddie wondered which it would be. *We will soon know,* he said in silent finality.

He had stayed on the bus because there was security in its movement and isolation, but now, three hours and fifty-four minutes before he was supposed to meet his wife and children in Nuevo Laredo, Mexico, he was 350 miles away from Laredo—more than seven hours away by fast car. Sometime just after midnight he had decided on the course of action that would cut the distance.

When he and Jilly arrived in Houston they would take a cab to Houston Intercontinental Airport and fly back to Laredo. Once in Laredo again, they would rent a car and drive to La Posada Hotel and Eddie would go inside and get his fake Canadian ID papers and his pistol and then Jilly would drive him across the International Bridge into Mexico and leave him at Mexican Customs.

But as always, there were so many *ifs,* so many *woulds.*

If he could go undetected in Houston.

If TDC had abandoned the search for him.

If Marzack was acting on his own.

If there was a plane to Laredo that would arrive before noon.

Would Jilly continue to help him?

Would she wait for him in the car at the hotel?

Would she willingly drive him across the border?

If; would? Eddie's mind opened for the flood of questions, but he closed the gate.

Act. Do. Now, Eddie told himself as he sat on the bus. *Don't worry. Worry counts for nothing. Just perform. Performance is all that matters.*

He and Jilly had talked some on the bus, but mostly they had been silent, lost in their own thoughts or sleep. At the Frio River, Eddie showed her where he bailed out of the Cotulla stock trailer and how he made his way to the railroad bridge for the knapsack Chris left for him. And from Laredo to the Frio he had given her a short narrative of his run. The telling had brought them closer together, and Eddie knew that when Jilly finally said the first words to him that were completely devoid of posing and nonsense.

"I think I know how you felt. A little of how you felt," she amended quickly, her voice slim and brittle. "That man last night . . . To have something . . . some rage like that behind you; I couldn't stand it. I *couldn't.*" She shuddered at the thought.

They talked about Marzack. Eddie told her about his first escape six years before, about his fight with Marzack, about the scar over Marzack's eye, about Marzack's hatred for him.

"But would that be enough for something like this?" she asked.

"I don't know" was all Eddie could answer.

The image of Marzack would not go away. Eddie played back the scene in the hotel hallway a hundred times, looking for anything that would give him some sort of edge, or something concrete to defend against.

Contact kills, he kept telling himself, as before. *But surprise kills, too. And there is no real defense against surprise.*

But there was something. Marzack had tripped his hand.

In the playback of the hotel scene, Eddie seized on three words Marzack used.

"Runner" was the first word. Marzack *knew* he was running. That meant Marzack had deduced Eddie's plan and had been following him.

The other two words were "Jilly Buck." Marzack knew her, too. That meant he had traced the SAM-7 license plate. That meant he probably knew about the rapist. It also meant he knew about

SAM-1. But apparently SAM-1 made no difference to him, because he had fired at them. He even screamed he didn't care *who* Jilly was. When you added it all up, it came down to the fact that Marzack was a fanatic, or that his desire to catch or kill Eddie was fanatical.

But in his playback, Eddie knew he had tipped his hand, too.

"Wait! My . . ." he had shouted.

He had announced to Marzack that he had left something in his room.

Did Marzack hear it? Did it register with him? Did he go back to the room? Could he get in the room? Would he be waiting? Would waiting be the only alternative left to Marzack since he had lost them the night before?

Eddie could only speculate. But if Marzack had been clever and competent enough to get as far as he had, he wouldn't let anything pass his ears without cataloging it and seizing on it. To eliminate surprise, Eddie had decided he would assume Marzack knew he had left something in the hotel room and would have to come back for it at all costs. *He will be there and he will try to kill me. We will go one-on-one before the day is over, and one of us will win and the other will lose. The winning will be permanent, and so will the loss.*

As the bus emptied, Eddie studied the sidewalk outside his window. He could see no one in a TDC or police uniform, and more important, he did not see Marzack. He motioned with his head for Jilly to get up, and he stood up with her and waited for her to enter the aisle in front of him, and then they walked off the bus together.

Jilly was stiff with weariness and fright, and she balked slightly in the bus's doorway.

"It's all right," Eddie said to her. "Just walk straight for the lobby. I'll do the looking." He was again aware of Jilly's terrified whine as she began to descend the steps of the bus.

They seated themselves in a front booth in the big, open antiseptic bus-station cafeteria, which was crowded with weary travelers, stale cigarette smoke, and screaming babies. Over coffee, Eddie told Jilly what he intended to do and what he expected of her.

"I'm sorry for all this," he told her firmly. "I don't have any right to keep you involved, but I can't let you go. You must see that, see that I don't have any choice. But I won't let you get hurt."

She stared back blankly across the table and didn't answer, but her silence was not a pose; she was scared.

"The first thing is the plane schedule," Eddie told her. "If there's no plane to Laredo, I don't know what I'll do. Just let you go and end it here, and try and get across the border as best I can, or something, I guess."

The remark triggered an automatic response within Jilly, and she came alive. "If there's no plane, I'll charter one. That's probably the best idea anyway," she said, looking him straight in the eyes.

It wasn't funny, but Eddie laughed out loud.

"I've got a better idea," he said at the end of his grim laugh. "Why don't you just buy me Mexico and solve *all* my problems."

Jilly laughed too.

"Take care of it with petty cash," she said, trying to keep the laugh alive as long as possible.

Jilly made the call to the airport, and when she came back to their table the look on her face was all Eddie needed.

"We're booked on Air Texas for a ten-fifty arrival in Laredo. Coach," she added, mugging. "There's no first class."

They laughed again, and went straight for the taxi stand in front of the bus station for the ride to the airport. In the taxi they were silent, thinking their own thoughts. They did not touch as they rode, but Eddie was aware that Jilly sat more to his side than hers. It was a good sign. And with the terror starting all over again, Eddie was acutely aware that he needed a good sign.

Eddie bought the tickets with cash in the name of "E. Buck and J. Buck." Then he and Jilly walked through the great main lobby of the airport and upstairs to a swank dining room that overlooked the runways.

Eddie was fascinated by the sight of the airplanes. There seemed to be hundreds of the colorful and gleaming multimillion-dollar machines. It was an awesome sight for a man who had been locked away in a cage for six years. In prison you only saw the outside world, and then only in the one dimension of TV or radio or movies or newspapers or magazines. Now Eddie could touch the world again. But once you were put in prison, you had to be given the right to touch through parole or serving your time. As he looked out at the airplanes and around the restaurant, filled with elegant and important people who were on their way to or from elegant and important things, Eddie was aware that he was touching before the right had been given to him. All around him there was flow, and momentum, and style, and choice: freedom. Taking the freedom before it was given was one thing, but keeping it was another matter. As Eddie took in the scene around him, he knew how badly he wanted to keep what he had taken, and, looking also at Jilly, this realization caused him anguish, because he knew, despite what he had told her about her safety, that he might stop at nothing to keep his prize, his freedom.

Two words entered his mind. *So easy. It is either so easy, or it doesn't happen at all,* he told himself with the warmth and ease of truth. *So easy, or not at all. He could taste freedom now, and he meant to keep it. To be free,* he said to himself as he looked out at the miles of runways with their beehive of planes landing and taking off, *and above all else to be with my family.*

He wanted it all so bad it stopped his breathing for a second.

They had breakfast and then Jilly led him to the Eastern Airlines Ionosphere VIP lounge. She settled them in a corner on a deep and comfortable sofa and a waiter in starched black and whites brought them coffee in small heavy cups. Eddie sat and took in the room and its patrons; Jilly read the New York *Times*.

So much, he told himself as his eyes drank in the surroundings. *I've missed so much.*

And as he looked on, something about the room—its feel, its smell, the movement—triggered long-ago images in his mind, images that stretched in a lightning flash from Blowing Rock to Key West. All his life he had plunged headlong after what he kept calling "something better." But his *better* was a material better. Never the better of the mind; he had stood outside and watched the summer people of Blowing Rock, and the winter people of Key West, and had longed for the materials of their life, but never the idea. Suddenly it occurred to him that that *idea of freedom* was what mattered. For a moment the realization and its simplicity overwhelmed him, and he froze and turned pale.

"Christ," he said out loud.

Jilly dropped her paper to her lap and looked at him. They were sitting only inches apart, and before either one of them could speak, he leaned over and kissed her on the mouth, a long, full kiss that she accepted automatically. When the kiss was over, they sat and looked deeply at each other and did not speak for what seemed like a very long time. Finally, it was Jilly who gently broke the silence.

"I don't know what that was all about, but thank you," she said like a young girl.

"It was about everything," Eddie answered quietly. "And thank *you*," he added like a young boy.

They sat and looked at each other for a time, and when the looking became too obvious, Jilly reluctantly went back to her paper. Eddie sat then and was left with her taste and feel and softness. His heart ached for a woman, but not for Jilly; he longed for Chris, his one great love.

In Texas prisons they stripped you naked at the end of the day and paraded you before the guards for searching; took away everything, dignity most of all. But most of the cons in TDC did not have much to take away. But it bothered Eddie; he felt that he had everything in the world to lose—that everything could be taken from him. But he was so close to having it all back. So close to finally getting and keeping what was his. So close.

So much; so easy. And all about to start again. For the last time. For winning or losing. For freedom or for no freedom. For . . .

37
Marzack / 9:17 a.m. /
Saint Augustin Plaza, Laredo, Texas

Marzack smelled bad and his clothes were creased into a print of his sitting position for the past sixteen hours. He was constipated and his head hurt; he remembered with grim amusement that at court, with everyone in civvies, you could always tell the detectives because they were constipated, and the patrolmen because their feet hurt. On a stakeout you wiggled your toes and fingers a lot and kept your shoulder muscles working, but the only relief your bowels got was when you got out of the car for a full stretch, and you couldn't afford to get out of the car often or you would attract attention to yourself and blow the stakeout.

But there was no amusement now for Marzack; he had blown another stakeout. And worse, there was only two hours and forty-five minutes left until Marzack believed Eddie would cross the border; two hours and forty-five minutes and no movement at all at the hotel.

He had figured it all out now. Eddie's run was for four days, and he would cross to Mexico on the morning of the fifth day. Noon of the fifth day. The wife and kids, not Jilly—she was a fluke—would be waiting across the border. Eddie would go to them and they would live in Mexico or Central or South America, getting their start with the money from the sale of the Blowing Rock farm. A perfect setup.

There were ample extradition treaties with Mexico, but either they didn't work, or they took too long to work, or they worked only on the highest level. Once across the border, Eddie was home free. Marzack knew this. He had to get Eddie north of the border; south was too late. South was Kings-X from the children's game, all the way down the line; just like in the cowboy movies. But deducing the plan was nothing. Nothing meant nothing without Eddie, without a capture or a kill. And that didn't seem likely, with less than three hours to go.

With the rich bitch, so many alternatives are possible, Marzack boiled as he sat in his car and stared with hate at the hotel across Saint Augustin Plaza. *So many alternatives that could negate anything the runner left behind in his hotel room; if he did leave something behind. . . .*

Marzack had been getting the eye from the Laredo PD since midnight, but they hadn't stopped to question him. He wouldn't show them his bogus FBI badge if they did, but he decided he would show his TDC card if he had to, rather than leave his stakeout. He sat in the car and had a breakfast of hot coffee he bought around the corner at a café, and rum from his bottle, and a sack full of glazed doughnuts that had gone flat and shriveled. The sun was out, and his eyes ached at the glare that came into the plaza. Cars were moving; Mexican day laborers, who had come over the International Bridge, filed past him with noise and momentum. Marzack rubbed his eyes and the stubble beard on his face and sipped his rum-laced coffee and began to feel obvious and exposed. He didn't know how much longer he could stay in the car, how much longer he *should* stay in the car. It was not like the old days in Passaic at all, and it had not been so for hours, not so since he blew the stakeout. Marzack finished his miserable breakfast and sat and looked at the hotel and wondered what to do. He felt desperate; he *had* to get Eddie.

You sonofabitch. He chewed the words inside his head. *I've got to get my hands on you. I've got . . .*

He couldn't take the thoughts further; they hurt too badly.

38

Eddie and Jilly / 10:50 a.m. /
Laredo International Airport, Laredo, Texas

Eddie was totally in command. He looked out of the small porthole of the Air Texas jet, but he saw nothing that seemed like harm. No TDC uniforms, no Laredo PD, no Marzack.

Marzack is here. Somewhere.

He believed that absolutely; and believing it, was ready to defend against it. On the plane, Eddie and Jilly had been safe, but there had been no thoughts of safety; the thoughts were of Marzack and what had to be done in Laredo for Eddie to cross the border by noon. Now, there were seventy minutes until he crossed; seventy minutes to win or lose. They got up in the flow of those who were exiting the plane, and as they stood, Eddie bent forward toward Jilly and spoke to her in a way he might have spoken to Chris.

"I won't let you get hurt," he said.

Immediately, he wished he meant it, but he didn't. He meant to get across the border to his wife and children, to freedom.

Jilly seemed to be with him completely. She rented the car, a new Ford Thunderbird, in her name, while Eddie stood back and watched. They had no luggage, so they were out of the airport and headed for downtown Laredo in less than fifteen minutes. When they were seated in the rented car, with Jilly driving, Eddie turned to her with words he had held inside all during the flight.

"You know Marzack will be waiting," he said to her.

"I know," she answered.

They were silent for a second and then Jilly spoke again. "With the man in the car—the man you knocked out—I was just mad, and disgusted with myself. With this man Marzack, I've known fear. I don't like the feeling. I want you to beat him. I want the feeling to go away. For both of us."

She fell silent, but he could see she still had something to say. He waited.

"I want you to know this, too," she told him. "I want you to know why I've helped you."

He listened intently. Her face became hard. "I've never seen anybody like you before," she began cautiously. "I've never seen anybody who *wanted* something so badly. Somebody who was actually trying to *do* something. I might just try it myself," she said with complete sincerity.

He looked at her as deeply as one human being can look at another; there were so many things he wanted to say to her, but all his heart and mind could manage was a short and dignified: "Thank you."

That was enough. Jilly started the car and they drove off toward Laredo.

Eddie had never been in war, but what they were doing seemed to him exactly like a beachhead landing, a landing that now had an even hour of time ahead before the objective could be reached.

They drove from the airport to the center of Laredo without speaking, Jilly engrossed in her driving, Eddie constantly on the lookout for Marzack or the police, or TDC searchers. As they entered the maze of narrow city streets from the airport highway, Eddie checked his watch—11:06.

Fifty-four minutes to go! His mind burned. He wanted to slip into thoughts of Chris and the children arriving or already being just across the border from him, waiting. But he stopped himself. *You must not think about them. You must not think or do anything that is not directly concerned with getting across the border. Watch and act! Watch and act!*

He obeyed, but the temptation was maddening.

They entered Saint Augustin Plaza from the northeast side; Eddie made Jilly stop just in front of Saint Augustin Cathedral's great white bulk. From that vantage point Eddie had a 360-degree view of the plaza and La Posada Hotel to the south across Zaragoza Street.

For a brief few seconds Eddie sat and looked at the hotel. It was an absolutely impossible situation. But it made everything else that had happened to him useless if he didn't go back inside the hotel. If he did not have his ID papers, all the knowledge he had gained on the run, all the lessons he had learned, counted for nothing.

"I don't see anything," he said finally to Jilly. "But then," he added with a gray smile, "if the police or TDC are here, they wouldn't exactly stand around outside and advertise."

Jilly tried to smile, but couldn't.

"But you can bet Marzack is here," Eddie said into the car's silence. "And you can bet he's hidden."

Jilly still could not speak, but her eyes mirrored words.

"So . . ." Eddie said, fumbling for words of his own, knowing it was time to go.

"Yeah," Jilly responded into the silence, able to find only the one word.

This time it was Eddie who couldn't speak. It was time to go, and when it was time to go, that was all there was to do. Words were useless. He reached for the car's door handle. But Jilly's eyes kept on betraying her thoughts; finally she spoke. He took his hand away from the door and faced her.

"I'm sorry about the shower, and about parading around, and . . . and about my bad mouth."

"It's okay," he said without hesitation.

"It's not okay," she came back, her voice stronger. "But I'm sorry, and I'm telling you I'm sorry."

He nodded.

"I don't ever remember *feeling* sorry for anything," she told him. "And I've never *said* I'm sorry in my life."

He flashed her a little smile.

He started to say something. But he didn't. He reached over very carefully and touched her cheek with the outside of the forefinger of his right hand, very gently and very carefully, and then he got out of the car and was on his way to the hotel.

As he crossed Zaragoza Street and started to descend the narrow paved driveway to La Posada's basement garage, Eddie heard Jilly inch the car up to the corner of Saint Augustin and Zaragoza. He did not turn; he looked at his watch and kept on straight ahead.

Eleven-ten exactly, his mind registered. *Letter-perfect, on schedule.*

He had exactly five minutes to get to the room and retrieve the fake Canadian papers and his pistol and run up the driveway, where Jilly would have turned right onto Zaragoza and would be waiting for him. If he did not make it in five minutes, Jilly was to leave without him and that would be the end. He would try to make a dash down Zaragoza for the International Bridge a block away and cross the border on his own if he could.

Five minutes, his mind flashed.

Act.

Perform.

Move!

Suddenly it was like his jagged movements to the Cotulla stock trailer five days before. But it was different now; he was on the Outside, he was in civilian clothes, not TDC coon stripes . . . and his family was so near.

Marzack . . . Eddie tried to shut his name from his mind, but he could not. *He's here somewhere. He's here!*

Eddie bolted on down the empty driveway and stopped at its open, gaping concrete-pillar doors. He stuck his head around the corner, eyes darting, taking in everything.

Nothing.

He was coil-spring tight, but not scared. He moved around the corner and into the cool and dim garage—a replay of his dash to the stock trailer. The similarity struck him, but he did not dwell on the thought.

No thinking! Move! Go! Move!

He broke for the elevator fifty feet from where he was standing, regarding Jilly's gold SAM-7 Mercedes out of the corner of his eye as he moved.

Nothing! No Marzack!

But he's here . . . where? Where?

Where?

But there was no interference. No one to stop him, no one to be seen. He thrust himself up hard against the elevator door and pushed the Up button; in seconds the door opened. His heart stopped as the doors parted; still there was no one. He brushed inside the box and pushed the Two button, and the doors whisked shut and he felt himself being hoisted up. For a second he half-relaxed inside the security and isolation of the elevator. The stairs were too open. The elevator was safe and could give the element of surprise if Marzack was waiting on the second floor.

A gun, his mind blazed as he heard the elevator's whirring motor stop and felt it come to rest on the second floor with a dull thud. *If I only had a gun I wouldn't need to rely on the whim of surprise.*

Another momentary pause, the doors parting. *Nothing! Where is he? Where . . . ?*

He threw himself out of the door and plunged to the right, stopping just behind the wall's corner. After a second more he stuck his head out into the space where he had seen Marzack the day before. For an instant he couldn't breathe.

Nothing! Nothing!

The void was maddening, insane. He stared ahead at Room 216, four doors down the hall. Insane. He looked left. Still there was nothing; no one. *No Marzack!*

Jilly had wanted to stop and buy him a pistol or a shotgun, but he would not let her. As it was, she could claim kidnapping and free herself of all but embarrassment if they were caught; if she bought a gun, she was part of the thing. But as Eddie turned his eyes to Room 216 once more, he was acutely aware of how much he wished for a gun. But there was none, so all he could do was reach in his trouser pocket for the room key and jerk out into the hall and dash for the room.

Go . . . go . . . go . . . go!

In a flash he was standing before the room door and stabbing the keyhole with the key. Then the door opened and he careened inside, searching wildly for Marzack.

But again—maddeningly—there was nothing. He banged the door shut and then made straight for the open bathroom door.

Nothing! Nothing! No one! No . . . Marzack!

He tore off the top of the toilet back, his heart stopping again for this final moment of truth.

Here . . . here . . . here! his mind roared as he saw the papers and pistol wrapped in their plastic bag.

But Marzack?

Where?

Where?

Where?

In that instant he heard the patio door open, and he had his answer.

The patio!

God . . .

I . . .

The patio!

Marzack!

God . . .

Eddie turned and stood there frozen with the bag in his hand. Marzack seemed as big as a mountain, his face radiating hate.

"You cocksucking sonofabitch," Marzack grunted, his riot shotgun leveled exactly at the base of Eddie's nose. "Drop that shit and *freeze!*"

For a second Eddie's eyes focused with crystal clarity past Marzack to the opening of the patio doors and Mexico across the river.

Chris . . . Angie . . . Bobby . . . Freedom . . .

He started to lunge into the death of the shotgun barrel. But something stopped him.

Then there was Marzack's command. *"Drop it!* And fall on the floor, facedown!"

Eddie complied like a zombie, his mind going idiot-blank in a black and hopeless void.

11:16. He was a minute late. Jilly's mind ached.

Jilly had turned the corner from the cathedral onto Zaragoza Street and was sitting at the entrance to the hotel's garage driveway, her eyes riveted to the driveway, which was empty.

11:17. Two minutes late.

She became frantic. Her eyes searched 180 degrees in front of the car for Marzack; *nothing.* The rearview mirror; *still nothing.*

11:18. Three full minutes late.

He was in trouble. Now there was no doubt. Jilly racked her brain for a remedy.

What? What? ˎ

But he had been explicit.

"If I'm not back in exactly five minutes, *five minutes,* not six, not seven, you leave. *Period.* Longer than five minutes, and I've had it."

11:19. Four minutes late.

Jilly's fingers dug into the rented car's steering wheel. She looked a last time at the driveway.

Eddie? Eddie? But he did not come.

She searched frantically to her front and back, and then, in a frenzy, she put the car in drive and roared off.

Eddie . . . Eddie . . . !

Marzack had Eddie sitting up on the bed; he was sitting in a chair four feet away, with the shotgun pointed straight into Eddie's face. Marzack had left the plastic bag, with Eddie's fake papers and pistol, on the bathroom floor where Eddie dropped them. He did not want what was inside the bag, he wanted Eddie. He sat and looked at Eddie in the manner of a hunter looking at his prey before he fires his weapon. And as he sat and looked, Marzack played with the idea of blowing Eddie's head off with one blast of .00 buckshot. But he didn't want to shoot Eddie; he wanted to *have* him. Eddie was a collar. He had made the perfect collar! He had found clues and had followed them—had read them perfectly—and had made his collar! He had opened the room door with a credit card and had been on the patio for more than an hour and had become stiff as he crouched out of sight, but all that was forgotten now, and Marzack was aware he had never felt better in his life.

"I had you figured every fucking inch of the way," he said to Eddie, opening his trench coat with his left hand, then adjusting his hat.

There was no reply. Eddie sat stone-faced with his hands behind his head—thinking; waiting for an opening.

For the five minutes he had had Eddie, all Marzack had done was gloat and give commands and threaten with his shotgun. Now he wanted to talk; he wanted Eddie to know fully what was happening, and how he had captured him.

"I was on your ass from the first second," Marzack said with total satisfaction. "You hooked a ride with the L-Bar-T, right?"

Silence.

"Yeah . . . right," Marzack said, ignoring the silence, needing no words from Eddie, just his attention.

"Then you picked up a little package from the wife at the Frio River Bridge."

He smiled viciously into Eddie's icy face.

"Then it was boogie-woogie across the desert until you met up with the Potts brothers' family flea circus?"

Eddie's head jerked at the mention of the Potts brothers; the jerk was more than enough to delight Marzack.

"They put one on you, huh?"

Eddie's mouth tightened.

"But you got in some licks, too," Marzack yielded.

Eddie's eyes twitched.

"Then a little more boogie-woogie without all your goodies, and hello Jilly Buck and pussy-hound friend.

"Then, wham; good-bye, pussy-hound."

Marzack smiled a twisted smile, then continued.

"A free ride across the border with the Queen Bee." He shoved the shotgun barrel closer to Eddie's face. "But uh-uh, enter me . . ."

Marzack trailed off for a second; Eddie thought he was about to pull the trigger of the shotgun.

"But, bang-bang, you're not dead," Marzack ended, almost touching Eddie's nose with the gun barrel.

"Bang-bang," he repeated with pleasure. "You're all mine."

All mine, Eddie's mind registered. *Not TDC's; all his. One-on-one, just like I thought,* he said to himself as he watched Marzack's smug face.

"So you got me," he said.

Marzack's eyes widened with still more pleasure.

"You bet your ass, runner," he replied.

"Do you kill me or take me back?"

Marzack's eyes narrowed. "Shut your fucking mouth!" he ordered. "You just sit. Your ass is bagged. You just sit."

"I don't belong in prison," Eddie went on, unmindful of Marzack's orders.

"Goddamn you, I said shut the fuck up!"

"I've done plenty of time for nothing."

Marzack jammed the barrel into Eddie's nose.

"I made it," Eddie kept on. "You got me, but I made it. We both won," he told Marzack fearlessly.

"Shut up or die!" Marzack bellowed.

"*I made it!*" Eddie shouted back, his face on fire. "Kill me! Shoot me! I'm not leaving this room for prison! I beat all of you, and you know it! I beat—"

The room's door flew open, and a maid's service cart was thrust inside, coming straight for Marzack across the carpeted floor. Eddie's hand was already up for the shotgun, but it missed its mark and Marzack bolted around and shot the cart.

Boom! A cannonlike explosion. The cart flying into a hundred pieces.

"Sonofabitch . . ."

Marzack's back was turned. Eddie was on him instantly, his fists like clubs. Eddie's hand reached the shotgun. Then the gun butt was in the air and falling on Marzack's head with a thud. Jilly came plunging into the room, screaming, eyes searching wildly for Eddie. Their eyes met. Eddie had the shotgun and was over Marzack's half-conscious body. Jilly thought he was about to shoot.

"No!" she screamed, her hands on the sides of her head.

Eddie's mind registered the scream, and he snapped. His eyes searched for the plastic bag. Jilly's eyes followed him. She was closer to it than he.

"Get it!" he commanded. "Get it!" She complied, and in a second more they were both running for the door.

"Go! Go!" he urged her from behind, running with the shotgun at port arms; waving it at the dazed people who came out of their rooms and stood gaping in their doorways.

At the head of the stairs Eddie saw two policemen dashing across the hotel's courtyard. Jilly saw them an instant later.

"My car!" she screamed at Eddie. "Go for my car!"

Eddie followed her down the stairs, but behind them he thought he heard Marzack.

Eddie held the shotgun between his legs with the barrel on the floorboard of the Mercedes. Jilly moved the big gold car up the driveway's incline at a fast but not frantic clip. Eddie stopped her with his hand at the entrance to Zaragoza Street. His eyes took in all of Saint Augustin Plaza. Police cars, with sirens and lights flashing, were coming down Saint Augustin Street in front of the cathedral to the right and down Flores Street to the left.

"We may get by to the right," he said quickly to her. "But they've got us bottled off to the left for the bridge."

"Get down!" Jilly cried suddenly. "Down!"

Eddie complied without words, plunging down on the seat with his head against Jilly's leg, the shotgun held barrel to the door, with his finger on the trigger. Jilly moved the Mercedes out across Zaragoza Street and in the opposite lane from the oncoming police car on Saint Augustin Street. Eddie could feel Jilly's car slowing still more. His hands tightened on the shotgun. Then he heard Jilly give out a friendly "Hi!" to the cops in the cruiser as she passed them with her SAM-7 plates blazing away to match—and overpower—the intensity of the police car's siren. From his vantage point Eddie did not believe the policemen could hear the "Hi!" but he knew they could see the SAM-7 license plates. He had to hope that was enough. Suddenly he felt the car lunge forward again.

"Keep down!" Jilly cried excitedly. "I think it's all right, but keep down."

Eddie held his position and felt the Mercedes begin to speed up the narrow street. Seconds went by, and then he saw Jilly's hand reach for the horn. When the horn's defiant blasts began to fill the air, he sat up in the seat. Jilly was flying up Saint Augustin Street, running red lights and crowding autos out of her way. Eddie got his bearings to the left, with the courthouse, and to the right, with the Plaza Hotel building. From his maps he knew they were on line with San Bernardo Street to the west, and that San Bernardo was a straight shot north out of town through a thickly populated residential and commercial area.

"Turn one street up in front of the Plaza Hotel," he told Jilly, his voice even and in control. "Fast, but not crazy," he instructed.

She slowed the car slightly.

"Okay . . . okay," she said, her voice settled somewhat.

The plastic bag was on the floorboard. Eddie reached down and got it and took the fake Canadian papers out and stuffed them in his coat pocket; then he laid the pistol on the seat between him and Jilly.

"Take the next left past the hotel and we'll stay on San Bernardo through the houses and shops and look for something. A cruising cab or a truck, or a place to hide for a few minutes. *Something*," he told her, unable to keep an edge out of his own voice.

Jilly turned north on San Bernardo without speaking, accelerated to sixty, and began weaving in and out of the medium traffic.

Marzack stormed out into the hallway, holding his head and cursing the people who filled up the narrow aisle. He could hear the police sirens clearly as he ran for the stairs.

Stairs . . . driveway . . .

Kitchen, his mind told him.

Kitchen to the left.

He darted down the stairs, and on the first floor he raced down the hallway looking for an exit. He found it around another right—a small hallway that opened onto the end of the hotel's enclosed patio. Ahead, past a line of open Spanish arches, he saw a series of doors to the left.

The kitchen . . . the kitchen . . .

He raced for the doors and burst inside. As he hoped, it was a passageway that led to the kitchen. He plowed into the kitchen's double swinging doors and sent a waiter and one of the chefs flying with trays and pots.

"Get the fuck . . ."

His eyes darted around the big room for another door. Again, to the left, he found it.

"Move, assholes!"

His huge pistol was out now; people were screaming and falling on the floor out of his way. In an instant more Marzack burst out the far door and was in a thin alley that led to Zaragoza Street. When he barreled out onto the sidewalk and across Zaragoza, bound for his car at the end of the plaza, the police were bursting in the hotel's front doors and converging on the stairs from the basement.

Runner . . . you bastard!

Runner, you are still mine!

Goddamn you, still mine! he raged, never letting go for a second.

They couldn't find anything.

No place to hide. No cabs. Nothing.

Eddie checked his watch—11:28. *Thirty-two minutes to get across!*

They were still going north. Police cars were passing them, racing back into the city, sirens and lights blazing. It seemed hopeless to both of them.

"Will they cut off the bridge?" Eddie asked her.

"I don't know," Jilly replied. "If they do, it will take time to close it from the Mexican end."

"But they can stop it from this end with police cars," Eddie injected sourly.

"Yes," Jilly responded.

"We've got to move now," Eddie said firmly. *"Now*, before they close it off."

Ahead there was a vast intersection as the city became a line of fast-food restaurants, shopping centers, and warehouses and motels out to I-35.

"Turn right at the next light," Eddie told her. "We're going back to town. "You can let me off if things look tight, but I'm going to cross *now."*

Jilly looked over at him gravely but said nothing. She knew there was no other alternative. At the light she made a right and they were on San Dario Boulevard going back to the heart of the city. Four blocks down the street, they saw Marzack coming the other way; he saw them in the same instant.

"Make a turn!" Eddie yelled. "Make a turn!"

San Dario was a one-way road going south into town, San Ursula went north out of town, the streets divided by a median that gave Laredo its grand Spanish-boulevard entrance and exit. Jilly bolted the car forward on San Dario and made a left on Clark Street, speeding across the boulevard to San Ursula, smashing the bumper of another car as she plowed around the ninety-degree turn. As soon as they were going north again, they saw Marzack right behind them with his pistol held out the window of his car. He was crazed. Eddie plunged into the backseat and opened the window on the driver's side and stuck the shotgun barrel out and took aim at the grille of Marzack's Olds. He was about to fire when he heard Jilly scream.

"School! School to the left!" she cried.

Eddie saw it while the words were still in his ears. He pulled the shotgun in the car and stared behind at Marzack's wild face. Then he heard Jilly's horn sound alarmingly as they plunged into a school zone with children on both sides of the street.

"Jesus!" Jilly screamed. "Jesus!"

Eddie's head whipped back and forth from Marzack to the street ahead. Marzack was seventy-five yards back and gaining on them on the big, exposed street. Eddie's eyes groped for a turnoff. He saw it ahead where Saunders Street bisected the boulevard to the east.

"Right! Go right at the next turn!" he shouted to Jilly.

Jilly complied, but the light was turning red as she entered the intersection. Cars were already starting from both sides of Saunders; she screeched around the corner and swerved to miss an oncoming truck. Eddie kept his eyes behind; Marzack never checked his speed. He entered the intersection, and the two lines of cars parted like pigeons in a park.

"He's coming! He's still coming!" Eddie called to Jilly.

"What? What do we do?" she shouted.

Saunders Street ran straight to the end of the city to the east, back to Laredo International Airport. They both knew where they were headed now, and they both knew what was between them and the airport: Catholic cemetery and the Laredo City Cemetery, acres of graves and a labyrinth of roads, all inside a high stone wall.

"The cemeteries," Eddie said first, as Jilly was about to say the words herself. "Go for the cemeteries!"

Marzack would not be cut off. He bulled his way through traffic behind Eddie and Jilly, smashing two cars, totally unmindful of anything but Jilly's gold Mercedes. As Eddie watched, he was sure they could not last much longer. Either they would wreck or Marzack would finally ram them, or worse, they would soon attract police. But ahead on the right there were the cemeteries; they might lose him there.

Jilly swerved onto the main cemetery road, a narrow street that cut the two cemeteries in half: Catholic to the west, City to the east. They could see no one on the properties; Jilly rammed ahead, but as she did, Eddie saw Marzack make the turn himself. Eddie's head whipped about, and he tried to size up the miniature lanes between the graves; they were too small, an impassable maze.

"Find a mausoleum!" Eddie shouted to Jilly from the backseat. "Something big. Something I can shoot from."

Jilly lunged the car off down the street; four lanes down she made a screeching right on line with a row of great marble mausoleums. Eddie was out of the car in seconds and braced with his shotgun on the side of one of the marble fortresses that had a painted roof with a delicate winged angel on top. Marzack was twenty-five yards away when Eddie shot: the .00 buckshot rippled the tin of the Olds's hood like choppy water, the lead balls entering the right side of the windshield, not Marzack's side. But it was enough! Marzack had to stop. He plowed to a halt and began banging the remains of the shattered windshield out with his pistol. Eddie took aim and started to shoot again, to kill Marzack; but again, Jilly stopped him.

"No!" he heard her scream. "No . . . please, no!"

He turned to face her.

"Let's go now!" she cried. "Now!"

He bolted for her car.

Jilly exited the cemeteries and flew back into town through the empty residential streets. For exactly one minute it seemed they had lost Marzack, and they headed for the border, but at the railroad-track crossing on Montezuma Street they saw him behind them, his pistol pointed directly out of his empty windshield.

Eleven-thirty-five! Only twenty-five minutes left! Only twenty-five! Eddie told himself as he watched the mad scene from the backseat, his shotgun held inside, out of view.

Less than a mile from the bridge!

A mile from Chris and the children!

A mile from freedom!

"Slow down!" he shouted suddenly at Jilly. "Slow down. I'm going to shoot him. I'm going to kill him. Slow down!"

They were eight streets up from Saint Augustin Cathedral, going south on San Eduardo through a poor Tex-Mex neighborhood known as South Laredo. Jilly slowed the car and Eddie turned his upper body out of the window and aimed the shotgun directly at Marzack's open windshield fifty yards away.

Marzack saw him, and fired first with his pistol.

The bullet missed Jilly's car.

Eddie fired. But the car was banging across the railroad tracks, spoiling his aim. He missed completely.

As Eddie pumped another round of .00 buck in the shotgun, Jilly turned left on Corpus Christi Street without being told and was headed straight toward a high concrete overpass. She took it like a roller coaster. The Mercedes left the pavement a full five feet in midair and crashed down on the far side of the rise forty feet from where the tires left solid ground. Ahead, in the opposite lane, a garbage truck was moving slowly up the hill. Jilly raked the whole left side of the Mercedes along the length ŏf the truck, but the motion stabilized her leap. Off to the left there was a dirt road bordered by unpainted wood houses; instantly she saw she was headed into a short dead-end street with a junk-strewn field at its end.

"Turn and stop and face him!" Eddie screamed. "Turn and face him! I'm killing him! *I'm killing him!*"

Jilly bulled on to the end of the street and made a fierce U turn that had the Mercedes pointed back toward the open street. The instant the car stopped, Eddie was outside with the shotgun.

"Get down! Down," he ordered Jilly as he raced to the front of the car and took up a firing position behind the front door.

Marzack came around the corner, accelerating to full speed. Eddie stood tall and took careful aim from left to right across the front of Marzack's shattered Olds. It would do no good to kill him, the car would keep moving. Eddie had to cripple the car. Then he could kill Marzack with his pistol.

There were three shots left in the shotgun. Eddie sent all three into the tires and radiator of the Olds; ten feet from the Mercedes, the

Olds finally blew up. But it was too late. It struck the Mercedes on the right side and flipped over.

Eddie stood back in shock and watched. Then he raced for Jilly. She was on the floorboard of the big car, scared white-faced but unhurt. Instantly Eddie feared another explosion.

"Get out!" he called to her as he forced the door open.

She jostled herself out of the car in a frenzy and stood clinging to him in terror. Eddie shook himself loose and threw the shotgun down and reached in his belt for his pistol.

"Stay!" he shouted to her as he raced off toward Marzack's burning car. "Stay!"

All around them a crowd of silent, curious Tex-Mex men, women, and small children began to gather. Eddie regarded them as he ran, his eyes bolted on Marzack's flaming car, but his thoughts on only one thing.

The police!

Police will come! his mind cried.

Eddie could not see Marzack behind the flames that came from his car's motor, but suddenly the driver's door banged open. Eddie held his pistol in both hands like a marksman and took aim just over the top of the door where Marzack would emerge. In another instant the big man tumbled out. He was bareheaded, and blood covered his forehead. There was blood on his trench coat. He was clearly in shock, but still functioning. Still in pursuit! Eddie got ready to fire. His eyes met Marzack's. His finger tightened on the trigger. He was about to kill him. But then Marzack broke the spell with words.

"Runner . . ." he groaned, his eyes glassy.

Eddie held fast on his trigger.

"I got your ass," Marzack groaned on, then tumbled straight to the ground, his pistol falling from his hand as he fell.

Eddie ran to him. Jilly followed. The crowd pressed in, in a tight circle. Marzack was alive. Eddie couldn't tell how badly he was hurt. He stood over him and cocked the hammer of his pistol. Marzack looked up at him and manufactured a tight smile.

"I had your ass figured to a T," he mumbled, his mouth bloody.

Eddie tried to pull the trigger, but he couldn't. "Don't go south," he said instead, his voice surprisingly calm, his eyes directly on Marzack's. "Don't you go south!"

There was dead, still silence.

"I don't have to," Marzack said. "I nailed you from A to Z."

Before they could exchange another word, they heard police sirens. Eddie turned, and his eyes froze on Jilly's.

"Oh, God," she whimpered, her hands coming up to her face.

Eddie turned and frantically searched the open dirt street ahead: two police cars were turning the corner in a cloud of dust and noise and flashing lights. Marzack raised his head slightly and saw them. His face turned sour and mad. Eddie saw the expression clearly; then Jilly saw it. There was a pause, and then Marzack reached inside his coat pocket. Eddie trained his pistol on him, thinking he was going for a weapon.

"*Eh* . . ." Marzack grunted resentfully.

Eddie eased up on his pistol. He and Jilly waited like children to see what Marzack was doing. From his pocket Marzack produced a small black leather object, looked at it for a second, then tossed it up to Eddie. Eddie caught it and held it for a second; then he opened it. Inside there was a gold FBI badge. Eddie's eyes went from Marzack to Jilly, then back to the badge. He couldn't speak. But he looked down at Marzack again. Their eyes were all the words they needed.

Eddie was the prey. Marzack was the hunter. Marzack had made his capture. A kill was not possible. Now others were closing in for the kill and the flesh. It was the oldest rule of hunting known to man or beast: if the hunter cannot have the flesh, others are not entitled to it. For a last time the eyes of the two men held each other. There was understanding.

Then for a last second Eddie's eyes were on Jilly's. For an instant she could not speak. Then words came.

"I know now this was not a game," she managed before the tears came. "I know that."

Eddie was as silent as stone; then he spoke.

"That's all there is to know," he said.

Their eyes held each other for a final time, and then, as in slow motion, Eddie turned and headed straight for the police cars that wallowed to a halt on the dirt street.

The four policemen in the two cars came out with their pistols drawn. Before he could think, Eddie faced them with his own pistol back in his belt, the fake FBI badge held out as his only barrier. Without thinking, he spoke.

"I don't belong here," he said. "I'm not supposed to be here. One of you get me out of here. I'll square it with your chief later. *But I'm not supposed to be here!*"

Two policemen sped past him; the other two were on him like wary dogs.

"What have you got? What have you got?" one of the policemen shouted at Eddie excitedly, his pistol pointed into his chest.

"See it! See it, and do what I tell you!" Eddie shouted back, trying to sound commanding.

One of the young policemen took the FBI badge and examined it; then he examined Eddie's face. The young cop was bewildered. He handed the badge to his partner.

"Shit," the other cop said.

Then the first policeman called to the other team who were standing over Jilly and Marzack and the wrecked cars.

"FBI!" he shouted. "Says he can't be seen here!"

"Hell," came back a defiant cry.

"Get me out of here now!" Eddie commanded. "There is more here than you know. *Get me out! I can't be seen here!*"

One of the other team members raced back to Eddie and the two young cops. The other man was a sergeant, a big tough-looking man in his forties. He took the badge and examined it and then handed it back to Eddie.

"What the *hell* is going on?" the sergeant demanded.

"Look at the plates on the Mercedes," Eddie came back.

The sergeant turned and looked. Then he looked again at the FBI badge in Eddie's hands.

"*Now!*" Eddie bellowed in the sergeant's face. "Get me out of here now! I'll clear it with your chief, but do it *now!*"

The sergeant turned red with anger and frustration. For a second he didn't speak; then he gave his command.

"Move him! Move him, dammit!"

Eddie did not turn back to Jilly and Marzack; he ran straight for the police cruiser.

The moment filled up with one single thought.

I made it.

I made it. . . .

Backward words and looks would have been meaningless.

39

Eddie / 11:45 a.m. / International Bridge / Laredo, Texas–Nuevo Laredo, Mexico

Eddie looked out of the police car's windshield for a motel or hotel. He found a small hotel at the corner of Market and San Enrique streets. Suddenly everything began to seem so easy.

"Stop here," he commanded the young policeman. "This is my hotel. I'll call your chief from here. You go back to the wreck scene."

The policeman stopped the car in front of the hotel's doors and made a quick U turn and was gone. Eddie stepped inside the hotel for just a second. A pretty young woman was behind the desk. She smiled at him and spoke.

"May I help you?" she said.

"No," he answered clearly. "I'm just fine. Just fine. . . ."

Then he turned and walked out the door; twenty yards down the street, there was an empty passing cab, the first he had seen in the city.

So easy, he said to himself as he hailed the cab. *So easy.* He dropped his pistol into a covered city garbage can just outside the hotel's door and stood and waited for the cab.

It was nine blocks to the International Bridge. There was a solid line of cars and trucks and buses wedging across the quarter-mile-long span—noise and excitement and momentum, and a mass of Mexican day laborers already starting their noonday crush back across the border for lunch. To the left, as the street sloped down to the bridge, was U.S. Customs; to the right, two center tollbooths for vehicles and a single tollbooth for walkers.

Eddie got out of the cab and paid the fare, and adjusted his suede coat and wool shirt and smoothed back his hair with his right hand, the palm ending on his neck, which was suddenly stiff and painful. He stood and held himself by the neck for a second; then he turned to face the city. As he looked, he wanted to feel something, some loss or gain. This would be the last time in his life that he would stand on the soil of the country of his birth, and he knew it. But he felt nothing, only the dry pain in his neck, which passed then as suddenly as it had come on.

At the passing of the pain Eddie turned and faced the bridge once more. A peace came over him, and he felt it flow through his body like a tonic. The peace made him smile, and with the smile on his face, and his hands in his pockets, he walked down the slope to the walkers' tollbooth and paid his nickel toll and started walking across to freedom. God, he felt good. As if everything in the world was his, which it was.

He joined the crush of people and vehicles on the bridge and was lost in the safety of their numbers. On the far side of the bridge he stepped onto Mexican soil and turned right and walked around the side of a fortresslike white-and-green building. He was cleared through Mexican Customs with a six-month visa as Mr. Edward J. Lanson of Windsor, Ontario, Canada, in ten short minutes. Outside the customs building he turned and walked due east for Morelos Park. The thing he desired most on earth was there, and now, after so long, it would again be his. His heart was beating out of his chest as he moved.

JG FISH FLYING FISH

Morelos Park

Nuevo Laredo, Mexico

Thursday, November 1, 11:59 a.m.

Angie was skipping cracks in the stones of a path near a fountain and watching the hands of a clock on a small church steeple that said half a minute before high noon. Bobby was hanging from the branch of a squat little tree. Chris was sitting on a bench with her legs crossed, looking off at a row of open shop doors.

Eddie was fifty yards from them, and he wanted to shout, but sounds would not come in his throat. All he could do was move toward them with his arms outstretched awkwardly at his waist.

Then Angie saw him, her head flicking up just slightly from the stones, her eyes sparkling. Then Bobby dropped to the ground and saw him, surprised and grinning from ear to ear. Then Chris saw him. She bit at her lip and was on her feet, her hand covering her mouth.

There was a silence, and the park stood still.

Then the four started to move.

Angie broke the silence.

"Daddy! Daddy!" she screamed, her young arms stretched out delicately as she began to run. "You're early! Daddy, you're early!"

Suddenly they were all running, but it was no effort at all.